"THOSE WHO HAVE YET TO DISCOVER THE JOYS
OF A MICHAEL McGARRITY NOVEL ARE IN
FOR A REAL TREAT."—*The Denver Post*

MICHAEL McGARRITY

"DELIVERS A BREATHLESS URGENCY."
—*Chicago Tribune*

"KEEPS YOU TURNING THE PAGES,"
—*Los Angeles Times*

"MAY BE THE BEST WRITER OF THE GENRE
WORKING TODAY."—*Tulsa World*

Praise for *Everyone Dies*

"A former police investigator, [McGarrity] infuses his fiction with a wealth of authentic details."
—*Roanoke Times & World-News* (VA)

"Readers familiar with the series will be happy to settle back with the chief, his complicated family, and the men and women of the department for another enjoyable installment." —*Publishers Weekly*

Praise for *The Big Gamble*

"Michael McGarrity delivers a breathless urgency to his seventh mystery, in which the intricacies of police investigation are as important as the dynamics between an estranged father and son." —*Chicago Tribune*

"McGarrity shines as he portrays the details of a finely wrought murder investigation, bringing to the table his experience on the 'job.' . . . There are no stereotypes, just living, breathing people. *The Big Gamble* brings into play greed, evil, power, and the lives of those who strive to control and manipulate others for their own pleasure and profit. This is a gripping tale told with intensity and skill." —*The Denver Post*

"There are times when all the lush prose and psychological insight in the world can't beat a straightforward, well-written police procedural. Such is the case with Michael McGarrity's *The Big Gamble* . . . a compelling portrait of a simple investigation that unexpectedly mushrooms into a multiagency task force of complex proportions . . . will keep you turning the pages. The action . . . is brisk and nonstop."
—*The Washington Post Book World*

"A series standout . . . smartly detailed police work . . . keep[s] you turning the pages." —*Los Angeles Times*

continued . . .

"Stealthily, meticulously McGarrity stalks his prey, unearthing a wonderfully sordid tale . . . a full-blown scandal that rocks all of New Mexico." —*The Providence Journal-Bulletin*

"McGarrity [and] fellow New Mexican Tony Hillerman share admirable strengths: convincing details, complex characters, clean writing, and compelling settings. That crime thrives in the Southwest is no blessing; but that such perceptive storytellers tell the tales is pure delight."
—*The Seattle Times*

"A former deputy sheriff for Santa Fe County, McGarrity brings remarkable verisimilitude to his re-creation of police procedures. In fact, this series has come to have an almost-documentary feel to it, something like the television series *Cops* . . . as fresh and carefully prepared as ever."—*Booklist*

"Like Tony Hillerman before him, Michael McGarrity puts the state of New Mexico on the map. His style is smooth, subtle, and his storytelling abilities keep the reader in thrall, wondering what will happen next. *The Big Gamble* is no gamble at all for readers; it is a surefire winner for anyone who likes a fascinating police procedural."
—*Midwest Book Review*

"Satisfying adventure . . . deft, tidy, and character-driven. . . . No one does the small-city police procedural more authoritatively than McGarrity." —*Kirkus Reviews*

"Well-crafted, entertaining, action-packed . . . an intriguing killer." —*Lansing State Journal*

"Captivating . . . a satisfying journey that takes readers into the complex workings of clever minds, both criminal and judicial. McGarrity knows whereof he writes, and his professional insights illuminate nearly every page."
—*Crosswinds Weekly*

"Masterful." —*The Sunday Oklahoman*

Everyone Dies

A Kevin Kerney Novel

Michael McGarrity

AN ONYX BOOK

ONYX
Published by New American Library, a division of
Penguin Group (USA) Inc., 375 Hudson Street,
New York, New York 10014, U.S.A.
Penguin Books Ltd, 80 Strand,
London WC2R 0RL, England
Penguin Books Australia Ltd, 250 Camberwell Road,
Camberwell, Victoria 3124, Australia
Penguin Books Canada Ltd, 10 Alcorn Avenue,
Toronto, Ontario, Canada M4V 3B2
Penguin Books (NZ), cnr Airborne and Rosedale Roads,
Albany, Auckland 1310, New Zealand

Penguin Books Ltd, Registered Offices:
80 Strand, London WC2R 0RL, England

Published by Onyx, an imprint of New American Library, a division of Penguin
Group (USA) Inc. Previously published in a Dutton edition.

First Onyx Printing, August 2004
10 9 8 7 6 5 4 3 2 1

 REGISTERED TRADEMARK—MARCA REGISTRADA

Printed in the United States of America

PUBLISHER'S NOTE
This is a work of fiction. Names, characters, places, and incidents either are the
product of the author's imagination or are used fictitiously, and any
resemblance to actual persons, living or dead, business establishments, events, or
locales is entirely coincidental.

For Charmay B. Allred

Acknowledgments

Carole Baron, Brian Tart, Lisa Johnson, Kathleen Matthews-Schmidt, Robert Kempe, Anthony Ramondo, Mitch Hoffman, Amy Hughes, Betsy DeJesu, and Anna Cowles are without a doubt the best group of people I've had the pleasure to work with as a writer. Thanks for the encouragement, support, and outstanding creativity you have brought to this shared enterprise.

Chapter 1

Jack Potter, perhaps the most successful and best known attorney in Santa Fe, had recently attended a gay rights costume ball dressed as Lady Justice. The following morning a photograph of a smiling Potter, wearing a shimmering frock, a curly wig, and holding the scales of justice and a sword, appeared on the front page of the local paper.

Today Jack Potter wore a tank top, shorts, and a pair of expensive running shoes that looked brand new to Detective Ramona Pino. He was faceup on the sidewalk with a bullet hole in his chest. He'd bled out in front of his office across from the county courthouse early on a warm July morning. From the blood trail on the sidewalk, Pino could tell that Potter had crawled a good fifty feet before turning over on his back to die.

Ramona was more than slightly pissed at the man who'd discovered Potter. Alfonso Allesandro had spotted the body as he passed by in his newspaper truck, and had called the city editor on a cell phone before dialing the cops to report the crime. As a result a photographer had hurried over from the newspaper offices a few blocks away and walked through the blood trail taking pictures before the first officer arrived.

Both men were now waiting in the panel truck under the watchful eye of a uniformed officer while Pino worked the cordoned-off crime scene with the techs, searching for shell casings and anything else that looked like evidence.

Little orange evidence markers were placed at the cigarette butts lying in the gutter, at a broken toothpick found a step away from Potter's body, and next to the small puddle of fairly fresh crankcase oil in the street. One tech dusted the parking meters for fingerprints, and another worked on the door and front porch to Potter's office.

Ramona inspected the small fenced lawn in front of the building looking for any signs that shrubbery and grass had been disturbed or for fibers, threads, or hair that might have been transferred by contact. Finding nothing, she sent a tech who'd finished taking snapshots of the bloody footprints to secure the photographer's shoes so a comparison could be made. The photographer opened the truck door, pulled off his shoes, and shot Ramona a dirty look as he handed them to the tech.

Ramona smiled, but not at the photographer. The newspaper's truck bore an advertising slogan, EVERYONE READS IT, and in black spray paint someone had added:

AND WONDERS WHY

By the time an assistant district attorney, a medical examiner, and Lieutenant Sal Molina showed up, the courthouse was about to open for business. A small crowd of lawyers, clerks, judges, and officers scheduled for court appearances had gathered across the street and were scrutinizing her every move, which made her a little uneasy.

The ME, a roly-poly man with skinny arms showing below a short-sleeved shirt, went off to declare Potter officially dead. Ramona turned her back on the crowd and briefed Molina and the ADA in a low voice.

"Potter was shot in the chest at what appears to be close range," she said. "We have no witnesses to the crime and so far no substantial evidence."

"Was it a drive-by?" Molina asked.

"I don't think so," Ramona replied. "Potter took just one bullet. If the killer had been firing from a moving vehicle, he probably would have emptied his weapon at his target."

"The shooter could have been parked at the curb."

"Possibly," Ramona said. "But if the killer was in a vehicle, I doubt it was a passenger car."

"Why do you say that?" Molina asked.

"The entry and exit wounds don't look that much out of alignment," Ramona answered. "From a car, the shooter would have been firing up at an angle."

Molina nodded in agreement. "Have you found the bullet?"

"No," Pino said as she gazed down the street. At least a dozen buildings would have to be checked for the spent round, including an elementary school, an office building, and a resort hotel two blocks away across a thoroughfare that circled downtown Santa Fe. It would take hours to do the search, probably with no results.

"Maybe we'll get lucky," Molina said, reading Pino's

pessimistic expression. She was a pretty young woman with even features and soft brown eyes that often fooled people into thinking she could be easily conned or manipulated.

"What if Potter knew his killer?" Barry Foyt, the ADA, asked.

"That would be great," Molina said. "Otherwise we've got either a random shooting or robbery as the possible motive."

"Was there anything in his pockets?" Foyt asked.

"Just his keys," Ramona answered, showing the key ring in a plastic bag, "and he's still wearing his watch, although it's not an expensive one."

"So maybe we should rule out robbery as a motive as soon as possible," Foyt said, inclining his head toward the single-story adobe building that housed Potter's offices.

"Are you giving permission to search?" Ramona asked.

"Plain view only, for now," Foyt said, "including his car."

"You got it," Ramona said.

"Does he have any employees?" Molina asked, looking at the civilians who had congregated at both ends of the street behind patrol cars blocking the intersections. Uniformed officers stood by their vehicles holding them back.

"He has one secretary," Foyt replied. "I don't see her here yet."

"ID her for us when she shows," Molina said, turning his attention to Pino. "Six detectives are rolling. Let's get the uniforms started identifying onlookers and taking statements. Assign a detective to search Potter's office and put one on his car. Find his wallet. That could help us rule out robbery as a motive. Have the others canvass the neighborhood, and start the techs looking for the bullet."

"Will do, Lieutenant," Ramona said. Even with the additional help, it was going to be a busy day. Once a residential neighborhood, the McKenzie District west of the courthouse was now a mixed-use area of professional offices, private dwellings, apartments in converted houses, several bed-and-breakfast inns, retail specialty shops, and some eateries that were popular with locals. A lot of people would need to be canvassed on the assumption that someone might have noticed a suspicious person, seen a vehicle, or heard the gunshot.

"I wonder if Potter ran every morning before he started work," Molina said.

Foyt shrugged. "I know he liked to run, but I don't know if he kept to a set schedule."

"We'll find out," Ramona said.

"Have you called Chief Kerney?" Molina asked Pino.

"Negative," Ramona answered. "I wanted to secure the crime scene and get an evidence search under way first."

"I'll call him," Molina said, turning to Foyt. "Anything else you want to add, counselor?"

Barry Foyt glanced ruefully at Potter's body. He'd been handling murder cases for the DA's office for the last five years and had been called out to most of the major homicide crime scenes. But this was the first time the victim had been someone he knew and liked.

"Jack was good people," Foyt said brusquely. "Let's get a suspect in custody fast, Lieutenant."

"If only it were that easy," Molina said, thinking maybe he'd been stupid to let Kerney talk him out of putting in his retirement papers. Potter's murder could turn into a real bitch of a controversy real fast if progress on the case stalled.

If he'd been smart, he could have been out on a lake trout fishing without a care in the world, instead of facing the potential indignation of every judge, lawyer, prosecutor, and gay activist in Santa Fe.

Molina scanned the growing crowd before addressing Ramona. "I know you caught the case, Detective, but I'm taking over as primary on this one."

"I understand, Lieutenant," Ramona said.

He sent Pino and Foyt off to brief the detectives who were piling out of unmarked units, flipped open his cell phone to call the chief, and hesitated.

Kerney had picked up his pregnant wife at the Albuquerque airport last night before starting a two-week vacation. Their baby was due any day, and on top of that Kerney was having a new house built on some ranch land he'd bought outside the city.

But the chief's policy was clear: No matter where he was or what he was doing, he was to be informed immediately about every homicide or major felony that occurred within the city limits.

Reluctantly, Molina dialed Kerney's number.

Lt. Colonel Sara Brannon handed the telephone to Kerney and watched his expression change from consternation to vexation as he listened to Sal Molina. She'd just told him that when her maternity leave ended she would start a tour of duty at the Pentagon in a plum strategic planning position that would put her on track for promotion to full colonel. He wasn't at all happy about it.

"What is it?" she said after Kerney hung up.

"Nothing good," Kerney answered. "A lawyer has been shot and killed outside the courthouse."

"You'd better go," Sara said, shifting her weight in the kitchen chair to ease the pain in her back. In the last two weeks being pregnant had become increasingly uncomfortable.

"They can get along without me for a few more minutes," Kerney replied, giving Sara a long, unhappy look across the kitchen table. "I thought you were trying for an assignment closer to home."

"Believe me, I did." As a Military Police Corps officer, Sara wore the insignia of crossed pistols on her uniform. "The only possibility was with the 14th Military Police Brigade at Fort Leonard Wood in Missouri. But there were no slots available at my rank."

Kerney nodded and studied his wife's face. Fast approaching her mid-thirties, Sara was fifteen years his junior. Even with the extra pounds she'd gained during pregnancy, she was lovely to look at. She had strawberry-blond hair, a slender neck, a small line of freckles along the ridge of her nose, sparkling green eyes capable of both warmth and chilling scrutiny, and lips that could smile generously or tighten quickly into firm resolve.

"What about resigning your commission?" Kerney asked. "I recall a conversation we had about that possibility."

"I'm not ready to do that," Sara said. "You knew I was a career officer when you married me."

"Things have changed, we're about to become parents."

"Thanks for the reminder," Sara said forcing a smile and patting her tummy. "I'd totally forgotten."

"We can talk about it later," Kerney said flatly as he got to his feet. Sara's sarcasm annoyed him, but he didn't want to quarrel.

"I thought you had the time," Sara said.

"Not for this discussion," Kerney replied with an abrupt shake of his head.

He left the kitchen and returned wearing a holstered sidearm and his shield clipped to his belt. He gave her a perfunctory kiss on the cheek and went quickly out the door.

Determined not to cry or throw her coffee cup against the wall, Sara decided to draw a warm bath and take a long soak in the tub.

Kerney arrived at the crime scene to find Potter's body covered with a tarp. A large number of onlookers were clustered in the courthouse parking lot watching television reporters broadcast live feeds about the murder to network affiliates in Albuquerque. One reporter started shouting questions at Kerney from across the street.

He ignored the woman and took a quick tour of the evidence markers which, except for the bloody footprints, looked like nothing more than street litter. But if they found a suspect, DNA testing of the cigarette butts that had been marked as evidence might prove valuable.

He bent down and uncovered Potter's body. Jack's handsome, wide-eyed features were frozen in shock, and his bloody hands were pressed against a dark stain on the tank top just below the entry wound in his chest. Potter had died hard.

Jack had started his law career with the district attorney's office a few years before Kerney first joined the police department, and Kerney knew him well, professionally and socially.

After a fairly long stint as an ADA, Potter had opened a private practice specializing in criminal law, quickly becoming one of the most sought-after defense lawyers in the city. When he came out of the closet as an advocate for same-sex marriages some years later, it didn't hurt his reputation in Santa Fe one bit.

Of all the prosecutors Kerney had worked with in the district attorney's office, Jack had been the best of the lot. Outside of the job, he was charming, witty, and fun to be around.

Kerney flipped the tarp over Jack's face and stood. Inside Potter's office he found Sal Molina talking with Larry Otero, his deputy chief and second-in-command. He nodded a curt greeting to both men and turned his attention to Molina. "Fill me in, Sal, if you don't mind repeating yourself."

"Not a problem, Chief," Molina said. "Potter was shot once in the chest at close range. I'm assuming you saw the blood trail on your way in."

"I did," Kerney replied.

"He crawled down the sidewalk and died in front of his office. The ME estimates Potter was shot about fifteen minutes before his body was discovered. We're canvassing the area, but so far we haven't turned up anyone who either witnessed the event or heard the shot."

Kerney glanced around the front office, once the living room of a modest residence. It was nicely appointed with matching Southwestern-style furniture consisting of a large desk, several chairs, a couch, and a coffee table. Two large museum-quality Navajo rugs hung on the walls, and a built-in bookcase held neatly organized state and federal statute books. The door to Potter's inner office was closed.

"Have you ruled out robbery?" Kerney asked.

"Pretty much," Molina replied, "as well as burglary. We've only done a plain-view search so far, but the office and his car appear undisturbed. There are no signs of breaking and entering and the vehicle hasn't been tampered with. Both were locked, and Potter had his keys in his possession when he was shot."

"Also, his wallet containing three hundred dollars and his credit cards is in the bathroom, along with an expensive Swiss wristwatch," Otero said.

"Where's his secretary?" Kerney asked.

"She showed up a few minutes ago," Molina said. "Detective Pino has her over at the courthouse, conducting an interview."

"Is Pino the primary?" Kerney asked.

"No, I am," Molina replied.

"That's what I wanted to hear," Kerney said. "Get the secretary over here soon. Have her double-check to see if anything is missing."

"That's the plan," Molina said.

"What have you learned from her so far?" Kerney asked.

"She says that unless Potter had a court appearance or trial scheduled, he worked abbreviated hours during the summer months," Molina replied. "He'd come in early, go running for a half hour or so, and then shower and change here before starting his day. He usually finished up by mid-afternoon."

"Several neighbors have seen Potter running in the morning, and he keeps a change of clothes in his office closet," Otero said.

"So Potter kept to a daily schedule," Kerney said, "which means this might not be a random shooting."

"That's the way we read it," Molina said.

"Have you contacted Jack's life partner?" Kerney asked. Norman Kaplan, Potter's significant other, owned an upscale antique shop on Canyon Road.

"According to Potter's secretary, he's in London on a buying trip and not due back for three days," Otero said. "I called his hotel, but he's not there. I'll try him again later on."

"Are there any other next of kin?" Kerney asked.

"Not that we know about yet," Otero answered. "But the story is already on the airwaves, thanks to the photographer who showed up before our people arrived on the scene."

"What happened?" Kerney asked.

"He walked through the blood trail, took pictures, and called the newspaper on his cell phone to tell them Potter had been gunned down," Molina explained. "Detective Pino had to order him away from the crime scene."

"Do we have this bozo in hand?" Kerney asked.

"Yeah, he's outside in the panel truck cooling his heels, waiting to give a statement," Otero said. "He's not too happy about it."

"Have a detective take his statement and then arrest

11

him for tampering with evidence and interfering with a criminal investigation," Kerney said.

"Those charges probably won't stick, Chief," Otero said.

"I don't give a damn if they stick or not," Kerney said. "Let the DA sort it out."

Otero eyed Kerney, who was usually levelheaded when it came to dealing with the media. He wondered what was biting the chief. It had to be more than a stupid photographer's mistakes. "Are you sure that's what you want us to do?" he asked.

Kerney bit his lip and shook his head. "You're right. It's a dumb idea. Put a scare into him, instead."

"We can do that," Molina said.

"Get a handle on this fast, Sal," Kerney said. "Let's find someone with a motive—friends, clients, enemies, you know the drill."

Molina nodded.

"I'll talk to the reporters," Otero said.

"Give them the usual spiel, Larry," Kerney said, heading for the door, "and keep me informed. Call me on my cell phone."

The bald-headed man waited inside the courthouse until the cops finished canvassing the onlookers and moved away. Then he joined a cluster of people who were watching TV reporters talk excitedly into microphones with their backs to the crime scene as camera operators got good visuals of Potter's tarp-covered body lying on the sidewalk.

He smiled when a stern-looking Kevin Kerney came out of Potter's office and walked quickly down the street. Several newspaper reporters jogged behind crime scene tape that held them at bay, yelling questions that Kerney waved off.

Soon Kerney would suffer from far more than the unpleasantness of Jack Potter's death. With all that had been put into play, plus what was yet to come, Kerney would quickly realize his world was about to disintegrate. If Kerney proved slow on the uptake, the bald-headed man had devised ways to give him a little nudge or two in the right direction.

He turned on his heel and walked way. It was time to return to his war room and gear up for the next phase of the plan.

The spat with Sara had put Kerney in a bad mood, and Jack Potter's murder only added to it. He decided to cool down before going home, and drove to the South Capitol neighborhood where Fletcher Hartley lived. In his seventies, Fletcher was a highly regarded Santa Fe artist, a retired museum director, and an old friend who'd assisted Kerney in a major art heist investigation several years ago, during his tenure with the state police.

A colorful eccentric, Fletcher was a prominent fixture in the gay community and a potential source of good information about Jack Potter's personal life.

Fletcher's sprawling adobe was nestled at the bottom of a large sloping lot behind a beautifully landscaped, expansive front yard filled with hedges and trees that screened the house from the street. Situated in a neighborhood of older homes lined up in tidy rows, Fletcher's hidden rural oasis was the crown jewel of a charming, residential area that still retained a small-town feel.

Kerney rang the doorbell and listened to a Beethoven piano sonata that flowed through the open windows of the front room. Fletcher opened the door clutching a book. He wore his favorite kimono and a pair of screaming-pink silk pajama bottoms. Reading glasses were perched on his nose, which had recently been made perfect by plastic surgery. Fletcher fought the aging process by every possible means. In the past, his cheeks had been lifted and his wrinkles tucked to give him the face of a fifty-year-old.

Kerney had heard about the nose job, but hadn't seen it until now.

"I know," Fletcher said with a smile, noticing Kerney's quick appraisal, "I'm a vain old coot." He turned to give Kerney a view of his improved profile. "Do you like it?"

"You look great," Kerney said. "Sorry to bother you so early."

"Pooh," Fletcher said, smiling broadly at the compliment. "You know full well that I am always home to visitors. I thrive on distraction. Come in, dear boy. Join me in the kitchen for a cup of coffee."

Kerney sat at the large antique Spanish Colonial table, where he'd spent many pleasant hours chatting with Fletcher, and told him about Jack Potter's murder. On an open shelf above a kitchen counter, a small menagerie of hand-carved wooden folk art animal figures—two chickens, a rabbit, and a pig—overlooked the scene.

Fletcher's cheery expression vanished. "You can't be serious," he said, his voice filled with dismay. He filled Kerney's coffee cup with a shaky hand and replaced the carafe in the coffeemaker. "This is tragic."

14

Kerney nodded solemnly. "What can you tell me about Jack that I don't already know?"

"You can't be thinking that Norman had anything to do with it," Fletcher said as he sat across from Kerney.

"Norman is in London. He doesn't know what happened, unless of course Kaplan hired a contract killer."

"Don't be absurd," Fletcher replied. "This will break the poor man's heart. They were such a loving couple, perfect for each other. How familiar are you with Jack's private life?"

"Until he came out, I just figured him to be the confirmed bachelor type," Kerney said. "I've met Norman socially, but Jack never talked to me about any of his personal relationships or his family."

"Until Jack met Norman he'd kept his sexual orientation out of public view," Fletcher said. "His love for Norman helped him realize that being gay was something to openly celebrate. As far as family goes, he was an only child and both his parents are dead. He is close to an aunt who is retired and lives in Tucson. Jack and Norman visit her several times a year."

"Do you have a name?" Kerney asked.

"Maude is her first name, I believe," Fletcher said. "But I'm sure Norman will know how to get in touch with her, or Jack's secretary should."

"Did he have any lovers before Norman who caused him trouble?" Kerney asked.

"He had a long-standing affair with a rather troubled young man whom he supported on the Q.T. for several years. Jack paid the rent, gave the boy expense money when he wasn't working, and bought his clothes. It was a May-September affair. The lad was a good twenty-five years younger than Jack. It was also common knowledge that the boy was not mentally sound."

"How so?" Kerney asked.

"He was in and out of the psychiatric ward for fits of depression and suicidal tendencies. When he was stable, he worked as a waiter. But as time went on, he became more unbalanced, less able to hold a job, and totally promiscuous. Jack had no choice but to end it."

"Did it end badly?"

"In chaotic uproar," Fletcher replied. "But Jack kept it under wraps from the straight community."

"Do you have a name to give me?" Kerney asked.

"That's a story in itself. The young man's name was Matthew B. Patterson. It's now Mary Beth Patterson. He had a sex-change operation up in Colorado six years ago. It made a world of difference for him."

Kerney finished his coffee and put the cup aside. "In what way?" he asked.

"Matthew was small-boned, almost petite, and very feminine, with soft doe eyes and pretty features. But he wasn't at all the swishy queen type. There was a woman hiding inside his body, and once Mary Beth emerged his depression and self-destructive tendencies seemed to vanish, at least for a time."

"Aren't sex-change operations expensive?" Kerney asked.

"Indeed. Jack paid for it as a settlement to the affair."

"And to keep it quiet?"

"That also," Fletcher replied. "All this happened before Jack and Norman became an item."

"So did the problem with Matthew go away?"

Fletcher nodded. "Only to be replaced by the arrival

of Mary Beth on the scene. She came back fully expecting Jack to marry her, which of course he did not do."

"Then what happened?" Kerney asked.

"Mary Beth took on the characteristics of a hysterical, wronged woman. She tried every ploy to get Jack back, including stalking him for a time."

"Did she make any threats?"

"Not that I know of."

"How was the situation resolved?"

"When Jack rejected her advances, she mutilated herself with a knife by cutting her arms and then called for an ambulance to take her to the hospital. The doctors diagnosed her as a borderline personality. Jack paid for her medical care, sorted out her disability benefits, and got her into a group home for mentally ill adults. She met another patient there and fell in love with him. They've been living together ever since they moved out of the group home."

"How do you know all this?" Kerney asked.

"Partially from Jack, but Mary Beth's lover is my new gardener. I've only employed him for a couple of months. His name is Kurt Larsen. He's much older than Mary Beth and suffers from post-traumatic stress disorder."

"Where can I find Mary Beth?"

"They live in an apartment complex run by a mental health clinic."

"I know the place," Kerney said.

"I'm sure you do."

"Tell me about Larsen."

"Kurt is quiet but pleasant, except when something triggers his war experiences. Then he becomes agitated, out of sorts, and drinks heavily. When he comes to work sullen and hungover I always know that he's had one of his episodes. He's a Vietnam veteran, an ex-Marine."

"You've been very helpful, Fletcher," Kerney said as he went to the sink and rinsed out his coffee cup.

"I'd like to say it's always a pleasure to assist the police," Fletcher replied with a rueful smile. "But this is so very sad. I must do something to help Norman get through this."

Kerney nodded in agreement. "I may need to talk to you about this again."

"Of course, as you wish. But you can't just jump up and leave until you agree to bring your lovely wife here for dinner. I think it would be best to do it before the baby arrives and you both become totally preoccupied with the exhausting tasks of parenthood. Are you free Friday night?"

"That should work," Kerney said.

"You must promise not to be called away on some pressing police matter."

"I'm on vacation."

Fletcher raised an eyebrow. "Really? One would hardly know it."

Kerney laughed. "No police business, I promise."

"Perfect. I'll pull out my cookbooks and start menu planning. We'll have a grand feast."

"As always," Kerney said.

"Neither Mary Beth nor Kurt strikes me as a killer," Fletcher said.

"Killers come in all flavors," Kerney said, as he patted Fletcher on the shoulder and left to the soft sounds of Beethoven.

In his unit, he got on the horn to Sal Molina and gave

him the rundown on Mary Beth Patterson and Kurt Larsen.

"Well, at least now we've got something to follow-up on," Molina said.

"No luck at the crime scene?" Kerney asked.

"Not so far," Sal replied.

Kerney arrived home to find Sara waiting expectantly for him. Their first day of vacation together was to have started with a visit to the construction site of their new house. Up to now, Sara had only seen the photographs Kerney had mailed to her. Last night she'd been excited and eager to see it firsthand. But their early-morning spat had left Sara less than enthusiastic. She nodded curtly when he asked if she was ready to go, walked quickly to his pickup truck, sat looking straight ahead, and said nothing as he wheeled out of the driveway. Feeling guilty about the squabble, Kerney matched Sara's silence with his own.

Halfway through the drive, Sara looked at her hands, twisted her wedding ring with her thumb, and asked about the homicide.

Kerney gave her a brief summary. "It could be a tough one to solve," he said in conclusion.

"You were so long getting back, I thought you had abandoned our plans for the morning," Sara said.

"I wouldn't do that," Kerney replied. "I stopped by to talk to Fletcher. He had some interesting information about Jack Potter that might prove helpful."

"You could've sent a detective to meet with Fletcher," she said flatly, her eyes still fixed on the road ahead.

"Yes, but I wanted to cool down a bit," Kerney said. "Besides, seeing Fletcher got us a dinner invitation at his house for Friday night."

"If we're talking to each other by then, I suppose we should go."

"Aren't we talking now?"

Sara squinted against the sunlight and lowered the visor. "Not really."

They left the highway and drove the ranch road to the cutoff that took them through a pasture on their new property and up toward a long ridgeline. Kerney had spent several weekends improving the road with a borrowed grader, spreading and packing vast amounts of gravel to make it usable year-round. No longer rutted, narrow, and rocky, it climbed gently to a large sheltered bowl below the crest, where several low courses of new adobe walls stood on the recently poured concrete pad.

Sara made no comment about the road, nor about the red prefabricated galvanized steel horse barn that had been erected a good half a mile from the house. She was out of the truck and moving toward their contractor, Bobby Trujillo, before Kerney set the parking brake and killed the engine.

Trujillo met Sara halfway across the open field. Together they walked around the outside perimeter of the partially raised adobe walls, inspecting the work in progress. Kerney decided to let them go on without him and took a hike in the direction of the horse barn to check on Soldier, the mustang he'd trained as a cutting horse.

Soldier had been pastured at Dale Jennings's ranch down on the Tularosa for the past several years. Two weekends ago, after the barn and corral were completed, Dale, his boyhood chum and lifelong friend, had brought Soldier up by trailer along with his own mount. The two men camped out on the property overnight and covered all of Kerney's two sections—twelve hundred and eighty acres—by horseback the following day.

It had been Kerney's best weekend away from the job in several months. Dale had left shaking his head in wonder and amusement at the beauty of the land and its magnificent views of the distant mountains, the size of the house Kerney was building, and the fact that his old buddy had put up a six-stall barn that for now would serve one lonely animal.

The corral gate was closed and the stall door was open, but Soldier wasn't inside the arena or under the covered shelter that ran the length of the barn. Inside the corral, Kerney inspected the water trough and free-standing hay rack he'd filled yesterday before leaving to pick up Sara at the airport. Both looked untouched. He glanced into the empty stall, which he'd purposely left open to give Soldier access to the corral. The interior gate to the center aisle was closed and latched.

Kerney stood in the corral and did a three-sixty looking for his horse. He was nowhere in sight. Kerney doubted Soldier could have gotten out without assistance. He'd carefully padlocked all the other exterior doors to keep rodents and other small animals from gaining access.

He walked around the barn. Except for Soldier's stall it was secure. He unlocked the barn doors, pushed one back, and saw Soldier lying on the concrete pad that ran the length of the center aisle. He stepped in and inspected the animal. Soldier had been shot three times in the stomach and left to die. In his death throes, he'd kicked and dented the steel wall with his forelegs. Blood from the wounds had stained the concrete and soaked into the dirt floor in front of a stall door.

Because he was starting out with just one animal, Kerney had jokingly named the spread the One Horse Ranch. Now it wasn't even that anymore. He bent down and stroked Soldier's head. He'd been a fine horse, a smart horse. Who would do such a thing? And why?

Outside, he used his cell phone to call Andy Baca, his ex-boss and the chief of the state police. He told Andy what had happened to Soldier and asked him to dispatch a patrol officer.

"Do you want me to send an agent also?" Andy asked.

"No, I'll handle the crime scene myself," Kerney said.

"Are you sure?"

"Yeah," Kerney said.

"This doesn't sit right with me," Andy said.

"With me either," Kerney replied. "Somebody went out of his way to kill my horse as painfully as possible."

"You got any idea who did it?"

"Only a handful of people knew Soldier was on the property, and none of them carry any grudges against me, as far as I know."

"Well, somebody's sending you a message," Andy said.

"It looks that way."

"Maybe you've got a wacko on the crew building your house."

"Maybe," Kerney said. "But I've gotten to know the guys pretty well and none of them strikes me that way."

"You never know."

"True enough," Kerney said.

"Any leads on the Jack Potter homicide?"

"Nothing worth talking about yet," Kerney answered.

"Keep me informed, and if you need help, just ask."

"I will, and thanks." Kerney disconnected and called Tug Cheney, a veterinarian he knew from his days as a caretaker of a small ranch on the Galisteo Basin. Tug told him Soldier could be sent to Albuquerque for an autopsy or he could do a quick and dirty one himself.

"I know what killed my horse," Kerney said. "What I want are the bullets out of Soldier's stomach. When can you get out here?"

"Give me directions to your place and I'll be there in an hour," Tug said.

Kerney supplied directions, thanked Tug, stuck the cell phone back on his belt, and turned to see Sara walking slowly in his direction from the construction site.

Today he'd argued with a woman he adored, seen the murdered body of a man he liked, and found a horse he loved maliciously destroyed. It was a crummy way to start a vacation.

He started toward Sara to give her the news.

Chapter 2

Detective Pino finished her courthouse interview with Stephanie Dwyer, Potter's secretary, and escorted her across the now-empty parking lot past the crime scene. Potter's body had been removed, but the blood trail on the sidewalk made Dwyer start sobbing all over again. Ramona guided her into the office, spent a few minutes calming her down, and then left her with another detective to conduct a complete inventory to determine if anything was missing from Potter's office.

Outside, she found Lieutenant Molina waiting and gave him her report. Dwyer knew of no reasons for Potter's murder. There had been no threats made against him, no hate mail or mysterious phone calls received, and nothing in Potter's recent behavior had pointed to any kind of worry or undue emotional stress. Although Ramona had quizzed her closely about Potter's past and current clients, friends, and associates, Dwyer was unable to think of anyone who held a grudge against her boss. Additionally, Dwyer, who kept the financial books for the practice as well as Potter's personal and housekeeping accounts, reported that there had been no unusual or suspicious flow of money, which might point to extortion or payoffs.

"Did Dwyer have an alibi?" Molina asked.

"Yes, and I confirmed it by telephone," Ramona replied. "She dropped her daughter off at day care and went to an early morning yoga class for working mothers."

Molina held out a slip of paper. "Go talk to this person."

Ramona read the note. "Who is she?"

"A transsexual who stalked Potter some years ago, after he ended a relationship with her," Molina replied. "She lives with her current boyfriend, who runs a one-man gardening service. Both of them are head cases. The boyfriend isn't home—he's a gardener and leaves early for work. I've got Sergeant Tafoya looking for him. His name is Kurt Larsen."

"What kind of head cases are they?" Ramona asked.

"Larsen's a vet with post-traumatic stress, and Patterson gets hysterical and cuts herself with a knife to get attention. The shrinks call it a borderline personality."

"You talked to their shrinks?" Ramona said.

"No, I spoke with the caseworker who supervises the apartments where Patterson and Larsen live. It's an independent living program for mental patients run by a local agency. The caseworker's name is Joyce Barbero. See her first before you meet with Patterson."

"Will do," Ramona said.

"It might be something," Molina said halfheartedly. "As it is, we're getting nothing from the neighborhood canvass."

"Have we found the spent bullet?"

"The techs are still looking, but I wouldn't count on them getting lucky. Be careful with Patterson."

Ramona rolled her eyes in agreement and went off to meet with a loony-tune transsexual who liked to play with knives.

Patterson and Larsen lived in a single-story apartment building behind a large discount department store just off Cerrillos Road, the busiest, noisiest, ugliest street in Santa Fe. A high concrete block wall tagged with graffiti separated the two structures.

The building had eight units with entrances fronting the street. Patches of stucco had broken off the exterior, exposing the gray undercoat, and the painted wood trim around the doors and windows was chipped and peeling. Landscaping consisted of some low-maintenance native shrubs and a few large boulders in a gravel bed that ran the length of the building from the sidewalk to the front stoops. On the street, litter had accumulated under several broken-down vehicles that were up on blocks and in the process of being repaired.

A sign in front of an end unit announced the office of the La Puerta Mental Health Independent Living Center, and asked all visitors to check in. Ramona rang the bell and was greeted by Joyce Barbero.

A large, round, middle-aged woman dressed in a loose-fitting skirt and top, Barbero carefully inspected Ramona's credentials.

"I'm sure Mary Beth had nothing to do with the murder," Barbero said.

"We're just gathering information about Mr. Potter from people who knew him," Ramona replied. "Did you know him?"

"Not personally. Mary Beth talks about him occasionally in group therapy. His rejection hurt her deeply."

"Did he ever come here to visit Mary Beth?"

"Not that I'm aware of."

"Would it be possible to check on that?" Ramona asked.

"We keep a log of all visitors," Barbero replied. "Our rules require it."

"Both day and nighttime visitors?"

"Yes, we have shift supervisors who sleep over. Visitors must leave by nine P.M."

"Would you check your records?"

"It will take some time to go through the file."

"I'll stop back after I've talked to Ms. Patterson," Ramona said. "Does she have any violent tendencies?"

"Not towards other people."

"You're sure of that? I understand she was very angry with Potter."

"Angry, yes, but not aggressive. I described Mary Beth's behavior to your lieutenant. She can be self-destructive. But it's an attention-getting device, and she hasn't mutilated herself in a very long time."

"Are there knives in the apartment?"

"Of course."

Barbero directed Ramona to Patterson's apartment and watched from her front stoop. Ramona rang once and the door opened. If she hadn't been given a heads up about Patterson's sex change operation, she never would have guessed it. At five-three, Mary Beth matched Ramona's height. Her features were feminine, her figure shapely, and her makeup was perfectly applied.

For all of that Ramona still had to force back a smile; Patterson wore a knee-length, short-sleeved, light blue summer dress with a high neckline that looked like it had come from the costume department of a 1960s TV sitcom. It was topped off by a pink chiffon scarf tied under her chin that covered the curlers in her hair.

Mary Beth smiled shyly and touched the scarf. A series of long, thin scars ran up her forearm. "I wasn't expecting company," she said in a soft tenor voice. "Who are you?"

"I'm a police officer," Romana said, showing her shield.

Patterson took a deep breath and patted her chest. "Why would you want to talk to me? I haven't done anything bad to myself."

"I'm sure you haven't. May I come in?"

Mary Beth turned quickly and her skirt swished across her legs. "Only if you promise not to lie to me."

"I wouldn't do that," Ramona said.

"The police always lie to me," Mary Beth replied with a pout, as she sat on an oversized ottoman with a worn cushion, crossed her legs, and demurely pulled her skirt down over her knees.

The front room of the apartment was furnished with what looked like castoffs and thrift shop purchases. An old couch covered with a faded quilt faced a large laminated-wood wall unit that contained a television set with a rabbit-ears antenna. A small table radio tuned to a country station was playing a mournful ballad about the pain of lost love.

In front of the couch, a battered piano bench had been cut down to serve as a coffee table. A collection of cheap glass figurines of dancing women were carefully arranged on the shelf above the TV. On the wall behind the ottoman were a Marine Corps insignia plaque and a shadow box containing military decorations, lance corporal stripes, and expert marksman awards.

"How do the police lie to you?" Ramona asked.

"They tell me I need help and then they take me to the hospital," Mary Beth replied, still pouting. "I ask them not to do it and they say they have to. They could just leave me alone and go away, but they won't."

"Maybe they're just trying to help you," Ramona said.

Mary Beth arched her neck. "I don't need help," she said haughtily. "I'm much better now that I have my Kurt."

"I'm glad to hear that. I've come to ask you about Jack Potter."

Mary Beth winced as though she'd been slapped. "Don't say that name to me."

"We have to talk about him."

"Why?"

"He was murdered this morning," Ramona answered.

Mary Beth put a hand to her mouth and giggled. "Goodie," she said brightly.

"You don't mind that he's dead?"

She was silent for a moment and her face lost all expression. "I did everything for him. Anything he wanted. He said he loved me, but he didn't."

"That must have been hard for you."

Mary Beth's foot began wagging rapidly, bright red toenails showing through the open end of her sandal. She ran a finger up her arm, tracing one of the long, thin scars, and said nothing. Suddenly, she lunged off the ottoman and walked past Ramona to the bathroom.

Ramona followed and from the open doorway watched Mary Beth remove her scarf and start taking curlers out of her hair, dropping them in the sink one by one.

A baby blue shower curtain covered the tub and a shelf above the sink held a large array of inexpensive perfume and cologne bottles. On top of the toilet tank a pair of scissors were within easy reach.

"Let's go back in the living room and talk," Ramona said, stepping closer to the toilet.

Mary Beth shook her head in a fierce rebuttal. "If I talk to you, you'll just think I killed him."

"Why would I think that?"

The last curler dropped into the sink and Mary Beth started furiously brushing her thick, dark hair. "Because I used to say I wanted to. Because for a long time that's all I would talk about. Because I stalked him and that was a bad thing to do."

Mary Beth's high tenor voice lost its feminine veneer. She sounded like a frightened, prepubescent boy.

"Everybody has someone in their life they want to hurt or get back at," Ramona said. "Those feelings don't make you a murderer."

The hairbrush in Mary Beth's hand stopped in midstroke. "You're just saying that."

"No, I'm not," Ramona said. "Answer a few questions and we can clear everything up."

"What kind of questions?"

"Easy ones," Ramona said. "Have you been home all morning?"

Mary Beth relaxed a bit. "Yes, I only go out with Kurt because I don't know how to drive and it's too far to walk anywhere."

"That's important for me to know. Have you seen anybody this morning?"

Mary Beth put the brush down and ran her fingers through her hair to fluff it up. "Just Kurt. I fixed his breakfast and then he went to work."

"What time was that?"

She studied her face in the mirror, turning her head from side to side to view her wavy locks. "He gets up at five during the summer when he's busy. I had his breakfast waiting for him. I always fix his breakfast."

"When did he leave?"

"About a half hour later. I packed him a nice lunch: a meatloaf sandwich and some cookies that I made last night. He's a big man and he needs to have a good meal at lunchtime."

"It sounds like you take good care of Kurt," Ramona said. The comment earned her a pleased smile. "Has he ever expressed any resentment about Jack Potter?"

Mary Beth's smile dissolved. "What do you mean?"

"Is he angry about the way Potter treated you?"

Mary Beth tentatively shook her head, reached for the brush and started in on her hair again with a trembling hand.

"He's okay about Potter?"

"Why shouldn't he be?" Mary Beth said sharply.

"Did Kurt ever say he wanted to get even with Potter because of the way he treated you?"

"My Kurt is a good man," Mary Beth said, swiveling from the mirror to face Ramona. "Now you have to go."

"Does Kurt own a gun?"

"I don't like guns."

"But does he own one?"

"You think Kurt killed Jack and you're trying to get me to help you put him in jail."

"Not at all," Ramona replied. "What kind of gun does Kurt have, Mary Beth?"

"I'm not talking to you anymore," Mary Beth said sternly. She stormed out of the bathroom, walked to the front door, and opened it. "Go away."

"Does Kurt have a cell phone?" Ramona asked as she followed along.

"No, and even if he did he's much too busy to call me."

Ramona stepped outside. "Do you know where he's working?"

"Kurt didn't kill anyone. Can't you believe that?"

"I want to believe it," Ramona said, "but you're not helping me give Kurt a chance to clear his name."

Mary Beth responded by slamming the door in Ramona's face.

Ramona walked to the office thinking that no matter how batty Mary Beth might be, she still did one hell of a job of standing by her man.

Ramona checked in with Barbero, who reported there was no record of Jack Potter visiting the facility. She also confirmed that Mary Beth didn't drive, never used the city buses, and rarely went out alone.

"Do you know if Larsen owns a gun?" Ramona asked.

Barbero winced at the thought of it. "That's not allowed."

Ramona blew past Barbero's gullibility and asked for

Larsen's business number. She went inside, returned with a piece of paper and handed it to Ramona.

"It's a cell-phone number," Barbero said. "Did talking to you upset Mary Beth?"

"You could say that," Ramona replied.

Barbero gave her a pained look and scurried off to check on Mary Beth's emotional welfare.

Ramona dialed the number. Surprise, surprise, the line was busy. In her unit, she tried to make radio contact with Sergeant Cruz Tafoya, who had been assigned by Molina to find Larsen, and got no response. She called his cell phone and it rang through to his voice mail. She left a message that Larsen was possibly armed with a gun, then disconnected and asked dispatch for Tafoya's location. He was at a house in an upscale rural subdivision in the foothills above the village of Tesuque, a few miles outside of town.

"When he calls in, tell him I'm en route to his twenty," Ramona said. "Ask him to stand by."

By the time the veterinarian arrived, State Police Officer Russell Thorpe had taken Kerney's statement and photographed the dead animal, and then completed a field search with the chief around the perimeter of the horse barn looking for evidence. Kerney pointed out some shoe prints and tire marks in front of the corral, in a spot where no vehicle had been parked during construction.

After Kerney, his wife, and the vet went into the barn, Thorpe gathered soil samples, sketched and photographed the impressions, and mixed up a batch of dental plaster to do the castings.

Thorpe had recently transferred to Santa Fe from the Las Vegas district. He'd first met Kerney soon after his graduation from the academy when body parts of a decomposed butchered female had been found on land Kerney had inherited and then later sold to the Nature Conservancy.

At the time, Kerney was deputy chief of the state police. He took charge of the investigation and Russell worked on the homicide with him. In the course of that assignment, Thorpe fell asleep while on surveillance, causing him to lose contact with the murder suspect, who was later caught and convicted. Kerney saved Russell's budding career by giving him a butt-chewing rather than an official reprimand. Now Thorpe hoped to pay back the favor by doing thorough work and maybe even catching the bad guy.

He cleaned out the loose material from the indentations, sprayed a plastic coating on each, built a form around every impression, and carefully poured the plaster in stages, building each form up as he went to avoid letting the material run off and spoil the casting.

Russell left the forms to dry and walked to the barn. The veterinarian had cut into the hide of the horse, sawed through some ribs, and sliced and pinned back the stomach muscles. Now he was probing for a spent round with a pair of forceps. The concrete pad under his feet ran blood red, and the smell from the exposed guts wasn't pleasant.

A grim Kerney and his equally unhappy-looking wife stood behind the vet watching. Tug Cheney grunted, gently extracted a slug and dropped it into Kerney's gloved hand.

He inspected it, marked it, and put it in a plastic bag.

Thorpe asked to see the bullet and Kerney handed him the bag. The tip of the slug was dented, probably from hitting a rib. Other than that, Thorpe wasn't sure what he was looking at.

"Is it from a handgun?" he asked.

Kerney nodded. "Probably a .38-caliber revolver."

"How can you tell?"

"From the diameter of the slug and the fact that a semi-automatic round is usually fully encased in a one-piece metal jacket. The bullet you're holding doesn't have a jacket covering the lead core and it shows spiral grooves from the rifling of the barrel. It explains why we didn't find any spent cartridges."

Thorpe nodded and handed back the bag. "Anything else?"

"The hair around one of the entry wounds was blistered," Kerney replied. "That means the shooter fired from close range, no more than two inches. He deliberately gut shot Soldier, then fired two more rounds to finish the job."

"That sucks," Thorpe said.

Kerney nodded. Years ago, he'd been gut shot by a drug dealer, so he had a fairly good idea of the pain Soldier had suffered before dying. He wondered if there was a connection between the two events. That was unlikely: Kerney had put the drug dealer down permanently before passing out, so that particular dirtbag couldn't possibly be a suspect. So, who was?

If the way Soldier was killed wasn't a coincidence, Kerney thought, then the shooter was telling him that he knew his personal history, what he cared about, where he lived, and how easy it would be to get to him or those he loved.

"What do you want me to do next, Chief?" Thorpe asked.

"Get me a large plastic bag," Kerney said, noticing for the first time that Soldier was wearing a halter. Yesterday, he'd removed it and put it on a hook inside the stall.

He stepped to the head of the horse, took out a pocket knife, cut through the halter to avoid touching the buckle, and slipped it off. He held it by the edges of his gloved fingertips until Thorpe returned with the bag.

"When you're finished here, have the lab check for prints and compare them to mine," he said to Thorpe as he eased it into the bag and zipped it shut.

"Got another one," Tug said, lifting out the forceps and dropping a bullet into Kerney's hand. "I think the last one went straight through the stomach cavity. We'll have to lift him up to see."

Kerney marked and bagged the round. "We can use the contractor's backhoe to do that." He turned to Thorpe. "Have it brought over here, and then check the crew members' shoes and their vehicle tires against the castings."

"What about the subcontractors?" Thorpe asked.

"Good point. Trujillo can provide us with names and addresses. I'll follow up with them later."

"I can do it," Thorpe said. "Chief Baca said I'm assigned to the case until you release me."

"You wouldn't mind?"

Russell smiled. "I owe you one, Chief."

"Okay, it's yours. Take statements, too."

"Affirmative," Thorpe said, as he left to get Trujillo.

"What do we do with Soldier?" Sara asked.

"You can either have the carcass shipped to Albuquerque for disposal or you can bury him here on your property," Tug said.

"We'll bury him," Sara said, before Kerney could respond.

Kerney bit his lip and nodded in agreement.

Tug stripped off his gloves and gave Kerney a solemn look. "I'm done here. Sorry for your loss. He was a fine animal. Whoever did this should be shot."

"That's not a bad idea," Sara said.

She put her arm around Kerney's waist as they walked Cheney to his truck and thanked him. Across the field, Trujillo cranked up the backhoe while Thorpe checked the tires of the parked vehicles against the plaster castings.

"What's this all about?" Sara said as Tug drove away.

"I don't know yet."

"It's freaky."

"I know," Kerney said, looking at Sara with sad eyes. "About this morning. . . ."

"We don't have to talk about that now."

"I want to. Whatever you decide to do is fine with me, as long as I can keep you and the baby in my life."

"That's a sweet sentiment," Sara said, turning to look Kerney in the eye. "But it doesn't get you out of really talking things through with me."

Kerney nodded. "We don't have to have an ordinary marriage. Maybe that's best."

"Meaning?"

Kerney smiled weakly. "I'm not sure."

Kerney's deep-set blue eyes moved from her face to the barn. He pulled himself ramrod straight, his six-one

37

frame accentuated by big shoulders, a broad chest, and a slim waist set off by a rodeo belt buckle he'd won in a high school competition. Only a touch of gray at his temples and crow's feet at the corners of his eyes hinted at his true age. He cleared his sad expression and replaced it with a look of detachment that tightened his square jaw. But the corded muscles in his neck showed the pain and anger he felt over the loss of Soldier.

"I have to take care of Soldier," he said. "Bury him."

"I know you do," Sara said, as she lifted her head and kissed him on the cheek.

"What's that for?"

"For being who you are," Sara said, squeezing his hand.

Bobby Trujillo arrived with the backhoe and some chains. Kerney guided him into the barn, and Bobby used the forks of the bucket to lift Soldier's hindquarters so Kerney could wrap a chain around the animal and secure it to the bucket. They repeated the process at Soldier's shoulders, then Bobby raised the animal a few inches off the pad and backed slowly out of the barn.

Under the bloody mess, Kerney could see the third flattened bullet embedded in the concrete, but retrieving it would have to wait until everything got cleaned up.

"Where do you want the horse to go?" Bobby asked, when Kerney came out of the barn.

"I'll take care of it," Kerney said, "if you'll let me borrow the backhoe."

Bobby nodded and climbed down.

"I'll follow you in the truck," Sara said.

Kerney pulled himself into the cab, raised the backhoe, swung the machine around, and started for the rutted ranch road that led to the ridge top. He stared down at Soldier's stiff legs and exposed innards and looked quickly away to force down his anger.

Sara caught up with him in the truck as he climbed the ridge. He topped out and found a spot off the ranch road where a massive old piñon tree stood near a fair-sized boulder. He lowered Soldier to the ground, unchained him, and dug a deep trench. He used the forks of the hoe to nudge Soldier into the trench, put the chains away, and began covering up the hole.

Sara stood by Kerney's truck with moist eyes studying the intense expression on Kerney's face, thinking how hard it had to be for him to maintain his composure. Under much more tragic circumstances, he'd done this before when his parents had been killed in a head-on traffic accident while traveling to meet him at the Albuquerque airport upon his return from 'Nam. He'd placed his military decorations in their caskets, dug their graves by hand, and buried them in a beautiful grove of trees on Dale Jennings's ranch, where his parents had lived and worked for many years. Surely, that memory had to be coursing through his mind.

She watched him dig out the boulder, move it to the grave site, and place it on top of the mound of dirt. She could see his stiff hands working the levers and the hard set of his jaw as he packed and smoothed the earth around the rock.

It was a lovely spot to put Soldier to rest, with a view of the expansive ridge-top pasture land and the surrounding mountain vistas.

Sara thought about the new set of military decorations she'd requested and received through official

Army channels to replace the ones Kerney had buried with his parents so many years ago. They were in her suitcase. Kerney knew nothing about them. She planned to give them to him after the birth of their baby. Not for Kerney to keep, but to pass on to his son. Now, more than ever, it felt like the right thing to do.

He waved to her that he had finished, spun the backhoe around, and started for the ranch road. Sara followed as Kerney moved slowly down the ridge. The baby kicked her hard in the stomach.

She placed her hand on her belly. "I know you're there, little one," she said softly.

Ramona Pino met up with Sergeant Cruz Tafoya at the end of the driveway to a two-million-dollar estate in the hills behind Tesuque. Stout and balding with a scraggly black mustache and a toothy grin, Cruz greeted her with a quick nod of his head. He was wearing a Kevlar vest over his white cowboy shirt.

"So Larsen's armed and dangerous," he said.

"Armed at least," Ramona replied.

"Same thing," Tafoya said. "Is he a credible suspect?"

"We won't know until we talk to him," Ramona said. "But from what the girlfriend told me, he left home in plenty of time to kill Potter before heading off to work."

"Well, let's do it," Tafoya said. "Larsen got a phone call while he was here and told the estate manager he had to bid on a gardening job at a neighbor's house and would be back later to finish up. His tools are still here. The road dead ends on the hill behind us, and Larsen's truck is parked at the last house. Put on your vest and follow me."

"Let's hope he's there," Ramona said. "He may have been tipped off that we're looking for him." She popped the trunk of her unit and strapped on her body armor.

"By the girlfriend?" Tafoya asked.

"Yeah," Ramona replied.

"Is she really a girl?" Cruz asked.

"From the top of her curly head right down to her little red toenails. She's a marvel of modern medicine."

Cruz shook his head in disbelief. "Santa Fe, the city different."

The hilltop house had a steep driveway that curved to a level parking area overlooking the road. Larsen's truck was in plain view in front of a three-car garage. The garage doors were closed and no other vehicles were present. Ramona left her unit angled to block the driveway and walked up the driveway to Cruz, who'd positioned his unit behind Larsen's truck. Together they walked up stone steps through a patio door and into a large courtyard, where a fountain of cut polished stone columns trickled water into a bed of pebbles. An L-shaped portal covered both the entrance and a large living room with glass doors and windows that looked out on the courtyard.

They stood on either side of the oversized hacienda-style double doors. Cruz rang the bell while Ramona kept her eye out for movement inside the living room. The doorbell brought no response.

Tafoya tried again with the same result. "See anything happening inside?"

"Nothing."

Tafoya unholstered his sidearm. "Perimeter search," he said, pointing the direction he wanted her to go.

Ramona took out her weapon and began her sweep. Staying as concealed as possible, she checked every door and window, finished the circle, and met up with Tafoya at the back of the house, where a patio provided a spectacular view of the Jemez Mountains to the west and the Tesuque Valley below.

Ramona shook her head to signal no contact. Beyond the valley she could see the soaring roof of the Santa Fe Opera and the white tents of the adjacent flea market that bordered the highway.

"Some place," Tafoya said.

"There's a trail off the master bedroom door that leads up towards the mountains," Ramona said. "I saw some fresh footprints."

Cruz flipped open his cell phone and dialed the number of the alarm company he'd written down from the sign posted at the end of the driveway. He identified himself, gave his shield number, and asked for information about the owners and any occupants, employees, or personnel with authorized access to the property.

He listened and shrugged as though what he'd heard was no big surprise. "Can you let us inside?" he asked, nodding at Ramona as he listened to the response.

"Good deal," he said as he disconnected. "The alarm system is satellite linked. They're gonna shut it down and open the front door for us. The owners are in California, nobody is in residence, and the grounds are maintained by a landscape company. Larsen had no reason to be here."

They did a room by room search, found the house empty, and returned to the patio.

"Seems like our boy is on the run," Tafoya said, holstering his weapon.

"Do we call out the troops?" Ramona asked, as she pivoted to look at the Sangre de Cristo Mountains that filled the eastern horizon, most of it heavily forested wilderness roughly fifty miles long and twenty-five miles wide.

"Yep," Cruz said, reaching for his handheld. "He's a credible suspect now."

Four hours into his trek, Kurt Larsen stopped to get his bearings. After leaving the foothills, the trail had taken him deep into the forest, up a steep grade, over thick underbrush, and into a dense stand of pine trees where he had no line of sight to any familiar landmarks.

Not that he'd recognize anything but the highest peaks of the mountains. Since coming back from 'Nam, Larsen had never set foot in a forest. The jungle had hammered into his mind the dangers of closed-in spaces, which made him crazy with anxiety.

He waited until his breathing slowed, then listened for any sound that would tell him he was being followed. All he heard were birds chirping, squirrels scampering, wind whistling through the trees, and the dull whine of a jet passing overhead.

He looked up the trail, if you could call it that, and all he saw were more trees ascending a punishing slope. He hadn't encountered anyone since entering the mountains and hadn't seen any signs of recent use, such as footprints or litter. Maybe it was a hiking trail the forest service had shut down years ago, or an old game trail.

He sat with his back against a tree and tried to calm

down. He'd skedaddled right after Mary Beth's phone call with nothing but his handgun, a pocket knife, and his lunch. He opened the bag, peeled the meatloaf off the slices of bread, and chewed them slowly to let the juices wet his dry mouth. He would need to find water before too long.

Did the cops really think he'd killed Potter? Sure, he'd talked about beating the shit out of him for emotionally messing up Mary Beth. But that was in group sessions that were supposed to be confidential. Did Barbero fink on him? Did Mary Beth tell the cops he had a gun?

Larsen knew he wasn't supposed to own a handgun. But law or no law, it made him feel safe. So what if he was mentally ill? He wasn't psychotic or something like that, and nobody was gonna take his right to bear arms away from him. Not after what he'd done for his country.

He took the weapon, a Glock 9mm semiautomatic, out of the holster and checked the magazine. The weight of it in his hand felt reassuring.

He put it away, rewrapped the bread slices in wax paper to save for later, and started up the incline. If he just kept climbing he would eventually break through the timberline and get a bearing on the ski basin, where he was sure there was water.

The eggbeater sound of helicopter rotors made him freeze. He hated that sound. Startled, he could feel the panic building. He scanned a patch of sky through a break in the trees looking for the chopper, waiting for incoming enemy mortar rounds and rocket-propelled grenades to start blowing through the canopy, waiting to get knocked off his feet and feel shrapnel take a three-inch slice out of his left triceps.

Hyperventilating and sweating like a pig, he scrambled off the trail looking for cover, rolled over a dead log, and took out the Glock. The sound of the chopper receded only to be replaced by the crunching of feet through the underbrush.

Come on, you slope gook motherfuckers.

He saw the shape of a man dressed in black, just like a North Vietnamese dink. Saw the muzzle of his automatic weapon.

Where the fuck was his unit?

Three more shapes emerged from the shadows. Larsen squeezed off two rounds at the point man. Bark flew off the tree above the man's head, and the figure dropped to the ground. The three remaining slopes disappeared in the underbrush. He could hear them crawling toward him.

He screamed profanities at them and they answered with heavy fire from automatic weapons, the slugs pulverizing the decayed log, blowing through it. He belly-crawled backward toward a rock outcropping, firing two more rounds. Above him the chopper's rotors swayed tree branches and swirled pine needles and dirt into the air.

Larsen saw the point man rise to a kneeling position, saw him bring the weapon to his shoulder. He twisted his body and rolled toward the safety of the rocks.

The last thing he felt were bullets shattering his back.

Chapter 3

Midday turned hot, so Sara sat in the truck with the engine running and the air conditioning on waiting for Kerney to finish his investigation and take her home. The baby had shifted position and was now pressing against her bladder, making her feel a constant need to pee. On top of that, her feet were swollen, her backside hurt, and all she wanted to do was stretch out and take a nap.

Before retreating to the truck, she'd watched Kerney clean up the mess in the barn, dig out the third bullet imbedded in the concrete slab, and dust for fingerprints around Soldier's stall. Now, he stood next to the patrol car talking to Russell Thorpe, who'd finished taking statements from the construction crew and was loading all the collected evidence into the trunk of his unit.

Sara slipped her shoes off and looked up to see Kerney on his way to the truck. It was wonderful to see him walking without a limp. Some years before she met him, a gunfight with a drug dealer had shattered his right knee and blown a hole in his stomach. The original artificial knee had recently been replaced with a new high-tech model that smoothed out his gait, gave him greater mobility, and squared his shoulders a bit, now that he no longer favored his bum leg.

He got in the truck and gave her the once-over. "I'd better get you home," he said.

"I do need to put my feet up," Sara said.

"Sorry it took so long."

Sara shook her head. "Not to worry. I'm fine."

At the house, after a late lunch that Kerney prepared, Sara stretched out on the bed and fell asleep for what seemed to be a few minutes. The baby kicked hard and woke her. She went looking for Kerney and found a note from him on the refrigerator. He'd been gone for over an hour, called out to another shooting. This time, a suspect in the murder case had been killed by officers who'd tracked him into the national forest.

She stared at Kerney's scribbling, wondering if he'd ever have any time for her before the baby was born. She had combined some annual and maternity leave to give them a mere six weeks together before she was scheduled to report back to duty.

She felt a contraction, grabbed her stomach, and held her breath. Dammit, was she going into labor? Would she have to call for an ambulance to take her to the hospital? Anger about Kerney's absence welled up and made her teary-eyed in frustration. This supposedly happy time in her life was really starting to suck.

The moment passed with no more pains. Her legs ached, so she went back into the bedroom and put up her swollen, ugly-looking feet.

* * *

By the time Kerney arrived, police cars and emergency vehicles filled the driveway at the Tesuque house. Several detectives and a search-and-rescue team were busy strapping on backpacks, organizing gear, and getting ready to move out. Kerney spoke to one of the detectives who told him the trail from the house into the mountains was the quickest access to the shooting scene. They would hike up to the officers at the scene, conduct an investigation, and carry out Larsen's body.

Noting a conspicuous absence of other essential personnel who should have been assembling, Kerney walked up the driveway hoping to find them at the house. All he found were Larry Otero and Sal Molina watching Cruz Tafoya conduct a search of Larsen's truck. Kerney doubted that Tafoya had secured a signed warrant, but with the suspect dead it probably didn't matter.

"Are any of our people hurt?" Kerney asked.

"No," Larry Otero replied.

"What do you know so far?" Kerney asked.

"Larsen ran, Chief," Molina replied. "Detective Pino had reason to believe he was armed. We sent SWAT into the mountains to track him. They took fire and had to stop the action."

"Can you tie him to Potter's murder?" Kerney asked.

Tafoya pulled his head out of the cab of the truck. A box of 9mm rounds sat on the bench seat. "Only circumstantially at this point, Chief," he said. He gave Kerney a quick rundown of the facts.

Kerney shook his head in dismay. There were times when a criminal investigation went badly off track, and this smelled like one of them. "You'd better hope Larsen killed Potter," he said flatly.

"He was armed, and he fired at our people," Otero said.

"That alone doesn't make him a credible suspect," Kerney said. "From what I've heard, we have a *possible* motive, *conjecture* that Larsen *could* have been at the Potter crime scene this morning, and *no* hard evidence that puts him there."

"We have his handgun in custody," Molina said.

"Do you have the round that killed Jack Potter, so we can make a comparison?" Kerney asked.

Molina shook his head.

"Detective Pino is getting a search warrant for Larsen's apartment," Tafoya said.

"To look for what?" Kerney demanded.

"Any papers, documents, phone calls, or electronic mail concerning or pertaining to Jack Potter," Molina replied.

"That sounds like a fishing expedition to me," Kerney said. "Patterson has a history of serious mental illness. Did anyone stop to consider that when she called Larsen she may have over-dramatized her meeting with Detective Pino and scared him into running?"

"So why did Larsen shoot at our people?" Tafoya asked.

"Perhaps because he's also not right in the head," Kerney said through clenched teeth. "What instructions did you give SWAT?"

"To proceed with caution and attempt to apprehend only," Molina replied. "It was my call, Chief."

"Were they advised of his mental condition?"

"Yes, sir," Molina said.

"And told he was wanted for questioning only?"

"Yes, but they never got the chance to talk to him, Chief," Molina said. "According to the officers on the scene, Larsen spotted them on the trail, took cover, and started squeezing off rounds before they even saw him."

Kerney turned his attention back to Sergeant Tafoya. "Did you talk to any of Larsen's clients who saw him today?"

"Three of them, Chief," Tafoya answered.

"And?"

"The first two said that Larsen seemed okay. He got to his jobs on time, did his work, and left without incident. The third said that Larsen seemed agitated when he told her he needed to take a break and go meet with a prospective client."

Kerney looked hard at Tafoya. "Did it occur to you that a spooked ex-vet with a mental condition might not react rationally to being the target of a homicide investigation?"

Silence greeted Kerney's question.

"Or that it might have been smart to just hold back and wait for Larsen to come down out of the mountains on his own when he got tired, hungry, cold, and thirsty?"

Tafoya lowered his head.

Kerney looked at the sky. July was the monsoon month in New Mexico, and thick cumulus clouds were building over the mountains. "Or that maybe the rainstorm that's coming before nightfall would have driven him out of the forest?"

"What do you want to do, Chief?" Otero asked, in an attempt to buffer Kerney's displeasure.

"I'm assuming command," Kerney said. "I want the DA here now. Tell him we've got a police shooting that requires his personal attention. I want the crime scene techs rolling and at the shooting site before it starts to rain and destroys or contaminates the evidence. Bring up the mobile command unit. I want it operational in twenty minutes. Have you called for a medical examiner?"

"There's one on the search-and-rescue team," Otero said. "Anything else?"

"Hold search and rescue and the detectives back until the crime scene techs arrive. Get the Internal Affairs commander up here pronto. I want an internal investigation started immediately on both the shooting and the SWAT call-out. Get some uniforms to set up a roadblock below the house before the news media show up. They're gonna be on us like flies. I'll call the city manager and brief him."

As Molina and Otero reached for their handhelds, Kerney turned on his heel and walked away.

Ramona Pino knew that her affidavit for a search warrant didn't come close to establishing sufficient probable cause that Larsen had murdered Jack Potter. Barry Foyt, the ADA, approved the affidavit only because Larsen had bolted to elude questioning and had been killed in a shootout by officers attempting to locate and detain him. Likewise, the judge who signed the order had been equally unimpressed with Ramona's scanty facts, but went along with it because the suspect was dead.

Knowing she'd been cut a break, Ramona left the courthouse with an order in hand that made Larsen a bona fide murder suspect. Whether it would stand up under close scrutiny was another matter.

She made radio contact with Detective Matthew Chacon and asked him to meet her at Larsen's apartment. It was an ironclad rule to have at least two officers serve a search warrant, one to gather the evidence and the other to inventory seized items and control anyone on the premises, which in Mary Beth Patterson's case could well turn out to be a handful.

Ramona arrived at the apartment building before Chacon and spoke to Joyce Barbero in the office. She told Barbero about the search warrant, but made no mention of the Larsen shooting.

"Haven't you upset Mary Beth enough?" Barbero asked disapprovingly as she came to the front of her desk.

Through the open office door, Ramona saw Matt Chacon pull up to the curb in his unit. "I'll let you know when we're finished with the search," she said as she stepped outside.

Barbero watched from the doorway as Ramona warned Matt Chacon about Mary Beth's mental condition and went over the specifics of the warrant.

Thin with bushy brown hair, Chacon chewed on a toothpick as he listened and pulled the forms he needed out of his briefcase. He tapped his shirt pocket for his pen, found it, and uncapped the top.

"Are you gonna tell Patterson about Larsen?" he asked.

"I'm going to have to," Ramona said. "She's next of kin."

"Let's do it," Chacon said.

At the apartment, Mary Beth opened up the door and winced at Ramona. "Why are you back here?" she asked in a thin voice as her questioning gaze traveled to Matt Chacon.

"We need to look around your apartment," Ramona replied.

"I know my rights," Mary Beth said, her trembling hand toying with the doorknob. "You can't do that."

"I have a court order from a judge, Mary Beth," Ramona said.

"You're lying. Where's my Kurt?"

"I need to talk to you about him," Ramona said.

Her eyes dilated. "Why?"

"Because something bad has happened. Kurt is dead."

Mary Beth sagged against the door, dropped to her knees, her hand clutching the doorknob, and began rocking slowly back and forth.

Ramona stepped behind her, put both hands under her arms, and pulled her upright. She could feel the hardness of Mary Beth's breast implants against the palms of her hands. She walked her to the couch and sat her down.

"You have to listen to me, Mary Beth," Ramona said as she sat beside the woman.

Mute, Mary Beth clasped her arms around her waist and continued rocking, bending her torso back and forth, the movement building into a catatonic rhythm.

Nothing Ramona said broke through Mary Beth's stupor. Uneasy with the situation, she asked Matt to fetch Joyce Barbero, who came hurrying in, breathless and exasperated. She glanced at Mary Beth and shot Ramona an annoyed look.

"What happened?" Barbero demanded.

Ramona explained that Larsen was dead and Barbero's expression changed to angry condemnation. She asked Ramona to move aside, knelt down, and spent ten fruitless minutes trying to talk Mary Beth back to reality.

"She has to go to the hospital," Barbero said, shaking her head as she got to her feet.

Ramona called for an ambulance and then dialed Barry Foyt to ask for guidance on the situation.

"You're sure the woman isn't faking it?" Foyt asked.

"Positive."

"Did you tell her you had a search warrant?" Foyt asked.

"I did."

"And she's not a target of the investigation, right?"

"Correct."

"Do the search and leave copies of the paperwork behind," Foyt said. "I'll research case law and see if there's a precedent. If it gets challenged, we can deal with it later. Find something, Detective Pino. The Larsen shooting doesn't look good. My boss is in Tesuque now and he's plenty steamed about what happened."

Ramona held off on the search until the ambulance took Mary Beth away with Barbero in attendance. She spent the next two hours searching for documents, checking with the phone company to get a record of outgoing calls—none had been made to Jack Potter's office or home since the service had been connected—and looking through the files and e-mail on a laptop computer on a small table in the bedroom.

There was no e-mail to or from Potter, but next to the

computer sat an ashtray with a roach clip, a hash pipe, and a closed tin box containing a stash of marijuana.

The only mention of Jack Potter was in Mary Beth's diary on a bedside table. Several old entries written in a flowery hand expressed Mary Beth's anger and disappointment with Potter.

Ramona made a final sweep and told Matt to fill out the inventory sheet for the diary, laptop, grass, and drug paraphernalia.

"That's it?" Chacon asked.

Glumly, Ramona nodded as she surveyed the front room. No matter how meager and dismal, the apartment represented a new life that two emotionally damaged people had attempted to build together. Now, all of that had been destroyed.

As she closed the front door, she wondered—given the mistakes she'd made today—if the same now held true for her career.

Some time back at Sara's urging, Kerney had moved out of his cramped quarters and rented a place on Upper Canyon Road that was more than sufficient to accommodate both of them and the baby while their new home was under construction. It was a furnished guest house on an estate property owned by a megarich Wall Street stockbroker who rarely visited Santa Fe. Tucked against a hillside behind high adobe walls, the estate looked down on a small valley that once had been farmland but was now a wealthy residential neighborhood.

On the opposite hillside, trophy homes were perched in full view of the road that circled the valley, so that all who passed by could see the fruits of the owners' success. Only a very few of the homes on the valley floor were still owned by Hispanics, and those were mostly small and built on tiny plots of land where a half acre could sell for as much as a quarter-million dollars.

On the rear patio of the guest house, Sara waited impatiently for Kerney's return. He knew damn well she was scheduled to pick up her new car this afternoon from a Santa Fe dealership.

She'd sold her old vehicle at Fort Leavenworth and bought a new one with her own money. Kerney had offered to pay for it. But Sara was unwilling to become dependent on any man, even one she loved and had married. She didn't make a big salary as a lieutenant colonel, but she'd been raised by frugal ranching parents who'd taught her the value of living debt free. So she'd put aside money every month over the past several years to be able to pay cash when the time came to replace her car.

Kerney, who had also been raised on a ranch, was much the same way about money and had only recently begun, with Sara's encouragement, to spend some of the wealth he'd inherited from the estate of an old family friend.

Sara thought about the qualities she shared with her husband. Both of them had been raised to value work, thrive on it, take pride in it. That figured into her reluctance to give up her military career for full-time motherhood, just as it kept Kerney unwilling to retire from police work.

Could she really fault him for wanting to continue working at a job he loved? Or for responding to the demands of his job, when she would have done exactly the same thing?

She called for a taxi and within twenty minutes was at the dealership signing the paperwork. The car, a small SUV, was the safest on the market, a perfect size for a small family, and it came with all the bells and whistles. It would serve her well either at the ranch or on the D.C. beltway.

She drove the SUV home, hoping Kerney would be there so she could show it off to him. Instead, she found a dead rat under the portal by the front door. She stepped around it, went inside, and called the part-time estate manager who looked after the property.

"A rat?" the woman said in surprise.

"Yes," Sara replied. "Does this happen often?"

"No, it's never happened before. I'll have it removed."

"I'll take care of it," Sara said.

"Are you sure?"

"Yes. Have there been any workmen or exterminators on the premises today?"

"No one is scheduled to be there."

"Do you have poisoned bait traps put out?"

"No," the woman answered. "There's never been a need for them."

Sara thanked the woman, hung up, and went back outside to look at the animal more closely. With a small stick she turned the rat over. Its limbs were rigid and splayed out from the torso, the mouth was open, and there were no visible wounds. An experienced military police officer who'd commanded a criminal investigation unit, Sara had seen her share of death, including a few suicides by poison. She had a strong hunch the rat hadn't crawled onto the front portal to die.

She called Tug Cheney, explained the situation, and asked him to come over.

"Don't touch it," Cheney said. "I'll be there soon. What's going on? First the horse and now this."

"I think somebody doesn't like us very much," Sara said.

She thought about calling Kerney then dropped the idea, deciding it would be best to wait until Cheney finished his examination.

As a precaution, she locked all the doors and windows and took Kerney's personal handgun from a box on the bedroom closet shelf. She sat on the living room sofa, checked the rounds in the .38, and laid the weapon on the end table.

This was no time for someone to be threatening her or her family. Without hesitation, she would blow away anyone who came to do them harm.

She patted her tummy and hummed quietly as she waited for Tug Cheney to arrive.

With the information Bobby Trujillo had provided, Patrol Officer Russell Thorpe found it relatively easy to locate the subcontractors who'd worked on Kerney's new house. By the end of his shift, he'd interviewed everybody who'd been involved with site preparation, earth moving, concrete pouring, and the rough-in plumbing and electrical work. He'd also checked every possible vehicle for a tread mark match. The sum total of his efforts resulted in excluding everybody he'd interviewed as a likely suspect in the case, which wasn't a bad thing.

At state police headquarters, Thorpe dropped off the evidence at the lab for analysis. On his way out the door the thought occurred to him that it might be wise to talk to the building suppliers. He called Trujillo on his cell phone, got the names and addresses of the companies that had delivered materials to the site, and set out to make the rounds.

A bachelor with no one waiting for him at home, Thorpe didn't mind putting out the extra effort. He wanted to show initiative and make an arrest in the case. Besides pleasing Kerney, it would earn him some points with Chief Baca, which might help when he had enough time on the job to apply for a transfer to criminal investigations.

The suppliers consisted of an adobe manufacturer, a lumber company, and a ready-mix concrete outfit. The ready-mix plant and the lumberyard were nearby, so Thorpe checked there first and talked to the drivers, both of whom reported seeing no traffic on the ranch road or any suspicious activity at the job site. The adobe works was run by a tribal outfit on a pueblo outside of Espanola, a small city north of Santa Fe.

The drive to the pueblo took Thorpe along a busy highway that eventually ran north to Taos and then on to Colorado. He passed by two Indian casinos, through some badlands where the roadside businesses looked junky and languishing, and got caught in stop-and-go traffic as the road funneled down to the main drag in Espanola, which seemed to offer nothing more than a combination of strip malls, gas stations, fast-food restaurants, and mom-and-pop businesses housed in dilapidated buildings.

On the other hand, the pueblo outside of town had some charm. Located along the river in thick *bosque* with ancient cottonwoods lining the roadway, the main village was virtually hidden from the outside world.

In a large fenced clearing away from the village, Thorpe found the yard where the adobes were made. It consisted of a metal building and long rows of freshly made mud and straw adobe bricks that were drying in the sun. Bales of straw and mounds of clay were strategically located next to several large, motor-driven mixing tanks used to stir the ingredients to the right consistency. Hundreds of empty wooden forms were lined up ready to be used in the next production run, and a fully loaded flatbed truck was parked in front of the office.

Inside the building he introduced himself to a middle-aged man who didn't look happy to see a state cop in uniform on tribal land.

"What do you want?" the man asked suspiciously. His face was covered in a film of adobe dust and his large hands were calloused and rough looking.

"I'm investigating a crime in Santa Fe County," Thorpe said, "and I need to talk to your driver."

"I'm the manager and the driver," the man said. "What crime?"

"You delivered to a construction site where a horse was killed sometime yesterday." Thorpe gave him the location and the contractor's name.

"I wasn't at that site yesterday. Trujillo's next order isn't due for another week."

"When were you out there?" Thorpe asked.

"Five, maybe six days ago."

"Did you see anything out of the ordinary?"

The man shrugged. "Not really."

"What did you see?" Thorpe asked.

"I had three deliveries to make that day so I got out there real early. A vehicle passed me coming down the ranch road. I figured it was one of the crew off to get something he needed for the job. But when I got to the site there wasn't anybody around. I unloaded where Trujillo wanted the bricks and left before Bobby and his crew showed up. That's all I saw."

"What kind of car was it?"

"A van. One of those big, older models, maybe an eighty-two or eighty-three. A blue GMC with a crumpled front fender on the driver's side. I got a good look at it because he had to slow way down to get past me on the road."

Thorpe was impressed. The man had a good eye. "Did you see any passengers?"

The man shook his head. "Nope, at least not in the front. The rear windows had curtains."

"Who was driving?" Thorpe asked.

"A man."

"Anglo? Hispanic?"

"I didn't pay any attention to his face."

"Can you give me the exact date you were there?"

The man looked through his invoices and read off the date.

"Thanks for your help," Thorpe said.

"Did you stop at the tribal office before you came here?" the man asked.

"No."

"Well, you should have. This is sovereign land. You've got no jurisdiction to be here without permission."

Thorpe threw up his hands apologetically. "I'm sorry about that."

The man looked Thorpe up and down. "Dumb rookie mistake."

"Excuse me?" Thorpe said, taken aback.

"I said you made a dumb, rookie mistake. I spent ten years as a tribal police officer, and met a lot of young state cops who thought they could go anywhere they wanted. Had to throw a few of them off the pueblo a time or two. Would have done the same to you, if I was still in uniform."

"I can understand your point of view," Thorpe said, unwilling to apologize twice. He reached for his pocket notebook. "I'll need your name for my report."

"Donald Naranjo," the man answered as he handed Thorpe a business card. "You can call me here at the office if you've got more questions. Good luck with the case. Anybody who puts a good horse down for no reason needs his butt seriously kicked before he gets locked up."

"Maybe so," Thorpe said. "Thanks for your help."

Naranjo gave him a tight smile in reply.

Thorpe left, vowing to bone up on tribal jurisdictions. That issue aside, just maybe he had his first lead. He'd talk to Bobby Trujillo in the morning to see if anyone driving a blue van had been working at the job site. If not, he'd have to look for the vehicle, which could set back his investigation a good bit.

But either way, he still had a start.

Tug Cheney looked at the dead rat. "Most likely it was poisoned," he said. With a gloved hand he picked it up by the tail and put it in a box. "I won't know for sure until I cut it open."

"Can you tell me anything else?" Sara asked.

"I'm no expert on rodents," Tug replied. "But I do know rats are nocturnal. They feed at night and usually sleep during the day, so I doubt it crawled onto your front porch by itself. You're sure there hasn't been a pest exterminator out here recently?"

"That's what I was told by the estate manager," Sara replied.

"Let's look for a burrow," Tug said, eyeing Sara's bulging stomach. "If I remember correctly, rats have a fairly limited territory. Are you up for it?"

"Of course," Sara said. "I'm pregnant, not disabled. What exactly are we looking for?"

"Any kind of mound where the earth has been disturbed. It might look like a prairie dog hole, or be a smaller burrow system under a tree or shrub."

Tug viewed the lush landscaping surrounding the estate. Whoever owned the property didn't give a hoot about water conservation. Non-native annuals filled flowerbeds bordering the main house and driveway, a large swath of thirsty blue grass ran down to the adobe wall, and mature fruit trees and several big Navajo willow trees that required intensive irrigation shaded open patios around the huge, rambling structure.

"I've got to tell you," Cheney said, "this doesn't look like a good rat habitat to me. They prefer open, native grassland and more arid, sandy places."

They walked the property several times and found no evidence of burrows. Back at the guesthouse, Tug took a small address book out of his truck and flipped through the pages. "I know a retired wildlife biologist here in town," he said. "Maybe he can tell us something about the rat."

On his cell phone, Tug spoke to the biologist, a man named Byron Stoll. He described the situation and the dead rodent. The information intrigued Stoll, who agreed to come and take a look for himself.

Within ten minutes, Stoll arrived on a motorcycle. "Can't say I've heard of many kangaroo rats in Santa Fe," he said, pulling off his helmet and shaking Sara's hand.

A slightly built man in his sixties, Stoll had a full head of gray hair and a neatly trimmed matching mustache and beard. He went straight for the box containing the dead rat and opened the lid.

"This is a *D. merriami,* commonly known as the Merriam Kangaroo Rat," he said.

"How can you tell?" Sara asked, looking over Stoll's shoulder.

"Four toes per hind foot," Stoll answered. "The Ord rat has five, although that extra toe is sometimes hard to see because it's so tiny. But this is clearly a Merriam."

Stoll looked at Tug and Sara. "This animal shouldn't even be here."

"What do you mean?" Tug asked.

"There are three species of native New Mexico kangaroo rats. The Ord, Merriam, and the Bannertail. The Bannertail is easy to spot because the last one-third of its tail is white. When you called, I would have bet you had a dead Bannertail on your hands, because they have a preference for places where grass is readily available. But the Merriam is only found from about Albuquerque southward in the Rio Grande Valley, and over by Santa Rosa, along the Pecos River Valley."

"Which definitely means it was brought here," Sara said.

"Without a doubt," Stoll said.

"Maybe it was a pet that was turned loose by its owner," Tug said.

"That could be," Stoll replied. "They're relatively gentle and easily handled."

"I'd like to know specifically what killed it," Sara said, turning to Tug.

"It was undoubtedly poisoned," Stoll said.

"Where can we have it tested?" Sara asked.

"There's a lab in Albuquerque," Tug replied.

"No need for that," Stoll replied, smiling at Sara. "I've got a small lab at home. I'll run some toxicology tests after dinner and give Tug a call."

"I think it should be handled by a police lab," Sara said.

Stoll laughed. "It would still come to me in any case. I do contract work for a number of law enforcement agencies. Don't worry, I'll enter it into evidence and preserve the chain of custody."

"That will work," Sara said.

Stoll strapped the box with the rat on a rack over the rear wheel of his motorcycle, waved goodbye, and roared off.

"Call me after you hear from Mr. Stoll," Sara said as she walked Tug to his truck.

"I will," he said. "I think you and Kerney need to be cautious for a while."

Sara smiled. "Don't worry, I'm armed and dangerous."

*   *   *

Drenching rain beat down on the roof of the mobile command trailer as Kerney and the district attorney, Sid Larranaga, listened to Ramona Pino give her report. The thunderstorm had blown in just as the crime scene techs were finishing up at the shooting site, and the search-and-rescue team was carrying Larsen's body down the mountain trail, accompanied by detectives and Kerney's Internal Affairs commander.

"That's all you got from the house search?" Larranaga asked when Detective Pino stopped talking.

"Yes, sir," Ramona replied, pushing a strand of wet hair away from her face. She'd gotten soaked running from her unit to the command trailer, which only made her feel more miserable about the situation.

"I'm taking this to the grand jury," Larranaga said, running a hand over the lapel of his suit jacket. He glanced hard at Kerney and nodded toward the door.

"You're excused, Detective," Kerney said. He waited for Pino to leave before addressing Larranaga. "That's a premature call to make, Sid. Why not wait until you hear what my Internal Affairs commander has to say?"

Larranaga snorted and shifted his bulk in the chair. "It was stupid to call out SWAT and you know it. Even if your IA commander agrees with that assessment, the public is going to want an independent review made on this case. I'm charging the officers who shot Larsen with involuntary manslaughter. This was a lawful act, incautiously done, that resulted in the death of what clearly appears to be an innocent man. The grand jury can decide if it was justified or not."

"Is that the way you intend to present it?" Kerney asked.

"I don't know," Larranaga replied. "But I will tell you this: I've got growing reservations about this big love affair cop shops have with special weapons and tactics units. This whole thing with the combat boots, military-style fatigues, automatic weapons, and all that high-tech stuff is getting to be a bit much. You're supposed to police the community, not act like some sort of quasi-militia."

"SWAT has a role to play in policing," Kerney replied.

"Sometimes," Larranaga said. "But not when a poor, unbalanced sucker who's scared shitless is hiding in the woods because his deranged girlfriend has blown things all out of proportion."

"Are you going to sacrifice my people to make your point?"

"Do you disagree with my analysis of the situation?" Larranaga shot back.

"No."

Larranaga stood up. "Then make damn sure all the facts are available to present to the grand jury. The only defense you've got is to provide conclusive proof above and beyond the officers' statements that they were forced to stop the action when they came under fire. You'd better hope and pray the evidence is there. I want the reports on my desk by morning."

"What are you going to tell the media?" Kerney asked.

"For now, nothing," Larranaga said. "I'll announce my decision tomorrow after I've read your reports."

Larranaga flipped up the collar of his suit jacket and left, running through the rain to his car. Through the open trailer door Kerney saw Otero and Molina sitting in a nearby unit. He gestured for them to join him and spent a few minutes discussing Pino's report, Larranaga's reaction, and laying out exactly what he wanted to see on his desk no later than six o'clock in the morning.

Molina opened his mouth to speak, and Larry Otero cut him off.

"I'll take responsibility for authorizing SWAT," he said grimly.

"You'll do no such thing," Kerney answered sharply, as he moved toward the door. "This is my kitchen, and I'll take the heat."

Chapter 4

It took Kerney a minute to realize that the new vehicle parked next to his truck outside the guesthouse belonged to Sara. Stirred by the uneasy realization that he'd spaced out their appointment to take delivery of the car, he hurried inside to apologize. He shucked off his wet windbreaker, hung it on the hall closet doorknob, and called her name as he walked into the living room.

Sara answered from the kitchen. She sat at the table eating her dinner, a bowl of pasta with asparagus in a cream sauce. Kerney's .38 sat next to the place mat by her right hand.

He lowered himself into a chair, eying the handgun. "Sorry I couldn't get back in time to take you to pick up your car."

"I managed." Sara stood, moved to the stove, and spooned out a bowl of pasta. She seemed calm, not at all upset with him.

"You didn't have to make my dinner."

"Yes, I did. I need to practice cooking for two, at least for a little while. Besides, I was hungry."

He took the bowl from Sara's hand and reached for a fork. "What's up with the *pistola*?"

"We had a dead rat delivered to our front door this afternoon," Sara replied, returning to her chair, "by person or persons unknown."

Kerney set aside the fork. "And?"

Sara laid the story out, including the call from Tug Cheney confirming that the rat, according to Byron Stoll's toxicology test, had been poisoned with strychnine.

"It's commonly used in rodenticides sold over the counter," Sara added calmly.

"Rodenticides?"

"That what Tug Cheney calls them," Sara answered, stabbing the last asparagus spear. She chewed it slowly. "Anyway, the *pistola* is a precaution until we find out who is playing this unpleasant little game."

"I'll deal with it," Kerney said.

Sara shook her head, and pushed aside her empty bowl. "Don't go getting all macho on me, Kerney. I've already started the ball rolling. I spoke to both the city and the county animal control supervisors this afternoon and asked about any recent calls regarding dead rats."

She got up and fetched a notepad next to the kitchen telephone. "Two days ago, a rat was removed from in front of a house off Hyde Park Road, just outside the city limits. The woman who requested the service was afraid of contracting Hantavirus. She didn't realize that the disease was spread to humans only by deer mice droppings, not from rats. An animal control officer removed the rat and disposed of it. In his report he noted the animal appeared to have been poisoned. The woman found it in the driveway next to her car."

"Was it a kangaroo rat?" Kerney asked between fork-fuls of pasta.

"The officer thought so, but wasn't sure," Sara replied, returning to the table. "Requests to remove dead rats aren't all that common."

"Who was the woman?"

"Dora Manning."

"That name sounds familiar," Kerney said.

"I tried phoning her several times and got no answer."

His mouth full, Kerney nodded in approval before speaking. "Was the rat tested before it was destroyed?"

"Unfortunately, no." Sara went to the sink and rinsed out her bowl. "I think we should pay a visit to Ms. Manning's house after you finish your dinner."

"Why should we do that?"

"I got the phone company to give me the names and numbers of Manning's immediate neighbors, and one of them hasn't seen her for a day."

"How did you do that?"

"I asked questions."

"No, I mean find the neighbors."

"You're not the only member of this family with law enforcement experience. I commanded a military police unit, remember? The phone company was very cooperative. Anyway, I spoke to a neighbor. Manning is an older woman who lives alone. Her car is at the house but the neighbor hasn't seen her outside since yesterday evening, and she always lets him or his wife know when she's going out of town."

Sara held out her key ring. "Come on, I'll let you drive my new SUV." She eased the .38 into her purse.

Kerney dropped the fork in the bowl. "Okay, let's go. Good chow, by the way."

"You're too kind."

"Are you being sarcastic?" Kerney asked, as he followed suit and rinsed out his bowl in the sink.

"Perhaps a tiny bit," Sara said with a smile. "You can tell me about your afternoon in the car."

"It's a big mess, that's for sure," Kerney said.

Throughout the day, the bald-headed man had listened carefully to radio traffic on his police scanner, waiting for the call that would send animal control to Kerney's house to remove the dead rat.

He'd left it there fully expecting Kerney's wife to ask animal control to collect it and then think no more about it. But it hadn't played out that way. Perhaps she'd called Kerney by phone instead, or simply thrown the rat into the trash. Either way, the man was not disconcerted. He'd prepared his plan with those contingencies in mind.

When Kerney reported by radio that he was leaving Tesuque and going home, the man drove to the church at the bottom of Upper Canyon Road and parked. Within ten minutes of his arrival, Kerney passed by.

He drummed his fingers on the shoe box that contained another dead rat. Soon it would be dark enough to leave it, without being detected, for Kerney to find, accompanied by a note that would fully clarify the chief's predicament.

After nightfall, he drove to the end of Upper Canyon Road and walked down the hill to Kerney's house. The new car was missing from the driveway and there were no lights on inside. He stayed in the shadows, moved quietly to the portal, placed the rat on the floor, tacked the note to the door, and hurried away.

Soldier's slaughter and the discovery of the poisoned rat made Kerney apprehensive. But he stayed focused on the Larsen shooting during the drive to Manning's house. Likewise, Sara avoided the subject, limiting her comments to some questions about the SWAT screwup. It was as if they'd silently agreed to postpone any speculation about the day's events until they had a better understanding of them.

He could sense that Sara's worry matched his own, but she didn't appear rattled by it. He expected as much from her. Before their marriage, she'd won a meritorious promotion to her current rank for leading a covert mission in Korea that had successfully thwarted an assassination plot against the secretary of state.

Beyond that, Kerney had witnessed firsthand Sara's coolness under fire, when a military intelligence agent had tried to bushwhack them in order to cover up an illicit government spy operation.

The Manning house was in a foothills subdivision off Hyde Park Road, which climbed into the high mountains of the national forest and ended at the ski basin. Kerney followed a long, looping street with several cul-de-sacs that ran around a hillside. The storm had cleared out, and thick stands of pine blocked the weak glow of the moon. With no street lamps and only a few house lights showing, the neighborhood was masked in shades of darkness.

Sara consulted her notes and guided Kerney to the

right address. He drove by slowly without stopping. A car sat in the driveway in front of the unlit house.

"Based on what I learned today," Sara said, turning off the map light, "this is definitely not the natural habitat of *D. merriami*."

"Of the what?"

"The Merriam Kangaroo Rat, or either of the other two native species, for that matter. Stop next door."

Kerney swung into the driveway. Lights were on inside the house. Sara rang the doorbell and an older man answered.

"Mr. Saul?" Sara asked. "I spoke to you earlier today about Dora Manning."

"Oh, yes," Saul answered, nodding his head. "I went to Dora's house after you called, but she wasn't home. You have us quite worried about her. She never leaves town without telling me and my wife she'll be gone. We always pick up her mail for her."

"Does she often travel without her car?" Sara asked.

Saul nodded. "She doesn't like to drive in Albuquerque, so she takes a taxi downtown and rides the shuttle bus to the airport. Perhaps she had an emergency. Her older sister in California isn't in good health."

"How old is Ms. Manning?" Sara asked.

"About my age," Saul said. "In her late sixties, I'd say."

"Does Dora have health problems?" Sara asked.

"Not that I know of. She's very active."

"Does she work?" Kerney asked.

"She's an artist," Saul replied, "and works at home. We have several of her watercolors."

"And before that?"

"For many years, she was a clinical psychologist here in Santa Fe," Saul said, looking closely at Kerney. What had brought the police chief and a very pregnant woman to his front door to question him about Dora?

"You're the police chief," Saul said.

"I am," Kerney said quickly. "Have you had any problems with rats?"

Saul shook his head. "The only rat I've ever seen around here is the one Dora found in her driveway several days ago. She came and told me about it before animal control took it away."

"Do you have a key to her house?" Kerney asked.

"Yes, and a mailbox key as well. My wife picked up her mail this afternoon."

"Did you or your wife go inside her house?" Sara asked.

"No, we only check inside when she's on extended trips, just to make sure everything is okay." Saul's worried gaze shifted from Sara to Kerney and back again. "What's going on?"

Sara smiled reassuringly. "Probably nothing. Could we have the key?"

Saul nodded and left them waiting in the doorway. They could hear him talking in a hushed voice. After a few minutes, he returned with his wife in tow, who handed Kerney a key.

"Is there an alarm system?" Kerney asked.

"No," the woman said. "This is very disconcerting. Why are you concerned about Dora?"

"We're just checking on her welfare," Kerney replied.

He thanked the couple and asked them to remain in their house. They nodded in unison, eyes wide with misgiving.

At the SUV, Kerney got a flashlight and led the way along the dark street to Manning's house. He thought about asking Sara to remain behind while he looked around, but knew she'd have none of it.

"So, do you know Manning?" Sara asked, as they approached the house.

"Professionally, I did," he said. "She did a good bit of forensic psychology work for the courts before she gave up her practice to become an artist. I'd forgotten all about her. It was a long time ago."

He knocked hard and rang the doorbell several times before handing Sara the key. "Stay here. I'll scout the perimeter and look for any signs of forced entry," he said, reaching for his sidearm. Sara already had the .38 out of her purse and in her hand.

He checked every door and window and returned to find Sara with her back against the wall, her weapon in the ready position, and the key in the lock.

He shook his head. "Looks okay on the outside," he whispered. "We'll do a room search. Back me up."

Sara nodded and turned the key.

Together, they swept the house. In the master bedroom they found Dora Manning stretched out on an ornate Victorian bed with her throat cut. Her pajama top and the bed sheet were soaked in blood. On the wall behind the bed, the killer had left a message in red. In block letters, it read:

EVERYONE DIES

They retreated from the house. Kerney turned on the ceiling lights with the butt of his flashlight as they went from room to room, illuminating walls covered with Manning's framed egg tempera and watercolor paintings. There was no sign that the house had been burglarized or a struggle had occurred.

Under the portal porch light, Kerney holstered his weapon, called in homicide on his cell phone, and told dispatch to roll units running a silent code three.

"Get Chief Otero and Lieutenant Molina up here ASAP," he added before disconnecting.

"I don't like this at all," Sara said.

Kerney thought about the two murder victims, Jack Potter, a former prosecutor, and now Dora Manning, an ex–forensic psychologist. He thought about the message on Manning's bedroom wall, and the image of Soldier lying dead in the horse barn ran through his mind.

"Maybe you should go up to Montana and stay with your parents until after the baby is born," he said.

"I am not having this baby without you there to greet him," Sara said peevishly.

"I'd feel better if you did."

"No way, Kerney," Sara said.

"Until we know what 'everyone dies' means, it would be the best thing to do."

Sara shook her head fiercely. "I'm staying. It isn't negotiable."

"Fine. I'm sending you home with a patrol officer as soon as my people get here, with orders to sweep the house and remain with you until I return."

"Try to get home before morning," Sara said.

"We'll see how it goes."

She wrapped her arms around her belly, cradling and

protecting the baby. "This is an absolutely crappy thing to have happening right now."

He pulled her close. "We'll get through it, I promise."

Slowly, her arms encircled his waist and she held him tight.

The bald-headed man pulled to the shoulder of Hyde Park Road to let a line of police cars pass by. He followed and caught up in time to see the last unit turn off into the subdivision where Dora Manning lived.

He nodded approvingly. According to his timetable, if Manning's body hadn't been discovered by midnight, he would make an anonymous call to the police. He decided to go back to the war room and confirm it on the scanner.

Everything was working perfectly. He wondered where Kerney and his wife were. But it really didn't matter. Part of the plan was designed to get Kerney scared and scrambling for answers, which he would then supply.

So far, so good.

After Kerney's people arrived and were briefed, the patrol lieutenant and an officer in a second unit escorted Sara home. At the lieutenant's request, Sara stayed in the squad car until the two men checked the grounds around the guesthouse and the main residence. She could see the beams of their flashlights as they moved back and forth through the trees and shrubs, until they disappeared behind the buildings. Finally they returned.

"It's clear," the lieutenant said through the open driver's side window, holding out his hand. "Your house key please, ma'am."

"There's something tacked on the front door," she said, handing him the key.

The lieutenant turned on the unit's spotlight and aimed it at the front door. "Manny, go see what that is," he said to the patrol officer. "But don't touch it."

The officer hurried to the front door and came back at a run. "It's a typed note on white paper that says, 'Everyone dies. Two down, two to go, and then you're dead.' There's no signature, but there's a dead rat on the portal."

Sara bit her lip and wondered if she and her unborn son counted as two in the killer's mind. The odds were good that they did.

The lieutenant reached in through the open window for the microphone and called Kerney's unit number. It took him a minute to respond.

The baby moved, and Sara leaned back against the headrest wondering if she was about to give birth. She held her breath, hoping it was a false alarm. She wanted this madness over before Patrick Brannon Kerney came into the world. She listened as the lieutenant gave Kerney the news.

"Have you searched the house?" Kerney asked, his voice clear on the radio speaker.

"Not yet."

"Bring in another officer to assist," Kerney said. "I doubt whoever left the message is around, but play it safe anyway. Call me when you've finished the house search, and I'll send a detective to fetch the note. Is everything else ten-four?"

"Affirmative." After requesting another unit, the lieutenant dropped the microphone on the seat. "This won't take all that long, ma'am," he said.

"Good," Sara replied, trying not to wiggle, "because I have to pee."

Kerney sat in Sara's new car with Larry Otero and watched as a group of detectives huddled in the middle of the street while Sal Molina gave them the word that the scope of the investigation now included a serious threat to the chief and his pregnant wife.

The emergency lights from the police units, an ambulance, and the crime scene van blinked lollipop colors into the night, bouncing off the trees and the front of Manning's house. A cluster of neighbors, including the Sauls, stood behind the police line watching techs lug equipment into Dora Manning's house.

The killer's note and the explicit symbolism of a second dead rat on his doorstep ate like a worm in Kerney's gut, and assigning officers to protect Sara didn't ease his anxiety. Until he knew who the perp was and why this was happening, none of them was safe.

An unmarked unit passed through the checkpoint and pulled to the side of the street. Ramona Pino came over with a shut-down look on her face and handed Kerney the note retrieved from his front door. It was protected in a clear plastic bag.

He read it, turned it over to the back side, which was blank, and passed it along to Larry, who did the same before handing it back.

"I think the neighborhood knows that we've arrived in force," Kerney said, as he returned the note to Pino.

"Except for the patrol officer at the checkpoint, ask the officers and detectives to kill their emergency lights."

Kerney knew his orders sounded picky. But it was a lot better than cursing the nameless son of a bitch who wanted to kill his family.

Ramona nodded stiffly and walked away.

"She's not a happy camper right now," Larry said.

"She'll get over it," Kerney said, not in the least interested in Pino's emotional state. "What's happening with the IA investigation?"

"Lieutenant Casados has personally interviewed Pino, Tafoya, Molina, all on-duty commanders in the operations division, and the SWAT supervisor. I'm next on the list. I'm meeting with him in the morning. He'll want to see you after that."

One by one, the emergency lights went dark. Kerney nodded. Unless directed otherwise, Casados reported to the chief and no one else.

"We'll see what shakes out," he said. "Have Molina put Tafoya and Pino on desk duty starting tomorrow. I want a comprehensive search made to locate every case file and court record that involved Jack Potter, Dora Manning, and me. I don't care how many archives they have to dig through to get the information. It's time to start connecting the dots."

"You've got it."

"Also have the ME give us his best estimate of the time of Manning's death. To me, it looks like she's been dead for at least twenty-four hours, perhaps longer. That would mean the perp cut her throat before he shot Jack Potter."

"Why the different MOs?" Larry asked.

"We don't know yet if they're different," Kerney replied.

"He used a knife on Manning and a pistol on Potter."

"Because each circumstance and setting was unique. Potter was killed early in the morning on an empty street. I doubt our perp wanted to risk attacking him with a knife. It was far better to shoot him and then get the hell out of there in a hurry. On the other hand, Manning died in her bed, so I'm assuming she was killed at night. A gunshot could have alerted the neighbors. In that instance, it was better to use a blade."

"But there's no indication the perp played any mind games with Potter before he killed him," Larry said.

"We don't know that for sure," Kerney said as he started the engine.

"Going home?" Larry asked, as he opened the passenger door.

"Not yet. There are a few things I want to do first. Is the ADA on his way?"

"Yeah, Foyt should be here soon. I'll bring him up to speed."

On late rounds, Dr. Rand Collier read the admission report, the medication chart, and the nursing notes in Mary Beth Patterson's chart. After an hour of observation in the ER, Patterson's catatonic stupor had lifted, replaced by a moderate psychotic reaction stemming from the death of her boyfriend. The ER physician who'd examined Patterson cited nihilistic delusions, verbal requests to be punished, and a flat affect. An antidepressant had been prescribed and Patterson had been sent up to the psych unit for further observation and evaluation.

The nursing notes from the afternoon shift reported that upon arrival, Mary Beth had been placed on a close watch. She had remained passive and verbally unresponsive until early evening, when she had requested some juice at the nursing station. Since then, she'd been observed in her room watching television, and had partially eaten her dinner meal—all good signs.

He reviewed summaries of Patterson's prior admissions which detailed her self-destructive behavior, depressive episodes, and her sex-change operation, and read through the intake note prepared by the hospital social worker who'd interviewed Joyce Barbero, Patterson's counselor at the independent living center.

Collier, who was covering for the mental health clinic's psychiatrist, walked into Mary Beth's room and introduced himself.

"How are you feeling?" he asked, as he approached the bed.

Mary Beth pushed herself to a sitting position. "I need to go home. My Kurt will be worried about me. He doesn't know where I am."

"Would you like to talk about what happened to Kurt today?"

"Nothing happened to him," Mary Beth replied.

"Do you remember why you were brought to the hospital?" Collier asked.

"Why was I?" Mary Beth replied. "I wasn't sick or anything."

"You were upset," Collier said.

"No, I don't let things upset me anymore." She tugged

at the collar of her hospital gown. "I want my own clothes. I can't let Kurt see me like this."

Collier asked Mary Beth to tell him the day, month, and year. Her answers were way off.

"Do you know Joyce Barbero?" Collier asked.

"Is she one of the nurses?" Mary Beth replied, looking confused.

"I'm going to have the nurse bring you something to help you sleep," Collier said, as he scribbled a prescription note on the chart and a remark that Mary Beth was disoriented, possibly due to emotional trauma. "Rest tonight and we can talk again in the morning."

"I don't want to stay here."

"We'll see how you feel in the morning," Collier replied as he smiled and left the room.

Mary Beth sank back against the pillow and started scratching her arm with her long fingernails, drawing blood as she went.

At police headquarters, Kerney asked dispatch to pull all the logs for animal control calls that had occurred on nights and weekends over the past sixty days. During normal weekday hours calls went directly to animal control, which was housed on the grounds of the humane society shelter but under the control and supervision of the police department.

Kerney knew Jack Potter's house was inside the city limits. But he didn't know if Potter and his partner, Norman Kaplan, owned a pet. Still, it was worth checking out. Dispatch called and reported no contact by Potter to animal control. He contacted the animal control supervisor at home and asked him to go to the office right away and search the phone logs for Kaplan's or Potter's name. The supervisor said he'd call back in thirty minutes.

Kerney used his time making a list of what else needed to be done to start identifying candidates who might reasonably be suspected to hold a grudge against Potter, Manning, and himself. Checking court records and case files only started the paper search. Data from the sex offender registration files, intelligence reports, jail and prison release reports, and confidential files needed to be pulled to see if any red flags popped up. He ended his list with the names of a dozen or so of the most violent offenders he'd busted during his career who were mostly likely to seek revenge.

He looked at the names on the list. The men were all hardcore felons with extensive criminal records. It would be foolish to assume the killer's motivation could be tied to a single case that involved all three primary targets. A separate search would need to be done for threats against each one.

He scratched out a note amending the order he'd told Larry Otero to pass on to Sal Molina, and called Helen Mulz, his office manager. He asked to have her staff get all in-house documents gathered and on Sal Molina's desk by mid-morning with instructions to conduct both a combined and separate assessment of perps who might have reason to seek revenge against any one of the targets.

Molina wouldn't like getting Kerney's orders through Helen Muiz, but right now he didn't give a dead rat's ass about Sal's feelings. The SWAT screw-up still stuck in his craw and the jeopardy to Sara and the baby was too great to waste time worrying about protocol.

"I'll call my staff and have them get to work early," Helen said. "You've got me worried about you and your family, Kevin. Is Sara all right?"

Kerney smiled at her rare use of his given name. "She's doing okay."

"Are you sure you don't want to have Larry Otero pass on your orders to Lieutenant Molina?"

"Larry's got enough to do, and there isn't time for niceties," Kerney replied. "I'll leave my note on your desk. Wave it at Molina if he gets uppity."

"What a terrible day you've had," Helen said.

"It hasn't been a good one. I'll see you sometime tomorrow."

Soon after he hung up, the animal control supervisor called.

"We haven't had any calls to that address, Chief," he said. "But I just checked the animal shelter's lost dog reports. Three days ago Jack Potter called asking if a five-year-old, mixed-breed, female Border collie named Mandy had been picked up or brought into the shelter. He said she'd gotten out of his backyard. She's still active on the lost animal list."

"You've been very helpful," Kerney said, pushing back his chair.

"If you don't mind me asking, Chief, first I get a call from your wife about a dead rat, and now you want to know about a lost dog. Does all this have something to do with Potter's murder?"

"You'll read about it in the papers soon enough," Kerney said. "Thanks."

EVERYONE DIES

*   *   *

Jack Potter's house sat on a hill above the Casa Solana neighborhood, once the site of a World War II Japanese-American internment camp. A newer adobe structure with large glass windows, the house commanded a view of the mountains and downtown Santa Fe.

He could see headlights of cars traveling on Paseo de Peralta, a street that looped around the historical core of the city, and a few of the traffic lights along Saint Francis Drive, the state road that led north to Taos. Behind the city the mountains were soft, obscure shapes in a star-filled night sky, and the semicircular sliver of the moon looked like the cutting edge of an old-fashioned sickle suspended in the air.

Kerney didn't bother ringing the doorbell; Norman Kaplan was still on a plane flying home from England. He walked around the darkened house and encountered a high six-foot fence and a locked wooden gate that enclosed the backyard. Kerney wondered how Potter's mixed-breed collie, which wasn't a big dog, could have jumped the fence. It didn't seem likely.

The closest house was about a hundred yards away. Kerney spoke to Potter's neighbors, a younger couple who were surprised to find him at their doorstep. He showed his shield and explained the reason for his visit.

"What does Mandy have to do with Jack's murder?" the man asked. A chocolate-colored Labrador padded to the open door and sniffed at Kerney's knee.

"Behave, Herschel," the man said.

The dog sat and smiled up at Kerney.

"I'm just wondering how Mandy managed to go missing from the backyard," Kerney said. "I didn't see any evidence that she'd dug her way out under the fence. Was the gate left unlocked?"

"Mandy isn't a digger, and Jack always kept the gate locked when he wasn't home and Mandy was outside," the woman replied.

"We don't know how she got out," the man said. "It's never happened before, and we've been Jack and Norm's neighbors for three years."

"I think Mandy was stolen," the woman said.

"What makes you say that?" Kerney asked.

"How else can you explain it? Mandy is an absolutely beautiful dog, very well behaved, and has a large, secure backyard to romp in when Jack and Norman are at work."

"Did he search the neighborhood for the dog?"

"Yes, along with Norman and the two of us," the woman said. "We went house to house, passed out posters, and even walked through the arroyos."

"I think a coyote got her," the man said.

"Perhaps," Kerney said, doubting it. Coyotes rarely took down large prey, unless it was sick or wounded.

"Do you think whoever took Mandy killed Jack?" the woman asked.

"Anything's possible."

Kerney thanked the couple and went home, where he found Sara asleep in the bedroom and two uniformed officers on duty. After being assured that the house was secure and all windows were closed and locked, he released them to return to patrol.

Unwilling to risk waking Sara, he sat quietly on the living room couch and mulled over the pattern that seemed to be developing in the cases: dead kangaroo rats delivered to doorsteps, a prized horse killed, a cherished dog stolen. All seemed acts intended to intimidate, to create a climate of fear, and demonstrate the killer's superiority and intelligence.

The threatening note left on his door announcing two more deaths before his own meant that he was supposed to be the final target. Did it also mean the killer wanted Kerney to lose Sara and the baby before he died himself? Or was it a ploy to throw him off?

IIe used the cell phone and called Larry Otero, who was still at the Manning crime scene.

"Jack Potter had his dog stolen three days ago," he said. "Have the detectives find out if Manning had a pet, was a recent crime victim, or had suffered any kind of personal or family loss."

"Will do," Otero said. "She didn't have any pets, so that's one thing we can forget about. How far back do you want them to go?"

"Six months, for now," Kerney said. "Do we have flight information on Norman Kaplan?"

"Nothing specific, just that he's on his way."

"Put someone on it," Kerney said. "I want him met at the Albuquerque airport, accompanied home, and given protection."

"I'll see that it's taken care of," Otero replied.

"Where are you with the crime scene?"

"Molina and his people are still gathering evidence and talking to neighbors. You were right about the time of death; Manning was killed before Potter was shot."

"I'll see you in the morning."

He checked the lock on the front door one more time, pulled off his boots, and stretched out on the couch. With all that had happened, with all there was still to face, he wondered if he could sleep. It didn't seem possible.

When the nurse brought the sleeping medication, Mary Beth kept her mutilated arm under the covers, tucked the pill under her tongue and pretended to swallow it. She spit it out as soon as the nurse left the room, her mind racing with images of Kurt dead, all cut up and bleeding. He was dead, dead, dead.

Had she killed Kurt? She decided no one else could have done it. But how and when?

For hours, she moaned quietly into the pillow, stuffing it in her mouth, covering her face. But she still kept breathing, kept thinking, kept seeing Kurt standing naked like a statue with his arms at his sides, bleeding from every pore of his body with a sickly smile on his face until he disappeared behind a creamy red shroud.

Her visions never lied. She needed to stop her mind from remembering how she'd killed her Kurt.

She waited until the nurse made a late-night round, then got out of bed and went to the bathroom. The mirror was metal and fixed to the wall. The toilet had no tank, just a flush valve. The light fixture had a plastic cover screwed in place over the flourescent tube. There was nothing around she could use to stop the bad vision of Kurt and the terrible thoughts about herself.

She opened the venetian blind next to the bed and looked out the window into the dark night, running her finger along the sharp edge of a plastic slat. With both hands, she bent the brittle slat until it snapped, and then broke it once more to free it from the cord that held it in place.

In the bathroom with the door closed, she pressed down hard, drawing the sharpest point of the slat up the length of her arm, cutting deeper than her fingernails ever could. The pain felt so good it made her shiver.

She did the other arm, and then her thighs. Lovely red blood stained her gown. She took the gown off and cut into the soft flesh under her breasts and watched red droplets course down to her belly button.

She put her hands together and looked at her wrists. The veins were right at the surface. She dug the slat into the fattest one, gritting her teeth until she broke through and blood squirted out in pulses. She clenched her fist, gouged between two tendons, popped open the other vein, and watched the blood flow freely into the sink.

She switched hands to repeat the process, her fingers shaking as she tried to stab into the vein. She punched repeatedly until the slat pierced it. Then she sawed the last one open, her blood lubricating every cutting stroke.

She dropped her hands to her sides, smiled at herself in the metal mirror, and saw Kurt smiling back at her. She could feel the blood draining from her body, her head becoming light and empty of bad thoughts. It felt so very, very dreamy.

Now she could sleep. She sank to the floor and closed her eyes.

The telephone rang and instinctively Kerney reached for it on the bedside table, his hand grabbing empty air.

Groggily, he got up from the couch, hurried to the kitchen, and picked up on the third ring. The stove clock read 4:00 A.M.

"What is it?" he asked.

The third-shift dispatcher told him Mary Beth Patterson had been found dead in her psych-unit hospital room.

"How did it happen?"

"An apparent suicide, Chief. She cut her veins open with a piece of a venetian blind."

"Who's on it?"

"Lieutenant Molina and Detective Pino."

"Have them call me back when they know something," Kerney said.

"Ten-four."

Kerney dropped the phone in the cradle. Day two of his vacation had just begun and it had already gone from bad to worse.

Chapter 5

In the early morning light, Detective Ramona Pino walked slowly down the street where Jack Potter had been killed. Yesterday's search by the crime scene techs for the spent bullet had been unsuccessful, and Ramona wanted to look for it on her own before starting her normal shift.

But more than that, Ramona wanted a break from the biting anguish she felt about the deaths of Larsen and Patterson. If she'd handled the investigation differently both of them would be alive. For the first time in her career as a cop, she had to seriously question her abilities and judgment. She knew Lieutenant Casados was doing the same, and she fully expected that he would drop Patterson's suicide on her as part of his IA investigation.

Yesterday's session with Casados had been grueling enough with only one innocent person's death to account for. Maybe she should just turn in her shield and walk away from it all.

She rejected the idea with an unconscious shake of her head. There was important work to do. Chief Kerney and his family were at risk, apparently targeted by a revenge killer, who could easily be someone unknown to the chief with a motive that was equally unclear, which meant finding the link between the perp, the chief, and the two victims might not be an easy task.

Beyond that, there were aspects of the perp's MO that didn't fit the typical pattern of revenge killers. Usually, such homicides were planned blitz attacks against unsuspecting victims that occurred with no forewarning, or were impulsive murders of opportunity that happened in public view, often without any thought given to escape.

But this perp wasn't playing by the rules. In the Manning homicide, he'd alerted his victim of his intentions with a dead rat in her driveway and, according to information received overnight from the Taos Police Department, was most likely the unknown subject who had broken into an art gallery a month ago and stolen twelve of Manning's paintings by cutting them out of their frames.

He'd followed the same MO with Kerney by first destroying the chief's horse and then leaving two dead rats at his house. Additionally, his messages, left at the Manning crime scene and tacked to the chief's front door, made it clear that there were more killings to come, which wasn't something a revenge killer would ordinarily do.

In an attempt to confirm part of the killer's MO, Chief Otero had officers searching Potter's neighborhood in the hopes of finding the carcass of the missing Border collie. If they came up empty, Ramona still thought it highly probable that the killer had an agenda for the dog.

Pino ran down two other possible types of multiple killers worth considering. Spree killers didn't fit because the perp had planned and carried out his attacks methodically. A serial killer didn't work because there appeared to be no sexual component to the crimes. That left vengeance as the motive, which brought her back to the still unanswered questions, who and why.

She continued down the street, inspecting anything that might have stopped the bullet. Somehow, without willing it, her mind had erased the image of Patterson's naked, mutilated body. All that floated through her head was the face of the hysterical psych-unit nurse who'd found Mary Beth lying in a pool of blood on the bathroom floor.

She stopped to inspect a tree trunk. There was no traffic, no people were out and about, and the only sound came from a singing towhee who ended a long series of clinking sounds with a trill. It cut short a repeat of its refrain, flew out of the high branches above Ramona's head, and perched on the roof of the elementary school a half-block away.

The last of the old downtown schools, the building had been saved because of community protests to keep it open. Two rows of high, old-style windows, designed to let as much sunlight as possible into the classrooms, ran across the front of the building. A small street-side playground enclosed by a low wall served kindergarten students. It contained new, brightly colored slides and play equipment. Just beyond, steps led up to a formal portico entrance. Jutting out from the rear of the building was what Ramona guessed to be either an assembly hall or the school gym. Behind the gym was a dirt-packed playground for the older children enclosed by a chain-link fence.

Ramona climbed the low wall and inspected the street-side playground equipment before moving on to the portico, where she stood on the top step trying to remember the good times of her early school days in Albuquerque. But her mind kept going back to the face of the hysterical psych-unit nurse.

She examined the large square-beam columns and the gray plastered walls for any sign of recent damage. The initial autopsy report indicated the round had clipped Potter's sternum before passing through his chest cavity and out his back. That could have changed the trajectory of the bullet.

Ramona also knew from the pathologist's findings that the muzzle-to-target distance was less than three inches, which meant that the killer had made sure Jack Potter knew he was about to die. Additionally, the diameter of the entry wound suggested that the killer had used a large-caliber handgun.

She looked both high and low. Finding nothing, she reached the intersection where Griffin Street and Paseo de Peralta met just as the traffic light changed and the DON'T WALK sign started flashing. Part of the glass looked broken. She crossed the empty street, looked up, and saw a small hole at the bottom of the sign with spider-like cracks radiating out in random directions.

She keyed her handheld and told dispatch to send a tech to her location pronto. Forty minutes later, she had the partially flattened large caliber bullet in hand, secured in an evidence baggie.

She walked back to her unit wondering if Potter's

sternum had caused an upward deflection of the round, or if the killer had angled his weapon slightly to fire into Potter's chest. Perhaps both factors had come into play. But just maybe the perp was a couple of inches shorter than Potter, no more than five-seven or five-eight in height.

The entry and exit wounds had looked to be aligned when Ramona examined Potter's body on the sidewalk. But that didn't mean there wasn't a variation between the two. She would call the pathologist and ask some questions. Depending on his answers, she might have the beginnings of a physical description for the perp. If not, she at least had the first piece of hard physical evidence in the Potter murder. She would drop it off at the state crime lab for analysis before her regular shift started.

A few minutes before Russell Thorpe left for work Chief Baca called to tell him the horse-shooting incident was now part of a major felony investigation that included, among other things, two homicides and a threat against Kerney's and his family's lives. Baca asked for an update, and Russell filled him in on the blue GMC van and his plan to canvass the few ranchers who lived close to Kerney's property along Highway 285, starting with his nearest neighbor. Baca gave the go-ahead, adding that he wanted an in-person report when Thorpe finished.

From his apartment in town, Thorpe took the Interstate north and turned off on Highway 285, driving along a ten-mile strip of the rural residential sprawl southeast of Santa Fe. He left the highway just before the Lamy turn-off, where the sweep of the Galisteo Basin stretched to the Ortiz Mountains, closed the ranch gate behind his unit, and drove past the cutoff to Kerney's ranch. Several miles beyond was the head-quarters of the Sombrero Ranch, owned by Jack and Irene Burke, the couple who'd sold Kerney his land. The Burkes were first on Thorpe's list of neighbors he wanted to talk to.

The ranch house, an old adobe with a screened-in, low-slung front porch, sat in a grove of ancient cotton-wood trees at the edge of a wide, sandy arroyo. Beyond the arroyo the tracks of the Atchison, Topeka & Santa Fe Railroad crossed a dry creek bed over a long wooden trestle. The place felt like it was a hundred miles from Santa Fe, locked in a time warp of an era long past. Thorpe had seen a lot of late-nineteenth-century ranch houses while stationed in Las Vegas, and the original part of the building was at least that old, if not older.

A smaller, much more modern residence with a slanted tin roof, probably a foreman's cottage, stood steps away from a free-standing garage that contained three pickup trucks and a small farm tractor. Behind the garage was a long, rectangular building covered with sheets of tin that served as a shop and equipment shed. On a patch of grass by the walkway to the main house stood a six-foot-high piece of petrified wood that had once been a tree trunk. A mud mat at the front step read WELCOME.

Thorpe knocked on the partially open door, called out, and got no response. About a quarter-mile away, several horses lazed in a corral outside a pitched-roof, slat-wood barn. Back at his unit, Thorpe watched a pickup truck come into view around a low hill. It passed the barn and accelerated when the driver saw Thorpe's patrol car.

A man pulled to a stop and looked Thorpe over through the open window of his truck. "What brings the police here?" he asked with a smile. "I thought you guys never left the pavement unless you had to, and I sure as hell didn't call you."

"Jack Burke?" Russell asked with a laugh.

"That's right," Burke replied, as he got out of the truck.

Through the open door, Thorpe saw a holstered pistol on the passenger seat and a hunting rifle in a roof-mounted rack. "Why all the weapons?" he asked.

Burke pushed his cowboy hat back on his forehead and frowned. A middle-aged man with graying hair and a thick neck, he had large hands with stubby fingers and thick arms that filled out the sleeves of his cowboy shirt.

"Because the more people who come to Santa Fe, the more trouble I've got," he said in a disgruntled tone. "People cutting fences so they can drive their ATVs on my land, dumping garbage in arroyos because the county landfill is closed and they don't want to take it back home, cutting firewood illegally, shooting at my windmills, killing the antelope, and hauling off gravel from an old quarry. I've even had to chase off a few folks I've caught digging up plants to take home and put in their yards. It doesn't matter how many no trespassing signs I put up, some people have no respect for private property."

"Have you called the police?" Thorpe asked.

Burke eyed Thorpe as though he was plain crazy.

"Why? So they can take a report and file it? I gave up on that a long time ago. All it does is waste my time. Best I can do is catch 'em when I can and scare the bejesus out of them."

"Have you run anyone off recently who was driving an eighty-two or eighty-three blue GMC van with a crumpled driver's side front fender?"

"Care to tell me why you're asking?"

"Yesterday your neighbor, Chief Kerney, found his horse dead inside the barn, shot three times."

Burke's face flushed with anger. "Anyone who'd do a thing like that needs a dose of his own medicine. That was a damn fine animal, good-natured and well-trained. Had stamina, too. I remember when Kerney bought him at a BLM mustang auction. He turned that animal into a fine cutting horse with good cow sense."

"Have you seen a blue van?" Thorpe asked, trying to keep Burke on topic.

Burke nodded. "When we sold Kerney his land we gave him an easement to use our road so he wouldn't have to build a new one from the highway. With all the construction going on up at his place, it doesn't make much sense to keep the gate locked, so I asked Kerney to make sure that the crew working at the site closed the gate when they came and went. The boys have been real good about it, except for one time last week when me and the wife came back from town."

"What happened?" Thorpe asked, trying to hurry Burke along.

"My wife had just closed the gate when this blue van came barreling down on us kicking up a cloud of dust. I went over and asked the driver if he'd left it open. He said he was sorry and wouldn't do it again. I figured him to be one of the construction crew."

"Did you get a good look at him?"

"You bet, so did my wife. He was no further away than you are to me."

Thorpe got the day and time of the incident, and a physical description: a white male in his thirties with long blond hair, no mustache, and no beard.

"Height?" he asked.

"He stayed in the van," Burke said, "so I can't be sure, but I'd say average."

"What's average to you?"

"Five-ten, with a skinny build," Burke replied. "Now that I think of it, his hands were kinda soft-looking."

"I'm going to need you and your wife to come to state police headquarters today," Thorpe said, "so we can work up a composite sketch of the suspect."

"Isn't what I just told you good enough?"

"The man who shot the horse intends to kill Chief Kerney."

Burke's expression darkened. "I don't like the sound of that at all. Kerney's a good man. I've been looking forward to having him as a neighbor. Wouldn't want anything to change that. My wife's at her sister's house. I can pick her up and be there whenever you want us."

Thorpe checked his watch and said he would meet Burke at headquarters in two hours. That would give him time to brief Chief Baca and do his paperwork.

"I'll see you then," Burke said.

Russell nodded and drove off. Before returning to Santa Fe, he made a quick stop at the construction site, and spoke to Bobby Trujillo, Kerney's general contractor. As expected, nobody matching Burke's description of the driver of the blue van was or had been working on the job.

Awake and up before Kerney, Sara stepped out of the shower, toweled herself dry, and stood in front of the mirror, examining her body. Her face was just a tiny bit fuller, her breasts had gotten huge, but her belly looked enormous. At least her legs hadn't changed during pregnancy, and her arms were still firm. It was a small consolation; she was retaining fluids and felt like a bloated cow. She wondered how long it would take to lose the extra weight she'd gained after the baby was born.

Kerney knocked on the bathroom door and opened it a crack when she answered. His hair stood up in a cowlick on the back of his head and his blue eyes were ringed with dark circles.

"Are you all right?" he asked, peeking inside.

"You've got to stop asking me that," she replied. "I'm fine. The baby will let me know when it's time to go to the hospital."

"I wasn't thinking about the baby," Kerney replied.

In the background, Sara could hear the voice of an early morning local televison news anchor reporting the breaking story of the Manning homicide. "Stop staring at me," she said, wrapping the towel around her body.

"I think you look beautiful," Kerney said.

"Thank you. But as far as I'm concerned, the beauty of impending motherhood is nothing more than a male myth."

"Meaning?"

"How would you like it if, within a matter of months,

your face puffed up, you grew a pot belly, and your chest looked like milk-cow teats?"

"I thought being pregnant was supposed to be a sensual experience for women."

"I'm still waiting for that to happen. Can I have a few minutes alone in the bathroom?"

Kerney nodded sheepishly and closed the door. Sara put on a loose-fitting short-sleeved summer dress that accented her legs and softened the roundness of her stomach. She applied a bit of mascara, a touch of lipstick, ran a comb through her short, strawberry blond hair, and decided maybe she didn't look so bad after all. At least, not when she was fully clothed.

In the kitchen, Kerney served her breakfast, a heaping concoction of scrambled eggs, melted cheese, and bits of ham, onions, and green peppers. He seemed very pleased with himself, so she thanked him with as much enthusiasm as she could muster, wondering where men got the idea that a pregnant woman needed to eat meals fit for a starving stevedore.

She took a bite and chewed slowly, nodding her head. "Very good."

Kerney accepted the compliment with a smile.

"After the baby is born, and I feel normal again, I want you to take me out dancing. Now that you have a new knee, there's no excuse not to."

"I think I can do that," Kerney said. He started to say something more and stopped, and his smile vanished, replaced by a preoccupied look.

"Have you gone quiet because you want to preserve an illusion of normalcy before we start talking about who's trying to kill us?" Sara asked.

"Something like that. Mary Beth Patterson committed suicide in her hospital room late last night. I got a call from Sal Molina confirming it while you were in the shower."

Sara reacted to the news without emotion. Since last night, her only focus had become survival for her family. That wasn't about to change until the problem got solved.

"You're going in to work, I take it," she said.

"I have to," Kerney said apologetically.

"I wouldn't expect you to do anything less," Sara said. "What happened after you sent me home last night?"

Kerney told her about setting into motion a records search for the killer, and the mysterious disappearance of Jack Potter's dog.

Sara shrugged off the tidbit about the dog as she pushed food around the plate with her fork. It fit the killer's already established pattern, but added nothing of substance to the investigation. "Assigning only two detectives to do a records search seems a bit skimpy on the resources to me."

"More people will be assigned," Kerney said, "and I plan to help out myself."

Sara wiped her lips with a napkin and shook her head. "Think about it, Kerney. We've got two homicides, one police shooting, a suicide, the killer's promise to carry out two more murders—which could very well mean our son and me—and his threat against you."

"I know all that, Sara."

"If anyone else were the target, you'd be calling out the cavalry. Do you think you can't ask for help because you're the police chief? Or is it because you don't think you're allowed to be scared about what's happening to us?"

"I am scared. But that isn't going to get in my way of doing the job."

"It's my job too. I'm going to work with you."

"This is a police matter."

"I've got a valid United States Army criminal investigator ID card in my wallet. Give me a desk, a computer, and a telephone, and I can run every potential suspect you have through the military records center in St. Louis to see if they have prior service. Under federal law, none of your people can do that. Who knows what we might learn? Wouldn't you like to have that information?"

Kerney bit his lip and nodded. "It wouldn't hurt."

"Well then, shower, get dressed, and let's go."

Sara scraped and stacked the breakfast dishes while Kerney got ready. He returned in uniform, freshly shaved, with his cowlick now firmly under control. He stopped her as she moved toward the front door and hugged her for a long minute.

"What's this for?" she asked, looking up at him.

He could feel the hardness of her belly against his body. He kissed her gently on the lips. "I just needed a hug."

Outside, a state police cruiser was parked conspicuously across the street, positioned to allow the occupant a full view of the driveway to the house. Kerney got Sara settled in the passenger seat of his unit and pulled out into the road, flashing his headlights at the vehicle. The officer, a young woman who Kerney knew in passing from his time as deputy chief of the state police, got out of the unit and came around to Kerney's window.

"What brings you to my driveway, Officer Rasmussen?" he asked.

Yvonne Rasmussen bent low to look at Kerney, touched the brim of her cap, and nodded to Sara. "Chief Baca's orders, sir."

"Which are?"

"Twenty-four-hour security at your house until further notice."

Sara smiled approvingly.

"I see," Kerney said. "What else has Chief Baca arranged?"

"I wouldn't know, sir," Rasmussen replied. "He did ask me to remind you that you have no authority to countermand his orders."

"I wouldn't think of it," Kerney replied, as he waved at Rasmussen and drove off.

Sara laughed and broke into a big smile. It was the first genuinely happy sound either of them had made since yesterday morning.

"What?" Kerney asked.

"He knows you well," Sara said, "and he isn't about to let you play the lone wolf this time. I'm going to shower him with kisses the next time I see him," Sara replied.

"That will embarrass him."

"He'll just have to cope with it."

At headquarters, the parking lot for official vehicles contained an unusually large number of units, including some unmarked sheriff and state police cars, one of which Kerney recognized as Andy Baca's. They went in through the back entrance to find cops everywhere, working at folding tables set up in hallways, filling the first-floor conference room, and spilling over into the reception area of Kerney's second-floor office suite. Most were off-duty personnel, but Barry Foyt and two other lawyers from the district attorney's office were there along with several sheriff's investigators and state police agents. All were busy on telephones or reading case files.

Andy Baca, Larry Otero, and Helen Muiz were in Kerney's office sitting at the small conference table that butted up against the desk. Sara limited her shower of kisses for Andy to one sisterly peck on the cheek while Kerney went to his desk and waited for an explanation.

None came, so as Sara took a seat next to Andy he asked for one.

"Larry and I thought it best to centralize the investigation and bring in more resources," Andy replied, scratching a jowly cheek. "The DA and the sheriff agreed to get on board, and your off-duty personnel just started showing up this morning as volunteers. Seems like nobody wants to see you wind up dead. Although for the life of me, I can't understand it." He broke into a big grin. "So, we need to catch this guy, so we can get all these folks back to normal duty before we run out of money to pay for the overtime."

Kerney shook his head in disbelief, a smile flooding his face. Of the three, only Andy had the chutzpah to mastermind this ploy. But he knew Helen and Larry had tagged along as willing co-conspirators.

"Okay, where are we?" he asked.

"We have a possible suspect that Russell Thorpe got a line on," Andy said. "Unknown white male, thirty-something, driving a blue GMC van, who was seen twice on the ranch road to your new place. Thorpe is meeting with Jack and Irene Burke right now to have a composite sketch made."

"They saw him?"

"Up close and personal," Andy replied. "A man delivering adobes to the building site also spotted him on the ranch."

"Excellent work."

"Detective Pino found the slug that Jack Potter took in the chest," Larry Otero said. "We're waiting to hear if a match can be made to the bullets that killed your horse."

"More good news."

"The caliber doesn't match Kurt Larsen's gun."

"I didn't expect it would," Kerney said.

"Lieutenant Molina has, according to your instructions, started a full case review," Helen Muiz said. "With the extra manpower available, we've expanded it a bit to include all felony cases within the first judicial district, the county, and the state police district office, so that we don't miss any possible suspects."

"That's smart," Kerney said.

"First up for review are the people on the list you prepared last night," Larry said. "Tafoya and Pino are working those cases. We've got a team pulling names of new possible suspects, another team working prisons, jails, probation and parole personnel to track them down, and Foyt is heading up the court records search."

"Give me all those names and identifying information," Sara said, "and I'll cross-check them with the armed forces record center in St. Louis."

"I'll get that to you right away," Helen Muiz said, smiling at Sara and writing herself a note, "and set you up with a desk and computer."

Andy stared at Sara's belly and gave her an uneasy look.

"Don't say a word, Andy," Kerney said.

Sara patted Andy's arm. "I promise not to have the baby at police headquarters."

Dubiously, Andy looked away.

"What else?" Kerney asked.

"You're booked with meetings," Helen answered. "Sal Molina, Lieutenant Casados, and the district attorney at his office, in that order."

"Larranaga is taking the police shooting to the grand jury," Larry Otero said.

Kerney nodded. "Has he met with the media?"

"Yeah, but he toned his rhetoric down a bit," Larry replied, "and said he was doing it in the best interest of all parties concerned. He didn't publically slam the SWAT call-out or dwell on the Patterson suicide."

"Fair enough," Kerney said.

The meeting broke up and Sara stayed behind for a moment.

"I like your Helen Muiz," she said.

"I wonder why?" Kerney replied, knowing full well both women possessed similar attributes: natural femininity and singular tough-mindedness.

"And I'm in love with Andy Baca."

"Stay away from him. He's a married man." He gave her a kiss and sent her on her way just before Sal Molina knocked at the open door.

Sal looked bleary-eyed and ready to nod off, but his head seemed to be working clearly. He sat at the conference table occasionally running a hand through what remained of his hair, and asked Kerney to come up with some more possible suspects.

Kerney added the names of a serial rapist he'd caught on the strength of nothing more than a shoe print outside a bedroom window, a stepfather who'd molested his wife's ten-year-old daughter, and a punk who was pulling twenty-five years for murdering an old lady because she'd refused him a glass of water when he was drunk and thirsty. He dug deep into his memory and added several more names, including several individuals he'd shot and wounded over the course of his career.

"I gotta ask you a few more questions, Chief," Sal said as he straightened out his slumping shoulders. "Have you pissed off somebody's husband or boyfriend that I need to know about?"

"No."

Sal gave him an uncomfortable glance. "Were you ever intimately involved with Jack Potter or Dora Manning?"

Kerney put his arms on the desk, clasped his hands, and looked Molina in the eyes. "You mean sexually, don't you?"

"Yeah."

"No, I was not."

"What about Norm Kaplan?"

"Same answer."

"Did you ever have a confidential informant you either had to lean on hard or bust? A guy who might still be pissed off about it?"

"Two," Kerney said, and gave Molina their names.

"Did you ever put somebody in the slam you knew didn't belong there?"

"You're asking if I falsified evidence or gave perjured testimony."

"Yeah."

"No, I haven't done that."

"How about any threats you might have made to a perp?" Molina asked.

Kerney thought about Bernardo Barela, a young man who'd raped, murdered, and mutilated a woman near Hermit's Peak, and then killed his accomplice, a state police officer's son, to keep him silent.

As far as Kerney knew, Barela was on death row awaiting execution. He'd personally promised Bernardo that he would hunt him down and kill him if he ever got released, and that vow still stood.

Kerney nodded and gave Sal a brief summary of Barela and his crimes.

"Anyone else?" Sal asked.

Kerney shook his head, unclasped his hands, and leaned back in his chair. "No."

Sal closed his notebook. "That's it, Chief."

"What about the Patterson death investigation?"

"From all indications, it was a clear-cut suicide," Molina replied. "Detective Pino is pretty shook up about it, and Cruz Tafoya is in the same boat about the Larsen shooting."

Kerney responded with silence.

"They're good detectives, Chief."

"They'll just have to sweat it out until Lieutenant Casados finishes his IA investigation."

"When will that be?" Molina asked, as he got to his feet.

"I'll let you know, Sal."

Molina stood at the door and nodded. "Sorry about all those questions, Chief."

"They were the right ones to ask," Kerney replied.

Lieutenant Robert Casados had two pastimes: weightlifting and singing baritone in a barbershop quartet. At six-foot-two he was a bit taller than Kerney, and carried himself with the easy poise of a big man used to being treated with deference. His size and voice gave Casados a command presence, which usually made just about everybody, including cops, eager to cooperate with him. Along with his physical attributes, Casados had an analytical mind and a degree with honors in sociology.

Sitting with Casados at the conference table, Kerney listened while the lieutenant laid out his findings. The SWAT call-out had been premised solely on Detective Pino's unconfirmed belief that Larsen was armed with a gun, followed by the supposition of both Pino and Sergeant Tafoya that Larsen was attempting to elude them.

"Pino had no actual knowledge that Larsen had a gun," Casados said, as he referred to a note. "She based her premise on Patterson's non-verbal reaction to the question. In fact, the counselor Pino spoke to, Joyce Barbero, made it clear that guns were not allowed at the independent living center."

Casados set his note aside and reached for another slip of paper. "However, the presumption that Larsen ran to elude the police does have credibility. Patterson placed a call to Larsen's cell phone minutes after Pino left the apartment. Why he ran is still in doubt, although it could very well be because he knew it was illegal for him to possess a handgun."

"Why do you say that?" Kerney asked.

"Twice in Santa Fe and once in Albuquerque he tried to buy a pistol, and was turned down each time when the records check came back identifying him as mentally ill. He got red-flagged through an out-of-state arrest stemming from a road rage incident some years back where he'd brandished a weapon at a passing motorist who'd cut him off in traffic. He got a deferred sentence based on his military record, his previous psych history, and a court-ordered agreement to enter and successfully complete a treatment program, which he did. As far as I know, it was his first and only offense."

"How did Larsen go from being an informant wanted for questioning to a murder suspect?" Kerney asked.

"According to everyone I've talked to and the tapes of the radio traffic, he didn't," Casados replied. "The orders were to proceed with caution and find and apprehend only. Sal Molina made it clear that Pino and Tafoya briefed him fully by phone before he bumped the request up to Deputy Chief Otero to call out SWAT."

"Do you think Molina is covering for his people?"

"Only insofar as he's willing to take the hit on this as their supervisor," Casados replied. "Sal has nothing to lose, he can retire and go fishing. Tafoya and Pino still have most of their careers in front of them. He'd hate to see their chances for advancement get derailed."

"So what went wrong?" Kerney asked.

"Since it wasn't a hostage situation, nobody thought to put a negotiator on the team that went looking for Larsen. That might have made all the difference."

"Nobody on the team tried to talk Larsen into surrendering?"

"After Larsen opened fire, the SWAT commander ordered Larsen to toss his weapon and give up peacefully. All four officers said he responded with more gunfire."

"They had cover and concealment?" Kerney asked.

"Affirmative, although the evidence at the scene shows that Larsen came close to taking out the point man."

"How many rounds did the team fire?" Kerney asked.

"In all, thirty-five," Casados said, giving Kerney an uneasy look. The figure was exact; policy required every officer to account for all department-issued ammunition down to the last cartridge. But that wasn't what bothered Casados.

"Did all the officers fire their weapons?" Kerney asked, reading Casados's discomfort.

"Yes, sir."

"That's a hell of a lot of firepower to stop the action of one man with a handgun. How many shots did Larsen get off?"

"I checked his magazine. Larsen fired four times, and he wasn't carrying any spare clips."

Kerney's expression turned sour. "What else, Lieutenant?"

"Larsen took three rounds in the back, Chief."

"Shit," Kerney said.

"According to the team, Larsen was belly crawling to safety and firing at the same time. The point man caught him with a burst when he rolled towards some rocks."

114

Kerney pushed back his chair and stared out his office window. This wasn't good. In fact, it sucked.

"Do you want me to write up my report and submit it?" Casados asked.

"Not yet. I want you to tack the Patterson suicide onto your investigation," Kerney replied, as he got up and walked to the window. "Go over all that happened with Patterson and Detective Pino from first contact to the time she was hospitalized."

"Yes, sir. Is that all for now?"

Kerney turned and nodded. "Thanks, Robert. You've done a good job."

Casados assembled his paperwork and left quietly.

The DA wasn't going to like what Kerney had to tell him, and he was due at Sid Larranaga's office in fifteen minutes.

Kerney didn't like it either. The problem was much bigger than the tragic mistakes that had been made by his people. Maybe Sid was right about the overeagerness of cop shops to use special weapons and tactics in every apparent high-risk situation.

He thought about it a bit longer. No matter what kind of discipline had to be served up to individual officers, the overriding problem was officer training. Sworn personnel needed to deal effectively with mentally ill informants, suspects, witnesses, and victims, no matter what the situation. He would get the ball rolling on a mandatory in-service program. It wouldn't stop the uproar from the community, but it was still the right thing to do.

He looked for Sara on the way out, found her in Sal Molina's office at the computer, and told her he'd be back shortly. He clamped his mouth shut to avoid asking if she was all right.

She waved him away with her hand, and he left the building trying to convince himself the day could only get better.

Chapter 6

Mechanical problems with the plane delayed Norm Kaplan's arrival in Albuquerque by over four hours. From the second-level observation deck, Santa Fe Police Officer Seth Neal, who'd been cooling his heels all that time, watched the plane land, turn, and taxi slowly to the terminal. He walked to the gate and asked the woman at the check-in counter to have a flight attendant advise Kaplan that a police officer would be waiting for him when he deplaned. He reassured her that everything was cool, and the woman's somewhat startled, questioning look disappeared.

Neal, who normally rode a motorcycle during the summer months and drove a squad car the rest of the year, didn't particularly like the assignment he'd been given. As a traffic officer, Neal's notion of a good day at work consisted of writing tickets, running speed traps, investigating accidents, pulling dignitary escort details, and busting drunk drivers.

Conspicuous in his uniform with tight-fitting pants and motorcycle boots, Neal stood to one side of the open jetway door as the first-class passengers hurried past, casting curious glances in his direction. A tall man dressed in jeans and an expensive pumice-colored linen sport coat broke ranks and veered toward him.

"Mr. Kaplan?" Neal inquired.

Kaplan nodded. A pained, tired expression carved deep lines around his mouth. "Have you caught Jack's killer?" he asked.

"No, sir. I'm here to escort you to Santa Fe."

"Why?"

"The detectives need to speak with you as soon as possible," Neal replied.

"I have my own car," Kaplan replied.

"Yes, sir, I know. I'll take you to it, and follow you to Santa Fe."

"Why do you need to do that?" Kaplan asked, his eyes searching Neal's face.

"It's just a precaution," Neal replied. "Did you check any luggage?"

"What kind of precaution?" Kaplan asked, his voice rising.

Neal touched Kaplan's arm to get him moving. "The detectives will explain it. Do you have any luggage checked?"

Kaplan nodded and Neal prodded him down the long corridor toward the lower level. In the baggage claim area, Neal kept Kaplan away from the passengers who ringed the carousel waiting for their luggage to arrive as he searched the crowd looking for any suspicious characters.

As luggage began tumbling down the conveyer belt, Kaplan asked questions about the investigation. Neal told him what he knew, which wasn't much, and Kaplan groused about the scantiness of the information.

Kaplan spied his bag, grabbed it, and Neal drove him to the off-site lot where his car was parked. He made Kaplan wait in the unit and did a visual inspection of the vehicle. He returned and ordered Kaplan to stay in the squad car.

"Why?"

"There's a dead dog on the driver's seat," Neal said.

"Oh my God," Kaplan said, his voice cracking. "What kind of dog?"

"I don't know," Neal said, as he reached for his cell phone to ask Santa Fe for instructions. "But we're gonna be here for a while."

He didn't tell Kaplan that the dog had been beheaded.

Sid Larranaga paced in front of his big oak desk, built by prison inmates. On it was a plaque with Larranaga's name carved in script, bordered on each side by the sun symbol of the state flag, which had been borrowed from a nineteenth-century Zia Pueblo pottery design.

Originally the symbol—a circle with lines radiating out in the four major directions of the compass—represented the stages of life, the cycle of the seasons, and the sacred obligations of the Zia people: clear minds, strong bodies, pure spirits, and devotion to the welfare of the tribe.

The design had been adopted in 1925, but to this day there were tribal members who didn't appreciate the state ripping-off a hallowed religious symbol without the Pueblos' permission.

Kerney waited for Sid to stop pacing. No longer the Young Turk politician who'd been swept into office and reelected district attorney a second time, Larranaga had put on some weight. His pudgy stomach jiggled a bit over a tightly cinched belt.

Sid sank into an overstuffed chair, took a cigar out of a humidor that sat on the corner of the desk, clamped it between his teeth, left it unlit, and stared at Kerney with a perplexed frown on his face.

He pulled the cigar out of his mouth and pointed it at Kerney. "You can't possibly believe that Larsen's death was justifiable. Thirty-five rounds fired by your people and Larsen shot three times in the back. Give me a break."

"That's not the issue," Kerney replied.

Larranaga snorted. "If that's not a perfect example of overkill, I don't know what is."

"It's impossible to precisely forecast the level of threat to an officer. Larsen ran to elude questioning, and Detective Pino's assumption that he was armed proved to be correct. That made it a high-risk situation. Furthermore, Larsen initiated a deadly assault, which put the officers' lives in jeopardy."

"I'm not questioning that," Sid replied, dropping the unlit cigar into an ashtray. "What I have a problem with is the fact that your people had an overwhelming advantage over Larsen. Why didn't they retreat, take cover, and give him a verbal warning?"

"My people were fired upon by a concealed subject in dense cover without provocation," Kerney replied. "They had no time to retreat, but a warning was given."

"Yeah, while they were pumping automatic fire at him," Larranaga replied. "Some warning."

"You don't know that," Kerney said. "Are these the kind of tactics you plan to use with the grand jury?"

Sid's expression turned angry and his hand gripped the arm of the chair. "Maybe," he snapped, "and just maybe I'll tantalize them further with the fact that Larsen wasn't a fugitive from justice, didn't kill Jack Potter, and had an extensive psychiatric history."

"Will you carefully leave out the point that he had a prior arrest for assault involving a handgun and, as a mental patient, was in illegal possession of a 9mm semi-automatic? What are you trying to do, Sid, be the crusading DA who cleans out a nest of trigger-happy cops, so you can get a leg up on an appointment to the bench?"

Sid took a deep breath and shook his head. "Don't bait me, Kerney. This isn't political. Look, I told you yesterday, you needed to show me evidence that the officers were forced to stop an attack. You've managed to do that, just barely. But you know the disparity of force was overwhelmingly in favor of the team that went in to get Larsen."

"That doesn't mean you have to ask the grand jury to return a true bill of indictment charging involuntary manslaughter against the officers," Kerney said. "Do you really want to take this to trial? What if a jury doesn't agree?"

Larranaga threw a hand in the air. "What's my alternative?"

"Have the grand jury investigate the department's use of force policies, SWAT procedures, and guidelines for dealing with mentally ill subjects. I'll cooperate fully."

"A slap on the wrist isn't going to cut it."

"I'm talking about using the incident to make constructive changes."

"Besides that wonderful plum, what else are you willing to give me?" Sid asked.

As with most police departments, the SWAT team consisted of personnel who served on it in addition to their normal duties, which gave Kerney some disciplinary options. "I'll permanently remove the SWAT commander from his position and place the other three officers on suspended SWAT status pending completion of remedial training."

"Not good enough. I want the officer who actually shot Larsen also kicked off SWAT."

"Agreed."

Sid rubbed his lips together. "And the grand jury can have complete access to whatever, with nothing held back, including the Patterson debacle?"

"Bring it on," Kerney replied.

"This could cost you your job."

"I think the grand jury will find much to praise by the time their investigation gets underway."

"Don't ask me to stall on this," Sid said.

"I wouldn't think of it."

Larranaga picked up the cigar, started chewing on it, and wiped a bit of tobacco off his lower lip. Kerney wasn't wrong about his political agenda, and a grand jury probe into department operations that weren't perceived as anti–law enforcement could give him front-runner status for an interim appointment to the bench. Eventually, he'd have to run in an election to be retained in the position, but as the incumbent he'd have the advantage.

"Okay, I'll go along with you on this," Larranaga said.

"Thanks, Sid."

Larranaga smiled. "Yeah, sure. Just remember, I can't subpoena a dead police chief, so go catch the guy who wants to kill you."

"That's a great idea," Kerney said as he left Sid's office.

After receiving Officer Neal's report of a dead dog in Kaplan's car, Sal Molina pulled Ramona Pino off the records search to go and investigate, called the Albuquerque Police Department to ask for assistance, and ordered Neal to take Kaplan to the nearest police substation and wait there for Pino's arrival.

It was a still, hot day in Albuquerque when Ramona arrived at the parking lot near the airport. A relentless sun pushed the temperature near the century mark and dust kicked up by dry, early morning canyon winds hung in the hazy air. The lane to Kaplan's car had been blocked off with bright yellow police tape. Two local crime scene techs and a detective waited in the air-conditioned comfort of their vehicles.

With the heat from the pavement boiling through the soles of her shoes, she walked around Kaplan's car with the detective, who'd introduced himself as Danny Roth.

Probably in his late forties, Roth was a transplant with a decidedly East Coast accent who'd gone Western. He wore boots, a bolo tie around the open collar of his cowboy shirt, and a pair of stretch cotton and polyester jeans. Tufts of dark chest hair curled above the open shirt collar.

There was no sign of forced entry. In unison, they shaded their eyes and looked through the tinted side windows and windshield. The headless dog, which had the markings and coloration of a Border collie, sat upright, resting against the back of the driver's seat. There was a white envelope on the dashboard behind the steering wheel. They could see no discernible blood in the passenger compartment.

With a slightly leering smile, Roth held out the car key Kaplan had given him. "Want to open it up?" he asked in a cavalier, joking tone, as he sidled close to her.

"I'll let your people do that," Ramona said as she backed away. She didn't need Roth wasting her time with any cute moves. She had a boyfriend, an APD vice sergeant, who wasn't overly hairy, and didn't leer. Besides that, the inside of the vehicle probably smelled like dead dog.

The car was a high-end, imported sedan that came with an antitheft system and keys with built-in electronic circuits coded to open the doors and start the engine.

"How did the perp get into the vehicle without setting off the alarm?" she asked.

Roth shrugged a nonchalant shoulder. "When Kaplan gave me the key, he said the system was working, and the lot manager said no car alarms have gone off since Kaplan arrived at the lot."

"You asked him to check the records?"

"Yeah, for the eight days the vehicle has been here."

"You'd think that somebody parked nearby would have noticed the dog," Ramona said.

"Depends on when the perp put the pooch in the car," Roth said.

"Good point. Okay, let's have the techs dust the outside for prints and then open it up," Ramona said.

Roth waved at the other police vehicle and two techs, both with surgical masks hanging around their necks, came over and started rummaging through their cases.

Ramona glanced around the lot while Roth tried to chat her up. The eager look in his eye and the absence of a wedding ring made her shut down even more. Except for the entrance and exit lanes by the attendant's booth, a high chain-link security fence enclosed the property, and the long rows of parking spaces had light poles at each end to illuminate the lot at night. She doubted the perp had scaled the fence or walked onto the lot carrying a thirty-pound, headless dog, no matter how well concealed it might have been.

She ignored Roth and walked fifty yards to the attendant's booth through heat waves that shimmered up from the hot pavement.

"What's going on down there?" the female attendant asked, as she waved off a car trying to enter and pointed to a sign that read LOT FULL. "I had to close the lot and we've got two people waiting in the manager's office because you cops won't let them leave."

"It shouldn't be long now," Ramona said. "I'll speak to them. When did you start work?"

"Seven this morning."

"Has anything out of the ordinary occurred?"

"Like what?"

"Somebody leaving without paying, or coming and going in a short period of time."

"Everybody pays," the blonde said. "You gotta go through this gate in order to get out. It's the only way. And this is a long-term lot. People don't just come and go. Some of these cars are here for three or four weeks."

"So nobody did a fast turnaround," Ramona said, "or failed to pay."

"Not since I've been here."

"How about earlier this week?"

"Same thing, and I've been here for five straight days."

Ramona got the shift-change times from the blonde and asked for the manager. The woman pointed at a small building outside the fence next to a staging area where idling shuttle buses were parked. Inside, Ramona reassured two unhappy customers that they wouldn't have to wait much longer, and met with the manager, a Hispanic male with nervous black eyes, a slightly crooked nose, and a mouth twisted in annoyance. His name, Leon Villa, was embroidered beneath a company patch sewn above the pocket of his short-sleeved shirt.

"Are you going to tell me what's going on?" Villa asked, staring at Ramona's shield. "The other policeman told me nothing. Is somebody dead?"

"No one's dead," Ramona replied. "I need to talk to the booth attendants who worked the afternoon and late-night shifts during the last eight days."

"They're not here."

"Of course not," Ramona said, wondering whether Villa was rattled by the presence of cops or a bit dim-witted. "Do you have their names, addresses, and phone numbers?"

Villa nodded, paged through a three-ring binder, and read off the information as Ramona wrote it down.

Back at the crime scene, the techs, their faces partially hidden behind surgical masks, were working on the inside of the car. A rancid, maggoty odor wafted out of the vehicle. The dog had been removed from the driver's seat, bundled in a dark green garbage bag, and left on the pavement. There was no sign of blood on the seat or the floor mat.

Detective Roth handed her the blank envelope from the dashboard of Kaplan's car and the note it contained. Both were protected by clear plastic sleeves. The note read:

KERNEY
THE DOG DOESN'T COUNT
STILL TWO TO GO
CAN YOU GUESS WHO DIES
BEFORE YOU?

"Who's Kerney?" Roth asked.

"My chief."

"No shit? What do you know about that? Bet he's got to be sweating a bit."

Ramona nodded as she studied the note. "This type looks identical to the message that was tacked to the chief's front door."

"It looks like a common font," Roth said.

"How can you be sure?"

"I do the monthly newsletter for my kid's soccer league," Roth said, looking at it again. "In fact, I use this typeface all the time. It's called Arial Narrow."

"Did the techs lift any prints?"

"Not from the note or envelope," Roth replied. "But there are lots of partials from the car."

"I need to have the carcass examined."

"Sure thing. We use a vet here in town who does a

good job with animal forensics. I'll have it dropped off after we finish up with the inspection at the lab. But from first look, Fido was probably left outside for a couple of days after he was killed. The techs found some dirt and pine needles matted in the dried blood on his fur."

"That's good to know," Ramona said. "A trace evidence analysis might give us a general idea where the perp stashed the dog. Can you arrange to have the vehicle towed to Santa Fe? I don't think Kaplan will want to drive it home. Not until it's fumigated at least."

"You got it," Roth said, giving her the once-over for the second time.

Ramona smiled tightly in response, left Roth in the hot sun, went to her unit, cranked up the air conditioning, and started calling the off-duty attendants on her cell phone.

She hit pay dirt on the second call. Yesterday afternoon, a man driving a van had entered the lot only to drive out after a few minutes. As a precaution, the attendant had written down the van's license plate number on the lot ticket.

Ramona made an appointment to interview the attendant, hung up, and went immediately to the manager's office to search for the ticket. Wearing gloves, she went through the date and time stamped tickets until she found it. She slipped it into an envelope, and called in the license number from her unit. The plate had been stolen three weeks ago from a car in Socorro, eighty miles south of Albuquerque.

"We're almost done here," Roth said with a big smile, as he slid into the passenger seat next to her. "Want to grab some lunch?"

"Not today."

"You don't take meal breaks?"

"I've got work to do," Ramona said, hoping Roth would take the hint and go away.

"We still don't know how the perp got in the car."

"I'm working on it, Detective," Ramona said flatly.

Roth got the message and shrugged. "Hey, let me know how it turns out." He handed Ramona his card. "The vet's name is on the back. I'll have our lab get a report up to you by tomorrow."

"Ask him to rush it," Ramona said.

"Anything for a fellow officer."

"Thanks, Detective."

Ramona left Roth and went to meet up with Officer Neal and Norm Kaplan. When she'd secured Potter's keys into evidence, only one car key had been on the ring. She was betting Kaplan would tell her that, just like any other couple, both men carried keys to each other's cars. The perp must have taken it after shooting Potter.

Which meant that from the start everything the perp had done had been carefully thought out. She wondered if Kaplan was the next target. It wasn't far-fetched to think so. But why, was the unanswered question. And what did the perp have planned for the dog's severed head?

She switched the radio frequency to the secure channel, keyed the microphone, asked for Lieutenant Molina by his call sign, and brought him up to date when he answered.

At state police headquarters, just a bit further down Cerrillos Road from Kerney's office, State Police Officer Russell Thorpe was pumped. After several hours of intensive, detailed questioning, Jack and Irene Burke's description of the man in the blue van had yielded a good sketch of the subject. Thorpe asked the couple to look at mug shots, which they willingly agreed to do, and left them with a technician to scroll through the department's computerized data files.

At the lab, he checked to see if the tests had been completed on the bullets removed from Kerney's horse, and got more good news: the rifling of the spent .38-caliber rounds matched a dented, partially flattened bullet that had been retrieved earlier in the morning near the Potter homicide scene. Forensic evidence now conclusively tied both cases together. Thorpe took the stairs two steps at a time and asked to see Chief Baca.

Ushered quickly into Andy's office by the receptionist, Thorpe stood in front of the desk, handed over the artist's sketch of the suspect, and gave the chief his news, dampening an almost overwhelming eagerness to blurt it out. Although he was hardly a seasoned veteran, he had no intention of looking like a bonehead rookie in front of Baca.

Andy smiled when Thorpe finished his report. "This is good," he said. "Things are starting to come together. One of Chief Kerney's detectives phoned in a sighting of the blue van at a parking lot near the Albuquerque airport, with plates stolen out of Socorro County. The driver left a decapitated dog in a vehicle belonging to Potter's lover."

Russell felt stupidly out of the loop. "Sir?" he asked, hoping that would be enough of a hint to get some clarification from the chief.

"I'm sorry," Andy said. "Let me bring you up to speed. The dog was Potter's lost mixed-breed collie, and it was left with another threatening note to Kerney. At this point we don't know if the perp has targeted Potter's lover as his next victim or is just playing mind games with Chief Kerney. An APB went out on the van thirty minutes ago."

Thorpe nodded.

"Make a copy of the sketch, leave the original with my secretary, get down to Albuquerque, and hook up with Detective Pino. She's about to meet with a witness. See if that person can confirm that our perp drove that van. I'll have Santa Fe PD dispatch let Pino know you're on the way."

"I've got the Burkes looking at mug shots," Thorpe said.

"I'll put an agent with them," Andy replied. "Call me as soon as you know something one way or the other."

"Yes, sir."

"And when you get back, report to Santa Fe Police headquarters. You're on this case until further notice."

"Thank you, sir."

"You've earned the assignment, Thorpe," Andy said, hesitating as he reached for the phone. "When Kerney was my chief deputy, he told me you had the makings of a good officer, and he was right."

Ramona Pino waited for Thorpe's arrival at a small city park near a technical college, within easy driving distance of the Albuquerque airport. Except for a busy one-way street that bordered the park and funneled traffic from the downtown core of the city, it was a pretty spot with big shade trees and a thick carpet of grass.

Norm Kaplan had freaked over the news that the dead dog was a Border collie. Kaplan had given the dog to Potter as an anniversary present. After calming the man down, Ramona had asked who knew about his flight home. Kaplan swore he'd told only Sal Molina, Potter's secretary, and the woman who managed his antique store. A call to the store manager revealed that some unnamed officer had phoned yesterday to confirm Kaplan's flight information.

Ramona checked in with Sal Molina, who validated her suspicion that the call was bogus. But how did the perp know which parking lot Kaplan had used? Maybe he'd just cruised all of them until he found Kaplan's car. There weren't that many, so it would have taken only a couple of hours at most to make the rounds.

While she waited, she spoke to the pathologist who'd examined Potter's body. The entry and exit wounds weren't aligned, and the exit wound was larger and more irregularly shaped, which was due to the bullet hitting the sternum. The path of the slug through Potter's body could mean the killer was smaller in height than his victim, but the pathologist wasn't about to bet on it.

Thorpe arrived, and while Pino looked over the sketch and the information about the blue GMC van, he caught her up on the forensic results from the examination of the bullets.

Ramona stifled any reaction. Under different circumstances, she would've been pleased to know she'd found an important piece of evidence that tied the perp to two crimes. But the news paled in comparison to yesterday's screw-ups.

"Do we have a make on the gun?" she asked. The number of rifling grooves in a barrel and the direction of their internal twists could sometimes be used to pinpoint the manufacturer.

"Nothing definite," Thorpe replied, "although it could possibly be a .38-caliber Taurus with a four-inch barrel. Who's our witness?"

"His name is Mark Cullum, age twenty-two, originally from Clovis. He attends the technical school in the mornings and works afternoons at the parking lot. He's expecting us."

Cullum's apartment was a first-floor boxy affair on a hillside street across from the park. A tall, pleasant-looking youth wearing jeans and a short-sleeved shirt with the tails out opened the door before Ramona had a chance to knock. He identified himself as Cullum, and asked the officers inside.

The front room was done up in pure college-student decor. An empty beer keg had been turned into an end table, a dart board was nailed to a wall, pine boards and bricks served as a bookcase, and a bicycle leaned against the side of a second-hand couch covered with a cheap throw. The place smelled of sweaty socks and Chinese take-out.

They stood in the center of the room. Thorpe pulled the sketch off his clipboard and handed it to Cullum, who looked at it, shook his head, and handed it back. "That's not the fella I saw," he said. "Not at all."

"What are the differences?" Thorpe asked.

"He had real short hair and a mustache, a real droopy one. And he was wearing aviator sunglasses."

"What about the nose, the chin, the shape of his head?" Ramona asked, taking the sketch from Thorpe and holding it up in front of Cullum's face.

"Maybe they're the same, but don't bank on it because of me."

"Did he have any scars or distinguishing marks?"

"None that I remember."

"What color hair did he have?" Thorpe asked.

"Black, like his mustache. He had a real good tan, like he'd been outdoors a lot, or he was dark-skinned. Other than that, I didn't notice much about him."

"Did you get a look inside the van?" Thorpe asked.

"I didn't pay it any mind."

"What did you notice about the vehicle?" Thorpe asked.

"It had a dinged-up front bumper and side window curtains. I think it was either blue or black. It was a GMC, that's for sure."

"Did he say anything when he left the lot?" Ramona asked.

"Yeah. I said something like 'that was mighty quick,' and he said that he needed to get something out of his wife's car."

"Did you watch where he went while he was on the lot?" Ramona asked.

"Nope. The shuttle had just brought in a load of customers, so I was humping it."

"Was he an Anglo, Hispanic, or Native American?" Thorpe asked.

"Anglo, I think."

"You're not sure?" Thorpe asked.

"Not really."

"Did he speak with an accent?" Russell had asked the Burkes the same question.

"Well, not an accent exactly. He sounded kind of country."

"Meaning?" Thorpe asked.

"You know, a twang, a drawl, kind of a nasal tone."

Russell nodded. Cullum's answer matched what the Burkes had told him. But that seemed to be the only similarity. Thorpe mulled it over.

"What made you write down the plate number?" Ramona asked.

Cullum shrugged. "We had a car broken into a couple months back, on my shift. My boss acted like it was all my fault, so now I'm extra careful."

They wound up the interview with a few more questions, thanked Cullum, and left the apartment.

"What do you think?" Thorpe asked as they waited for a break in traffic to cross the street. Motorists speeding by slowed down at the sight of Russell in his distinctive black state police uniform.

"Same vehicle, different driver," Pino replied, stepping off the curb. "It doesn't make sense, unless our perp has an accomplice."

"Cullum said the man had a drawl," Thorpe said as he kept pace with Pino. "So did the Burkes."

"You think he disguised himself?" Ramona asked as they walked under the welcome shade of the trees.

"It would be easy enough to do, a haircut, a dye job, a fake mustache, and sunglasses, and he's a different-looking guy."

"But why keep using the van?" Ramona asked as she

unlocked her unit. "It's been spotted three times already. The perp has got to know we're looking for it."

"Everything this guy does seems to have a purpose," Russell replied. "Maybe he stole the van as well as the license plate and plans to ditch it when he's done."

Ramona liked the way Thorpe's mind worked. She thought about all the dead animals, the threatening notes and messages left behind, Manning's paintings that had been cut from the frames in the Taos art gallery—each act carefully orchestrated. "There's got to be more to it than that."

Russell nodded in agreement. "Yeah, probably. I've been thinking he got lost trying to find Kerney's property. It's pretty much out of the way and not easy to find without directions. That's why he was seen twice on the ranch."

"But he knew generally where to look," Ramona said. "Which means he probably searched through public records for either the deed of sale for the land or the construction permit."

"Exactly."

Ramona reached for her cell phone. "I'll get my lieutenant to put someone on it. Thanks for your help."

"Any time, Detective."

Ramona watched Thorpe get in his unit and drive off. He was a good cop, a nice guy, and the time she'd spent with him had washed away almost all of her irritation about smarmy Detective Danny Roth.

Back at the office, Kerney spent a considerable amount of time fending off the news media, briefing the mayor and the city manager by phone on the status of all the investigations, and getting Larry Otero started on revising all relevant policies pertaining to use of force, SWAT operations, and dealing with the mentally ill. In conjunction with the initiative, he ordered the creation of a new in-service training plan for all sworn personnel.

Lieutenant Casados, who was next in line to see him, reported the results of the ballistics tests on the SWAT officer's weapons. Kerney told Robert what he was going to do, had Helen cut the orders, then called the SWAT supervisor and the officer who'd shot Kurt Larsen into his office and kicked them off the team.

Both men recoiled like they'd been hit in the gut and wanted to argue with him about it. Kerney told them to be glad they weren't off the force entirely and facing involuntary manslaughter charges, then sent them out the door.

He took a minute alone to settle down. He'd held his cool during the meeting, although it hadn't been easy, and he didn't want his anger with the two men to spill over to the rest of the troops. The attempt worked well enough when Molina came in to give a progress report. Kerney took notes as Sal talked, asked a few clarifying questions, and asked Molina to let everyone know they were doing a good job.

He decided to check on Sara, and went next door to the investigations unit suite, walking past detectives working at desks cluttered with pizza boxes, crumpled napkins, and soft-drink cups. Sara was still in Sal's office, sitting in a chair with her shoes off, her feet on a cardboard file box, and the telephone receiver cradled next to her ear. She looked tired, but he didn't dare say it.

She gave him a smile, flicked her hand to send him away, and kept talking into the handset. He smiled in response, hoping he didn't look too worried, returned to his office, and read over his notes from Molina's update.

The records search was going about the way Kerney figured it would: Names were going on a list and coming off just about as fast. A lot of potential suspects were still locked up and some were dead. Local ex-felons were being interviewed for alibis, and those living out of the area or in other states were being tracked down through probation and parole offices.

He thought about the message left for him in Kaplan's car. The perp was getting cocky, maybe even starting to feel invincible. If past behavior held true, leaving the dead dog with the note probably meant he was about to make a move on his next victim.

Ramona Pino and Russell Thorpe had done some good follow-up work to push the investigation along, and the city was saturated with patrol officers from every department looking for the blue van and the driver, be it a long-haired blond male or a mustached subject with matching, short dark hair. But unless they got lucky, they were still a long way from catching the guy.

He looked up to see Sara leaning against the door frame. She took her shoes off, padded barefoot to a chair, and sank down.

"You wanted to see me?" she asked.

"Let's get out of here," he said.

She nodded. "All I managed to accomplish today was absolutely nothing."

"That can't be true."

"Well, I crossed some names off the list." She placed

her hands on her belly. "Did you ever piss anyone off in your unit when you where in 'Nam?"

"Not enough to want to kill me."

She tapped her handbag. "I had Army archives fax me the complete company roster of your unit. It includes everyone who served with you during your tour. You can look through it when we get home, just to be sure."

"As you wish, Colonel," Kerney said, watching Sara rub her stomach. She looked uncomfortable. "How's Patrick Brannon doing?"

"He's restless. I think he wants to join the party fairly soon."

"How soon?"

Sara laughed as she pushed herself upright. "I'll keep you advised. Take me home, Kerney, and tell me what's new."

"He's still out there."

Her smile faded. "Tell me something I don't know."

Lights were on inside the town house. For Potter and Manning, the bald-headed man had worn a long blond wig and a theatrical nose purchased from a costume and special effects company. It was more a deceit than a disguise, designed to convince anyone who saw him that he was a very specific someone else.

Tonight was no different. After he backed the van next to the woman's vehicle, parked outside a two-car garage, he checked his appearance in the rearview mirror. The hair looked real and the nose was perfect. Good enough to fool anyone, even up close.

He opened the van's rear doors, and followed the

walkway at the side of the garage to a small enclosed patio. He paused to check for any activity in the neighboring units, saw nothing worrisome, and put on a pair of gloves before unlatching the gate. He sidled up to the sliding glass door and glanced inside the house. The room was unoccupied. He used a knife to jimmy the locks, and slipped inside.

He could hear the sounds of movement coming from an adjacent hallway. From the look of things, the woman was still in the process of unpacking and moving in. He found her in the guest bathroom breaking down empty cardboard boxes and stacking them neatly in the tub.

"Come with me," he said softly, pressing the blade of the knife against her throat as he grabbed her by the hair that fell to her shoulders.

The woman's mouth formed a silent scream. She was pretty in a used-up way, with interesting lines around her chin and eyes.

The bald-headed man shook his head. "Don't say a word."

He pushed her down the hallway, through the alcove, and into the garage, which was filled with stuff from the woman's recent move.

He leaned the woman against a wall, the knife still at her throat, and held out the specially prepared cookie he'd made for her. "Eat this."

The woman shook her head.

"Or die," the bald-headed man said.

"What is it?" the woman asked through thin lips, her body shaking uncontrollably.

"Eat it and I'll let you go."

The woman shook her head.

The man dropped the cookie on the floor and put away the knife. "Have it your way."

He spun her around, put his full weight against her back, pulled a length of rope from inside his shirt and tied her hands. He forced her to her knees, used more rope to tie her ankles, and rolled her over.

The woman looked up at him from the garage floor. "Why are you doing this?" she whimpered.

"You'll never know." He bent down, took a small box of rat poison from his shirt pocket, poured some into his gloved hand, squeezed her mouth open, forced the pellets into her mouth, and pressed her jaw shut.

She died fast, hard, and ugly. A bit too fast to be completely enjoyable.

A cat came in through a pet door and rubbed against the man's leg. He picked it up before it could sniff the cookie and stroked its back.

"We have lots to do, and not much time," he whispered to the cat before he broke its neck.

Stuck on protective service duty with Norm Kaplan for the remainder of his shift, Seth Neal was finally relieved by another officer, asked by his superior to work a double, and assigned to the roving patrol team that was looking for the blue van. By ten o'clock at night, the streets were fairly quiet and traffic was light on the through roads in and out of the city. Sheriff's deputies and state police officers were checking rural campgrounds and back roads, rangers were cruising in the national forest and at the state park, even motor transportation officers were out on the Interstate and state highways looking for the vehicle. In town, every parking lot, commercial district, and residential area was being patrolled.

It was a night when cop cars were everywhere but no motorist needed to fear getting a traffic ticket.

Neal took his meal break at headquarters so he could do his dailies from his regular shift and turn them in. Because it was part of a homicide investigation, he worked carefully on what he'd come to think of as the dead dog incident report. Neal knew the traffic code inside and out and could put together perfect paperwork for DWI arrests and accident reconstructions. But when it came to writing felony investigation narratives, he never felt all that competent about it.

Finished, Neal dropped the paperwork off on the shift commander's desk, told dispatch he was back in service, left the police parking lot, and hit the brakes when he saw a dark-colored GMC van with the back door open sitting in front of the nearby municipal court building.

He put the spotlight on the vehicle. It carried the plate stolen out of Socorro. He adjusted the light to shine inside the open door. He could see a naked human figure on the floor of the vehicle clutching what appeared to be the head of a dog.

Chapter 7

Exhausted but unable to sleep, Sara sat in the living room hoping the baby would either stop kicking or just get on with being born. She was weary of being pregnant, and thoroughly disgusted with the notion that, at such a supposedly wonderful time in their lives, she and Kerney were under siege.

Arriving home, she'd found no comfort in finding a state cop on guard duty outside, nor had she particularly enjoyed waiting in the car while Kerney conducted a room search before allowing her to go inside. The events of the last two days had become surreal and nightmarish.

Four hours ago, after an early light dinner, Kerney had gone into the bedroom to nap. He was still sleeping, stretched out on his side fully dressed except for his boots, his sidearm within reach on the night- stand.

The quiet house, the drawn shades, her reluctance to risk sitting on the patio to enjoy the cool night air made her feel caged. She sighed, got up, and went to the Arts and Crafts writing desk, one of a number of antique pieces she'd inherited from her grandmother, and tried to distract herself by studying the architectural drawings for the house.

Months ago, she'd shipped her heirloom furniture from Montana to Santa Fe and put it into storage, where—except for the desk and matching chair—it remained. But since Kerney had so few personal possessions, they would need a lot more than Sara's contributions to outfit their new home.

She studied the floor plan, visualizing where she might want to arrange the pieces she had and those that needed to be selected and purchased. Since they wouldn't be able to move in until well after Sara's maternity leave ended, furnishing and decorating the house would be an ongoing task with many decisions delayed until she could get back to Santa Fe on weekend trips.

However, she could do a number of things after the baby came: buy linens and housewares, perhaps some lamps and end tables, order a custom-made piece or two, and get a freestanding kitchen center island she'd spotted in a local store. But putting the house in any kind of reasonable order would have to be accomplished in bits and pieces.

That sucked, and she wondered if everything—the marriage, the baby, the new house—was nothing but a big romantic daydream on her part that had gone badly awry.

She blocked the negative thoughts from her mind. It wasn't like her to be so moody and disheartened. She *did* love Kerney and *did* want this baby. No matter that the task was daunting, she would turn the new house into a home, even if it took years.

The desk phone rang. Larry Otero needed to speak to Kerney. Sara asked why.

"We've got another homicide and another note," Larry replied.

"I'll get him."

She walked to the bedroom thinking one down, one to go, and for once she really didn't give a damn. The baby had stopped kicking and all she wanted to do was go to sleep.

She quietly opened the bedroom door, gently shook Kerney awake, and softly told him the killer had struck again.

Kerney rolled up to the crime scene. The blue van was awash in light and ringed off with police-line tape strung between the police cars that surrounded the vehicle. Andy Baca, Larry Otero, Russell Thorpe, and Sal Molina were standing at the perimeter with Officer Neal, all of them looking somber, watching the ME and two paramedics at the back of the van remove the body. Techs stood off to one side, waiting their turn at the vehicle, while two detectives videotaped and photographed the scene. Except for the sound of traffic coming from Cerrillos Road, silence hung thick in the air.

Kerney gave Andy and the others a quick nod. Nobody smiled. Sal Molina held out a bloodstained note encased in a clear plastic sleeve. It had a hole in it and read:

KERNEY,
DO YOU KNOW ME YET?
GUESS WHO'S NEXT.

"It was probably written with a fine-point permanent ink marker," Molina said.

"Has anybody had a look inside the vehicle?" Kerney asked.

"I did a quick visual check, Chief," Neal replied. "The victim is an unknown, naked white female, age probably late forties, I'd guess. Slender build, maybe five-six with long, light-brown hair. I saw no clothing or personal possessions inside the vehicle."

"The killer posed her," Otero said. "Wrapped her arms around the dog's head and placed it on her chest. The note was attached to the body by a knitting needle driven into the lower abdomen below the navel."

"Driven how deeply?" Kerney asked.

"Far enough to kill an unborn child," Larry said.

The appalled look on Kerney's face was palpable.

"We don't know if he did it before or after she was dead," Andy added, breaking the silence.

The men surrounding Kerney stared at the ground with expressionless eyes.

"Do we have an approximate time of death?" he asked, forcing himself to stay focused.

"According to the ME, it's a fresh kill," Larry said, lifting his gaze to Kerney's face. "Two, maybe three hours."

"And the cause of death?" Kerney asked.

"We don't know, Chief," Molina replied. "Except for the puncture wound to the stomach, there are no other visible traumas to the body. The ME thinks she may have been poisoned."

"What about the van?"

"The tire tracks match the imprints I took at the horse barn," Thorpe replied.

"Well, at least that's nailed down," Kerney said, trying to keep the alarm he felt out of his voice. He glanced at Larry. "What's under way?"

"We're running a records check on the van, and searching the missing-person database for a match," Larry replied. "Plus, Lieutenant Molina has a man inside the courthouse pulling the tape from the parking lot surveillance camera."

"Did he view it?" Kerney asked.

"We all did," Andy answered. "The perp's a ballsy bastard, Kerney. It shows him parking the van, opening the rear door, throwing a finger at the camera, and walking away. We'll have the lab enhance it to see if we can get an ID."

"What else was on the tape?"

"Nothing," Molina said.

"So where did the perp go?" Kerney asked. "Did he have another car nearby? Did he walk away?"

"We don't know," Larry said. "But Chief Baca and I have every available officer from both departments hunting for him. We're checking public transportation, cab companies, and all residential areas within walking distance."

"What about nearby hotels and motels?" Kerney asked.

"We're on it," Molina said quietly.

"I'd like to go out on patrol and help find this guy, sir," Thorpe said to Chief Baca, eager to get away from the tight-lipped gloom that permeated the group.

"Go ahead," Andy replied.

Thorpe hurried to his unit. Kerney turned to Sal Molina. "When the ME is finished, I want people all over that vehicle, top to bottom. I want to know where it's been and who's been in it. I want to know the name of every person who ever owned it, ever rode in it. I want every fiber, every hair, every piece of dirt, mud, or pebble stuck in the tread of a tire found and analyzed. If there's a leaf or twig caught in the undercarriage, I want it logged into evidence, and I want to know where it came from. Nothing comes out of or off that vehicle that isn't bagged and tagged."

"We'll do it right, Chief," Molina said.

"I want the entire vehicle dusted for prints: the engine compartment, wheel wells, and every other possible place that could have been handled or touched. When that's done, tow it, have it stripped down, and put everything under a microscope."

"My techs are on the way," Andy said.

"Good," Kerney said. "I want the autopsy started right now, and a plant biologist and soil expert looking at what we get off that vehicle as soon as possible. Let's get that videotape enlarged and analyzed pronto. Wake people up if you have to."

"Anything else?" Otero asked.

"That will do for starters. I'll be in my office."

They watched Kerney walk away, his back stiff with anger.

"God, I hated to tell him about the knitting needle," Larry said.

In unison, the men nodded glumly and then turned to the business at hand.

What was he missing? Who was this guy? In the quiet of his office, Kerney started from scratch and went through every bit of information that had been assembled so far. Amid the reams of contacts, follow-ups, and closed-case research conducted by the teams of officers and detectives, there wasn't one reasonable suspect in sight.

The phone rang and the light to his private line blinked. Kerney answered quickly, thinking it might be Sara calling to tell him the baby was on the way.

"Do you know me yet?" a man's soft voice asked.

Kerney didn't respond. He picked up a pen and started writing everything down.

The man chuckled at Kerney's silence. "You know nothing."

"You'd be surprised," Kerney said.

"So who's next?" the man asked.

"Let's get together and talk about it," Kerney said. "There's no need for this to go any further."

The man laughed. "I can't stop now, Kerney. I'm planning a two-for-one special, just for you. Haven't you got that figured out yet?"

"Do you think I'm going to let that happen?" Kerney asked, biting back his exasperation.

"You can't stop it. But before that, I'm going to make your world blow up in your face."

"Meaning what?" Kerney asked, as he kept writing.

"Since you deserve to lose the most, I've decided to improvise a bit, expand my horizons, and add a few more people to my list. It's time to wipe out your bloodline completely, Kerney."

"Tell me more," Kerney said.

"I can't do that," the man replied. "Time's up, Kerney, and the clock is ticking."

The line went dead. Quickly, Kerney reviewed his notes, which were almost a verbatim record of the conversation. He underlined the phrases "blow up" and "the clock is ticking." Had the perp given him a hint? Was there a bomb planted somewhere ready to go off?

His first thoughts turned to Sara at their rental house on Upper Canyon Road. The impulse to go to her drove him to his feet. He anchored himself back in the chair, used his handheld radio, and made contact with the state police officer on duty outside the house.

"Is everything okay?" he asked.

"Affirmative, Chief," Officer Barney Wade replied. "I just made a sweep around the property. It's all quiet."

"Have you seen my wife?"

"Not since she came home with you earlier, Chief. I think she's sleeping. I saw the bedroom light go off soon after you left. Do you want me to check on her?"

"The house may be rigged with a bomb. Wake her up, get her out of the house now, and move away from the property, and stay on the air while you do it," Kerney said. "I'll call out the bomb squad. Keep your microphone keyed open."

"Ten-four, Chief," Wade replied.

With a phone in one hand and his handheld in the other, Kerney listened to Wade pound on the door while the line to the bomb squad commander's residence seemed to ring endlessly. Finally, Lieutenant Alan Evertson picked up.

"I want you over at my house, pronto, Al," Kerney said as he listened to Wade talking to Sara. "The entire team, now. Call out SWAT on my command and clear the immediate neighborhood if you have to."

"Roger that, Chief," Evertson said. "Any idea of what kind of device we're looking for?"

"Not a clue, Al. The house is on a concrete pad, so there's no crawl space or basement."

"I'm out the door, Chief."

"Stay in close touch," Kerney said as he disconnected and pressed the handheld's talk button. "Wade?"

There was nothing but static from Wade's open microphone. Kerney's foot beat a tattoo on the carpet as he waited for the officer or Sara to say something. He could hear the sound of movement, the slamming of vehicle doors, the rumble of an engine turning over, but nothing else. He started breathing again when Wade spoke.

"Okay, we're clear, Chief. I've got your wife in my unit and we're proceeding down the street. She wants to talk to you."

"Sara?"

"A bomb, Kerney?" Sara said, her voice anxious and tight.

"Possibly."

"What now?"

"I'm at the office. Ask Officer Wade to bring you here after my people show up."

"Then what do we do?"

"I don't know yet."

"You are going to tell me what's happening, aren't you?" Sara asked.

"Yes, of course, when you're here. I'll talk to you then."

Kerney cut off the handheld and grabbed the phone. The perp had said he planned to add people to his hit list and wipe out Kerney's bloodline completely. Except for his adult son, Clayton Istee, and his family, Kerney had no other blood relatives.

Through an unusual set of circumstances, Kerney had only recently learned of Clayton's existence. A sheriff's sergeant in Lincoln County, Clayton, who was half Apache, lived with his family on the Mescalero Apache Reservation in southern New Mexico.

How could the killer know about Clayton when so few people did? Not even his staff knew, as far as Kerney could tell.

There wasn't time to speculate. Rapidly, Kerney punched numbers on the keypad and gritted his teeth as the phone rang. The sleepy voice of Grace Istee, Clayton's wife, greeted him on the fifth ring.

"Grace, it's Kerney. Let me speak to Clayton."

"He's not here. He started working swing shift today."

"When is he due home?"

"In a hour or so."

"Take Wendell and Hannah and get out of the house now," Kerney said.

"What?"

"Grace, just do it. Get far away from the house. Get in the car, go to your mother's, and don't stop for anything or anybody."

"Why are you telling me this?" Grace asked, her voice rising.

"Grace," Kerney snapped, "don't argue. Gather up Wendell and Hannah and leave the house, dammit. Get your cell phone and give me the number. I'll call you right back."

Grace read off the numbers. Kerney disconnected and punched in the new digits.

"Where are you?" he asked when Grace came on the line.

"In the children's bedroom," she replied, fear cracking her voice.

"They're okay?"

"Yes."

"Talk me through everything you're doing."

"You're scaring me, Kerney."

He could hear her rapid breathing. "You don't have time to be scared. What are you doing?"

"Wendell's awake and out of bed. I'm picking Hannah up right now."

He heard Hannah's soft moan as Grace lifted her from the bed. "Do you have your car keys?"

"Yes."

"Go, go now."

"Why am I doing this?" Grace asked hysterically.

"Are you outside?" Kerney demanded.

"Just about."

"Don't go to the car," Kerney said, realizing it could easily be booby trapped.

"What? I can't possibly walk to my mother's."

"Do as I tell you, Grace. Go to your neighbor's. Walk there and wait for Clayton."

"That's a half a mile away," Grace said. "Tell me right now what is going on."

"Are you and the children outside?"

"Yes," Grace shouted. "Answer my question."

"Someone may be trying to kill you with a bomb," Kerney said.

"We're running," Grace said.

"Good. Stay with me on the line until you get to your neighbor's," Kerney ordered.

In the earpiece he could hear Grace's labored breathing as she ran down the dirt road that led to the state highway that cut through the reservation. It seemed to take forever for her and the children to reach the safety of the neighbor's house.

Once they were inside, Kerney relaxed a bit, told her what he suspected, said he would contact Clayton right away, and asked her to stand by.

It took a few minutes for the sheriff's dispatcher to patch Kerney through to Clayton, who was in his unit thirty miles from home. Kerney explained the situation and reassured Clayton that Grace and the children were all right.

"You're sure about this?" Clayton asked, disbelief flooding his voice.

"I don't have time to give you all the details, but this is a serious, credible threat," Kerney snapped.

Kerney's harsh tone erased Clayton's doubts. "Okay, okay," he said as he hit his siren and emergency-light switches.

"I'll ask the state police to send out an explosive expert," Kerney said. "You get on the horn to your boss and the tribal police and fill them in."

"Ten-four," Clayton said.

"Be careful," Kerney said. "This killer is smart and dangerous."

"I'll talk to you later," Clayton replied.

The phone went dead. Kerney called Andy Baca, who was still at the crime scene in front of the municipal court building, and gave him the rundown.

"Have you notified the feds?" Andy asked. "It's their jurisdiction."

"There's no time for that," Kerney answered. "They'd be way too slow in responding. I need the explosives expert who's stationed at your Las Cruces office dispatched at once."

"I'll get him rolling code three immediately. It should take him about ninety minutes to get there, if he humps it. I'll put patrol officers ahead of him to clear the route."

"Thanks, Andy."

"This dirtbag may just be fucking with you, Kerney," Andy said.

"Maybe," he replied, "but I can't take that chance. Ask Sal Molina to meet me in my office ASAP."

"Ten-four."

Lieutenant Sal Molina arrived at the chief's office within a matter of minutes. Kerney showed him the notes he'd taken of his phone conversation with the perp and then told him who was at risk and why.

Sal Molina sat quietly, his hands folded in his lap, and let Kerney talk. The chief, obviously distracted and on edge, constantly shifted his gaze from the wall clock to the telephone on his desk, as he laid out the facts about Clayton Istee, his family, and his very reasonable suspicion that the perp intended to kill them all.

Although he tried to stayed focused on the information pertaining to the investigation, Molina found Kerney's tale riveting. Who would have ever thought it? It seemed like something right out of a novel or a movie. The college sweetheart, an Apache girl, who'd given birth to Kerney's son and kept it a secret from him for almost thirty years. The chance meeting between father and son, both of them cops. Kerney's discovery that he was a grandfather twice over. It was one hell of a story.

Molina wondered what kind of woman would deliberately get pregnant without a man's knowledge, bear his child while the father served as a combat infantry officer in 'Nam, and keep it a secret for so many years. It seemed selfish at the very least, perhaps even heartless.

But was it? Sal didn't know much about the Apache people or their traditions, so maybe it was a cultural thing. Or perhaps you had to know the woman to understand her reasoning.

Kerney cast another glance from the wall clock to the telephone and stopped talking. The handheld radio on his desk squawked traffic from bomb squad and SWAT team members en route to Upper Canyon Road.

"If your theory pans out, and I think it will, I'm going to have to let people know about this," Molina said.

"That's not a problem," Kerney said.

"I want to send a detective down there to work the case with the local cops."

"Of course."

"Did you recognize the perp's voice when he called?" Molina asked.

"No, but he seemed relaxed," Kerney said, "like he was totally in control of himself. He also sounded educated, and not very old."

"A young man?" Molina asked, as he started taking notes.

"Hard to say, but he didn't sound old. He was more a tenor than a baritone."

"He didn't attempt to disguise his voice?"

"Not that I could tell," Kerney replied.

"Why do you think he was educated?"

"He was articulate and had a good vocabulary."

"There are a lot of well-read, educated ex-cons walking the streets courtesy of the taxpayers' dollars."

Kerney nodded. "There was a hint of sarcasm in his voice, sort of a mocking tone. He thinks he's smarter than all of us."

"But he said nothing personal? Nothing that tied him to you?"

"I tried to get him to open up and talk, but he wouldn't bite."

"Do you think his call was designed to create a diversion?" Molina asked, putting his pen away. "To get you focused on something else?"

"No, I think he's raising the stakes. Everything he's done up to now has been carefully thought out."

"How does he know so much about you?" Molina asked. "It isn't like this thing with Clayton and his family is old news or common knowledge."

Kerney shook his head. "For starters, I'd be happy if we could find out how he got the number to my private line. No more than a half-dozen people have it."

"I'll put somebody to work on that."

"Was the videotape of the parking lot time and date stamped?" Kerney asked.

"Yes," Molina replied, looking at his wristwatch. "The perp left the van outside the municipal court just over three hours ago."

"That's enough time to drive to the reservation if you push it."

The phone rang. Kerney answered, listened for a moment, gave a hurried thanks, and hung up. "I asked for a trace on the perp's call," he said. "It was long distance, and made from Dora Manning's cell phone."

"Which means he could be in Clayton's backyard," Molina said, rising to his feet, "ready to carry out his threat."

"Don't wait to find out if this is a ruse," Kerney said. "Send a detective down to Mescalero now."

He reached for the handheld as Molina nodded and left the office, and called Evertson. The bomb squad and the SWAT team were on-site at his house.

"What have you got for me?" he asked.

"I'll call you back, Chief," Evertson said. "We're just starting the search."

A uniformed city police officer and Andy Baca were waiting for Sara at police headquarters when Wade dropped her off. The officer opened the back entrance, escorted them to Kerney's second-floor office, and then left to return to patrol. Kerney tried to smile when they walked in, but it was more a worried grimace, and his normally clear blue eyes looked troubled and uncertain.

Sara walked to him as he rose and gave him a hug. He held her tight for a moment, patting her reassuringly on the back as though to soothe himself.

They sat at the small rectangular conference table as Kerney talked over the noise of the radio traffic coming from the handheld on his desk. He told them about the conversation with the perp that had triggered his course of action.

"I just heard from Clayton," he added. "He's with

Grace and the children, the tribal police are on-site in force, and Paul Hewitt, the sheriff, is with them for added protection."

"That's good," Andy said with a nod. He was one of the handful of people Kerney had told about Clayton. "Everyone's safe."

"For now," Kerney replied. "When will your man arrive?"

"He's got about a sixty-minute ETA."

"So now we wait," Kerney said.

"While we're waiting, tell me about the latest murder victim," Sara said, trying to rid her mind of the panic Grace Istee must have felt during Kerney's phone call.

Andy cleared his throat and Kerney's gaze moved away from her. "What is it?" she demanded, reading their hesitancy. Andy smiled but his eyes didn't.

"What are you hiding?" she asked, switching her attention to Kerney. A hand covered his mouth. "Dammit, tell me."

"The killer posed his victim," Andy said, his smile vanishing. "He wrapped her hands around the decapitated head of Potter's dog."

"Wrapped her hands how?" Sara asked.

"As though she was cuddling a baby against her chest," Andy replied.

Instinctively, Sara's hands traveled to her stomach. She could feel the hard-stretched skin under the fabric of her loose top. "Did he leave a note like before?"

Kerney nodded. "It was addressed to me, and asked if I knew who he was and who was next to die."

Sara's hands trembled. "That son of a bitch."

"The note was found on her lower abdomen," he continued, "attached by a knitting needle that had been driven, we think, through the stomach wall into the uterus."

A sharp pain coursed up Sara's spine to her neck, as if all the tension of the last few days had suddenly been compressed into one enormous jolt that froze her muscles and immobilized her body.

"This can't go on," she said, forcing her mouth to work. "It has to stop."

The phone rang. Kerney turned the handheld radio volume down, punched the button to the blinking line, and activated the speaker function. "Go ahead," he said.

"It's Lieutenant Evertson, Chief. The house is clean, inside and out, and we didn't find anything on the grounds. No explosives. But the perp broke the utility company seal on the outside electrical box and left a note. It says, 'Bang you're dead.' "

Kerney's hand squeezed the receiver. He paused a beat before responding. "Get the note to Lieutenant Molina, give everyone my thanks, and send the teams home."

"Will do. I've got a couple of reporters down at a roadblock asking questions. Want me to tell them to call you?"

"Fuck 'em," Kerney said without thinking. He rarely cursed, but the words burst out of him as though he was voiding something rancid.

"Would you repeat that, Chief?"

"Be nice, but say there is no statement at this time, Lieutenant."

Kerney hung up, and Sara said, "I'm not going back to that house tonight."

"You can stay with me and Gloria," Andy said. "Besides, she needs the company and has lots of baby stories that will keep you entertained."

"Good idea," Kerney said before Sara could respond. "Raise your right hand, Sara."

"Why?"

"Because I'm swearing you in as a police officer. If *anyone* approaches you in a threatening manner, blow the sucker away."

"I can do that," Sara replied as she raised her hand.

Clayton's closest neighbors, Eugene and Jeannie Naiche, were an older couple with grown children living on their own. Until his retirement, Eugene had run the tribal youth recreation program. Jeannie, a skilled basketmaker, operated a studio and gallery out of the house. Built almost forty years ago, the rambling ranch-style residence had a pitched roof, a stone fireplace, a large deck off the back patio door, and a family room filled with books on the history and art of Native Americans.

Clayton sat on a couch in the family room with Hannah on his lap, Grace next to him, and Wendell snuggled close to his mother's side. All of them seemed emotionally empty, as though the experience of fleeing the house had transformed them into instantly displaced persons facing a strange, uncertain, and dangerous world.

Eugene Naiche sat in a rocking chair with a determined look on his usually jovial face, his hunting rifle resting against an end table. He rocked slowly with his hands on the arm rests, his stocky legs planted firmly on the floor.

Clayton's boss, Sheriff Paul Hewitt, stood at the side of a curtained window, peering out at the driveway, his face washed by the colors of the flashing emergency lights of vehicles passing by on the dirt road. In the kitchen, Jeannie Naiche was making coffee for the adults and hot chocolate for the children.

Outside, tribal officers patrolled the dirt road and conducted foot searches in the woods around Clayton's house. Volunteer fire department personnel were deploying equipment a safe distance away from the house, and the state police explosives expert, Perry Dahl, was walking a bomb-sniffing dog named Clementine around the outside of the structure. He hadn't reported in yet.

Clayton's handheld radio crackled. He let go of Hannah and turned up the volume.

"Clementine smells something," Dahl said. "Hold on."

Clayton peeled one of Hannah's arms from around his neck.

"Don't go, Daddy," Hannah said.

"It's all right, honey," he said gently, as he put his daughter on Grace's lap and stood. "I'm staying right here with you."

He walked to Paul Hewitt, and spoke softly into his radio. "Where are you?" he asked Dahl.

"At your back door about to take the cover off the entrance to the crawl space," Dahl replied. "Clementine's really excited. We're going in."

Clayton waited.

"Have you been under your house lately?" Dahl asked.

"Not for a while," Clayton replied.

"Well, someone has. There's a lot of disturbed dirt, and the insulation and plastic vapor barrier between the floor joists has been pulled out in places. Okay, I've found some wires, and Clementine just sniffed out a device. Make that two devices."

"What kind?" Clayton whispered, looking at Grace, who'd gone rigid, her arms locked around Hannah.

"Give me a minute," Dahl answered. "I have to crawl on my back to get to them."

Clayton turned away from his family and lowered the handheld's volume.

Paul Hewitt turned his radio down, put a hand on Clayton's shoulder and looked at his young sergeant. "Let's go outside."

Clayton nodded and glanced at Grace. "I'll be back in a minute."

Wendell pushed himself off the couch. "Can I come, too?"

"Stay with your mother," Clayton replied.

Grace grabbed Wendell's hand and jerked him close to her, her eyes filled with apprehension.

Clayton smiled at his family reassuringly, his heart pounding, and walked out of the room with Paul Hewitt. On the front step he could see the spotlight of a tribal police cruiser slowly moving down the dirt road. The flashing lights of fire department vehicles up ahead cut through the stand of trees, casting broken red beams that fractured the darkness.

"We've got a pound of plastique planted under the floorboards at each end of the house," Dahl said. "They're wired together and attached to a radio receiver."

"Can you disarm them?" Paul Hewitt asked.

"Hold it," Dahl replied. "Yeah, but not easily. Whoever built this thing added what looks like a pulse detonator wired into the radio battery. Any power interruption will set off one or the other packs of plastique. It's pretty sophisticated work."

"How long will it take you?" Hewitt asked.

"I'm gonna have to get my tools and try to figure it out. An hour, maybe more, once I get started. This is all miniature equipment."

"What's the range of the receiver?" Hewitt asked, the handheld an inch from his lips.

"I'd say maybe five miles," Dahl replied. "No more than ten."

Clayton glanced up at the heavily forested peaks that loomed over the narrow valley. He knew every gully, wash, stream, outcropping, and clearing in those mountains. There were countless places within a couple of miles that a man could easily hike to and have a clear line of sight into the settlement below.

"Get out of there now," Hewitt snapped. "The Sante Fe PD has advised that the perp may already be at our location, and there's no way we can clear that kind of radius at night."

"Ten-four," Dahl said. "I'm exiting the crawl space now."

"Roger that."

Paul Hewitt looked at his sergeant. "Now, do you want to tell me what this is really all about?"

"Some shithead wants to kill Kerney and his entire family."

"I know that. What's it got to do with you?"

"I'm his son," Clayton replied.

For once, Paul Hewitt couldn't think of a damn thing to say.

Clayton keyed his handheld and asked the tribal police to start patrolling the roads into the mountains.

For years, the bald-headed man had prepared to become a successful killer. On his own, in public and university libraries across the western states, he'd read the works of behavioral profilers, criminologists, psychologists, and forensics specialists. He'd delved into the history of crime and the psychiatric studies of the criminal mind, scrutinized all the relevant journals for articles on criminal behavior, reviewed the latest developments in the classification systems used to target potential suspects, and pored over volumes that dealt with the use of scientific evidence in criminal investigations.

He knew the current literature on revenge killers was at best nothing more than rudimentary. About all the cops had to go on, if the murders were skillfully planned and carried out, was the belief that the killer would have openly brooded or bragged about revenge to others.

He'd never done that. His revenge was a private, personal obsession that, since the age of seven, had formed the core of his identity, right down to the name he'd chosen for himself from a little-known footnote in American history: Samuel Green. The country's first mass murderer, Green had gone to the gallows in 1822, unrepentant, without admitting guilt, and leaving all to wonder exactly how many people he'd murdered during his two-year crime spree.

He admired those qualities, so Samuel Green he'd legally become, shedding his past but never the memory of it. He enjoyed his new name's legacy and the innocuous sound of it.

Green hiked from the Indian Health Service Hospital parking lot to the hillside outcropping that overlooked the Istee residence, thinking he'd diverted Kerney's attention to Sara and the unborn baby and away from Clayton, who should be just getting home from his shift. When he arrived, the sight through the night-vision scope of police vehicles patrolling the roads and a cluster of fire trucks parked on the dirt lane caught him by surprise.

At the neighboring house, all the interior and exterior lights were on. Two Lincoln County sheriff's vehicles—one of them assigned to Sergeant Istee—and a state cop car sat outside.

From the look of things, Green assumed that Istee had his family safely out of the house. It was the first time anything had gone wrong with his plan. Was it a setback? Perhaps his phone call to Kerney had been too precipitous, too revealing.

Green decided against that kind of thinking. After all, he'd led Kerney by the nose to his next targets, and the man had taken the threat seriously and acted quickly. That was to be expected.

He sat down and considered his options. Perhaps he should just walk back to the car and let the cops spend the next two or three hours trying to figure out how to disarm the explosives and blow themselves up in the process. But he hated the idea of chancing everything to fate and possibly seeing all his hard work go to waste. Better to salvage something then to walk away empty-handed.

Killing Potter and Manning had been nothing but a prelude, although they both deserved to die for their part in ruining his life. On the other hand, the woman he'd killed with the rat poison had been an innocent victim. But her death was essential to his plan.

Now it all came down to Kerney, who'd destroyed Green's manhood and taken away any chance for a family or a normal relationship with a woman. That should cost Kerney everything and everybody, although if Green had to settle for taking out the pregnant wife that might still be good enough.

Green retraced his way to his car, drove down the highway, made sure he wasn't being followed, and pressed the transmitter button. In the rearview mirror a sudden flash of light erupted into the night sky just as the sound waves from the explosion rolled through the open window.

The spectacle made Samuel Green smile. Maybe it would start a big fire on the Rez.

Chapter 8

The explosion brought Grace and the children outside. They gathered wordlessly around Clayton, watching flames from their burning house throw sparks into the air. The propane gas tank had blown up, spewing fire that licked at the large pine trees and spread through the native grass.

Grace gripped Clayton's hand as though she was trying to squeeze away the anguish that showed on her face. Wendell stood frozen between them, his arms wrapped around Clayton's leg. Perched on Grace's hip, Hannah, too young to understand, watched in wonder.

Fire trucks and personnel moved to attack the flames. Through the darkness and the growing light from the scattered fires Clayton saw the figures of Perry Dahl and his dog come out of the trees on the opposite side of the lane. He sighed in relief as Paul Hewitt moved off to meet them.

The reality of what he'd witnessed hit, and a biting, hollow feeling swept over him. All that he'd done to build a home for his family had been wiped out. Despondency, quickly replaced by anger, gave way to an ice-cold detachment that wiped all emotion from Clayton's mind. He wrapped himself in the feeling. This wasn't the time to feel sorry for himself. He had to think and act like a cop. He wondered how long he could pull it off before the shock of what had happened hit him again.

"Take the children and go inside," he said to Grace.

She was slow to respond. "Then what?"

"Call our families and wait for me," Clayton replied, as he watched Paul Hewitt and Perry Dahl talking thirty yards away in front of a police cruiser.

She let go of his hand, pulled Wendell away from Clayton, and turned to face him. In the reflection of her dark eyes flames danced like pinprick blood wounds. He could see tears forming and it almost made him want to cry.

"It will be all right," he said.

She shook her head in a silent rejection of such a ludicrous notion, turned on her heel, and went into the house, yanking a reluctant Wendell along. Clayton walked quickly to join Hewitt and Dahl. There was much to do, and if he kept his thoughts on the job, maybe he'd get through the night without losing his self-control.

Kerney got the call from Paul Hewitt telling him that Clayton's house had been destroyed. He left Sara with Andy, who promised to take her to his house and assign two state police agents to stay with her for personal protection. Before flying off in a borrowed state police helicopter to Mescalero, Kerney beefed up security by putting two of his own officers on duty outside Andy's home.

Ever since he'd been shot down during an extraction from a hot landing zone in 'Nam, choppers had been Kerney's least favorite mode of transportation. He sat stiffly in the passenger seat listening to the rotors cut through the air in monotonous mechanical thuds, bracing for the sickening lurch that would plow the chopper into the ground.

Below, in the weak light of the thin moon, Kerney could see the faint ribbon of empty roadway that dropped out of low-lying hills into the small ranching village of Corona.

The word meant "crown" in Spanish, but the village was no jewel by any stretch of the imagination. Corona had once been a thriving trade and agricultural center. But all that had slipped away years ago when the trains no longer stopped at the station. Now, like so many other rural towns and villages in New Mexico, it was just another decaying strip of old buildings interspersed with a few roadside businesses along a lightly traveled state highway.

They were halfway to Mescalero and the pilot had the chopper cruising at top speed, paralleling the highway that ran south to the county seat of Carrizozo. Once there, they would skirt the high mountains, cut across the mesa east of Ruidoso, drop through the narrow pass that led into the city, and follow it to Mescalero.

Kerney closed his eyes and thought about what he could possibly say to Clayton and Grace. The couple had been made homeless and all their possessions destroyed because of a sick killer bent on revenge that went far beyond the ordinary.

They would want answers, and Kerney had little to

give them other than some fairly reasonable speculation. He could tell them about the dead victims, the
dead animals, the stolen art, the killer's notes and phone
call. But even with all that, he still had no clear motive
for the crimes that might lead to a suspect, and only an
artist's sketch that could possibly ID the unknown perp
when and if he was found.

Kerney switched his thoughts to Clayton and Grace's
situation. Even with insurance, which he assumed they
had, there would be immediate and large out-of-pocket
expenses. Aside from temporary housing, the family
would need clothes, bedding, kitchen utensils, everything necessary to set up housekeeping again. Beyond
that, some of what had been lost could never be replaced, and rebuilding their home would only be a small
part of what it would take to restore the family to some
sort of emotional normalcy.

He wondered if Clayton would accept an offer of financial help. Although their relationship over the past
few months had improved slightly, they were still basically strangers to each other, and Clayton was an ex-
tremely proud man who might not take kindly to the
idea. Kerney decided he'd make an overture anyway.

Flying low through the pass to Mescalero, Kerney
could see smoke in the night sky. The pilot circled over
it, but the cover was too thick to give them a view of
what was happening on the ground.

They landed in the parking lot of the tribal adminis-
trative offices, where a state cop was waiting to take
Kerney to the Naiche residence. During the short drive,
Kerney learned that Clayton and Grace had lost both of
their vehicles in the blast, that the explosives expert and

his dog had escaped without injury just before detonation, and that burning debris had ignited a fire that scorched two acres around Clayton's house before it had been brought under control.

The dirt lane in front of the Naiche residence was lined with police, emergency, and private vehicles with firefighter license plates. Kerney entered the front room and saw Clayton, Paul Hewitt, and a group of tribal officers organizing a crime scene investigation and a first-light reconnaissance of the foot trails leading into the mountains. The explosives specialist, who was covered in dust, sat to one side in a chair with a clipboard on his lap and a dog at his feet, writing notes.

Paul Hewitt, a big, somewhat beefy man who had grown a neatly trimmed salt-and-pepper beard since Kerney last saw him, spotted Kerney first, gave him a curious look, and touched Clayton on the arm. All talk ceased as Clayton stepped away from the group and approached him.

"When did it happen?" Kerney asked.

"About an hour and thirty minutes ago," Clayton answered. "The firefighters have it just about put out and we're waiting for clearance to go in."

"Are Grace and the children all right?"

"Everyone's safe."

"And the damage?"

"According to the reports, it's all blown to hell. From what I saw, that's just about right."

Kerney searched Clayton's face looking for anger, shock, or outrage. All he saw was a slight tightness at the corners of Clayton's mouth. He scanned the group behind Clayton. The officers gazed at him silently.

"Tell us what you know," Clayton said as he rejoined the group.

"This guy isn't going to be easy to catch," Kerney said as he followed along and handed Clayton a manila folder he'd carried with him. "We've had two sightings, and have an inconclusive shot of him on a surveillance video tape. That folder contains a copy of a police artist's sketch of the perp along with physical descriptions we got from witnesses."

Clayton studied the material before passing it around. "This is it? You haven't made an ID?"

"He's still an unknown subject," Kerney replied.

"And you've got nothing from forensics?"

"We have a lot of evidence, but nothing that allows us to identify him yet," Kerney replied. "So far, he's killed three times. His victims have been a former assistant district attorney, a former forensic psychologist, and an unidentified woman whose body he left in a van outside the municipal court in Santa Fe earlier tonight.

"Before he strikes, he likes to get his victim's attention. He's left dead rats at houses, killed a pet dog, and swiped a number of valuable paintings belonging to one of the victims. After the first homicide, he's been leaving messages at the crime scenes. I'm his final target."

"You know that for sure?" Clayton asked.

"I do."

"How?"

"He slaughtered my horse, left poisoned rats outside my house, and called me."

"What did he say when he called?" Hewitt asked.

"That everyone will die. Then he asked if I'd figured out who was next on his list before he comes after me.

He also said he planned to wipe out my bloodline completely. That's why I called Grace and told her to get the children and leave the house."

"So who else is on his list?" Hewitt asked.

"My wife and our unborn child. But since he missed taking out Clayton and his family, he may try again before he moves on."

The hush in the room was broken only by the cough of one of the officers. The men tensed and exchanged hard looks. A killer who had targeted two cops was bad enough. But to go after their families went beyond the unthinkable.

Clayton bit his lip. "How did the perp find out that I'm your son?"

"I don't know," Kerney said. "But I plan to look into it. Who have you told on your end?"

"It's common knowledge on the Rez," Clayton replied.

"That could mean a couple of thousand people know about it."

"At least."

"You can't waste time trying to interview the entire tribe," Kerney said. "I'll work my list and see where it goes."

Clayton nodded. "When do we get all of your case material?"

"One of my detectives is en route. You should have it soon. What have you got going?"

"We're patrolling the tribal roads that lead to the trails into the mountains behind us," Paul Hewitt said. "But nobody has been spotted, and the perp's had more than enough time to clear the area. The feds are on the way, and once they get here, it's their ball game. So for now, we'll seal off the crime scene and get the sketch distributed to all personnel. That's the best we can do until daylight."

Kerney nodded and turned to Clayton. "I'd like a minute of your time."

The officers, including Paul Hewitt, took the cue and filed out.

"Thanks for calling Grace," Clayton said when they were alone.

"How is she doing?"

"She's pretty shook up, but coping."

"And the children?"

"Hannah's too young to know what really happened, but Wendell's taking it hard."

"What about you?"

Clayton glanced away. "I'm trying not to think about it." The strain showed clearly in his eyes.

Kerney changed the subject. "Aren't you and the sheriff outside your jurisdiction?"

"No, all department officers are cross-deputized under an agreement with the tribal government."

"Do you want me to talk to Grace?" Kerney asked.

"Yeah, she wants to know what's going on. She's at the back of the house with her parents and my mother."

"I'd like to help out financially. After all, I'm the reason you're all in this mess."

Clayton shook his head. "We'll be okay."

He took Kerney into a family room where Grace, her parents, and Clayton's mother, Isabel Istee, were waiting. Clayton introduced him to his in-laws, Orlin and Lillian Chatto, while Isabel took Hannah and Wendell out of the room. When she returned, Grace raised her dark eyes to Kerney's face.

"Why has this happened?" she asked. She wore borrowed clothes that hung loosely on her slender frame, and her narrow-eyed gaze held a tangible pain.

"It's complicated," Kerney replied. "To put it simply we have a killer who's seeking revenge. Who he is and why he's doing it are still unknown."

"Why did he try to kill us?" Grace asked.

"Because I'm Clayton's father," Kerney replied. "He wants all my blood relatives dead before he attempts to kill me. But I'm not his only target. He's already murdered three people, and we believe the killings have something to do with an old criminal investigation of mine. Two of the victims worked with the courts. One was a former prosecutor and the other was an ex–forensic psychologist."

"And that's all you know?"

"It narrows down the field considerably," Kerney answered. "We're reviewing every possible suspect."

"Will he try to hurt us again?"

"We won't let him do that," Kerney replied. "You'll be protected."

Grace looked at Clayton for confirmation, who nodded his head. "If you don't know who he is, how can you stop him?" she asked in a disbelieving tone.

"He'll make a mistake," Kerney replied, "or the evidence we've collected and the work we're doing will lead us to him."

"You're sure of that?"

"I am."

"You said he wants to kill everyone related to you."

"Yes."

"Including Sara?"

Kerney nodded. "She has twenty-four-hour police

protection, just as you and the children will have as soon as you leave here."

"And your baby. Has he been born yet?"

"He's due any day."

"Yet, with all of that you came here."

"Yes."

"Why?"

Kerney looked at Clayton. "Because for the sake of us all we have to catch this man."

"Yes, you must," Grace said, forcing a smile. "You saved our lives."

"I think it was more a question of lucky timing," Kerney said, as he looked directly at Clayton. "I would like to help you and your family recover from this."

Orlin Chatto stood up before Clayton could respond. Probably Kerney's age, he was barrel-chested with a slim waist. His nose was broad above a round, full chin.

"Perhaps such talk should wait," he said, "until all of us have had time to think about what has happened."

"Yes, of course," Kerney replied, getting to his feet.

Orlin nodded. "It is late and we should go. Grace and the children will stay with us."

"You'll have a police escort and an officer will be on duty outside the house," Clayton said to his wife.

"Will I see you in the morning?" Grace asked him.

"As soon as I can get free," he said.

Isabel, who'd remained frozen in silence on the couch during the conversation, her hands clasped in her lap, rose and went to gather up the children. When they came into the room, Orlin Chatto shook Kerney's hand, said good night, and ushered his wife outside. Grace, Clayton, and the children followed behind.

Kerney watched from the front door as Clayton put his family in his father-in-law's car. The state police officer took the lead in his unit and the two vehicles slowly drove away.

Isabel brushed past him in the doorway and turned to face him. An expression of cold anger, which had been carved across her face from the moment she saw him, remained.

Kerney looked at the woman who in his distant past had once meant so much to him. Eyes that had once danced with humor now flared with accusation, and her soft mouth was a thin, angry line.

As a cop, he'd taken the brunt of people's misplaced outrage many times before. But this time it felt justified. He waited for her to confront him, but she left without saying a word, stopping only to give Clayton a hug before hurrying to her car.

"Are you leaving?" Clayton asked as he drew near.

"Not yet," Kerney answered. "I want to see what turns up at the crime scene. It could yield some important evidence."

"Thanks for not going into too much detail with the family."

"It would have only served to upset them more than they already are. Grace handled it well."

"She's a strong person."

"Yes, she is," Kerney said, reaching for his cell phone. "I need to make some phone calls."

"I'll let you know when the feds get here."

Kerney searched Clayton's face. Although he was still

keeping the lid on, the strain had become more visible, especially around his mouth. He wondered when Clayton would let himself feel something. It needed to happen soon.

"Good deal," he said.

Clayton left Kerney at the house and checked in with tribal dispatch on his handheld. Officers were still out on the back roads, the fire was out, firefighters were scouring the surrounding woods looking for any flare-ups, and Perry Dahl had returned to the bomb site, accompanied by officers who'd secured the perimeter.

He disconnected and started walking through the trees in the direction of the spot where his home had once stood. He forced himself to move at a steady pace and tried to prepare himself for what he was about to see. Ahead, the spotlights and headlights of police cruisers and several fire trucks broke the darkness, illuminating the ruins of his home. Crime scene tape had been strung across his driveway, and officers were posted at strategic locations.

He approached quietly, not wanting to be seen. They'd lost all the landscape trees at the front of the house as well as a stand of pines on the back of the lot. The charred trunks of the tallest trees rose thirty feet into the sky.

Where the house had stood there was nothing but rubble. Large, twisted sections of the corrugated metal roof partially covered the few standing walls, and the metal headboard of Wendell's twin bed jutted through a shattered window frame.

He moved closer and looked away from the light, letting his night vision adjust. What appeared to be the refrigerator lay on its side next to his two burned-out vehicles, both of them resting on wheel rims over black puddles of melted rubber.

He saw a flashlight beam at the rear of the house and Dahl came into view, casting his light over the littered concrete pad where the new tool shed had been, then over the remnants of the propane tank scattered under some trees that had been burned halfway up the canopy. If the fire department hadn't been standing by before the explosion, the whole forest could have gone up in flames.

The swing set and slide had been taken out by the exploding gas tank, and the vegetable garden was nothing more than a scorched plot enclosed by the post-and-wire fence.

It was worse than he'd imagined. His hands were shaking, so he stuffed them into his trouser pockets. He started to sweat in the cool night as a lump rose up in his throat and he thought about what might have happened to Grace and the children. He waited for the dizzy feeling of shock to pass. Finally, his heart stopped pounding in his chest and the tremors in his arms and legs lessened.

He watched Dahl put his dog in his unit and drive away. Quickly, he made his way back toward the Naiches' house, trying to convince himself that the burning sensation in his eyes came from the lingering smoke and soot in the air. He saw Perry Dahl talking to Kerney and Sheriff Hewitt at the front of Eugene and Jeannie's house and hurried to join them.

"What have I missed?" Clayton asked as he reached the men.

Bits of ash clung to Dahl's short-cropped hair and speckled his unshaved face. His shoes and trousers were caked with black soot and mud. Clementine, his German shepherd, sat at his feet busily cleaning gobs of muck from her front paws.

"Not much," Dahl replied, as he reached down to scratch Clementine's head. "I just started my briefing. I'm thinking the plastique was homemade, which means there won't be any detection agent that could lead us back to a manufacturer."

Dahl unsnapped Clementine's leash. "The two charges were shaped to do maximum damage upwards through the floor. I'd say they were a pound each. One was placed next to the gas line that ran under and up into the house from the outside propane tank, which guaranteed a secondary explosion."

"Where was the second charge placed?" Clayton asked.

"Facing the house from here, on the left side," Dahl replied. He wrapped the leash around his hand and stuck it in his back pocket. "Which I assume is where the bedrooms were located."

Clayton nodded and said nothing.

"What kind of chemical agents were used?" Kerney asked.

"That will have to wait until we can run some tests," Dahl answered. "But it could've been anything from a potassium or chlorate compound, a phenol derivative, to an antifreeze concoction treated with calcium chloride then filtered to remove the water and the calcium chloride, which is my best guess right now."

"Why do you say that?" Hewitt asked.

"Because it acts like a nitro-gelatin explosive, which means it's highly flammable, and there was fire almost immediately after the explosion on both sides of the house."

"Do you have anything that can help us find the perp?" Kerney asked.

"The hardware that was used is our best bet," Dahl said. "Based on what I saw, I'm thinking he built everything from scratch, which means he had to buy the components somewhere. But more than that, I'd also be looking for someone with electronics experience, who is good with his hands, has had some formal training, and has a basic understanding of chemistry."

"An amateur couldn't do it?" Clayton asked, forcing himself to stay focused on the subject. He wanted to find the asshole and kill him.

"He'd have to be very gifted," Dahl replied. "No matter what you've heard about bomb-making instructions on the Internet, none of this stuff is *that* easy to do, especially the electronics."

"Give us an example," Hewitt said.

"A radio detonator was used to trigger the charges placed inside the house," Dahl replied. "To do that the perp had to accomplish two things to ensure success: first, use a microwave transmitter so the signal would penetrate into the structure, and second, shield the signal so that a random transmission wouldn't prematurely set off the plastique. That takes a high degree of knowledge and skill."

"So we start checking electronic suppliers to see who has been buying what," Kerney said, "and look for a perp with some formal training or education in the field."

"Yeah," Dahl said. "I can work up a list of what I think he used to build the device and start calling supply houses and retailers. And if I can find any intact pieces of the wire he used, that might be helpful. But don't get your hopes up. If he was smart, he bought from a lot of different places, probably off the Internet and by mail order."

"What else?" Clayton asked.

"I'll see what the feds have on known bombers with similar MOs. Also, most of these guys like to watch their shows, especially the big blasts, and this one was designed for maximum devastation. You might get lucky in the morning and find a shoe print or some trace evidence on a trail or at the spot where he detonated the explosion."

An unmarked car pulled up next to Clayton's unit and two feds got out.

Kerney looked at Clayton's mud-caked boots. He'd been to the site, of that he was certain. "Are you all right?" he asked.

"If you want to bail out, you can," Hewitt added.

Clayton shook his head and managed a thin smile. "I'm just pissed off, big time. It sucks to be a victim."

The two feds approached, flashed their shields, and immediately started asking questions.

Kerney had been unable to contact only one person on his list of those who knew about Clayton, the executor of Erma Fergurson's estate, a man named Milton Lynch. Lynch was a probate and tax attorney based in Las Cruces, a hundred miles away.

It was Erma's legacy that had made Kerney a rich

man, and Lynch had handled all the paperwork, including the college funds Kerney had set up for Wendell and Hannah.

At dawn, Clayton went into the mountains hoping to cut the perp's trail. Kerney radioed the chopper pilot and asked him to get clearance to fly to Las Cruces over the restricted airspace of White Sands Missile Range before he sought out Paul Hewitt.

"Will you give me a ride to the chopper?" he asked.

"Sure."

"Are you going to establish a fund to help Clayton and his family?" Kerney asked as he got in Hewitt's vehicle.

"You bet, as soon as I get to the office."

Kerney handed him a folded check. "This is an anonymous contribution."

"Whatever you say," Hewitt replied as he slipped the check into a shirt pocket.

"Good," Kerney replied.

"What's between you and Clayton is none of my business, Kerney," Paul said, keeping his eyes on the road.

"I'm proud to be Clayton's father, Paul," Kerney said as they coasted to a stop at the tribal offices where the chopper waited. "He's a good man and a fine police officer. When we have the time, I'll tell you the story of how we found out about each other. Or maybe Clayton will."

"I'll let you know if he does," Hewitt replied.

"Look after him, Sheriff," Kerney said as he got out of the car. "He's due for a letdown from all of this."

Hewitt replied with a nod. "I know it. You be careful."

He watched Kerney get into the chopper and take off before opening the folded check. He knew Kerney had inherited a pile of money through the sale of a ranch left to him by an old family friend.

He looked at the amount and whistled. Make that a *big* pile of money. Kerney's check would easily cover the cost of buying two new vehicles for the Istee family, free and clear.

It was a pleasant nighttime drive that took Samuel Green from the town of Tularosa, north to Carrizozo, and then west toward San Antonio and Interstate 25. Just past Stallion Gate, a restricted access road on the north boundary of White Sands Missile Range, Green left the highway and followed an unpaved county road that wound through some low hills on the east side of the Rio Grande Valley near the small city of Socorro.

Most of the land was controlled by the Bureau of Land Management, but there were a few private parcels tucked into the barren hills that overlooked the valley farms and the mountains to the west of the city. Green stopped at the gate to a private road, unlocked it, and drove up the hill to a small adobe house once owned by Noel Olsen. But now that Olsen was dead, he didn't own anything anymore.

Green had created his plan with two main goals in mind. First and foremost were the killings, and they were going well. The failed attempt to blow up the Istee family was a disappointment, but partially successful nonetheless in exacting heavy retribution against Kerney's family. He would let it go at that for now, and keep his option open to kill them later, perhaps as some sort of epilogue.

Green's second goal was equally simple, yet complex in its execution. He wanted not only to succeed with his plan but to survive it and enjoy the emotional fruits of his labor. To do that, he'd decided to give the cops a perpetrator to look for and never find. Thus, the recently deceased Noel Olsen.

Green slipped on a pair of plastic gloves, entered the house, and removed Olsen's hiking boots. Even with two pairs of socks, the oversized boots had been uncomfortable to wear and his feet were sore. He padded into the bedroom, put the boots in the closet, slipped on a pair of Olsen's running shoes, and turned to the body on the bed.

"You made a lovely bomb," he said as he pressed Olsen's thumb and fingers on Dora Manning's cell phone. He did it several times to make sure there were a number of partial and smudged prints for the police to find, and repeated the process with the radio transmitter used to detonate the plastique.

Green had kept Olsen captive and alive for the two weeks it had taken to order the parts and make the bomb. During the times he was gone, he'd sedated Olsen with a major tranquilizer and left him manacled, handcuffed, gagged, and chained to a fifty-gallon water heater in the utility room.

He left the room and dropped Manning's cell phone and the radio transmitter on the work table in the small second bedroom where Olsen had played with all his electronic toys and built the bomb. In the corner were the containers of chemicals Olsen had used to make the plastique, and buried under a stack of paper were receipts for some of the components that had been bought to make the hardware. The cops would find additional information on Olsen's laptop computer, which should also make them happy.

In the utility room, he bundled up the clothes Olsen had worn and fouled during his confinement, packed them in a travel bag along with the restraints, added some of Olsen's toiletries from the bathroom, and left it near the front door.

Back in the bedroom, he wrapped the body in a sheet and carried it out to the car, carefully staying on the gravel path to avoid leaving footprints that would show the weight he was carrying. He stuffed the body in the trunk, made a second trip for the travel bag, and closed the lid.

He went to the toolshed behind the house and checked on the two Merriam Kangaroo Rats he'd caught that were in a cage on a shelf. Their little eyes blinked rapidly in the glare of his flashlight. He fed them some poisoned bait and watched their contortions as they died. The cops, who got off on finding little details that corroborated their facts, would be pissing in their pants with excitement when they found the rats.

Green checked his watch. He figured it would be a good ten to twelve hours before the cops got here. First, they had to identify the body he'd left in the van, which should be done by now. Then, they had to make the connection to Olsen, which would take some head work and digging, but not that much. After all, the dead woman had at one time been Olsen's parole officer in Las Cruces.

At the age of twenty, Olsen and two undergraduate buddies from New Mexico State University had been arrested for the rape and murder of a woman in Santa

Fe. Because he hadn't participated in the rape, Olsen had been allowed to plead to a lesser charge in exchange for testifying against his co-defendants. He'd done his time, finished his parole, completed his engineering degree, and had his voting rights restored, which meant he wasn't going to be hard to find.

But what made Olsen the perfect suspect was the fact that Kerney had busted him, Potter had prosecuted the case, and Dora Manning had done the psych evaluation for the court. It had taken Green a year's researching to find the ideal candidate to become the cops' one and only prime suspect.

He got in Olsen's car and drove away. By the time the cops arrived, Olsen's body would be at the bottom of a lava tube in the El Malpais National Monument, his car would be at a chop shop across the border in Juarez, and Green would be on his way back to Santa Fe ready to implement the final phase of his plan.

Chapter 9

Last night, Kerney had spoken by phone with Milton Lynch's wife, who'd told him that her husband would be returning from Albuquerque to Las Cruces early in the morning to prepare for an afternoon court appearance. She assured him that Lynch would be at his office by eight o'clock.

As he flew over the Tularosa Basin above the highway that cut through the missile range, Kerney could see sections of the land that had once belonged to his family. The sun lit up the alkali flats and washed over the tips of the Hardscabble Mountains, part of the San Andres Range, south of Rhodes Canyon. In his mind's eye, he could picture the ranch house and the old road that snaked down the hills to the broad swales of tall grama grass that, in the wet years, spread out across the range.

Silently, Kerney studied the vast, empty reaches of the basin, broken only by some military roads and clusters of high-security testing facilities. This was the land he'd been born to, only to have the family ranch taken away by the government when he was a child. This was the land where his godson, Sammy Yazzi, a soldier stationed at the missile range, had been murdered. He looked over his shoulder at Sierra Blanca Mountain on the eastern fringe of the basin that defined the Mescalero homeland, now forever embedded in his memory as the place where Clayton and his family had seen their home destroyed.

The early morning light softened the black lava flows far to the north, made the pure white gypsum sand dunes sparkle, blunted the squat Jarilla Mountains west of Orogrande, and bleached the dry salt flats of Lake Lucero. It was a land of wind-blown drought, cactus and rattlesnakes, thorny mesquite, and boulder-strewn foothill canyons at the base of the mountains. Despite the harsh vastness, there was an intense, wild, undeniable beauty to the Tularosa.

The land held good memories, too. It was here, under the watchful eye of his father, that he'd been taught to cowboy and ranch. It was here that his lifelong friendship with Dale Jennings had begun. And it was here, just a few short years ago, that he'd first met Sara during her tour of duty at the missile range.

The chopper traveled through the San Agustin Pass and dropped down to the desert where the city of Las Cruces spread out before them. New residential subdivisions peppered the hills and stretched along the Interstate. Strip malls, business parks, and commercial buildings lined the highway that had once been a two-lane road into town.

The second-largest and fastest-growing city in New Mexico, Las Cruces was no longer the sleepy little ranching, farming, and college town of Kerney's childhood. But even with all the exploding growth, most of it fueled by the defense industry and migrating retirees, the green of the pecan orchards and farms along the Rio Grande River valley and the magnificent spire-shaped peaks of the Organ Mountains still gave the city a certain natural charm that the man-made sprawl had yet to diminish.

The chopper pilot had radioed ahead to have the parking lot at the district state police headquarters cleared for their landing. Motorists along University Boulevard and the nearby Interstate slowed to watch the chopper's descent.

As Kerney left the helicopter and went into the building, he checked the time. It was too early to expect Lynch to be in his office, so he would call Sara and then buy the pilot breakfast.

Sal Molina sat behind a mechanic's desk at the city maintenance yard garage and watched as the crime scene techs continued working on the blue van. The place smelled—not unpleasantly—of grease and motor oil, rubber and cold metal. It had taken several hours to complete the search for evidence on and in the van, and not one fingerprint had been found. Every surface had been wiped clean, and, according to the techs, the perp had even vacuumed the carpet and floor mats before he'd loaded up the body and parked it at the municipal court building.

Along with a plant biologist who'd just shown up, the techs were now working on the undercarriage of the vehicle, which had been raised on a hydraulic rack, looking for trace elements that could possibly tell Molina where the van had been. They were prying pebbles out of the tire treads, picking small strands of vegetation off the grease on the rear axle with tweezers, and looking for seeds and other plant matter that might be caught in the U-joints, springs, or clinging to various parts of the chassis.

Molina had worked the vehicle identification number and the license plate while the techs dusted for prints. A year ago, the van had been sold to a junkyard in El Paso and then bought for parts by one Lewis Lawless. According to the El Paso PD, Lawless had provided an address on the sales receipt that turned out to be a vacant city lot. It made Molina think that Lawless was a bogus name used by the perp as a derisive, cocky little joke.

He looked at the bagged and tagged evidence that had been removed from the van. It consisted of a used Band-Aid that had adhered to the lever of the brake pedal where it came in contact with the floorboard, some blond hairs that possibly came from the perp, and several other strands of hair that probably belonged to the victim. It was very slim pickings.

The body had been fingerprinted, but the victim's identity was still unknown. Although Molina had a detective checking the state and federal data banks, there was no guarantee her prints would be on file. Dental records would most likely wind up being how the body would be identified—*if* they could come up with a suitable missing-person candidate.

However, after checking with the National Crime Information Center, Molina had his doubts about making a quick ID. The woman had a butterfly tattooed on her right inner thigh, but there was no record of a missing person with such a unique identifier. It was no big surprise; a lot of people who disappear are never reported to the authorities.

Molina had been frustrated by unknown homicide victims before. He'd worked cases involving decomposed remains found by hikers in the foothills, bodies discovered in shallow roadside graves, scattered human bones recovered in arroyos after a heavy rain, and corpses that had been dumped at the landfill. In each of those situations the victim had remained nameless and the killer anonymous.

He thought about it a little more. Up to now, the perp had been an in-your-face killer with an agenda and specific targets. If he held to form, the dead woman had to be linked to Potter, Manning, and Chief Kerney, which meant he expected the police to puzzle their way through it.

Molina's cell phone rang and he answered quickly.

"I got a preliminary cause of death," the pathologist said. "Strychnine poisoning, specifically rat poison ingested orally."

"You're sure?"

"I haven't cut her open yet, but it looks that way. I found traces of the poison in the mouth, plus the jaw muscles were paralyzed and the lips were drawn back to expose the teeth."

"What else?" Molina asked.

"I think she was tied up and then the killer forced her mouth open and made her swallow the poison pellets."

"What makes you say that?"

"There are abrasions at the wrists and ankles, and bruising around the deltoid and pectoral muscles, most likely caused by the violent convulsions brought on by the strychnine."

"Will you be able to confirm that rat poison was used and not some other compound?"

"I took swabs of the mouth and picked up some good granular samples along the gum lines. I should be able to isolate the inert properties easily. The blood, urine, and tissue work should also show poison traces."

"What about the puncture wound to the lower abdomen?"

"I'd say it occurred after death," the pathologist said. "It's a clean entry, so I doubt the killer did it while she was experiencing poison-induced spasms. I'll know for sure after I open her up and see where the blood settled."

"Call me if you learn anything else," Molina said.

He put the cell phone down and studied the license plate that had been removed from the van. He'd hoped the perp would have left prints on the back side of the plate, but no such luck. It had been wiped clean. He looked up to find the plant biologist standing in front of the desk holding a baggie in his hand.

"This is interesting," the man said, shaking the baggie at Molina. It held a single stem and one partial leaf of a plant.

"Tell me why," Molina said.

"It's *Lupinus brevicaulis*," the biologist said as he pushed his eyeglasses back into place. "Short-stemmed lupine. It doesn't grow here."

"Where does it grow?" Molina asked.

"Mostly south of Albuquerque along the Rio Grande. But the range extends into the southwestern part of the state and north into the Four Corners region."

Molina thought about the report Chief Kerney had filed about the dead Merriam Kangaroo Rats found on his front step. According to the wildlife specialist who'd examined the animal, the rat's range was similar to that of the plant.

He checked his copy of Kerney's report to make sure. The rat's native habitat was also along the Pecos River south of Santa Rosa. "Would it be found in the eastern part of the state along the Pecos?"

"Nope. There you'd find the spurred lupine and the low lupine. Neither come close to looking like the petal and stem of this variety."

"How far south does it grow?"

"All the way into Mexico."

The van had been lowered from the rack and the techs were about to strip it into parts. "That's helpful," Molina said. "Have you got anything else for me?"

The biologist shook his head. "Nothing out of the ordinary. But the soil samples may show something once you get them analyzed. I'm done, Lieutenant. I'll send you a report for your file."

Molina nodded and jotted down what the biologist had told him. Another fact had fallen into place. Unlike most of the other pieces of evidence, this one was at least linked to something, in this case geography. But that left a hell of a lot of land to cover south of Albuquerque to pinpoint a location for the perp, and it might mean nothing at all to the outcome of the investigation. Still, it would need to be looked into.

Molina considered the fact that the perp had used poison on his latest victim. He'd also poisoned the rats left on Kerney's doorstep and probably the one Dora

Manning had found in her driveway. It was another interesting thread that probably wouldn't go anywhere.

What did matter was the fact that the perp kept changing how he carried out his lethal attacks. So far, he'd successfully used poison, knives, and guns, and made one failed attempt with explosives. He wondered what he had in store for Kerney, Sara, and the baby. Strangulation? Drowning? Suffocation?

Was the perp a cop? Sal didn't think so. Anybody could study basic police science and learn fundamental investigative and forensic techniques from a book or a community college class.

Molina looked out the garage door. Morning had come and a shaft of sunlight spread into the open bay. He wondered why the chief hadn't called to ream him out for sending Ramona Pino down to Mescalero. Surely Kerney had to know he'd done it to get her away from Lieutenant Casados and his IA investigation.

Casados would be fuming when he got to the office and learned about Molina's ploy. But Sal had a plan on how to deal with Casados, and he was pretty sure it would work.

Milton Lynch's bushy, untamed eyebrows cascaded down and interfered with his vision. He licked a stubby finger, ran it across his brows to get them to behave, and nodded at the police artist's sketch that Kerney had placed on his office desk.

"Yeah, I did talk to this guy," Lynch said. "Except he had his long hair pulled back in a ponytail and wore a suit."

"Tell me about him," Kerney said.

"He said he was writing a book about the ranchers

that had been kicked off the Tularosa Basin by the government during and after World War II. Said he was researching the failed attempts of descendants of the ranchers to get compensation from the government for the loss of their land. He wanted to talk to them and get their stories."

"So he asked for names?"

"Yeah, and you were just one of many I told him about."

"What about Clayton Istee and his family? Did you mention him?"

"I'm almost sure I did."

"How did he find you?" Kerney asked.

"I've handled probate for a lot of those ranching families over the years," Lynch replied. "Plus, because I've got records of old title searches and copies of last wills and testaments, I've given depositions in a number of civil cases brought against the government for damages and just compensation claims that the courts have rejected. What the government did sixty years ago is still a thorn in the side of many of the old-timers and their families who lost everything when the missile range was established. But of course, you know all of this."

Kerney nodded. "So he found you through court records?"

Lynch snickered. "He probably didn't have to dig that deep. About once a year the newspaper interviews me for a feature article when another court case for a rancher or an heir hits the docket. It's always big news around here."

"What exactly did he want from you?"

"Like I said, just the names of living family members and relatives," Lynch replied. "He wanted to concentrate on the human side of their stories and the losses they'd suffered at the hands of the government."

"Did he identify himself?"

Lynch nodded. "He gave me his business card and told me his name, but I can't say I recall it. This was five, maybe six months ago."

"Did you keep the card?"

"No, I tossed it."

"Try to remember the name," Kerney said.

Lynch shook his head. "Nothing comes to mind. But I do remember he was from Arizona. Tucson, I think."

"Did he make an appointment to see you?"

"No, he just walked in early in the morning and asked for a quick meeting."

"Was there anything unusual about him?"

"Not really. Five-ten, average build, maybe thirty years old. Except for the long hair, he was just a normal-looking guy."

"Did he have any quirks or distinctive mannerisms?" Kerney asked.

Lynch thought for a moment. "He kept rubbing his forefinger against his nose, and it was rosy in color. But it looked more like a skin condition than a cold or an allergy. He wasn't sneezing or anything."

"Did you notice anything else?"

"He had a bandage on his left hand between the thumb and forefinger, right in that soft spot. I figured he'd cut himself. Why are you asking about this guy?"

"Because he's a killer," Kerney said as he stood up and handed Lynch his card. "Call me if you remember the name he gave you."

Lynch's expression darkened. "Are you serious?"

"Very," Kerney said as he headed for the door, eager to get back to Santa Fe.

Sal Molina didn't have to wait until he got back to headquarters to have Robert Casados in his face. Casados stomped into the garage, curled his lip and said in a loud voice, "Stop fucking with me, Sal."

All the techs quit what they were doing and glanced at the two men.

"Let's take it outside," Molina said to the young lieutenant. He put down the inventory sheet of all the parts from the van that had already been inspected by the techs and got to his feet.

"You sent Pino out of town, and you knew I had an interview scheduled with her first thing this morning."

"Outside, Lieutenant," Molina said gruffly as he moved away from Casados.

The bright July sunlight made Molina blink. He walked Casados into some shade at the side of the garage. "Now, what's your gripe?" he asked.

"You heard me. I've got a job to do and you're messing with me."

"I sent Detective Pino to Mescalero because I wanted to talk to you before this goes any further."

"I could write you up for interfering with my investigation," Casados said.

"Do you want to flex your muscles or hear me out?" Molina asked.

"What do you want to say?"

"I put pressure on Pino to find a suspect in the Potter homicide, but she isn't going to tell you that. I told her to take a hard look at Mary Beth Patterson and Kurt Larsen, and she isn't going to tell you that either."

"That doesn't excuse Pino's lack of judgment," Casados said.

"Ain't hindsight a wonderful thing?" Molina shot back. "She had two mentally ill people known to hold a grudge against the victim, and one of them was armed and potentially dangerous."

"She still fucked up," Casados replied. "So did Sergeant Tafoya."

"No, Bobby, I fucked up," Molina said, poking himself in the chest. "I put the pressure on them. I requested the SWAT call-out. I *wanted* Larsen to be our perp, and because of that I didn't ask the right questions."

"Pino fed you misinformation because she didn't do her job right."

"She's not a social worker, dammit, and the tip that Larsen and Patterson might be credible suspects came from Chief Kerney. Are you also going to write him up for feeding me misinformation?"

"That's absurd."

"Pino acted based on what she'd been told to do by me, and the reasonable suspicion she got from her conversation with Patterson. You want accountability for this screw-up? You're looking at it."

"You can't cover for your people this time, Sal."

"Why not? I did it for you when you were in my unit. More than once, if I recall correctly."

"Are you asking me for a favor?" Casados demanded.

"No favor," Sal replied. "But I will give you what you need to put this to rest. You recommend to the chief that I'm to be severely reprimanded and asked to retire. I'll turn in my paperwork immediately."

"Why scapegoat yourself?"

"I *want* to retire, Bobby. I haven't slept in two days, haven't seen my wife, haven't even changed my shirt. I'm maxed-out on my pension benefits, so I'm not gonna get any richer. I just want to rest for a week and then go fishing."

"Tafoya's on the list for lieutenant and Pino's next in line for sergeant stripes," Casados said.

"Yes, they are, and you worked with both of them in my unit. Are they seasoned? Are they capable of command? Of course they are. But forget about all that. The final decision to promote rests with the chief. Let him sort it out. That's his job, not yours."

Casados bit his lip.

"There's one more thing," Molina said.

"What's that?"

"Chief Kerney knows I sent Pino down to Mescalero and I haven't heard a peep out of him about my decision. If he'd wanted to countermand my order and chew my butt out, it would have happened long before you got to work this morning."

Casados stood with his hands on his hips, tapping his fingers against the butt of his holstered sidearm. "Are you telling me Kerney's behind this scheme?"

"No, I'm telling you I know the man and I think he'll want to make a decision that's best for all concerned. All you have to do is give him the opportunity."

"If I go with this, you can't back out, Sal," Casados said.

Molina laughed. "Hell no. I'm doing myself a favor, Bobby."

"Okay."

"Good," Sal said as he walked back into the sunlight. "Now leave me alone. I've got work to do, and not much time to do it."

Detective Matt Chacon knew that unlike the TV cop shows—where actors sit in front of a computer monitor and instantaneously pull up a digital fingerprint record that matches a perp or a victim—trying to ID someone using prints in the real world can be mind-numbing work. There are thousands of prints that have never been entered into the computer data banks, and thousands more on file that, because of poor quality, are virtually unusable for comparison purposes. On top of that, figure in the small cop shops who haven't got the money, manpower, and equipment to transfer print records to computers, and the unknown number of print cards that were left in closed felony cases and sit forgotten in basement archives at police departments all over the country, and you've got a data-bank system that is woefully inadequate and incomplete. Finally, while each fingerprint is unique, the difference between prints can be so slight that a very careful analysis must be made to confirm a perfect match. Even then, different experts can debate the results endlessly, since it isn't an exact science.

Chacon had started his career in law enforcement as a crime scene technician with a speciality in fingerprint and tool-mark identification, so of course Lieutenant Molina had sent him off to the state police headquarters to work the state and federal data banks to see if he could get a match.

He'd been at it all night long and his coffee was starting to taste like sludge, his eyes were itchy, and his butt was numb. Using an automated identification system, Chacon had digitally stored the victim's prints in the computer and then started scanning for a match against those already on file.

The computer system could identify possible matches quickly, but then it became a process of carefully analyzing each one and scoring them according to a detailed classification system. So far, Chacon had examined six dozen sets of prints that looked like possible equivalents and had struck out. But there was another baker's dozen to review.

He clicked on the next record, adjusted the monitor to enhance the resolution of the smudged prints, and began scoring them in sequence. Whoever had printed the subject had done a piss-poor job. He glanced at the agency indentifier. It was a Department of Corrections submission.

Chacon finished the sequence and used a split screen to compare his scoring to the victim's prints. It showed a match. He rechecked the scoring and verified his findings.

For the first time, he looked at the subject's name. The victim was Victoria Drake, a probation and parole officer with the Department of Corrections, assigned to a regional office in the southern part of the state.

He printed out a hard copy, moved his chair to another monitor, accessed the motor vehicle computer system, typed in the woman's personal information from the record, and a driver's license photograph of Drake appeared on the screen. The dead woman in the van was most definitely Victoria Drake, although she'd looked much better in life than in death.

Chacon glanced at the hard copy. Drake had been fingerprinted fifteen years ago. He wondered if she was still employed by the department. He reached for the three-ring binder that contained addresses and phone numbers of every federal, state, and local criminal justice agency in the state and paged through it until he found the listing for the regional office.

Chacon paused and thought about giving Molina the word first. But since Drake had been a probation and parole officer, the lieutenant would want to know a hell of a lot more than just the woman's identity. He quashed the idea of calling Molina and dialed the number for the regional probation and parole office instead.

Sal Molina drove while Matt Chacon briefed him. Victoria Drake, age forty-three, had recently been promoted to a central-office job in the corrections department after serving as a probation and parole officer in Las Cruces and then as the manager of the regional office in Socorro. Divorced with one grown son serving in the armed forces, Drake had moved to Santa Fe less than a month ago and lived alone in a rented town house in a middle-class neighborhood off Rodeo Road.

Molina thought it interesting that once again the compass pointed south. He wheeled into the subdivision with the crime scene techs following close behind. It was one of those developments with a homeowners association and restrictive building covenants that hadn't existed in Santa Fe before the early seventies. Now they were sprinkled around the city and in several larger nearby bedroom communities in the county.

The streets were narrow curving lanes designed to create a tranquil feeling. The native landscaping in the common areas was the low-maintenance variety, with lots of carefully pruned piñon trees and gravel planting beds interspersed with artistically grouped boulders. The houses and town homes had been built in a standard cookie-cutter design, right down to the exterior plaster, trim paint, patio walls, walkways, and street-number signs outside each unit. Molina found it boring.

He barreled over the last speed bump, turned into Drake's driveway, and parked behind a late-model imported sedan. "Let's do a walk-around before we go inside," he said to Chacon.

At the back of the unit, they found the gate to the patio ajar and the sliding glass and screen doors jimmied open. They entered the combination living and dining room, an open space with a corner beehive fireplace and a high ceiling of plank wood and beams. To the rear was a long counter that separated the space from a step-up galley kitchen.

Drake had arranged the furniture in the room but hadn't finished unpacking from her move. Sealed cardboard boxes were stacked in a line under the counter, several framed posters leaned against a wall by the fireplace, crumpled newspaper littered the carpet, and knickknacks sat haphazardly on the dining table. It was impossible to tell if a struggle had taken place.

Molina scanned the stairs leading to a second-story landing that looked down on the living room and then dropped his gaze to the hallway off the kitchen that ended at the front door. "We'll hold the techs outside until we do a visual search," he said as he slipped on a pair of plastic gloves. "Take the upstairs and look around. See if the perp left us another love note."

Chacon went upstairs and Molina started his tour by examining the sliding patio door, which showed tool marks on the jamb, probably made by a knife. The perp had picked the easiest, quietest, and quickest way to break into the house.

The galley kitchen was neat and clean. There was a kitty-litter box and food and water dishes on the tile floor, but no sign of a cat. In the small second bedroom off the adjacent hall, a computer and printer sat on a desk and three empty freestanding bookcases stood in the middle of the room surrounded by boxes of books. The linen closest in the guest bathroom at the end of the corridor held carefully folded towels. The tub was filled with empty cartons that had been broken down into bundles and tied with twine.

Molina entered the garage through a door perpendicular to the front entrance and hit the light switch with his elbow. Except for a large, cleared space in the center of the garage floor, it was filled with empty cardboard wardrobe boxes, trunks, lawn and garden tools, and miscellaneous pieces of furniture.

A small, open box sat in the cleared area. Molina looked inside and found a cat with a broken neck, a package of rat poison, a knife, some rope, and a note, which read:

KERNEY
CAN'T WAIT TO
MEET THE WIFE
SEE YOU SOON

He bagged the note and carried it upstairs to Chacon. "Find anything?" he asked.

"Nope," Chacon replied, gesturing at the orderly, organized master bedroom. "What have you got?"

Molina held up the note for Chacon to read. "Found it in the garage," he said, "where I think he probably killed her. He's a tidy fellow; he left everything behind he used to break in, tie her up, and poison her in a box for us to find."

"How thoughtful," Chacon said.

Molina nodded. "Get the techs started. Maybe he forgot something when he cleaned up after himself."

Samuel Green's mother, his second victim, was buried under some privet bushes that formed a hedge along the backyard wall of the house where she'd lived. He'd killed her five years ago, buried the body, planted the privets, faked her move to Arizona, and arranged for a property management firm to lease out the house and send the rent checks in her name to a post office box in Tucson, which he then easily forged and cashed. After the last tenant had moved out, he leased the property as Samuel Green and moved back to Santa Fe.

The house was in an older subdivision off Old Pecos Trail on a dead end dirt lane surrounded by a high wall that hid the house from sight. Territorial in style, with brick coping around the roof line, milled woodwork lintels, and a Victorian-style porch, it had been built in the 1960s. Upscale in its heyday, it was in need of serious modernization, particularly the kitchen and bathrooms. When Green was a boy, there had only been two neighbors along the lane. Now the area was built up with newer, expensive pueblo-style homes, all of them behind gated walls.

Green appreciated his neighbors' need for privacy, although it was unlikely any of them could possibly know his true identity. Almost twenty years had passed since he'd lived in the house as a child and both of the original neighbors had moved away long before he'd murdered Mother.

He parked in the garage and walked into the house, his footsteps echoing through the dark, empty living room. After disposing of Noel Olsen's car, he'd taken a morning flight from El Paso to Albuquerque, ridden the shuttle bus to downtown Santa Fe, and picked up his car from the parking lot at a city recreation center within walking distance of the Plaza.

In the bathroom he peeled off the fake nose, removed the blue-tinted contact lenses, took off the blond wig, washed away the adhesive that had held it in place, and inspected himself in the mirror. It didn't take much to go from looking like Noel Olsen back to being Samuel Green. He put the disguise in the makeup kit, which also contained the black wig and matching mustache.

The stubble that had reappeared on his head made him frown. He shaved it with a razor until it was nice and smooth again, smiled at the results, and then stretched. It was time for a well-deserved nap.

He walked to the bedroom where his father, Ed, had tied a string around his penis and locked him in his room for wetting his bed. Where his mother had starved him for failing to do his chores or for bringing home bad grades. Where his few toys would be taken from him for the slightest infraction of any rule. Where if he "talked back" his father would put duct tape over his mouth. Where he'd been forced to sleep on the floor because he'd played with daddy's tools or disobeyed him. Where he'd been tied up for running around the backyard pretending to be a choo-choo train.

The room was his prison until the day he'd told his second-grade teacher about it. After that, it had only gotten worse.

Now the old bedroom was Green's war room, filled with all the tools and materials needed to carry out his plan. There were books on police procedures, homicide investigation techniques, and the latest developments in forensic science. Various photographs he'd taken of his targets were taped to one wall along with snapshots of where they lived and worked and corresponding hand-drawn diagrams he'd made of the various escape routes. He'd memorized, driven, and walked all of them repeatedly before striking.

On the large desk fashioned from plywood and lumber sat the police scanner, a laptop and printer, a camera with various lenses, his handgun, binoculars, a small color television, and brown accordion files that contained pertinent personal and background information on each subject.

On the wall above the box spring and mattress that served as his bed, Green had tacked up a large map that showed all the roads into and out of Santa Fe. He'd spent hours studying it on the off chance that something went wrong, so he could avoid roadblocks, lose pursuing cops, and get away successfully.

He grabbed a black marker from the desk, walked to the wall of photographs, and drew an X through all of

Victoria Drake's pictures. He wrote question marks on the photos of Clayton Istee, his wife, and their two children and then quickly blotted them out. It didn't matter if Kerney wasn't around to see it. He would finish the job and wipe out Kerney's bloodline completely. Besides, it gave him something to look forward to.

He stretched out on the bed and thought about his father, and how much fun it had been to find him in California years after his parents' divorce, kill him, carve him up, and dump his body parts in the Pacific Ocean. How his mother had squealed when he strangled her. How Olsen had pleaded for his life, and Potter had frozen at the sight of the pistol. How Manning had watched in fright as the knife approached her throat while he held her down, and how Victoria Drake had convulsed on the garage floor like a headless chicken.

He smiled in the darkness as he thought about more good times to come, then curled up in a ball and went to sleep.

Chapter 10

Kerney landed in Santa Fe and got briefed by radio as he drove to Andy's house on Palace Avenue to check in with Sara. Andy and his wife, Gloria, lived within walking distance of the Plaza in one of the few houses that hadn't been bought up by wealthy newcomers, turned into a bed-and-breakfast, or converted into upscale professional office suites. It was a low-slung, rambling adobe dwelling with a beautiful backyard garden tucked between two large Victorian mansions. The house had been in the Baca family for over a hundred years.

Gloria Baca greeted him at the door with a smile, took him into the kitchen, poured him a cup of coffee, gave his shoulder an affectionate squeeze, and left him alone with Sara. The room was bright and airy, with a skylight above the large, round oak kitchen table, and French doors that led to the portal and the tree-shaded yard beyond. Through the window over the sink, Kerney could see a state police agent roaming along the flower beds in front of the privacy fence at the back of the lot. Behind the closed kitchen door another agent stood guard in the living room. On the street, a city patrol officer was parked curbside at the front of the house.

Kerney sat at the table, which was large enough for eight people. He took a sip of coffee and tried to read Sara's mood. He couldn't tell if she was just worried about the events of the week, physically worn down, or both. Her face was drawn and her green eyes seemed remote, inward looking. Even her greeting had been cursory—a quick hug and the brush of her lips against his cheek.

He decided to approach with caution. "How are you feeling?" he asked.

Her eyes never left his face. "I'm tired," she said without affect.

"Has the baby been keeping you awake?"

"No."

Kerney waited for more. Silently, she toyed with her wedding band and looked out the kitchen window for a long moment.

"Talk to me, Sara," he said.

She adjusted a pot of azaleas on the table so that it sat perfectly centered on a handwoven mat, and pinched off a drooping flower. Finally she looked at him. "I'm on edge, Kerney, wondering what's going to happen next. If I wasn't pregnant I'd be hunting for this bastard, not sitting here feeling like I'm under house arrest."

Kerney nodded sympathetically, lowered his gaze, and took another sip of coffee. He was light-headed from a lack of sleep and ill-prepared to deal with Sara's complaint. There simply wasn't a less restrictive alternative he could think of that would keep her out of danger. He drank some more coffee. It wouldn't sit well in his damaged gut, but maybe it would keep him from nodding off, or better yet saying something testy. When he looked up Sara was smiling apologetically.

"I'm sorry," she said. "You don't need me sounding whiny. But I have these protective feelings that make me want to tear the throat out of the son of a bitch. I was awake half the night worrying about you, thinking the attack on Clayton was just a feint to draw you into the open."

"I had the same feelings about you when I left for Mescalero," Kerney said, managing a smile. "But the investigation is making some progress. We've got an ID on the woman in the van and have located the crime scene. Her name was Victoria Drake—she was a probation and parole officer who'd just transferred up here from Socorro. Sal Molina has people digging into her old cases to see if they can link any of her parolees to me or the other victims."

"That could narrow the field a bit," Sara said. "How many cases need to be reviewed?"

"Hundreds, probably," Kerney replied. "But from what I learned in Mescalero, we need to be looking for a suspect who has the skill to build a sophisticated explosive device. There can't be too many ex-cons like that."

"That's encouraging," Sara said. "But except for the attack on Clayton and his family, all the victims are from Santa Fe, not the southern part of the state."

"I'm thinking our perp was arrested and convicted of a crime here, paroled down south after he did his time, and may still be living there."

"Do you have anything to support that?"

"A biologist found some trace evidence on the van, a plant that's not native to this area. It matches nicely with the range of the Merriam Kangaroo Rat. Both exist within the Rio Grande corridor down around Socorro."

"Do you think he's been traveling to Santa Fe to commit the murders?" Sara asked as she studied Kerney's pale face and tired, watery blue eyes.

"Possibly," Kerney answered, stifling a yawn. "We're only a hundred and thirty miles up the Interstate from Socorro, and it's about the same driving time from there to Mescalero. That's not much of a haul, yet it's still far enough away to lie low after each attack. I've got Ramona Pino en route to Socorro from Mescalero to start an immediate follow-up on any likely suspects we identify through the records search, and Andy has people standing by to assist her. If we ID him and he's down there, we'll blanket the area with personnel until we find him."

Sara grimaced and wrapped her arms around her belly.

"Contractions?" Kerney asked.

Sara forced a smile. "No, just a swift kick from Patrick Brannon Kerney. I'll let you know when my water breaks." She pulled her shoulders back and stretched. "Now, what about Clayton and his family? From what you told me on the phone, they must be devastated."

Kerney nodded grimly and slugged down the rest of his coffee. It was going to be another long day and he was already running behind. "They are. But I only have time to give you a quick report right now."

*   *   *

After leaving Sara, Kerney went to the house on Upper Canyon Road to shower and shave. For good reason, the place didn't feel safe. Each sound he heard put him on edge, and he kept the bathroom door open and his semiautomatic close at hand. He dressed quickly in a fresh uniform, holstered his weapon, and walked into the bedroom.

Sara had asked for some fresh clothes. Kerney packed them in an overnight bag—two days' worth—along with her toiletries. He zipped the bag, took it into the living room, and dumped it on the couch. On the writing desk were the architectural plans for the new house, which Sara wanted him to bring to her. Next to the plans was a handwritten list of things Sara wanted for the new house: a kitchen island, lamps and end tables, bedroom linens and a seven-foot sofa, cooking utensils. On the architect's drawing she'd marked places where she planned to arrange the antique pieces she'd inherited from her grandmother.

Sara's wish list made Kerney ache for a return to sanity in their lives, and for everyday conversations about what furniture to buy, what trees should be planted around the house, and their ongoing debate about whether or not they should add a pergola to the patio inside the courtyard entrance.

Was it really only last night that Drake's body had been found in the blue van? Time felt drawn out and chaotic, and his life turned upside down by a nameless, faceless murderer.

He placed Sara's list on top of the plans, rolled them up, and snapped rubber bands around them, thinking that all he wanted to do was find out *who* to hunt down and kill.

Outside, Sal Molina stood waiting by his unmarked unit. "Have you got something for me, Lieutenant?" Kerney asked.

Sal shook his head. "Nothing about the murders, Chief."

"So what brings you here?"

"You didn't pull my chain when I sent Ramona Pino down to Mescalero last night."

"I thought about doing it," Kerney said. He debated saying more and decided not to.

"Bobby Casados is going to recommend that I be officially censured and forced into retirement," Molina said, as he shifted his weight uneasily from one foot to the other. "I wanted you to know it was my idea."

"Is this what you want?" Kerney asked.

"Yeah, it is. I put pressure on Detective Pino to make a quick arrest and I also made the call to bring in SWAT."

"A lot of mistakes in judgment were made, Sal, up and down the line," Kerney replied.

"That wouldn't have happened if I'd thought things through before I reacted. I finish my work week tomorrow. I'll have my retirement papers on your desk by the end of shift today."

"No deal, Lieutenant," Kerney said.

Molina shook his head abruptly. "There's no need for Pino or Cruz Tafoya to take a hit for this."

"That's not my point," Kerney said. "I can't have my best investigator walking out on me until this case is completely wrapped up. Then you can retire. We can talk about under what conditions you leave the department when the time comes."

"You may not have the luxury of waiting," Sal said. "There are seventy-five people from a group called the Friends of the Mentally Ill holding a protest vigil outside headquarters right now, and they want blood. The media is covering it big time."

"I'm not going to cave into that kind of pressure, Sal," Kerney said. "Not from a protest group, the DA, the city manager, or the media. If they want a pound of flesh, they'll have to wait, because I'm not about to lose my major felony case supervisor with three unsolved homicides and four attempted murder investigations under way. Are we clear on that?"

Molina nodded.

"Okay, let's go back to work."

Sal drove away and Kerney sat in his unit listening to the radio traffic. The size of the protest vigil had swelled to over a hundred, and people were walking along nearby Cerrillos Road carrying placards that accused the department of discrimination, police brutality, and violating civil rights. He scratched out some notes and called Helen Muiz, his office manager, on his cell phone.

"Will you be joining the party?" Helen asked. "It's turning into quite an event. The gay pride people have just showed up to add their voices to the chorus of protest."

"I'll be there in a few," Kerney said. "Let the media know that I'll be giving a prepared statement but taking no questions."

"Oh, I'm sure that will please them no end."

By the time Kerney arrived at headquarters, Helen had arranged for a podium to be set up outside the visitors entrance. He stepped out the door with Larry Otero in tow to find a semicircle of TV cameras facing him, and the parking lot filled with people, with more arriving from lines of cars parked along both sides of the street that paralleled Cerrillos Road.

Plainclothes officers and some of Andy's agents were spread throughout the gathering, and uniformed personnel were stationed at the back of the parking lot, eyeing people as they came in. Larry Otero had officers taking photographs from inside the building just in case the perp had decided to join the throng.

In the front row he spotted a solemn-looking Fletcher Hartley holding a handwritten sign that read JUSTICE FOR ALL. It was the least inflammatory placard among the many that were being thrust up and down in the air by the noisy crowd.

Kerney walked to the podium, pulled out his notes, paused a minute to let people quiet down, and then made his statement. He spoke about the unfortunate death of Kurt Larsen and Mary Beth Patterson's suicide, and how the department would improve and strengthen policies and procedures to ensure that no similar tragedy happened again. He mentioned the development of mandatory training that would require all sworn personnel to gain the knowledge and sensitivity needed to deal with emotionally disturbed and mentally ill citizens, and called upon professionals, advocates, and family members to assist in that process.

Without giving specifics, he talked about the internal affairs investigation and the disciplinary action he'd already taken regarding the SWAT call-out that had resulted in the shooting of Kurt Larsen.

Finally, he said, "The loss of innocent lives is unacceptable and has deeply affected the men and women of this department. More officers may be held accountable as our probe continues. However, the ultimate responsibility for the conduct of the department is mine alone, and you have every right to expect me to meet my obligations, which I will do. But for now, I ask for your patience as we use all of our time and resources to apprehend the killer. Thank you."

Kerney turned away as reporters called out questions at him about the murders and the status of the investigations. "How do you think it went?" he asked Otero, as he pushed open the door to the reception area.

"Good," Larry replied. "They listened, didn't hiss or boo, and best of all, nobody tried to shoot you."

Ramona Pino rolled into Socorro, keyed her radio, and asked the state police dispatcher for directions to the district office, which was a few miles outside of town. From a long-ago high school New Mexico history class, Ramona knew some basic information about the city. She knew Socorro in Spanish meant "help" or "assistance," and that the city had been given the name by conquistadors because of the nearby Pueblo Indians who'd provided them with food. During the middle to late nineteenth-century, the town had been the center of one of the richest mining districts in the southwest. Now it served as a hub for area farms and ranches and was home to New Mexico Tech, a state university. It was also the birthplace of Conrad Hilton, the man who'd started the famous hotel chain.

With an enrollment of slightly over twelve hundred students, the school was consistently rated as one of the best in the country. Ramona had researched the institute as a college choice before deciding to drop science as a major in favor of criminal justice. Given the very real possibility that her cop career was going down the tubes, maybe she should have stuck with science.

The main drag through town wasn't much to look at, just the usual conglomeration of local businesses, fast-food joints, gas stations, motels, and a few strip malls. The district state police headquarters was a modern, single-story, sand-colored concrete block building with pale gray stone coping, situated next to the Interstate.

Inside, the duty officer buzzed her through the security door and directed her to a bullpen area, where she spotted Russell Thorpe and two investigators working over some papers.

Thorpe grinned at her as he got to his feet. "Good, you're here."

"I'm surprised to see you," Ramona replied, smiling back and thinking that Thorpe was not bad looking with his boyish face and six-foot, hard-body frame.

"My chief sent me down," Thorpe said as he picked up a file and put it on the seat of an empty chair.

"What have you got?"

"A possible hard target, named Noel Olsen. We're trying to track him down. Chief Kerney busted him and two other guys for a rape-murder in Santa Fe. Olsen turned state's evidence and pled to a second-degree felony on the rape and as an accessory to the murder. The judge made the prison time concurrent on both counts, so Olsen did only four and a half years at the medium-security prison in Las Lunas, and was paroled to Las Cruces after his release. Drake was his P.O. before she got promoted to run the Socorro office."

"Why is he a target?" Ramona asked.

Thorpe ran it down. Olsen had been a third-year engineering student at New Mexico State when he'd been busted. After he was paroled, he'd finished his degree and taken a master's in electrical engineering, with a specialty in energetic materials.

"Bombs," Ramona said.

"Yeah, that and more," Thorpe replied. "Artillery weapons, ballistic experiments, rocket propulsion systems, explosives, nuclear blast and shock effects, land mines—you name it."

"The fact that Olsen knows how to make a bomb won't get an arrest warrant signed," Ramona said.

"The first of the court trial documents just got faxed to us from the Santa Fe District Attorney's Office," Thorpe said with a nod at the file he'd placed on the chair. "Jack Potter prosecuted the case and Dora Manning did the psych evaluation on Olsen."

"That should do it," Ramona said, smiling back at Thorpe's infectious grin. "Where is he?"

Thorpe shook his head. "Don't know. He's on vacation from his job at a New Mexico Tech research and testing facility. According to the personnel office, he works as a research tech at an explosives mixing facility on a forty-square-mile field laboratory outside the city."

Ramona whistled. "Do we know where he lives?"

"Yeah, but he's not answering his phone. We've got a make, model, and license number for his car, and his driver's license photo is a close match to the police artist sketch. We're doing a casual patrol in the area, just in case he shows. But we didn't want to move on a search warrant for his residence until we tied him to the other victims."

"Are the arrest and search warrant affidavits done?"

"Just about," Thorpe answered.

"Have you called Chief Kerney?"

"Not yet."

"I'll do it, and then we'll go see a judge."

A state police SWAT team surrounded Olsen's house. Uniformed officers blocked off the county road in both directions. Ramona scanned the structure through binoculars. A fixer-upper with a sagging porch roof, it had cracked and broken plaster that exposed the adobe walls, old-fashioned single-pane sash windows, and a rickety screen door that clanked against the door jamb when the wind gusted. To one side stood a weather-beaten shed and the remnants of an old windmill that leaned precariously at an angle.

There was no sign of activity and no vehicle in sight. Ramona waited five minutes and then had SWAT move in. The team quickly cleared the premises, the outbuilding, and a large area of the dusty brown hillside behind the house. With Thorpe and the two state police investigators at her heels, she stepped inside the house and began a visual search.

An hour later, they had compelling evidence that tied Olsen to the explosion in Mescalero and the murders of Victoria Drake and Dora Manning.

By phone, she reported to Lieutenant Molina. "We've got a pair of Olsen's boots that match the shoe prints Deputy Istee found on the trail behind his house, Dora Manning's cell phone, receipts for the parts Olsen bought to make the triggering and detonation devices, all the raw materials used to make the plastique, the formula for the bomb he left on his computer, two dead Kangaroo Rats we found in a toolshed, plus a partially used container of over-the-counter poison bait."

"Excellent," Molina said. "Have you found anything that might tell us where Olsen is?"

"We're about to start looking," Ramona said. "What I've given you so far is just from a preliminary once-over. But I can give you information on Olsen's vehicle."

"Read it off."

Ramona fed Molina the data. "Looks like our boy isn't as smart as he thinks he is," she added. "How did we miss him during our initial records search?"

"He had a clean record in the slammer and as a parolee. He was a model prisoner, made no threats against Kerney or the victims, didn't violate his parole conditions, and supposedly rehabilitated himself. Besides that, at the time we weren't looking for a perp who knew how to blow people up. I'll get an advisory out for Olsen and his car. Keep me informed."

Ramona disconnected and turned to Thorpe and the two investigators. "Okay," she said, "let's tear this place apart."

"What do you remember about this guy?" Molina asked Kerney, as he put a thick packet containing Noel Olsen's case file, court trial documents, prison records, and parole officer reports on the chief's desk and settled into a chair.

"You worked the case with me, Sal," Kerney said. "He was an upper-middle-class kid who went out drinking and hoping to get laid with two of his college buddies. They picked up a woman, fed her some crap about taking her to a party, drove her out to the boonies and gangbanged her. The fun times went a little too far when they wound up strangling her and burying the body."

"I don't mean the case," Molina said, realizing that Kerney was tired and not tracking very well. "What do you remember about Olsen as a person?"

"He was an only child and a spoiled pretty boy," Kerney said, "who played the lady's-man role. The murder probably never would have happened if Olsen hadn't tried to sodomize the woman. According to his buddies, that's what caused her to fight back. She bit and scratched him and he slapped her around. The other two kids joined in to beat and strangle her."

"Did he strike you as cold-blooded?"

"Not really. He started out acting the tough guy during interrogation, but broke down real fast, which is why he got to plead to lesser charges. I thought he was just as guilty as his cohorts, and so did Jack Potter, who cut him a deal in order to get murder-one indictments on his chums. To me, Olsen's machismo act was a cover for his unresolved homosexuality. Dora Manning didn't see it that way; she found him to be narcissistic with sociopathic tendencies."

"Well, Manning may have missed the boat," Molina said, as he pointed to the files on Kerney's desk. "According to the prison records, a con made Olsen his bitch less than a month after he entered the general population at Los Lunas."

"You got a name?"

"Yep, Kerry LaPointe, out of Curry County. He's back

in the slammer doing a hard twenty at Santa Fe Max for armed robbery, possession of meth, and assault with intent to kill a police officer. He's an Aryan brother. Matt Chacon is on his way to interview him now."

"Let's locate Olsen's parents and talk to them," Kerney said, "and have Detective Pino do the same with his coworkers and friends in Socorro."

Molina nodded. "Did Olsen ever threaten to get even with you?"

"No. In fact, he apologized to the victim's family at the sentencing hearing."

"Do you think he's our guy?" Sal asked.

"Although the evidence is compelling, I have trouble understanding his motive," Kerney said. "Potter cut him a really sweet deal compared to his two pals. What about that list of possible suspects I gave you?"

"We've tracked all of them down except two," Molina replied, "and those we've talked to have tight alibis. We're still looking for the others."

"Okay, Olsen looks promising," Kerney said, "but I want all the pieces to fit together, Sal. Olsen's college pals should still be doing time for felony murder and aggravated rape. Have Chacon talk to them while he's at the prison. Have him find out if prison made Olsen vengeful."

Molina pushed his chair back from the table. "If it did, he's waited a hell of a long time to act on it."

Samuel Green had trained himself to sleep an hour or two at a time and wake up refreshed. He dressed in his jogging outfit, drove to the church at the lower end of Upper Canyon Road, parked, and took off at a fast pace up the street where Kerney lived, past the expensive adobe houses and estates that overlooked the dry Santa Fe River.

Aside from the workout it provided, running cleared Samuel Green's mind. He liked the random thoughts he had when he ran, the ideas that came to him, the things and people he saw. Except for a wave from one pedestrian walking a dog, and a car that slowed as it passed him by, nobody paid any attention to him as he pounded out an eight-minute mile along the fairly steep grade of Upper Canyon Road. He was just another anonymous jogger getting some exercise.

Yesterday, he'd run past a female state police officer stationed in front of Kerney's house. Today, the cop was gone. He stopped in front of the driveway, put his hands on his knees as if he was catching his breath, and glanced at the guest house. The new vehicle Kerney's wife had bought was parked next to the pickup truck, but the unmarked police car Kerney drove was gone.

He stretched his right leg and rubbed his calf so that anyone who might be watching would think he had a cramp. All the curtains at the front of the house were drawn, but that didn't mean anything. It was the cop's absence that told him Kerney had moved his wife.

Green smiled, straightened up, and ran on. He liked the fact that Kerney was no dummy. It made things all the more interesting.

Detective Matt Chacon stopped at the guard station at the state pen a few miles outside Santa Fe on Highway 14 and waited while the correctional officer cleared him to enter.

After an infamous riot in 1980 that had resulted in the death of several guards and the murder of some thirty inmates, most of whom were found in bits and pieces spread throughout the facility, the state had embarked on a massive new prison construction program. High-tech penitentiaries were built around the state, including the super max for men here at Santa Fe. The old facility had been closed but left standing, and was now rented out to Hollywood film companies shooting on location. A short distance down the road were the Correction Department training academy for guards and the central administration offices. Across the highway stood the county detention center and a brand-new county public safety building that housed the sheriff's department, the county fire chief's office, and the regional emergency communication center.

The guard finally waved him through. Inside the prison he was handed a phone message from Molina asking him to also interview Charles Stewart and Archie Schroder, Olsen's partners in crime. It took twenty minutes for his first subject, Kerry LaPointe, to be brought to the interview room.

No more than five-six, LaPointe had light-brown hair, an acne-scarred face, a pumped-up frame, and an Aryan Brotherhood swastika and Nazi SS lightning bolt tattooed on his forearm.

Chacon asked him about Olsen.

"He was a pussy," LaPointe said with a smug smile. "I made him my bitch as soon as he hit the general population at Lunas. Wish I had him here with me now. Why are you looking for him?"

"Multiple murder counts," Chacon replied.

LaPointe laughed. "You've got to be kidding."

"He did it once before," Chacon said.

"Yeah, but he's no stone-cold killer," LaPointe replied. "Icing that slut with Stewart and Schroder was just a gang-bang that went bad. He tried to put on a hard-case act when he came out of reception and classification, but nobody bought it."

"Did he ever talk about a payback? Going after the people who put him in the slam?"

LaPointe shook his head. "He whined a lot about how his life was ruined, that's about it. Like I said, he was a pussy. Hell, I even branded him."

"Branded him?"

LaPointe stroked the soft spot between his thumb and forefinger. "AB right here for the Brotherhood, so everybody knew who he belonged to. Didn't want no niggers or spics thinking he was fair game."

"Did he ever talk to you about getting even with anybody?" Chacon asked.

"All he rapped about was getting out and proving to everybody how wrong they were about him, like he was going to show the world how fucking brilliant he was."

After a few more questions that got him nowhere, Chacon moved on to Stewart and Schroder. In individual interviews, both men talked about how the woman had agreed to take on all three of them, Schroder from behind, Stewart getting a blow job while Olsen played with her nipples and waited his turn. How when Olsen had tried to butt-fuck her, she'd spit Stewart's cum in his face. How Olsen had threatened to get a safety flare from his car, stick it up her ass and light it if she didn't cooperate. How the slut had tried to run away, which started the beating that led to her death.

Stewart swore Olsen incited the beating, got off on it. Schroder confirmed Stewart's statement, said Olsen had a real mean streak. Both thought he could kill again.

"So what if he turned queer?" Schroder said. "I don't think that changed his personality. He didn't give a shit about anyone except himself. He'd be all charming on the surface and would get real cold if things didn't go his way. He liked to get even with people who fucked with him, find sneaky ways to do paybacks."

Stewart said that nothing was ever Olsen's fault, that he expected special treatment, and that he liked to talk about how smart he was and how dumb other people were, especially women.

Chacon asked if they thought Olsen had the capacity to organize and carry out revenge killings.

"Why not?" Stewart had said. "I'm sitting here locked up because he played the cops and the DA for chumps."

"Oh yeah," Schroder said. "He was a natural born actor, and I've got to give it to him, he was one smart motherfucker."

In the prison parking lot, Chacon sat in his unit and played back the taped sessions a bit at a time as he wrote up his field interview reports. He finished and put the clipboard aside. So which Olsen was real? Was he the psychopathic genius who could outsmart everybody or a weak sister, a sadistic braggart, or a fairy to an Aryan brother?

Matt cranked the engine and left the prison grounds thinking maybe Olsen could easily be all of the above.

*　　*　　*

The search warrant had been written broadly enough to allow for the seizure of Olsen's personal, medical, and financial documents; his computer; any and all items used in bomb-making; articles of apparel and footwear; any and all poisons, weapons, or tools used as weapons; samples of material from blankets, linens, textiles, carpets, and rugs; any stolen property of the victims; and any personal hygiene products, hairbrushes, combs, or toothbrushes that could yield forensic or DNA evidence.

While Ramona and her team hadn't gotten lucky and found a handgun, there were a number of knives that could have possibly been used to slash Dora Manning's throat. Moreover, in Olsen's office they'd discovered a scrapbook in the black vinyl binder that contained newspaper clippings about Jack Potter and Chief Kerney going back a number of years, and an arts calender notice in the Taos paper announcing Manning's upcoming one-woman show.

That got them looking for the paintings that had been stolen during the break-in at the Taos gallery. Thorpe found them wadded up and stuffed into a fifty-five-gallon drum in the toolshed.

Ramona left Thorpe and the two investigators in charge of inventorying and boxing up the evidence for transport to Santa Fe, and drove to New Mexico Tech. Next up were interviews with Olsen's coworkers and supervisor, which Ramona hoped would yield some information about where Olsen was spending his alleged vacation.

Buffered by pleasant, tree-lined residential streets, the

college was a short drive from the main drag. The school grounds were even more delightful to the eye. A lush golf course, set in stark contrast to the brown foothills of the Socorro Mountains, separated two campuses. The main campus consisted of a blend of modern and territorial buildings surrounded by wide lawns fronting a curved main roadway. The west campus was less charming and more industrial in appearance, with blocky warehouses, storage facilities, a surplus property yard, and a number of research buildings, which included the headquarters of the testing center where Olsen was employed.

Ramona met with Morris Day, Olsen's supervisor, who offered her a coffee in a mug bearing the logo of the Bureau of Alcohol, Tobacco & Firearms.

"You do training work with law enforcement agencies," Ramona said. "One of my coworkers took your course on terrorist bomb threats."

Day, a thirty-something man with curly light-brown hair cut short and a protruding chin below a slightly turned-up nose, nodded. "It's one of the most popular courses we offer to government entities. We have students from federal agencies, friendly foreign governments, and many state and local police and fire departments who come here to learn antiterrorism and counterterrorism measures pertaining to the use and identification of explosive and incendiary devices."

"Sounds interesting," Ramona said. "I'd like to take it."

"I'll give you an application packet before you leave," Day replied.

"That would be great," Ramona said. "Tell me about Noel Olsen. Did you know he was a convicted felon when you hired him?"

"Of course," Day replied. "Even though he's not working in a classified or a security-sensitive job, we did a very thorough background check before we took him on. He came highly recommended by his professors at State and his parole officer. Is he in trouble?"

"I just need to talk to him."

"My secretary told the other officer who called that he's on vacation," Day said as he toyed with his coffee mug. "He asked for leave rather unexpectedly, but it came at a time when we could spare him."

"Did he say what he planned to do on his vacation?"

"Noel likes to travel, especially to Europe. He said he had a last-minute offer from a friend to go on a hiking tour in Scotland that was too good to pass up."

"Did he mention the friend's name?" Ramona asked.

"No."

"Did he request his leave in person?"

"No, he called me at home on a Friday night about two weeks ago and asked for fifteen workdays off."

Ramona found that interesting. Why would Olsen, who had planned his crimes so carefully, wait until the last minute to arrange to go on holiday? It didn't make sense. "Had he ever done that before?" she asked.

"Ask for an unscheduled vacation? No."

Ramona asked about Olsen's personality and learned he was well-liked, a hard worker, and had recently been upgraded to senior technician at the explosives mixing facility on the school's testing grounds. He had no close friends at work, but always showed up for office parties and picnics, and played on the center's coed volleyball team.

After she finished questioning Day, he drove her out

to the facility where she spoke to Olsen's coworkers, who confirmed that Olsen was a good guy who kept his head into work and his personal life to himself, which meant absolutely nothing. There were any number of sex offenders and murderers who masqueraded as ordinary people until something set them off.

Back at the center, Ramona thanked Day for his time and left, still nagged by the thought of Olsen's abrupt request for a vacation. Perhaps Olsen had timed his leave to overlap with the arrival of Kerney's wife, and since he didn't have an exact date had to play it by ear.

But how did he know, even in a general way, when Sara Brannon would be coming to Santa Fe to have her baby?

In the kitchen, Samuel Green heated up some canned soup, poured it into a bowl, and carried it to his bedroom. He sat on the bed facing the small color television and watched the local noontime news out of Albuquerque. An anchor woman with big hair and bright-red lips smiled into the camera as she read the Teleprompter headline about the protest outside the Santa Fe Police Department.

Green turned down the volume when the picture switched to the intro of Kerney's statement to the press. The camera panned over the crowd, and Green saw himself standing in the front row next to an old fag holding a JUSTICE FOR ALL sign. He looked good on camera, better then he'd expected.

He hit the mute button on the remote, and thought about how Kerney had to die. He'd done everything possible to make Kerney believe his next victim would be his pregnant wife. But that was not to be the case. In fact, until she delivered, Sara Brannon was in no danger at all.

Above all else, Green wanted Kerney to watch his wife and newborn child die before he killed him.

Chapter 11

Through a stream of fax messages and phone calls, the Santa Fe PD had kept Sheriff Paul Hewitt advised of the progress of the investigation. As soon as he got the word that a credible suspect had been identified in Socorro, Hewitt called Clayton Istee, who was with his family at his in-laws' house. He gave Istee the skinny on the ID of Victoria Drake, her tie-in to Noel Olsen, and the search under way at Olsen's house.

"They've found evidence that connects Olsen to the bombing and all but one of the homicides," Hewitt added.

"I'm going up there," Clayton said.

"Stay with your family, Sergeant," Hewitt said. "They need you."

"My family's fine," Clayton replied. "Grace and the kids are taken care of and well-protected."

"That's not what I'm talking about."

"I'm not going to sit here and do nothing," Clayton said heatedly. "One way or the other, I want in on the investigation."

Hewitt knew arguing wouldn't change Clayton's mind and ordering him not to go would be pointless.

"Okay, I'm placing you on training leave for the rest of the week. You're to observe methods and procedures used by the Santa Fe PD major felony unit. *Observe* is the key word. I'll let them know you're coming."

"Thank you," Clayton said.

"Don't overstep your bounds, Sergeant," Hewitt said. "It could cost us both, big time."

"Who's the contact in Socorro?" Clayton asked.

"Detective Pino."

"Ten-four," Clayton said.

He made the drive to Socorro running a silent code three all the way, trying not to think too much about Grace and the children. Wendell, usually so talkative, had fallen silent. Hannah refused to leave her mother's side and didn't understand why she couldn't go home. Grace vacillated between black despair and frantic bursts of energy, one minute refusing to look at anybody, the next minute whirling through her parents' living room straightening up the numerous toys that relatives had brought over for the children, especially the Lincoln Log set Wendell kept building into houses and then destroying.

He felt guilty for leaving Grace to do all the phone calling to the bank, the mortgage company, government agencies, and the insurance agent to get their claims started and replace all the important documents that had been destroyed. But in his current state of mind he would have been useless at doing any of it himself.

Last night's events continued to swirl through Clayton's head. He forced the images away by concentrating on the fact that there was now a viable suspect. The possibility of being in on the arrest cheered him, even if all he got to do was watch the Santa Fe PD take the SOB down.

He arrived at Olsen's house, where Ramona Pino, whom he'd met last night, and three men were loading up an evidence trailer.

"Have you found Olsen?" Clayton asked as he approached Pino.

"Not yet, Sergeant," Ramona replied, eyeing Clayton speculatively, thinking the man needed to be with his family and not playing observer on a case involving himself and his family, which was way outside the rules. She wondered how Clayton had talked his boss into it.

She introduced him around and gave him a rundown on the incriminating evidence that had been seized from the house. "We matched the photo you took of the shoe print on the trail behind your house with a pair of hiking boots from Olsen's closet," she added.

"Let me see them," Clayton asked without changing expression.

Russell Thorpe climbed into the trailer and returned with an evidence box containing the boots. Clayton opened the box and examined them, paying particular attention to the heel of the right shoe, looking for wear along the outer edge. There wasn't any.

"I'd like to see all of the footwear," he said.

"I checked them already," Thorpe said, "to see if I could get a match with the shoe impressions I found on Chief Kerney's property."

"And?" Clayton asked.

Thorpe shrugged. "Nothing. Olsen must have gotten rid of them. But what's strange is that all the shoes in Olsen's closet are a size and a half larger than the prints left outside Chief Kerney's horse barn."

"Let's take a look," Clayton said.

Inside the house, Clayton sat on the bedroom floor and examined every right-foot shoe in Olsen's closet while Ramona and Thorpe watched.

"What are you looking for?" Thorpe asked.

"For something I learned in the FBI footwear and tire tread evidence course I took," Clayton said. "People walk heel to toe. The deepest impression is usually from the heel, which, along with the arch, bears most of the body's weight. The impressions I saw on the trail had a slightly deeper heel strike along the outer edge of the right shoe, which should show up as a wear characteristic on the bottom of these shoes."

Thorpe studied the heel of a right-foot athletic sneaker. "I don't see it."

"Because it's not there," Clayton said. "His stride indicated he was moving at a fast walk and not carrying anything heavy which might have shifted his balance."

"How can you be so sure?" Ramona asked.

"The depth of the print is the key, along with the distance between the tracks he left behind."

"So what does that tell us?" Thorpe asked.

"I'm not certain," Clayton replied. "You said the casting impressions you made in Santa Fe were a size and a half smaller."

"Yeah, but I left those with forensics," Thorpe said. "I compared my photographs with Olsen's boots and came up with the difference in size."

"I'd like to see those pictures," Clayton said.

Thorpe nodded, left, and returned with the photos. "Why would Olsen cram his feet into a smaller shoe?" he asked as he handed them to Istee.

"I don't know," Clayton answered, as he studied the

photos. Thorpe had done it the right way by laying a ruler alongside each print before taking the picture. He memorized the tread design. "Maybe he's got an accomplice." He looked up at Pino. "Who's been on the property today?"

"Aside from the officers who are here, a six-man SWAT team."

"Wearing combat boots, right?" Clayton asked as he got to his feet and handed Thorpe the photos.

Ramona nodded.

"I'm going to take a look around," Clayton said.

"Aren't you here only to observe?" Ramona asked.

"Looking around is observing," Clayton replied.

"There have been people trampling all over the place," Thorpe said.

"It's never too late to look," Clayton replied as he left the room.

It took Clayton thirty minutes to find two prints that matched those Thorpe had found on Kerney's land, one partial impression in the toolshed on an oil stain under the fifty-five-gallon drum where the stolen paintings had been stashed, and an almost perfect print in a shallow arroyo near the old windmill.

He showed them to Pino and Thorpe. "Where are the shoes that made these?" he asked.

"He's kept them to use again," Thorpe suggested.

Ramona shook her head. "It doesn't make sense. Why would Olsen leave all the evidence that we can tie to the crime scenes in plain view for us to find, except for one pair of too-small shoes?"

"Exactly," Clayton said, looking at Pino and Thorpe. "Now, what about the blue van?"

"I didn't find any tread marks from it," Thorpe

replied with a boyish grin. "But I suppose it's not too late to look again."

"Smart thinking," Clayton said, giving Thorpe a small smile in return.

"I'll get the photos," Thorpe said.

With the photos in hand, Clayton, Pino, and Thorpe began a grid search of the driveway, an area around the front of the house, and a section of the country road. A short time later, Clayton stood on the part of the gravel driveway Olsen used as a turnaround and studied some overlapping tire tracks. He knelt down, spotted two impressions identical to the treads from the rear tires of the blue van, looked around a bit more, and called Thorpe and Pino over.

"The car was towed behind the van," he said when they arrived. He showed them how the passenger car's tire impressions cut across the front treads of the van at a sharp angle. "I think that pretty much wipes out the accomplice theory. Why bother to tow a vehicle if you've got a second driver?"

"It also explains what he used for transportation after he left the van in front of the municipal court," Ramona said.

"But what about the shoe prints?" Thorpe asked.

"It's gotta mean something," Clayton said as he watched the two agents who'd been loading evidence lock the doors to the trailer. He turned to Pino. "You said most of what you seized inside the house was in plain view."

"Pretty much," Pino said.

"And you didn't have one solid lead about Olsen's identity until he killed his former parole officer."

"Basically, yes," Thorpe replied.

"Well, for a guy who's supposedly real smart, that was a pretty stupid thing to do," Clayton said, "because it brought you right to his front door."

"So he screwed up and made a mistake," Thorpe said.

"I wouldn't bet on it," Clayton said with a dismissive shake of his head. "Everything I read in the case files Detective Pino gave me last night argues against that kind of a screw-up. Until Drake's murder, all you had were little bits and pieces of miscellaneous evidence and no hard-target suspect. Then, bingo, everything falls into place, neat as a pin."

"You're saying it's far too convenient," Ramona said.

"Staged might be a better word," Clayton replied.

"Except for the shoe prints," Thorpe said.

"Maybe he isn't coming back here," Ramona said.

"That's possible," Clayton said. "What showed up when you tossed the house?"

Ramona shook her head. "Not much. We pretty much found what we were looking for on the first pass."

"Let's take a closer look inside for more anomalies. He'd need money if he plans to disappear after he's done with the killing."

"More observing, Sergeant?" Ramona asked.

"Exactly," Clayton answered.

"We didn't find any money," Thorpe said.

"It won't hurt to look again," Clayton replied.

"I guess not," Thorpe said, with a grin.

Sergeant Cruz Tafoya went hunting for Nocl Olsen's parents, Stanley and Meredith, who were listed in the phone book but either away from home or not taking calls. Stanley, according to the information contained in

241

the old case file, was a dentist, so Tafoya went to Olsen's last known office address only to learn that he'd sold his practice some years ago and taken a job with the Indian Health Service.

Tafoya checked with the Indian Hospital on Cerrillos Road and learned that Olsen was still employed by the IHS, but out of town doing his monthly rounds of regularly scheduled appointments at clinics on the Navajo Reservation. He asked about Mrs. Olsen's whereabouts and was told she didn't work and was something of a recluse.

The home address for the couple didn't register with Tafoya, so he looked it up in the county street map guide. The Olsens lived in Eldorado, a rural, middle-class subdivision ten miles southeast of Santa Fe along U.S. Highway 285.

Thirty years ago, when the subdivision was new and still relatively undeveloped, Tafoya's uncle, Benny, had managed the privately owned water utility that served the small cluster of new houses near the old ranch headquarters that had been turned into a real estate office.

As a young kid, Cruz had spent many summer weekends with Uncle Benny, now long retired, who'd lived in a cottage at the stables. Together, they rode horseback over the thousands of yet untouched acres that gave spectacular views of three mountain ranges in the distance, or drove into the back-country hills over rough roads on land slated to remain as open space.

Cruz knew that the subdivision had grown into a bedroom community of several thousand homes. But without a reason to visit over the years, he hadn't given it much thought. Seeing it up close after so long made his jaw drop. All traces of the vast stretches of piñon-studded ranchland were gone. The main trunk roads had been paved, and houses on acre or more lots were scattered in every direction.

A shopping mall, a branch bank, and a professional office building stood within shouting distance of the highway. Further down the road, past a number of Santa Fe–style, faux-adobe houses, an elementary school and a fire station stood on pastureland where antelope had once grazed.

Cruz pulled to a stop in front of the community library near the school, consulted his map, and then drove on to the west end of the subdivision, where a string of houses bordered an old post-and-barbed-wire fence. Beyond the fence, open land stretched for several miles, ending at the state highway that cut in front of the Cerrillos Hills and ran past the state prison.

Tafoya knew the day was coming when pricier houses on five-, ten-, and twenty-acre tracts that were way beyond the means of most native Santa Feans would fill up the land.

The Olsens' house was on a side road situated at the back of a lot accessed by a long, weed-infested driveway. Cruz entered the gate to a walled courtyard, walked up a flagstone path past barren flower beds, and rang the doorbell.

From the outside, the place looked neglected. The exterior plaster was badly cracked and the portal above his head showed water damage from a roof leak. A bird had built a nest on the outside light fixture next to the front door and there was a mound of dried droppings on the flagstone at his feet.

He rang the bell again and listened. From inside he could hear the sound of a blaring television. After waiting a few more seconds, he pounded on the door. An older woman with tousled gray hair opened up.

"Please go away," the woman said. Wrinkles around her mouth gave her a sad, dissatisfied look.

"Meredith Olsen?" Cruz asked, displaying his shield.

"Yes. Why are you here? We don't bother anybody." Her breath smelled of booze.

"I need to ask you some questions about your son."

"Noel? I can't talk to you about him." Mrs. Olsen's expression turned cagey. "Did Stanley send you here to trick me?"

"I've never met your husband," Cruz replied.

Mrs. Olsen raised her hand as if to stop him. "Why should I believe you?"

"Because I have no reason to lie," Cruz said.

Slowly, she lowered her hand and pulled her robe tightly around her thick waist. "We don't talk about Noel," she replied in a toneless recitation. "It's not allowed. That's all I have to say."

Cruz looked past Olsen into the darkened front room. He could hear the television broadcasting what sounded like big band dance music from an old movie. The weak flickering of the screen spilled out from an adjacent room.

Mrs. Olsen hadn't moved. He glanced back at her face and decided to try a ploy. "Noel is missing and I was hoping you could help me find him."

"Missing?" Mrs. Olsen's eyes blinked rapidly. "How can he be missing?"

"He's not at home and hasn't been at work for some time," Tafoya answered. "Can we talk inside?"

"Are you sure you haven't talked to Stanley?" she asked suspiciously.

"Never. Can we talk? I'm sure you want us to find your son."

Meredith Olsen nodded timidly and led the way into a family room. Fred Astaire and Ginger Rogers were dancing on the large-screen TV. Bookcases along one wall were filled with hundreds, perhaps a thousand, movie video cassettes. A fifth of scotch and a glass sat on a side table next to a reclining chair that faced the tube.

She picked up the remote control and pressed the mute button. "I knew something was wrong with Noel," she said.

"Why do you say that?" Tafoya asked.

"Every month, when Stanley goes out of town, I have lunch with him. We always meet in Albuquerque on a Saturday. He didn't come last week."

"Did you try to call him?"

Mrs. Olsen nodded. "From a pay phone. He didn't answer. He's always kept his word to see me since he got out of prison, whenever we could do it so Stanley wouldn't know."

On the television, Astaire and Rogers spun across the ballroom floor and swirled off camera. The scene shifted to a closeup of an unhappy looking bandleader. "Does he come to Santa Fe to see you?" Cruz asked.

"Never. He hasn't been in Santa Fe since the day he went away."

"He hasn't visited here recently, in the last week or so?"

Mrs. Olsen shook her head. "Why is Noel missing? Has he done something bad?"

"No, nothing like that," Tafoya said. "His employer

reported that he hasn't been at work for the last two weeks. How do you stay in touch with him?"

"By letter. I can't call him from home. Stanley would know about it when he paid the phone bill."

"Does Noel call you?"

"Only very rarely when he has to cancel our lunches because of work."

"And he didn't call to cancel last Saturday?" Cruz asked.

"No." She touched a finger to her lips. "Now I'm worried."

"I'm sure he'll turn up," Tafoya said. "Do you have Noel's letters?"

Meredith Olsen stiffened. "You have to understand that Stanley has no son, and I'm not supposed to either."

Tafoya smiled sympathetically. "Your husband doesn't have to know about my visit."

"Promise?"

"Yes. Did Noel ever talk to you about getting even with the people who sent him to prison?"

Mrs. Olsen shook her head vigorously. "He made a terrible mistake and he knows it. He's tried hard to put that behind him and become a good person. It does happen, you know. People can change for the better."

"Would you get Noel's letters?" Cruz asked gently. "They could help us locate him."

"I don't see how," Mrs. Olsen said.

"The more we know about him, the more likely we are to find him."

She left and returned with a shoe box filled with letters. She gave Cruz the box reluctantly, as though turning over a priceless treasure.

He promised to return the letters at a time when Dr. Olsen wasn't home, said good-bye, and walked to his unit, thinking how the ripple effect of murder always seemed to destroy so many lives beyond that of the victim.

Tafoya called dispatch as he rolled out of the driveway, and gave an ETA to headquarters. He was eager to read what Noel Olsen had written to his mother.

The last room to be tossed again was the kitchen. In a coffee can at the back of the top shelf of a pantry, Ramona found Olsen's passport and six hundred dollars in unused traveler's checks.

"Seems you were right," she said as she showed the items to Clayton.

"That's our second interesting anomaly," Clayton said with an approving nod of his head. He opened the door to what he thought would be the back porch and found that it had been sealed off and turned into a utility room that contained a fifty-gallon propane water heater plus a washer and dryer.

Clayton stepped inside and closed the door. There were a number of what appeared to be scuff marks made by rubber soles on the door and the bottom horizontal plate showed a fresh crack. He knelt down for a closer look. Someone had kicked the door repeatedly, and not with the tip of a shoe. There were full footwear impressions on the painted wood.

He gauged the length of the room. It was just long enough for a man to lie prone. He swung around and examined the water heater that sat on a raised plywood platform. It was a fairly new fifty-gallon tank painted a light gray. At the base of the unit was a series of scratch marks that had exposed bare metal. He ran a forefinger along the scratches and looked at the light coating of paint dust and metal particles on his fingertip. From the feel of it, the scratches ran completely around the tank.

He turned to the washer and dryer. The unbalanced dryer wobbled badly when he jiggled it, and there was a dent on the side about six inches above the floor. He opened the dryer door and caught the strong odor of mildew. An unused fabric softener sheet sat on top of wadded-up clothes. The dryer hadn't been used in some time.

Clayton checked the washing machine, found it empty and dry, and went back to the water heater. There were a few brown spots on the side of the platform and a yellowish stain on the middle of the linoleum floor.

He went into the kitchen where Thorpe and Pino were looking behind the refrigerator and under the sink. "Let's get some techs out here," he said.

"What have you got?" Thorpe asked.

"It could be a crime scene," Clayton replied. "I think somebody was kept prisoner in the utility closet."

"Another victim?" Pino asked as she flipped open her cell phone and made the call.

"Yeah, maybe," Clayton said. "But who?"

"A third anomaly," Russell Thorpe said as he peeked into the utility closet and saw nothing that pointed to a person being kept captive. He decided not to question Sergeant Istee about it. "What next?" he asked.

Ramona held up the address book she'd found in a drawer next to the wall phone by the refrigerator. "First, I need to bring my lieutenant up to speed." She spoke to Thorpe, deliberately excluding Clayton. "Then, let's start calling people. If Olsen really is our perp, somebody he knows should be able to tell us something of value."

"I'll work part of the list," Clayton said.

"That's not the role of an observer," Ramona replied.

"Do you really want to waste time arguing with me about it?" Clayton asked.

Ramona paused and thought about it. Technically, she could order Istee to back off, but she didn't want to do it. He was sharp, experienced, and had been more than helpful. "Okay," she said, "you're in."

Samuel Green parked in front of the Laundromat on St. Michael's Drive, grabbed the pillow case filled with his dirty clothes, and walked inside. The place was empty except for a long-haired college kid who was sitting at a table next to the wall dispenser that changed bills into quarters for the machines.

Green dumped his pillowcase on top of a dryer, which made the kid glance up from his book. Green smiled and the kid nodded in reply and went back to scribbling notes on a yellow pad.

He stuffed his laundry into a machine, poured in some detergent, and walked to the change machine. The kid slid his chair out of the way so Green could get by.

"How you doing?" Green asked, as he inserted the bill into the machine and waited for the quarters to drop down into the slot.

"Good," the kid replied.

"Studying?" Green asked as he fished the coins out. The kid couldn't be more than twenty.

"Yeah, summer school. I'm taking a required history course."

"I like history," Green said as he started up the washing machine. "You can learn about a lot of interesting people."

The kid made a face. "Not me."

"Why not?" Green asked as he sat at the table.

The kid closed his book. "It's just a survey course of names, dates, and events that you've got to memorize, and the instructor is real lame."

"That's too bad, because history can be real educational," Green said. "Like this place, for example. It's got some history."

The kid laughed. "What kind of history does a Laundromat have?"

"There was a murder here a long time ago," Green replied. "An old lady was beaten to death with a hammer."

"You're kidding. Right here?"

"That's right. She owned the place and came in one night to fill up the soap dispensers and collect the money from the machines. She got robbed and killed."

"No shit? Did they catch who did it?"

Green nodded. "Yeah, a fourteen-year-old. They say he hit her ten times with the hammer. Burst her head open like a melon. There was blood all over the place."

"Gross," the kid said. "Did he get sent away for life?"

"You can't do that to a fourteen-year-old," Green replied. "In this state, young kids can't get sent to prison. They get adjudicated and sent to reform schools. Except now they don't call them that anymore. But they're still under lock and key."

"What happened to him?"

"They had to release him when he was twenty-one. Then he just disappeared."

"Maybe he learned his lesson."

Green nodded. "Yeah, he got reformed, I bet. I guess there's hope for all of us."

"That sounds sarcastic," the kid said. "Are you a cop?"

Green laughed. "No, but I guess you could call me a criminologist."

The dryer buzzer sounded. The kid gathered up his stuff and went to get his clothes. "So, you're a teacher."

"More like a student of criminal behavior," Green said as he followed along.

"Graduate school?" the kid asked, eyeing Green as he crammed his laundry into a backpack.

"Doing some research," Green replied elliptically with a nod.

"Well, with all the murders in town lately, you must be staying pretty busy," the kid said as he zipped the backpack closed.

"Ain't that the truth," Green replied with a toothy grin.

The kid strapped on the backpack, said good-bye, and walked across the street toward the college. Green sat on one of the dryers and looked around. Except for new machines and a fresh paint job, not much had changed since the night he'd killed that old lady.

Because it predated his transformation to Samuel Green, the murder didn't count in the usual sense. None of the early ones did. They all belonged to someone who'd not yet learned to be thoughtful, studious, and deliberate about murder.

Still, it had been a turning point in his life. Because no

one had believed that his parents abused him—they were, after all, respected, upstanding citizens—he'd spent seven more years in hell at home, only to be followed by incarceration at the Boys' School in Springer, where he'd surely been reformed.

He hadn't meant to kill the old lady, but she'd resisted, and he needed that money to run away. So he hit her with the hammer, and it felt so good he did it again and again until her head was a bloody mess and she was lying on the floor.

The washing machine slowed to a stop. He transferred the clothes to a dryer and started thinking about a way to find out where Kerney and his wife where staying. It could be anywhere: a hotel, a friend's house, one of those short-term vacation rentals, or even a bed-and-breakfast. Wherever they were, Green was pretty sure Kerney had arranged for 24/7 police protection to keep his wife safe.

Earlier in the day, he'd spent a couple of wasted hours listening to police radio traffic on his scanner, hoping he could locate them that way. When that didn't work, he thought about following cops around town to see if one would lead him to them, but abandoned the idea as impractical. He needed to do something that would draw Kerney and the wife out into the open.

What would get them scrambling? He ran down a list of possible events in his mind and stopped when he got to the house that Kerney was building. From what he'd seen at the construction site, a lot of money was being poured into it. Although the horse barn was metal and the house was being made with adobe, there was enough wood lying around to start a really nice range fire, which would probably bring Kerney and his wife running.

The idea of arson appealed to Samuel Green. All he needed to do was to find another way in to avoid being spotted by anybody on the main ranch road. That shouldn't be too hard. On the east boundary of Kerney's land a railroad spur and a maintenance road ran from the Lamy junction to Santa Fe. In the evening, he would check it out to see how close he could get by car.

Even if he had to hoof it a bit, the site was remote enough to give him time to get away before the fire trucks arrived. Then he'd find a place near the highway to wait for Kerney to appear. After that, he'd just follow him back to town.

It should work. But if it didn't, there was still the fire to look forward to. He could picture flames raging in a night sky, turning the grassland charcoal black, burning up all the construction material lying around, maybe even getting hot enough to buckle the steel horse barn and kill all the big piñon trees.

It was too bad that the explosion and fire in Mescalero had been kept from spreading, too bad that he'd been forced to leave in a hurry and miss the enjoyment of it all.

Green took a deep breath to calm down and think straight. Before he got too excited about the plan, he needed to make a trial run to see if it was feasible. He'd do that tonight.

The dryer buzzer pulled his thoughts away from the scheme. He folded his clothes neatly, placed them inside the pillowcase, and took one last look around the Laundromat. It had been a real kick to visit the scene of his first crime and tell the college kid about it.

Bone-tired from a lack of sleep, Kerney sat at his desk and tried to stay focused as Sal Molina and Cruz Tafoya gave him an update. Clayton Istee was in Socorro with Ramona Pino and Russell Thorpe. Although there strictly to observe, Clayton was helping out with the canvass of Olsen's friends and acquaintances to gain information about his recent behavior and state of mind.

"That's fine with me," Kerney said, brushing aside the unasked question about Clayton's role in the investigation.

"So far, they've got nothing," Tafoya said, "except for the fact that nobody's seen Olsen for the past two weeks. He didn't have many friends, and those who have been interviewed reported he seemed okay. No aberrant behavior, no verbal preoccupation about his criminal past, and no talk about a last-minute vacation to Scotland."

"That fits with what Olsen's supervisor and coworkers told Detective Pino," Molina added.

"Also, the letters Olsen sent to his mother over the years contained no hint that he was plotting revenge or planning to go on a murder spree," Tafoya said.

"I doubt he'd admit that to his mother," Kerney said. "What about Chacon's interviews at the penitentiary?"

"It was a mixed bag," Molina replied. "The two other perps in the rape-murder case thought Olsen was more than capable of killing again. Of course, they laid the whole thing at Olsen's feet. The Aryan brother who turned Olsen into his bitch doesn't buy it. He pretty much said Olsen was a poser and a whiner while he was in the slam."

Kerney looked at Tafoya. "Do you think Olsen's mother held back information about his whereabouts?"

"No, I think she was genuinely upset that he's missing."

"So, except for Charles Stewart and Archie Schroder, who probably have their own agendas, nobody else sees Olsen as a stone-cold killer," Kerney said.

"That's affirmative," Molina said, "and according to Probation and Parole, Olsen was the star of Victoria Drake's caseload, a model parolee who went on to get a full pardon and his voting rights restored."

Kerney picked up the list of seized evidence Ramona Pino had faxed to Molina and waved it at him. "How do we explain all the goodies that were found at Olsen's house? Or the fact that we have a police artist sketch that looks a hell of a lot like Olsen, and that's based on information from reliable, local witnesses?"

"Who encountered him near one of the crime scenes," Tafoya noted.

Molina shrugged. "It gets even more confusing. Sergeant Istee found tire tracks from the blue van at Olsen's house, so we know for certain the vehicle was there. He also found evidence that someone may have been kept prisoner in a utility room inside the house, and two footprints that match those found on your property but don't square up with Olsen's shoe size. The crime scene techs are on it."

Kerney rubbed his hand over his chin. "Anything else?"

"Olsen left his passport and six hundred dollars in traveler's checks behind," Molina said. "They were hidden in a coffee can in the kitchen pantry. Why would he do that if he wasn't planning to go back there? And if he was planning to return, why would he leave so much physical evidence that connected him to the murders lying around for us to find?"

Kerney held up two fingers. "Add to that these two questions: Who, if anyone, was held captive, and why did Olsen kill Victoria Drake? Olsen had to know it would lead us right to him."

"He made a mistake," Tafoya replied.

"That's what I was hoping for last night," Kerney said. "But I'm not so sure this is it."

"He wants us to know who he is," Molina said.

"Maybe, but let's dig a little deeper."

"We have one new possible lead," Molina said, pulling a piece of paper out of his case file. "The techs found fingerprints in the engine compartment of the van that belong to an ex-con in Tucson. The guy's an auto mechanic who did a dime for armed robbery. I've got the Tucson PD tracking him down."

"Good," Kerney said as he pushed his chair back and stood. "Get Pino started on looking into Olsen's finances. If Sergeant Istee is willing to continue to help out, all the better." He picked up his file folder. "Is this everything?"

"Right up to the minute," Molina said, "except for the photographs we took of the protestors outside the building. Olsen wasn't with them. Do you want me to get you copies?"

"Not now," Kerney said as he walked to the door. "I'll be at Andy Baca's house if you need me."

Kerney left headquarters and drove to Andy's house with an eye glued to the rearview mirror looking for a tail. There was none. He waved to the patrol officer parked at the curb and walked to the front door, wondering if he had anything positive about the investigation to tell Sara. It sure didn't seem so.

Chapter 12

The three agents left for Santa Fe with the evidence just as the crime scene unit arrived. While techs examined the utility room, Clayton, Thorpe, and Pino went looking for the people in Olsen's address book that they hadn't been able to contact by telephone. All were local and relatively easy to track down at work.

Clayton finished his in-person interviews first and drove back to Olsen's house. Everyone he'd talked to was unaware that Olsen was supposedly on vacation in Scotland, but they all simply shrugged it off as Noel's quirky ways. According to the informants, Olsen had a habit of dropping out of the social scene for long periods of time, only to eventually resurface at his favorite watering hole, some community event, or a party. Apparently, the two most consistent things Olsen did was work hard at his job and play on a coed volleyball team during the fall league season.

Several people noted that Olsen had a strong bias against gay men and, to their knowledge, never dated any women, at least none that they knew of. When they encountered Olsen in town after one of his frequent unsocial spells, he'd be polite and joke about having been in one of his solitary moods. No one found him or thought him any stranger than the other techies or eggheads who worked at the college.

Inside Olsen's house, the crime scene techs had expanded their search to the bedroom. Clayton went into the home office and paged through the folders he'd emptied out of a file cabinet and dumped on the floor earlier in the day. One of the folders contained bank statements, the most recent a month old. It showed a combined checking and savings account balance of just over five thousand dollars. No checks in large amounts had cleared.

He scanned more files and found an annual pension fund statement which hadn't been touched, an up-to-date home mortgage payment book, and credit card statements with low balances.

Clayton searched unsuccessfully for Olsen's checkbook and then went back to the bank statement. According to the closing date, Olsen should have received a new statement. Clayton didn't remember seeing any unopened mail in the house.

He checked to make sure the mail hadn't been overlooked, and then walked to the mailbox at the end of the long driveway. It was stuffed full, mostly with junk flyers, a few credit card solicitations, an appointment reminder from a dentist, the latest issue of an engineering society magazine and the bank statement.

He opened the envelope. Olsen had written a two-thousand-dollar check made out to cash.

Clayton dialed Pino's cell-phone number. "This is

Sergeant Istee," he said when she answered. "Are you free to talk?"

"Yeah," Ramona said, "I just finished my last interview. Are you done?"

"Yes. When, exactly, did Olsen ask his boss for vacation time?"

"Just a minute," Ramona said. "Here it is. On the twelfth of this month."

"He cashed a check for two thousand dollars the day before," Clayton said.

"So he did take quite a bit of money with him."

"Yeah, but not all of it. He left over three thousand in the bank," Clayton replied.

"Which brings us back to the question of why he left his passport and traveler's checks behind," Ramona said.

"It was the largest withdrawal he'd made in the last eight months. I'm going to the bank now."

"You'll need a court order to get the records."

"I'm not interested in the paper trail," Clayton said. "I want to see the video surveillance tapes."

"Ten-four," Ramona said. "I'll meet you back at Olsen's."

"The techs are still working the scene."

"Have they got anything?"

"I haven't asked."

"I'll see you there," Ramona said.

Russell Thorpe sat in his unit outside what once was Walter Holbrook's house and wrote up his last field interview note, which didn't take long to finish. Holbrook had quit his job at the college some time back, divorced his wife, and moved to California. The ex-wife, who ran a private counseling practice out of the house, hadn't heard from him in months. She remembered seeing Noel Olsen at Holbrook's volleyball games and talking to him casually once or twice. She gave Russell a phone number where the ex could be reached.

Russell had hoped to score some important new information about Olsen. Instead, all he got were comments that the guy didn't like queers, didn't have a girlfriend, didn't talk about his personal life, but played a solid game of volleyball.

He put his clipboard away, closed the driver's-side window, and turned up the air conditioner a notch. State police cruisers were painted white over black, and heated up quickly in the New Mexico sun. On day shifts in the summer, they turned into blast furnaces the minute the air conditioning was cut off.

Russell thought about the blue van. The whole deal with the vehicle bothered him. Assuming Olsen was the perp, why had he used it to go back and forth to Santa Fe? Why did he go to the trouble to buy the junker, get it fixed up, and steal plates for it? Was it part of a plan to keep Chief Kerney from zeroing in on him? If so, why deliberately blow the scheme by killing Victoria Drake?

He wondered if he'd discovered another anomaly. The thought made him think about Clayton Istee. He liked the man and the way he processed information, paid attention to the details, and asked smart questions. Even Ramona Pino, who was no rookie, had seemed impressed with Istee.

Russell decided to follow Clayton's example. Along the road to Olsen's house he'd seen Bureau of Land

Management signs posted on fences. He reached under the front seat for a binder that contained reference materials and pulled out a map from a plastic sleeve that showed all the public land holdings in the state. Except for several small private inholdings, the hills east of Socorro where Olsen lived were owned by the state and federal agencies.

Why had Olsen picked such a remote place to live? Did he simply want privacy while he plotted and carried out the murders? If Clayton was right about someone being kept prisoner in the utility room, that made sense. But what if he was wrong?

Russell's first assignment as a rookie had been at the Las Vegas District, which covered a lot of big empty territory. He knew by experience that country people were usually very observant.

Maybe one of them had seen the blue van, or knew something interesting about Olsen. Thorpe figured it might be worthwhile to talk to the neighbors.

Noel Olsen did his banking at a state-chartered institution situated on the main drag close to the old plaza. A block away down a side street was one of the best western-wear stores in the state. Locally owned, it catered to real ranchers and cowboys, which meant that Clayton could always find jeans that fit, hats and boots that didn't cost an arm and a leg, and reasonably priced western-style shirts that weren't ridiculously gaudy. There were equally good deals on clothes for Grace and the kids.

Many of the store's customers were Navajos from the remote Alamo Band Reservation in the northwest corner of the county, and the place had a homey feel to it, with polite, friendly clerks who made shopping there enjoyable.

On family trips to Albuquerque, they'd often stop to do a little shopping at the store and have lunch at the restaurant in the old hotel a few steps away.

Inside the bank, Clayton met with a vice president, showed her the canceled check, explained the nature of his inquiry, and asked if he could view the video surveillance tapes for the day in question.

The woman, a round-faced Anglo with an easy smile, took Clayton to a back room, found the tapes, and sat with him while he watched the monitor, using the remote to fast-forward through the frames of customers at the teller stations inside the bank. Olsen wasn't on the tape.

"What, exactly, are you looking for?" she asked.

"I'm not sure," Clayton replied. "Can I view the tape from the drive-up window camera?"

The woman got up and replaced the tape. Clayton pressed the fast-forward button, and froze it when a van came into view. He did a slow-motion picture search, watching Olsen lower the van window and reach for the transaction tube. He stopped the tape. The passenger seat was empty.

Clayton advanced the tape frame by frame and watched Olsen conduct his transaction. He didn't look very happy, and twice he turned his head and said something over his right shoulder. A curtain on the side window blocked the view into the rear of the van. But it didn't matter. Clayton was certain another person was in the vehicle with Olsen. He ran through the frames again just to be sure.

"I may need a copy of this," he told the woman.

"You saw something?"

"Yeah," Clayton said, thinking that he might have been wrong about Olsen working solo. "But don't ask me what it means."

Two of the private parcels were tracts of vacant land, and a third looked to be an abandoned mining claim. Thorpe took the turn-off from the county road and traveled over rock-strewn ruts deep into the hills to a small ranch house situated in a shallow finger of a valley.

It wasn't much of a place to look at. The front porch of the weather-beaten house was filled with wooden crates, barrels, and piles of rusted junk. To one side stood an empty corral made out of slat boards, a windmill that fed water to a stock tank, and a broken loading chute. Except for an old pickup truck with current license plate tags parked on the side of the house, the place seemed unoccupied.

The sound of Thorpe's cruiser brought a man out of the house. He stood with his hands in his pockets and watched as Russell approached.

"Don't get many visitors out here," the man said. Tall and deeply tanned, the man's face showed years of wear and a day's growth of white whiskers. "Especially law officers."

"I expect not," Russell replied, extending his hand. "I'm Officer Thorpe."

The man shook Thorpe's hand. "Frank Lyons. What can I do for you?"

"Tell me what you know about Noel Olsen."

"Can't say I know much," Lyons said. "I met him

when he bought the place and moved in some years back, and I wave to him when I see him on the road. Occasionally, I'll run into him in town. That's where I hang my hat. I only come out here once in a while to keep an eye on things. Damn land isn't good for squat."

"Have you ever seen him driving a blue van?" Thorpe gave Lyons a full description.

Lyons shook his head. "Nope, just that little car he scoots around in."

"When was the last time you talked to him?"

"About two months ago, when we were both fueling our vehicles at a gas station."

"What did you talk about?"

"I asked him if he'd gotten a letter from the BLM, offering to buy up his property. They want to purchase all the inholdings and turn these hills into a wildlife preserve, which is just dandy with me. They quoted a fair price. Of course, knowing the government, I'll probably be long gone by the time the deal closes. Still, it'll put some cash money in my grandchildren's pockets."

"What did Olsen have to say about the offer?"

"He didn't like it. Said he was gonna turn them down, which I think would be plain stupid, because if the feds want your land, they'll find a way to get it. Just ask some of the old-timers who got booted off the north end of the missile range back in the fifties."

"Did he say why he didn't like the offer?" Thorpe asked.

"Said he liked his privacy," Lyons said with a laugh. "Well, he's sure got that. About the only thing worth a plug nickel in these hills is the view across the river to the mountains."

"Have you ever visited Olsen?"

Lyons shook his head. "He put a gate across his access road soon after he moved in. I took that to mean he wasn't interested in having unexpected company come calling."

"Are there any other neighbors?" Thorpe asked.

"Not nearby and living on the land," Lyons replied. "Jett Kirby owns a couple of sections, so do Cisco Tripp and Roman Mendez. But, like me, they live in town."

"Thanks for your time," Thorpe said.

"Has Olsen got trouble?" Lyons asked.

"He's gone missing."

"Sorry to hear that," Lyons said. "Good luck finding him."

Thorpe drove away in full agreement with Lyons's take on the land. It was parched, rocky, and desolate, chalk-colored and brown, and only cactus and scrub brush seemed to thrive on it. But when he topped out of the small valley the view was stupendous. Below was the fertile green expanse of the Rio Grande River valley, and beyond that were the mountain crests west of Socorro, blue-black against a bright afternoon sky.

Russell wasn't sure he'd learned anything worthwhile doing his one-man canvass. But he'd run it by Clayton Istee and Ramona Pino anyway.

Clayton and Thorpe arrived at Olsen's house within minutes of each other, and Ramona convened a conference at the front of Clayton's unit. Inside the house, techs were vacuuming floors, looking for latent prints, and gathering hair and fiber samples.

"What have we got?" Ramona asked as she leaned against the hood of the Lincoln County 4×4 patrol vehicle.

"Where do you want to start?" Clayton asked.

"Let's stay in sequence," Ramona said. "The interviews first."

Thorpe nodded. "I didn't learn much on my end, except that Olsen doesn't like gays, doesn't have a girlfriend, keeps his personal life private, and plays well with others on the volleyball team."

"Roger that," Ramona said. "I heard the same thing."

Clayton nodded. "Apparently, he hasn't had an intimate relationship with a woman since he moved to Socorro. At least not one that anyone knows about."

"Maybe he's asexual," Ramona said.

"That would be quite a behavior change for a convicted rapist," Clayton said.

"No one I talked to said anything about him being gay, bisexual, or asexual," Russell said, "and they all seemed like straight people to me."

"You can't always tell by appearances," Ramona said.

"Maybe he's just a gay-basher," Thorpe said as he hunkered down in front of the 4×4.

"What did you learn at the bank?" Ramona asked Clayton.

Clayton looked vexed. "It's another one of those anomalies. I reviewed the surveillance tapes. Olsen drove the van to a drive-up window to cash his check, and he had somebody with him when he did it."

"You've lost me," Thorpe said.

Clayton explained about the bank statement and the two-thousand-dollar withdrawal.

"So maybe he does have an accomplice," Ramona said. "Did you get a picture of the passenger?"

Clayton shook his head. "There wasn't one to get.

Whoever was with him was in the back of the van, out of sight. But Olsen talked to that person twice, speaking over his shoulder."

Clayton looked at the house. "Maybe it was the person Olsen had chained up in the utility room, if the techs haven't blown away that little theory of mine."

"The techs say the small stains on the water heater platform are blood," Ramona said, "and the dried fluid on the utility room floor is probably urine. They also found multiple prints on the platform and identified five different sets of latents in the bedroom."

"That's interesting," Thorpe said, as he stood up. "The guy doesn't date women, hates queers, but he's had five different people in his bedroom."

"It's more than interesting, especially if the prints in the utility room are from a possible unknown victim," Clayton said.

"I agree," Ramona said. "I asked the people I talked to if they hung out, partied, or had dinner with Olsen at his house. None of them had ever been here."

"I heard the same thing," Clayton said.

"Ditto that," Thorpe said. "I also talked to a neighbor, about the only one Olsen has, who hasn't set foot on the place since Olsen moved in. He said the BLM wants to buy all the inholdings and turn these hills into a wildlife sanctuary. Olsen told him he wasn't going to sell."

"With all the evidence we found, that's not surprising," Ramona said.

Clayton glanced to his left and right, looking for fences. He spotted one a good distance off on a rise. "I wonder how much land Olsen owns."

"From what I could tell, looking at my map, I'd guess no more than eighty acres," Russell replied. "It shows as a rectangle that runs straight back from the road."

"You can hide a hell of a lot of stuff on eighty acres," Clayton said. "Maybe we should take a look."

"It wouldn't hurt," Ramona said.

Sal Molina and Cruz Tafoya met the agents who'd brought the evidence up from Socorro at state police headquarters. Because Sal didn't want any screw-ups in the chain of custody, he'd decided to receive the seized items on the spot and immediately submit all of it to the state police lab for analysis.

With the three agents helping, they got the paperwork done and the evidence into the lab in less than an hour.

Henry Guillen, a senior tech who specialized in hair and fiber analysis, stopped Molina as he carried the last box into the lab.

"Come see me before you leave," Guillen said.

Sal nodded, dropped off the box, and waited for the receiving tech to inventory the contents and sign the chain of custody receipt. He grabbed Tafoya, who was on his way out, and asked him to have the fingerprint tech take a fast look at the cell phone and the scrapbook. Then he went looking for Henry Guillen, who was peering into a microscope, scratching the back of his neck with one hand and adjusting the lens with the other.

"Did you get the official word that the vic in the van died from rat poison?" Guillen asked without looking up.

"I did," Molina said.

"What an ugly way to die," Guillen said, glancing away from the microscope. "All those convulsions and muscle spasms. No wonder she flipped her wig."

"What are you talking about, Henry?"

Guillen tapped the microscope and stepped away from the table. "These hairs and fibers were found in the van. Take a look."

Molina looked into the eyepiece and saw what appeared to be several blond strands of hair. "They look the same to me."

"It's really a combination of human hair and modacrylic fiber of exactly the same length," Guillen said. "Modacrylic is a long-chain polymer used in clothing, bedding, paint, carpets, curtains, upholstery—all kinds of stuff. The only producers are in Japan. These strands came from a wig."

"How can you tell?" Molina asked as he raised up from the eyepiece.

"The combination of hair and fiber, plus the ends are curled, which means they were doubled over and machine sewn into the wig cap."

"Can you identify the manufacturer?"

Guillen laughed. "Sure, give me a round-trip plane ticket, a hefty expense account, and a year in Asia, and I'll get back to you."

"Why Asia?" Molina asked.

"Because that's where most of the cheap wigs and hairpieces are made."

"Victoria Drake was a brunette," Molina said, "with a full head of hair."

"Well, somebody who was in the van wore a blond wig," Guillen said. "Maybe your suspect or some other victim."

"I'll check it out," Molina said, as he patted Henry on the back.

He went down the corridor to the fingerprint section, where Cruz Tafoya was watching the tech at work. "Anything?" he asked.

"The cell phone has Olsen's prints on it," Tafoya said. "He's checking a page in the scrapbook now."

The tech had carefully peeled off one of the newspaper articles taped to a page and was scanning both documents with a laser light. He turned them over and repeated the process.

"No prints here," the tech said, "and none on the inside or outside of the binder. But I've got a lot left to examine."

"Let's us know what you find," Molina said.

Outside, there was a steady whine of traffic along Cerrillos Road. Molina watched it for a moment before turning to Tafoya. "Henry Guillen says somebody in the van wore a blond wig. Olsen has long blond hair, or at least he did. Call his mother and ask her if he's balding and wears a wig to hide it."

Tafoya checked his pocket notebook for a number and dialed his cell phone. It ran a long time before Meredith Olsen picked up and answered in a blurred voice. Cruz asked the question.

"Oh, no," Meredith Olsen replied. "He has shiny, long, baby-fine hair. I used to curl it for him when he was a little boy. He looked so beautiful."

Cruz thanked Meredith Olsen and clipped the cell phone to his belt. "No wig," he said.

"It could be that Clayton Istee's theory about another victim is on target," Molina said.

"You'd think Olsen's prints would be all over that scrapbook he put together on Chief Kerney," Tafoya said.

"I know it," Molina said.

Cruz Tafoya shook his head. "Things aren't jibing."

"I know," Molina said.

The men separated and walked to their units. As Molina pulled out of the parking lot, he considered the inconsistencies in the case, tried to reconcile them, and came up short. There were still too many unanswered questions that cast doubt in his mind.

The large guest room at Andy and Gloria's house had a separate entrance off the rear patio, a private bath, and two comfortable easy chairs positioned in front of a window that provided a view of the backyard. An antique pine chest under the window was filled with toys used to entertain visiting grandchildren, and a large walk-in closet contained two folding beds and all the necessary linens to accommodate four guests.

Kerney's attempt to brief Sara on the case had suffered from a stream of constant interruptions as phone calls came in from various personnel. It seemed that everybody in the department felt a need to keep Kerney fully informed about each and every new development, no matter how small.

Sara sat in a chair watching Kerney talk to Sal Molina on his cell phone. From what she'd overheard, it was clear the investigation was far from being wrapped up. The evidence seized in Socorro had raised troubling questions, as had the interviews conducted with Olsen's friends and acquaintances. The possibility that Olsen had an accomplice was still up for grabs, as was the theory that there might or might not be another victim.

Sara had tried to keep a sunny disposition and hold back on expressing the feeling of imprisonment that continued to annoy her. Although the two state police agents remained discreetly in the background, their presence was a constant reminder that she was under guard. And Gloria Baca's gracious attempts to put her at ease during the course of the day hadn't diminished her growing sense of uselessness. It wasn't a feeling Sara liked.

Half-listening as Kerney talked to Sal Molina, she told herself the situation was, after all, dangerous. When that didn't work, she told herself that Kerney's effort to keep her out of harm's way was instinctual and protective. She found no comfort in either thought.

Since the day Sara had entered West Point, she'd functioned in a male-dominated world, never once thinking that she couldn't be a man's equal. The bureaucratic barriers didn't faze her, nor did the chauvinistic attitudes of some of her superiors and colleagues. Eventually, the glass ceiling would be shattered and no rank or duty assignment, including combat arms, would be closed to women.

She knew Kerney wasn't a chauvinist, or simply pretending not to be, as many men did. His endearing ability to accept her as an equal without the need to dominate or control had drawn her to him in the first place.

When Kerney disconnected, Sara decided to approach him head-on with the fact she could no longer tolerate the situation. She held up a hand to keep him from talking.

"We have to reclaim our lives, Kerney," she said. "It doesn't matter if a bomb goes off in five minutes, hours, or days and blows us both to kingdom come, I can't stand being held hostage any longer. I want to go back to our own place, visit the new house, and do some shopping for the baby."

Kerney put the cell phone down, rubbed the palms of his hands over his eyes, and let out a deep breath. "That's not such a good idea right now," he said as he raised his head to look at her.

"Maybe not," Sara said, "but we've come through tough times before and survived them. We can do it again."

"Under completely different circumstances," he said.

"I'm not asking for your permission," Sara said. "I want you to call Larry Otero and tell him we're not to be bothered for the next twenty-four hours. Then turn off that damn cell phone and we'll go back to our place and try to organize one day of normal living with no agents hovering around and no interruptions before the baby comes."

Still thinking of all the reasons it was a bad idea, Kerney studied the determined look on Sara's face. "You're sure you want to do this?"

"It's time to stop hiding and go home."

"Will you accept having an officer stationed outside?" Kerney asked.

Sara nodded. "That's agreeable."

"Okay. So what do you want to do first?"

"I'd like to take an evening drive in my new car to see how our house is coming along."

Kerney smiled and flipped open his cell phone. "Give

me a couple of hours in the rack, and it's a date. Why don't you tell Gloria about our change in plans, and I'll let Andy and Larry Otero know."

Sara got out of her chair, kissed him, and went to speak to Gloria. Patrick Brannon gave a wiggle and something told Sara the twenty-four hours she'd demanded might not be as normal as she hoped.

Doing a comprehensive field search of eighty acres was no small task. Using the boundary fences as a guide, the three officers spread out and walked the perimeter of the property before separating at the back fence to sweep down the hill toward the house.

Shrub vegetation, mostly creosote, sage, and broom snakeweed, dominated several rocky terrace slopes, and there were clusters of hedgehog, prickly pear, and barrel cactus growing in pockets of coarse sand. Limestone, sandstone, and shale lined shallow runoff gullies, and gusts of wind raised dust swirls that dulled the pale-green, drought-stricken bunchgrass.

Halfway down the slope, Russell Thorpe spotted a series of five rock cairns arranged in a neat line on a sandy fold in the hillside. He walked to them, wondering what they signified, and noticed that one looked fairly recent. Each cairn was round and no more than three feet high.

He stepped back, knelt down, and pawed at the sand until he hit rock about a foot down. Fifty feet away from the cairns was a small quarry cut into the hillside. There he found a rock pile that matched the stones on the mounds. A wheelbarrow turned upside down leaned against the pile.

As he retraced his footsteps, marking each one with a

stone, Thorpe called out for Clayton and Ramona. They converged on him from the north and south.

"The one on the south side looks to be the most recent," he said as Clayton made a wide loop around the cairns and Ramona took photographs. "The sand gives way to rock about a foot down."

"I make each one to be about ten feet in diameter," Clayton said as he eyed the cairns, "and whatever is under them has drawn coyotes. There's old scat everywhere."

Ramona lowered the camera. "Let's rope off this area and get the techs up here." She slipped on plastic gloves, walked to the newest cairn, and began carefully removing rocks.

"Shouldn't we wait for them?" Thorpe asked before he keyed his handheld.

"There's enough work here for everybody," Clayton said as he joined Ramona at the mound.

Within two hours, three bodies had been partially exhumed.

Two hours of sleep left Kerney feeling better. He came out of the bedroom determined to put the investigation aside and enjoy the evening with Sara, although he did plan to remain cautious and armed. He clipped the holstered .45 to his belt.

The bulge of the .38 in the purse on the kitchen table told him Sara was of a like mind.

"Are you ready to go?" he asked as he entered the living room.

Sara nodded, eased herself off the couch, and held out the car keys.

"Don't you want to drive your new car?" Kerney asked.

"I do, but I'm afraid Patrick Brannon will be a distraction. He's getting restless and acting up."

"Maybe we should just stay here."

Sara shook her head as she put the keys in his hand. "Not a chance. I need to see a beautiful New Mexico sunset on our land, and talk you into letting me add the pergola on the front patio of the house."

"I'm having second thoughts about the swimming pool," Kerney said.

"Because of the water we'd use?" Sara asked.

Since he was warned not to run on the leg, the pool was to be the alternative way to keep his new knee operating at peak efficiency. But he'd been raised on a desert ranch where water was precious, which made the whole idea of a swimming pool uncomfortable.

"It's an indulgence we can do without," Kerney said. "Plus, even with the recent rains, we're still in a drought and probably will be for some time to come."

"Besides, what would the neighbors think?" Sara said with a teasing laugh. "If we installed a pool, none of them would believe for a minute that either of us was really ranch-raised."

Kerney smiled. "It might cause Jack and Irene Burke to wonder."

"I'm way ahead of you." Sara stepped to her grandmother's desk, gathered up the architectural plans, and brought them to Kerney. The swimming pool had been crossed out.

"I think a terraced flower garden with a few shade trees off to one side would be nice. It doesn't have to be something we do right away."

"Let's go see if it'll work," Kerney said.

The doorbell rang. "Whoever it is," Sara said, "send them packing."

Kerney opened up.

"Maybe you shouldn't have turned off all your phones," Andy Baca said with a shake of his head. He was dressed in civvies with his sidearm on his belt. Gloria waved at Kerney from the passenger seat of Andy's pickup truck parked in the driveway.

"This better be important, Andy," Kerney said.

"Look, you don't have to do anything, but I thought you'd want to know that five bodies, all male, have been discovered buried on Olsen's property. We don't know who they are yet or how they died. I've got my people working on it with Pino, Thorpe, Istee, and a team of forensic specialists. They're still uncovering the remains. It will probably take them most of the night to wrap up the preliminary work and get everything up to the medical examiner's office in Albuquerque."

"Dammit," Kerney said.

"It's being handled," Andy said as he turned to Sara. "You know, Gloria mentioned that we still haven't seen the new house you're putting up. She said you're going out there. How about giving us a tour?"

"You're very sneaky, Andy," Sara said, as she stepped to Kerney's side.

Andy grinned. "That's if you don't mind us tagging along behind you."

"Come along," Sara said. "Just let me get my purse."

Chapter 13

Fast-moving clouds drifted over the Jemez Mountains, diffusing the glare of the sun in short bursts, revealing it again and again as shafts of brilliant light cut through the billowing white cumulus caps. Not yet low enough on the horizon to light up the sky with colors, it studded the tips and underbellies of the clouds with a soft pink hue. Passing shadows dotting the basin gave way to patches of dense blue sky that turned hot white as the sun broke through, lighting up a distant peak and exposing a carmine-colored hillside in high relief.

The breathtaking vista pushed all the fears and worries of the week from Sara's mind. She felt lighthearted as she walked Andy and Gloria through the clutter of what would one day be her very first house, showing them the footprint for each room. The crew had started laying the interior adobe walls, and for the first time Sara could see actual room dimensions rather than have to imagine them from the plans.

She'd brought her camera, and as she took snapshots, she excitedly pointed out window placements, fireplace locations, how the entry alcove would give way to the great room, and the view she would have from the kitchen window over the sink.

Finally, she took them out on the recently poured slab for the portal that ran the length of the house, where they stood and looked down on the canyon below. A huge cottonwood glistened pale green along the edge of an arroyo that fanned out across the canyon floor. A slash of exposed limestone glimmered in the escarpment that hid the railroad spur from view.

"We'll hear trains," Sara said, pointing at the ridgeline that hid the tracks from view.

"I love the sound of trains," Gloria said.

"You'll have clear night skies and the Milky Way above you," Andy said.

"And coyotes howling," Kerney added, squeezing Sara's hand.

They stopped talking momentarily to watch a small herd of antelope warily enter the canyon, led by a male who first scanned for danger before beginning to graze. The females and juveniles quickly followed suit.

Sara adjusted the camera lens to zoom in on the herd and snapped the shutter.

"How beautiful," Gloria said in a whisper. "It's paradise."

They walked the perimeter of the house. The curving wall for the courtyard patio had been poured, and Sara showed Gloria where she planned to put the planting beds, how the flagstone walkway would veer off from the main path to an adjacent patio that would be accessed through French doors.

"With a pergola, it would be a perfect, sheltered place to breakfast," she said, eyeing Kerney. "We'd have a lovely view of the pasture, horse barn, the hill beyond, and the tips of the mountains in the distance."

Kerney laughed, put his arm around Sara's waist, and patted her tummy. "Okay, we'll build the pergola," he said as the early evening shadows began to lengthen. He turned to Andy and Gloria. "Are you up for a short drive? I want to show you something."

"What's that?" Andy asked.

"A special place."

The foursome piled into Sara's vehicle. Kerney drove up the hill past the spot were he'd buried Soldier, wound through the rolling grassland and into a draw bracketed by a low, rocky ridgeline, and pulled to a stop where marsh grass and cattails encircled a pond at the foot of a hillock.

"My God," Andy said, climbing out of the SUV, "you've got live water."

"Which has never run dry," Kerney said, following Andy to the edge of the pool.

"Unbelievable," Andy said. Any constant source of live water away from the rivers and streams was a rarity to be treasured in arid New Mexico.

"A hacienda stood here two hundred years ago," Kerney said, pointing to the rubble of the rock footings. "For a long time, it was the main stop on the cartage road from Galisteo to Santa Fe."

"And it's on your land?" Andy asked.

Kerney nodded and pointed at animal tracks in the soft earth at the edge of the water. "Yep, and it comes with a resident bobcat, who hunts rabbits here at night. I've found fresh tracks and kill sites just about every time I've come out here."

He watched Gloria and Sara kneel down to examine pieces of partially exposed petrified wood scattered under the base of an ancient willow tree on the other side of the pond.

Suddenly, Sara stood upright and looked at Kerney with a serene smile on her face. "It's time to go," she said.

"We've got a good twenty minutes before sunset," Kerney replied, glancing at the sky.

"It's time to go to the hospital," she said as she patted her belly and moved toward the SUV.

"Right now?"

"I think so."

Kerney gave his cell phone to Andy and raced to Sara's side. "Call the doctor. Press speed dial, then nine. Tell her we're on the way."

Sara laughed. "Slow down, cowboy. I don't need you four-wheeling me over hill and dale. We've got time."

"Let's go," Kerney said, easing Sara into the vehicle, not realizing that both Andy and Gloria were already on board.

He ground the gears putting the vehicle into motion, and Andy laughed at him from the backseat.

Samuel Green left his car on a point beside the railroad tracks where the sand looked too deep to pull through, checked his watch to time himself, and started walking at a fast pace in the direction of Kerney's property. He ducked through the barbed-wire fence, scrambled to the top of the ridgeline, saw the outline of a pickup truck at the construction site, and dropped quickly to the ground.

He slipped off the backpack, took out a pair of binoculars and carefully scanned the vehicle. It wasn't Kerney's truck. He wondered if security had been hired to watch the place at night after the crew went home. That would put his plan in jeopardy.

After making sure the truck was unoccupied, Green scanned the building site and horse barn several times for movement before deciding the pickup had probably been left behind by one of the workers.

He waited a few more minutes before he moved quickly off the ridgeline, loosening small rocks that cascaded down the slope in front of him. At the base of the incline he zigzagged in a lope across the rangeland, using small stands of piñon trees for cover, keeping his eyes fixed on the truck and house just in case someone came into view.

Green stopped at the last grove of trees about two hundred yards from the truck and used the binoculars again to search for activity before moving into the open pasture. The dry grass cracked under his feet. It would burn nicely.

Halfway across the field he heard the sound of a train clattering over the tracks, followed by the blast of its horn. Over his right shoulder the headlights of a car appeared at the top of the hill behind the horse barn. Green wheeled and ran back for the cover of the trees, cursing his bad luck and hoping he hadn't been spotted.

"Oh, the sound of a train," Gloria Baca said from the backseat as they passed Soldier's grave again. "How lovely."

At the top of the hill, Kerney saw the figure of a man

freeze in the pasture, turn, and start running for the trees. He pressed the accelerator.

"He'll make the trees before we can reach him," Sara said, reaching for her camera. "Stop the car."

"We've got to get you to the hospital."

"Stop the damn car, Kerney," Sara said as she set the camera on automatic zoom.

Kerney hit the brakes. From the backseat he heard Andy calling out his troops on the cell phone. Sara leaned out the passenger window and took pictures just before the man reached the cover of some trees.

"Okay, let's go," she said pulling her head back into the car.

"Drop me off at my truck," Andy said, as Kerney drove down the hill.

"Don't chase him," Kerney said.

"I've got units rolling code three," Andy said. "I'll head for the highway and coordinate from there."

"Have someone meet the train in Santa Fe," Kerney said.

"Why the train?" Andy asked as he jumped out of the SUV.

Kerney watched in frustration as the distant figure of the running man disappeared over the ridgeline. "There's no reason for the engineer to sound his horn. The nearest railroad crossing is several miles from here. Something caught his attention, and the runner is heading for the tracks."

"Consider it done," Andy said, as he held out his hand. "Give me the camera, so I can get the film developed."

Sara passed it through the open window. "Don't you dare lose my pictures of the house."

"Wouldn't think of it," Andy said as he gave her Kerney's cell phone and reached for his own. "Gloria will stay with you."

"Good," Sara replied, reaching back for Gloria's hand to give it a squeeze. "At least I'll have someone with me who knows what I'm going through."

A contraction made her catch her breath and let go of Gloria's hand. "Start driving, Kerney," she said. "And this time, please go a little faster."

"Catch this guy, Andy," Kerney said as he hit the gas, leaving Baca standing by his pickup, choking on the dust thrown up by the rear tires.

Three squad cars with flashing emergency lights sped by as Samuel Green impatiently waited at a traffic light near the Interstate that would take him back to Santa Fe. It wasn't the cops that worried him; he'd ripped a gash in the palm of his hand climbing through the barbed wire fence to get to his car. A deep cut that bled freely, it had soaked through the rag he'd wrapped around it.

The light turned green and he drove to town with his hand throbbing in pain. At the hospital parking lot, he inspected the wound. It ran from just above the wrist to his forefinger, and he'd lost a patch of skin. He needed stitches and a tetanus shot for sure.

He clenched the rag in his hand to slow the bleeding and thought things through. The car at the ranch had been too far away for anyone in it to get a clear look at him. Besides that, the light had faded and he'd been running with his back to the vehicle, so nobody saw his face. Finally, the cops would be looking for Olsen anyway, not him.

But his plan to burn Kerney's ranch and bring him out in the open was now off the table. He couldn't risk going back. He'd have to find another way to learn where Kerney was hiding out.

He decided to calm down, stop thinking about Kerney, and get his hand fixed. He would use a fictitious name and pay cash for the hospital bill, so he couldn't be traced.

Inside the urgent care center, a nurse looked at his hand and took him directly to an exam room. She cleaned and inspected the wound as he fed her a line of bull about cutting himself as he was taking down an old fence on his mother's property.

She shook her head sympathetically, placed his hand in a bowl of peroxide solution, let it sit there for a few minutes, and then elevated it on a tray table. "When was your last tetanus shot?" she asked.

"Years ago when I was a kid," Green replied.

"Leave your hand where it is," the nurse said. "I'll be back in a few minutes to give you a shot and stitch you up."

Sara was taken directly from the admitting area to labor and delivery, where the doctor was waiting. Dr. Carol Jojoya finished her exam of Sara, stripped off her gloves, and stepped back from the bed. Jojoya had a slightly dimpled chin, thick, curly dark hair, impish brown eyes, and an easy, calming manner.

"I think we'll keep you overnight," Jojoya said to Sara.

"What's wrong?" Kerney asked, jitters getting the best of him.

"Nothing," Jojoya said with a reassuring smile. Her eyes held a hint of amusement. "The baby isn't quite ready to make his appearance, but there's no sense in having Sara go home just to turn around again and come back."

"You're telling us everything?" Kerney asked, as he stepped over to Sara, who shook her head to signal that he was acting silly.

"My only concerns," Jojoya said, "are that Sara has a narrow pelvis, and is about to deliver her first child. Sometimes those factors can make childbirth a bit difficult on the mother."

"How difficult?" Kerney demanded.

Jojoya laughed. "Not to worry. Your wife is very physically fit. It's just that first births can take a little more time. At the worst, your wife will probably be exhausted and sore when it's all over."

"That's it?" Kerney asked.

"That sounds like enough to me," Sara said.

"Relax, Chief Kerney," Jojoya said. "Everything is normal. We'll leave Sara here and wait for nature to take its course."

"I want her in a private room," Kerney said.

Jojoya shook her head. "She doesn't get a room until she's done her job."

"Then I'll stay with her," Kerney said.

"Go away, Kerney," Sara said with a wave of a hand. "Just post a security guard nearby and get back here in time to meet me in the delivery room."

"I'm not going anywhere," Kerney said, "and it will be a police officer who's stationed outside, not a security guard."

"What on earth for?" Jojoya asked, her voice ringing with surprise.

"Don't ask him to explain," Sara said. "Just accept it as a good thing to do."

Jojoya looked at the couple, decided not to probe, and patted the edge of the bed. "I'll be around," she said. "Just press the buzzer when the contractions start up again."

Jojoya left and Kerney leaned over and kissed Sara's cheek. "You're all right?"

"Peachy," Sara replied, looking decidedly uncomfortable.

"I'll arrange a few things and be back in a flash."

Sara gave him a weak smile and waved him away with her hand.

In the area just outside Sara's exam room, Kerney met with Gloria Baca, filled her in on Sara's condition, and made arrangements by cell phone to post one officer at the hospital and have another take Gloria home.

Gloria went in to see how Sara was doing, and Kerney used the time to call Andy Baca.

"So, are you a father?" Andy asked.

"Not yet," Kerney replied. "It may be some time before the baby comes, so I'm here for the duration. I'm sending Gloria home with one of my officers. How's the search going?"

"We missed him," Andy said. "But the train engineer reported he blew his horn as a warning because a car was parked on the railroad right-of-way access road. Maximum speed on the spur line is fifteen miles per hour, so he got a pretty good look at the vehicle. It was an older, full-size domestic sedan, possibly an Oldsmobile or Buick, white in color, with Arizona plates. I've got people out there now looking for evidence, but they're probably not going to find much until daylight."

"Where are you?" Kerney asked.

"Halfway to town, taking Sara's camera to the lab. I've got a tech standing by to print the photos she took. I'll bring them to you ASAP."

"Thanks, Andy."

"Best to Sara," Andy replied before he cut the connection.

Kerney looked through the open door into the waiting room. A young mother paced the floor holding a crying infant, and an older man with a swollen cheek sat reading a magazine. A bald-headed man with a bandaged hand came out of an exam room, glanced at Kerney, and walked off in the direction of the billing office, holding a piece of paper. From the blood on his pants, it appeared he'd cut himself badly.

Kerney felt more awake than he had in several days. The pending arrival of Patrick Brannon had gotten his adrenaline pumping. He found Jojoya, who told him it might be some time before the baby was delivered, and went to check on Sara.

"You again," she said, as he gave her another kiss.

"Yeah, me," Kerney said. "Looks like we're gonna be here for a while."

"Why don't you find something to do?" Sara said. "I don't need a nervous, expectant father hovering over me."

"Am I acting silly?" Kerney asked.

"Almost."

Kerney sat in the chair next to the bed, called Sal

Molina and told him to gather up Cruz Tafoya plus all the case materials from the Socorro crime scene investigation and get to the hospital pronto.

Sara smiled as he hung up. "That's better."

"I'm staying until the officer arrives."

"You're damn right you are," Sara replied.

Samuel Green quickly paid his urgent-care bill with cash and returned to the waiting area to find Kerney nowhere in sight. His initial shock of seeing Kerney had rapidly given way to the happy thought that he no longer needed to search for him. But now Kerney was gone, and Green wondered if he was back to square one. He decided not to hang around inside hoping Kerney would reappear, and walked through the automatic doors to the parking lot just as two city police squad cars pulled to the curb.

Green tensed up until the two cops passed him without a second look. He stepped between one of the police cruisers and the SUV parked in front of it and stopped. The temporary license sticker in the rear window of the SUV was made out to Sara Brannon. Because of the pain in his hand, he'd paid no attention to the vehicle on his way in.

Had Kerney brought his wife in to have the baby? Or had she called Kerney and driven herself to the hospital? Were the two cops inside to provide security, or was Kerney there on official business?

Samuel Green needed clarity. He walked to the side of the building. There were no ambulances, police, or fire department vehicles outside the emergency room entrance, and he couldn't find Kerney's unmarked unit in the almost empty parking lot.

Kerney might have left, but Green doubted it. He sat in his car waiting to see what happened next. Within several minutes, a hospital security officer took up a position outside the urgent care entrance, and a second security guard entered the lot in a hospital vehicle, cruising past parked cars.

Green drove off the hospital property to a nearby medical office building where he had a clear view of the entrance, and settled down to watch. When Kerney came outside, moved his wife's vehicle from the curb to a parking space, and went back into the hospital, Green knew for sure the baby was on the way.

Now he could start thinking about the exciting times that lay ahead. The mental picture of a helpless Kerney watching as he brought the hammer down on the baby's head made Green chuckle in anticipation.

After the officer came, Kerney got permission from the hospital administrator on duty to use a staff training room. Sal Molina and Cruz Tafoya showed up within minutes and immediately asked Kerney about Sara's condition. Although he remained anxious and concerned, he told them everything was just fine.

They joined him at the long table and Molina arranged a number of digital photographs in front of Kerney.

"Pino sent these up by computer," Molina said, as he leaned over Kerney's shoulder. "They're shots of five circular burial mounds, about ten feet in circumference and three feet tall, taken before excavation began."

Molina lined up another set of pictures. "These are shots of the individual mounds with the remains exposed. We don't yet know the causes of death, and it will take dental records to identify the victims. But we do know that Olsen mined rock from a nearby quarry to build them. His fingerprints were all over the wheelbarrow and tools left at the pit."

Molina took a seat and continued. "Based on the decomposition of the bodies, the ME thinks there's about a five-year span between the earliest and most recent burial, which he believes is no more than six months old, but that's a guess."

Cruz Tafoya passed Kerney a list of names on a printout. "All the victims are male," he said. "Using that information, the ME's suggested time frame for the burials, and statements by Olsen's friends that he didn't like gays, we searched the missing-persons data banks. Hits came back on five gay, single men who've gone missing from Albuquerque over the last four and a half years; a hair stylist, bartender, nurse, bank clerk, and flight attendant."

"It's like Olsen built a burial shrine to commemorate each murder," Molina said.

"And he probably isn't finished killing," Tafoya said. "Clayton Istee located another sandy shelf about a hundred feet away from the existing cairns where Olsen had dug a sixth circular round hole down to bedrock."

"We're guessing it's for the prisoner Olsen had chained up in the utility room," Molina said. "The techs say the bloodstains probably post-date the last burial."

"Which may explain who Olsen had in the back of his van when he went to get money at his bank," Tafoya said.

"That makes no sense," Kerney said. "Why would

Olsen take a prisoner he plans to murder with him to Santa Fe just before he embarks on a killing spree?"

"Maybe he likes to play with them before he kills them," Tafoya said.

Kerney shook his head. "I don't buy it. The Santa Fe killings are motivated by revenge, and the Socorro murders are clear-cut serial sex crimes. These are two distinctly different signatures."

"Which gets us back to the notion that Olsen either has an accomplice or is acting on someone's behalf," Molina said. "Remember, we've got two sets of footprints and so far only one suspect."

"What is the lab telling us about the new evidence that's been collected?" Kerney asked.

"There are no fingerprints on the scrapbook found in Olsen's house," Molina said. "But Olsen's prints are all over Manning's cell phone, and the hair and fiber from the wig found in the van match some found in Olsen's bathroom."

"Olsen wears a wig?" Kerney asked.

"Not according to his mother," Tafoya said. "He's got a full head of shiny, blond, baby fine hair."

"Do we have anything new that absolutely puts Olsen in Santa Fe?" Kerney asked.

"Not really," Molina said. "The enhancement of the video surveillance tape outside the municipal court building was inconclusive. What we do have are eyewitness descriptions of an unknown male subject who looks like Olsen, evidence seized in Socorro that ties him to the crimes, and the blue van he left behind with Drake's body in it."

"Which, according to the entry and exit visa stamps in

Olsen's passport," Tafoya said, "was purchased from the El Paso junk dealer while he was out of the country."

"He could have bought it from another party after he returned," Kerney said.

"That's what we thought," Molina said, "until the Tucson PD got back to us on their meeting with the ex-con who installed the rebuilt engine. Allegedly, he never met with the customer in person. One morning when he came to work, the vehicle was outside his shop with the keys in it and a new engine in the back. The transaction was conducted entirely by phone. He got a money order in the mail for the labor, and when the work was done, he was told, again by phone, to leave the van outside with the keys under a floor mat. The next day it was gone."

"The calls to the mechanic were made from public pay phones in Tucson," Tafoya said, "on days when Olsen was working at his job in Socorro."

Kerney glanced nervously at the cell phone on the table next to his hand and then looked away at the chalkboard, which was filled with notes on how to evaluate terminally ill patients for placement in hospice care. It seemed like a dismal way to end a life.

He pulled his thoughts back to the subject at hand. "We saw a trespasser on my property just before sunset," he said. "The distance was too great to make an ID, but Sara was able to take a few telephoto pictures as he ran away. Chief Baca is having them developed."

"Do you think it was Olsen?" Molina asked.

"Whoever it was, it's highly suspicious," Kerney said. "The property is posted and there's no access for a casual hiker to get on the land easily, other than by fence-jumping."

"Speaking of photos," Tafoya said, "do you want to look at the ones we took at headquarters during the protest demonstration?"

Kerney nodded and Tafoya handed him a packet, telling him each unidentified subject was marked by a small x. He fanned through them, and froze at the close-up image of the bald-headed man he'd seen in the waiting area outside the urgent care center.

Kerney had screwed up big time by not looking at the pictures earlier in the day. His face flushed in silent anger at the blunder. Put a blond wig on his shaved head and the man could easily pass for Noel Olsen. Or maybe it was Olsen.

He pushed back from the table, got to his feet, and tossed the photograph on the table. "This man was in the hospital less than an hour ago. Get a search started, secure his admission and treatment records, talk to security and medical personnel, and look for somebody with a bandaged left hand."

Kerney's cell phone rang before Molina or Tafoya could react. He picked up, and Carol Jojoya told him the baby was on his way.

"Make it snappy, Chief," Jojoya said, "we're going into delivery right now."

"Are there any bald-headed strangers near your location?" he demanded, thinking about the knitting needle in Victoria Drake's abdomen and the killer's two-for-one threat.

"No," Jojoya said.

"Where's the uniformed officer?" Kerney said, striding for the door.

"Right behind us," Jojoya replied.

"I'm on my way." He turned to the two detectives, the blood from his pounding heart thundering in his ears. "The baby's coming. Find the son of a bitch *now*."

He raced for the stairs, taking them two at a time with Molina and Tafoya on his heels, calling for backup on their cell phones.

Sara didn't give a damn that her legs were spread wide open and people were staring at her crotch. She was sweating profusely and panting hard. Deep heaving sounds in a stranger's voice came booming out of her chest.

What was taking so long? Why was Jojoya telling her to relax when she wanted it over and done with?

The last contraction hit like a great purging that emptied her from head to toe. All she could think of was meeting Patrick Brannon Kerney, seeing him, holding him, talking to him face-to-face for the very first time.

Without thinking, she let go of Kerney's hand and reached out for her baby, who seemed to be singing instead of crying, making the sweetest little la-la sounds.

With her arms still outstretched, she watched Kerney cut the umbilical cord and Jojoya wash the waxy, blood-drenched coating off her son as the pain of the afterbirth hit her.

"He has your hands and feet," Sara said with a gasp as Jojoya wrapped Patrick in a blanket and handed him to her. "Quite the handsome lad."

"That's because his mother is a beauty," Kerney said, as he sponged her face with a towel. "How are you?"

Sara gazed at Patrick Brannon, who stared at her peacefully with pretty blue eyes as if to say everything was going to be just fine. "I'm very happy to finally meet our son," she said.

Kerney touched his son's cheek with a gentle finger. "Me too."

The baby gurgled and Kerney quickly pulled his hand away.

"He won't hurt you, Kerney," Sara said with a giggle.

Kerney's eyes danced as he squeezed her hand. "I'm overwhelmed by it all. It's a miracle."

Sara's expression turned serious.

"What is it?"

"Let's keep him safe," she said in a whisper.

"Always," Kerney whispered back.

When more police cars arrived at the hospital, Samuel Green went back to the house. In the war room he sat on the mattress, snacked on canned sardines and crackers, and mulled over his fuck-ups. Doing a reconnaissance of Kerney's ranch hadn't been a bad idea, but he should have thought things through better before acting. He was pissed off at himself for not checking the train schedule for the spur line.

He'd caught a look at it before it had rounded a bend. The engine had been pulling two old Pullman cars and a flatbed filled with tourists taking a sunset excursion ride. The way the train had crawled along the tracks, only a blind person would have missed seeing his car.

The license plates on it were stolen and the registration was phony, so that shouldn't cause a problem. But he couldn't afford to be driving a vehicle the cops were looking for. He'd leave it locked in the garage, call a cab in the morning, and buy a clunker for cash at a used car lot on Cerrillos Road.

Green brushed cracker crumbs off his shirt, thought about his next mistake, and decided that being spotted at Kerney's ranch wasn't worth worrying about. The distance between him and the vehicle had been too great and the light too poor for anyone to make an ID. But the cops might find some blood traces on the barbed wire where he'd cut his hand, and decide to question the urgent care staff at the hospital. If so, the nurse who'd stitched him up could give them a real good description, as could Kerney.

Green licked the oil from the sardines off his fingers, walked into the backyard, and took a piss on the bushes that grew over his mother's grave. He couldn't risk having the cops find his war room. He zipped up, went inside, stuffed his weapon, binoculars, and camera equipment into his backpack and moved everything else into the garage. He grabbed the makeup kit, wig, and toiletries out of the bathroom, changed into a fresh pair of pants, and closed all the windows.

It wasn't likely the cops would be able to unmask him. He'd made the legal name switch to Samuel Green with forged papers bought in Mexico to insure that Richard Finney disappeared without a trace. So if the cops came to the house, they'd be looking for a person who no longer existed. But why make it easy for them?

He went into the garage, turned off the furnace pilot light, uncoupled the gas line, and wrapped the blood-stained trousers around the pipe to slow the flow of gas into the house. In the kitchen, he slung on his backpack, lit the stove burners, and left the house on foot, cutting through the groves of piñon and juniper trees that surrounded the neighboring homes.

Green was a half-mile away when a fireball blew through the roof of the house. He watched it blossom into the night sky for a moment and walked on, skirting the major streets and sticking to the residential areas. He'd get a room in a motel on Cerrillos Road, where he could sleep and plan his next move. He had a lot to think about now that things were a bit out of kilter.

Chapter 14

Some years before Clayton met his father, Kerney had worked as a temporary forest ranger in Catron County and conducted an investigation into endangered wildlife poaching. Members of the county militia who were behind the poaching scheme had tried to kill Kerney by rigging an explosion and fire at his rented house trailer, which destroyed all his personal possessions. Because of the militia's involvement, the incident had captured national media attention.

As he stood at the counter of the western-wear store in Socorro paying for some new clothes, Clayton suddenly realized that Kerney was the only person he knew other than himself and his family who'd suffered a devastating loss of property. What if Kerney had come to Mescalero not out of guilt about what might have happened to Grace and the children, or simply to offer money? What if he'd come because he cared, wanted to lend support, and Clayton had been too thick-headed to see it? Maybe his stupid pride had gotten the better of him again.

He took his parcel of clothes, walked out into the hot

morning sun, and drove back to his motel room. Six hours of sleep had refreshed him, and his earlier phone call to Grace had reassured him that they would be able to make a fresh start. Paul Hewitt had started a fund on the family's behalf, and an anonymous Ruidoso businessman had donated fifty thousand dollars to kick it off. But even more encouraging was the news from Grace that Wendell had calmed down, Hannah was acting less clingy, and the tribal council had voted to give them a choice building lot and free use of a double-wide mobile home until they could rebuild.

Clayton peeled off his grubby uniform shirt and dirty blue jeans and dressed in the new clothes. The Olsen crime scene had shut down at two in the morning, with the understanding that the investigation was shifting back to Santa Fe. Paul Hewitt had given Clayton the green light to stay with it.

Grace hadn't been happy with the news, but Clayton appeased her by promising to be gone only one or two more days, which wasn't a dodge on his part. Because of what had happened, he desperately missed his family.

He stuffed his dirty clothes into the plastic garment bag, left the room card key on the bedside table, and went to his unit. He'd gas up and head for Santa Fe.

A late night report from Santa Fe had brought unsettling news. An unknown trespasser had been spotted late in the day on Kerney's ranch, and a possible suspect, not thought to be Olsen, had been seen at the hospital shortly before Sara went into labor.

Clayton left the hotel parking lot fairly certain he now had a baby brother. It was weird to think he actually had a sibling. As a child, he'd yearned for one. Because of the age difference, he couldn't be a brother in any ordinary way. But he could do his very best to be Patrick Brannon Kerney's friend.

He thought about Grace's reaction if he did anything less and laughed out loud. She'd hand his head to him on a platter.

Carol Jojoya was late on her morning rounds due to the arrival of another baby. Kerney used the time to tell Sara about the unknown subject he'd seen in the admitting area and the unsuccessful search for him.

"Also, Andy's people found blood traces on the barbed-wire fences near the train tracks," Kerney said, "and the man I saw here had a bandaged hand. Enlargements of those pictures you took show the back of a bald-headed man."

"Is it Olsen?" Sara asked.

"We've yet to ID him," Kerney answered. "But I doubt it. The blood stains found in Olsen's utility room match his type. Forensics has sent his hair samples and the blood work analysis to the FBI for DNA analysis."

"There are two killers?" Sara asked.

"Each with a completely different MO," Kerney said. "Personally, I think whoever is hunting us has been using Olsen as his cover."

"This isn't what I wanted to hear," Sara said, with a shake of her head.

Jojoya's arrival interrupted the conversation. She examined Sara and Patrick Brannon, proclaimed them to be healthy, and signed the discharge form. Kerney drove away from the hospital with Sara in the backseat next to Patrick, who was securely fastened into an infant carrier.

They had a police escort fore and aft. On the floorboard at Sara's feet were three floral arrangements that had been sent to the hospital, including one from Andy and Gloria.

"Have you called my parents?" Sara asked.

Kerney shook his head. "Not yet. I wanted to get you safely home first."

"I'll do it," Sara said as she adjusted Patrick's blanket to free his little arms.

"Unless you ask them not to come, they'll be on the way here with your brother and his wife as soon as you hang up," Kerney said.

"I wouldn't think of asking them to stay away," Sara said.

"Then we'll just have to fill them in when they get here."

"Well, at least we won't have to do that with Clayton and Grace," Sara said. "Have you called them?"

Kerney shook his head as he turned onto Canyon Road, where tourists jaywalking to get from one art gallery to another slowed traffic on the narrow street.

"Why not?"

"Clayton's on his way to Santa Fe, and I don't have a phone number for Grace."

"You're not avoiding it, are you?" Sara asked.

Kerney shook his head.

"Don't go quiet on me, Kerney," Sara said.

Kerney let out a deep breath. "I'm not going to try to push Clayton into accepting a family he doesn't want to be part of. He may not want to be Patrick's brother any more than he wants to accept me as his father."

"You can't just leave it at that."

"I haven't," Kerney replied. "I've asked dispatch to send him to our house as soon as he makes radio contact. We'll see what he does."

The lead unit pulled to a stop on the far side of the driveway. Kerney parked in front of the house and helped Sara out of the backseat as the two units turned around and left. She reached in and released Patrick's restraints, and he snorted in his sleep as she cradled him in her arms.

"We're home," he said, reaching for Sara's purse and one vase of flowers, "and it's just us."

"You're staying?" Sara asked as she walked to the front door.

"Yes, I am," Kerney answered as he unlocked the door.

Sara paused in the doorway and kissed him on the cheek.

"What's that for?"

"Doing the right thing," Sara said. "This is our first day as a family, and except for the three of us I want the world to go away at least for a little while."

Patrick opened his eyes, cooed and waved a tiny hand.

"But I'll make an exception," Sara said, "if Clayton decides to stop by."

Kerney smiled, pleased that he hadn't mentioned the police sharpshooter concealed on the hill behind the house and the detective stationed at a bedroom window of the neighbor's house across the street.

Samuel Green had gone to bed thinking that it might be best to let time work to his advantage. If he backed off for a couple of weeks, maybe even left town, Kerney and his wife would probably let their guard down. Surely, the new baby would distract them and he could find an opportunity to strike safely and without much difficulty.

In the morning, from his motel room, Green called the hospital, identified himself as a worried relative from out of state, asked about Sara's welfare, and learned that she'd delivered a healthy baby boy last night.

In the bathroom, he carefully cut down the blond wig so that it just covered the tips of his ears and draped slightly over his shirt collar at the back of his neck, put it on, and added a cap. Then he glued a big fake mole under one eye, added a blond mustache, and admired the results. No cop looking for a bald-headed man would give him a second glance.

In good spirits, he grabbed his backpack and walked past the Indian School to a used car lot, where he spent time picking out a car, haggling over the price, and signing all the required paperwork. After exchanging cash for the car keys, he drove to a diner a block away and ordered breakfast. On the empty table next to him a departing customer had left the daily paper. He scooped it up before the waitress could clear it away, eager to see if the house fire had made the front page. There it was, headline news complete with a color photo of the burned-out wreckage. The caption called it a suspicious fire under investigation.

The story described all the usual stuff: the extensive damage to the structure, the number of fire trucks called out, how long it took to battle the blaze, the neighbors' reaction to it, and a quote from an arson investigator on the scene, who wanted the unknown occupant to come forward.

Green smirked in satisfaction and turned to an inside page of state roundup news, which carried the headline:

FIVE BODIES FOUND IN SOCORRO

Always interested in murder, Green read the story quickly and stopped short at the mention of Noel Olsen's name as the primary suspect in the investigation. He almost snarled at the waitress when she slid the plate of bacon and eggs in front of him and refilled his coffee cup.

His breakfast forgotten, Green read the story again, and a deep anxiety washed over him. His choice of Olsen as an unwitting beard had been flawed in an unimaginable way. How could he have possibly known that Olsen had been secretly killing queers for the past five years?

Distressed, Green put aside the paper, pushed his plate away and silently cursed Olsen. If he had it to do all over again, he would kill the son of a bitch much more slowly and painfully.

He forced down thoughts of Olsen and concentrated on his predicament. All he'd learned about crime and cops told Green that Kerney now knew it wasn't Olsen who was stalking him. He pulled the plate of food to him and chewed a piece of bacon. He had to assume that he was now vulnerable, which meant that time was no longer on his side. He would move fast, get the job done, and vanish.

He reached for another bacon strip and started

mulling over a strategy. First on the docket, he had to locate Kerney and his family. Then he needed a way to get to them without raising alarm or suspicion. Finally, and most importantly, he had to escape cleanly.

He broke the fried egg yokes with a slice of toast and started running down schemes in his mind. As soon as Green decided that it really didn't matter how Kerney died or in what order he killed the family, ideas began to flow.

Propped up on the bed with Patrick in her lap, Sara called her parents in Montana. While she talked, Kerney carried in the two remaining bouquets from the car, placed them on a dresser, and then moved the crib into their bedroom, so that Patrick would be close at hand once Sara decided to let go of him.

He sat gingerly on the edge of the bed and looked at his wife and son. Patrick was sleeping soundly. Kerney studied his face, the little wisps of hair on his head, the shape of his nose and chin, noticing for the first time his resemblance to Sara. He felt a powerful, almost overwhelming connection to his son that came out of nowhere and both surprised and sobered him with its intensity.

He switched his attention to Sara, who smiled at him as she continued talking about the beautiful baby boy in her lap. Her tired eyes sparkled as she stroked Patrick's head and described once again to her mother how perfect he was, noting his weight, height, and calm disposition, laughing with joy as she said it.

The alarming sound of the doorbell pulled Kerney up short. He walked into the living room reassuring himself that all was well, peeked out the window, and saw a flower delivery truck in the driveway. He opened up, accepted another bouquet of flowers, tipped the driver, and took them to the bedroom. The attached card was from the city manager.

He handed the card to Sara as she passed the phone over to him, and he spent a pleasant few minutes confirming Sara's assessment of Patrick's perfection for his in-laws, reassuring them that their daughter was all right, and jotting down their travel plans. They would arrive in two days.

Sara took the phone back, said a long good-bye, and placed a call to her brother and sister-in-law, who would also be coming to Santa Fe, although for a much shorter time, since the ranch needed minding.

After the conversation ended, Sara handed Patrick to Kerney and asked him to put him in the crib. Gently, he took his son in his arms, turned to the crib, and set him down.

"You need to rest," Kerney said, as he returned to Sara.

"First, a kiss," she said.

He kissed her on the forehead, eyelids and mouth, and squeezed her hand.

"How do you like fatherhood so far?" she asked sleepily.

He felt his life had changed in a hundred different ways, but didn't have adequate words to express it.

"You've given me a great gift," he finally said.

"Speaking of gifts," Sara said, "there's something in the top dresser drawer."

Kerney stepped to the dresser and took out a package wrapped in silver paper tied with a ribbon. "What's this?"

"A birthday present for Patrick. Open it."

He untied the ribbon, loosened the paper and looked at the glass-framed, velvet-lined box. Inside were duplicates of all of his military decorations from his service in Vietnam. A lifetime ago, he'd buried the original medals in his parents' freshly dug graves on the Jennings ranch west of the Tularosa.

Speechless, he held the box out, looking at Sara.

"I want our son to know what a remarkable man his father is," Sara said.

Kerney put the box aside and took Sara in his arms.

Clayton topped out on La Bajada Hill ten miles outside Santa Fe just as the temperature gauge red-lined and steam started seeping from under the hood of his unit. He pulled into the rest stop that gave visitors a view of the city in the distance and the mountain range beyond, checked to see what the problem was, and discovered the water pump had failed.

He called state police by radio, identified himself, and asked to have a tow truck dispatched to his location. While he waited next to his unit, Clayton thought about the unkept promise he'd made to Grace months ago to bring the family to Santa Fe for a weekend outing. As soon as things settled down he'd do it. Actually, with Sara having the baby, he knew Grace would now give him no choice in the matter.

A state police cruiser came toward him on the Interstate. It slowed, drove onto the left shoulder, cut across the median and oncoming traffic through a break in the northbound flow, and stopped next to him. Russell Thorpe got out.

"Got problems, Sergeant Istee?" Thorpe asked jokingly, gazing at the steam billowing from the engine compartment.

"The water pump went out," Clayton said, returning Thorpe's smile, "and you don't have to be so formal."

Russell's smiled broadened. "Good deal. Santa Fe dispatch passed on a request from Chief Kerney. He'd like you to stop by his house."

"Did the baby come?" Clayton asked.

"Last night," Russell replied, "and mother and son are fine."

"Great," Clayton said.

"I'll give you a ride there after the tow truck arrives. ETA is ten minutes."

"I'd like to get briefed on what's been happening up here first," Clayton said.

"I can do that while we wait," Russell said, opening the passenger door to his cruiser.

Clayton nodded and climbed into Thorpe's unit.

Samuel Green left the diner with a plan in mind. He gassed up his car at a self-serve station, then checked the yellow page listings for florists at a pay phone. After writing down the addresses of several that weren't in busy retail, shopping mall, or downtown locations, he cruised by the businesses. He decided to use a florist that shared a stand-alone building with a shoe store on Cerrillos Road, where the only vehicle outside either establishment was the flower delivery van.

He drove around the building before parking and

found four cars in reserved employee spaces near the back doors to the shops. Inside the flower shop he saw no surveillance cameras. A middle-aged woman and a kid in his early twenties worked at a table behind the customer counter unpacking fresh cut flowers from boxes and placing them in a glass refrigerated display case that stood against a wall.

Green approached them with a smile. "I need to send some flowers."

"What's the occasion?" the woman asked, wiping her hands on an apron. She had a soft, placid face and chubby arms.

"A birth," Green replied. "Put something nice together."

The woman smiled cheerily. "I'd suggest stargazer lilies, some roses, and spikes of liatrus, set off with ferns and some delicate baby's breath."

"That sounds perfect," Green said. Except for the roses and ferns, he didn't have the slightest idea what she was talking about. "Can you deliver?"

"Certainly," the woman replied. "What color roses would you like?"

"Red will do," Green replied.

She asked him to select a card from the rack on the counter and turned away to begin putting the arrangement together. The kid moved the boxes of cut flowers to a work table and continued unpacking them.

Using a fingernail to hold the card in place, he scrawled congratulations, added an exclamation mark, scribbled an indecipherable name, and left it on the counter. He watched as the woman stuck a stem with a whole bunch of purple flowers into a vase. It only took her a couple of minutes to complete the job. She tied a ribbon around the vase and carried it to the counter.

"That's so lovely," she said, as she admired her handiwork.

Green nodded in agreement. "How soon can it be delivered?"

"Is it going to the hospital?"

Green shook his head and gave her Kerney's address.

"We'll get it out right away," she said as she wrote the address on a delivery slip, put the card in an envelope, and attached it to the vase.

"Thanks a lot," Green said as he paid the bill.

"Thank you," the woman replied. "We love doing birth bouquets. It's such a special event to celebrate."

Green smiled. "Yeah, I know what you mean."

While Sara and Patrick slept, Kerney dozed on the living room couch until the ringing doorbell brought him to his feet. A quick check out the window revealed another delivery truck and a kid standing on the porch holding a vase of flowers.

Kerney opened up wondering if the house would be filled with bouquets by day's end. It was the third delivery since they'd arrived home.

He tipped the kid, put the vase on the coffee table, and read the card, trying to make out who'd sent it. He couldn't decipher the name, and the handwriting was unfamiliar. Maybe Sara would know. He'd ask when she woke up.

Minutes later the doorbell rang again. This time Kerney glimpsed a state police cruiser in the driveway and Clayton, who was dressed in civvies, standing at the door.

"Where's your vehicle?" Kerney asked when he opened the door.

"Getting a new water pump installed," Clayton replied with a wave to Russell Thorpe, who drove away. "It's good to see you."

"I understand I now have a brother," Clayton said as he stepped inside and shook Kerney's hand.

"Yes, you do," Kerney said, surprised that Clayton hadn't stressed a half-blood relationship to Patrick. He looked for an unspoken coolness in Clayton's expression and saw nothing but genuine pleasure. "Six pounds, ten ounces. Fortunately, he looks like his mother."

Clayton smiled. "That's good. Let's hope he's not as troublesome to deal with as I've been."

"You've been confusing to deal with, not troublesome," Kerney said with a laugh.

Clayton chuckled in agreement and looked around the room. "So where is he?"

"Sleeping. So is Sara. Come into the kitchen. We can talk there without disturbing them. You did good work down in Socorro."

"Not good enough," Clayton replied as he followed Kerney through the living room. "We still haven't caught him."

"I've got some ideas why," Kerney said. "Are you up to speed on what happened last night?"

"Yeah, the bald-headed man," Clayton said as he sat at the kitchen table. "Thorpe filled me in."

"Good," Kerney said. He filled two coffee mugs and brought them to the table. "But first, how are Grace and the children?" he asked.

"Doing better," Clayton answered. He sat back in his

chair and talked about how he'd hated to leave them while they were still so upset, how Wendell had gone a bit wild after the explosion, how Hannah had glued herself to her mother, how Grace probably felt abandoned by his decision to go to Socorro.

"Didn't Grace understand that it was something you had to do?" Kerney asked.

"Yeah, but that doesn't make it any easier on her," Clayton replied, launching in to all the things that needed to be done to get everything back to normal.

Kerney nodded sympathetically and listened, thinking maybe something good had come out of all the adversity and chaos of the past week. For the very first time in their relationship, Clayton was really talking to him.

Down the street from the flower shop Samuel Green waited impatiently for the kid in the delivery truck to return. What happened next would all depend on what the kid had to tell him.

Even though there was heavy traffic on Cerrillos Road, nobody had entered the shop since Green left, and only one customer had made a quick stop at the business next door. If the trend held, there shouldn't be any problem putting the second phase of his plan into action.

After ten more minutes, the kid arrived. Green left his car, circled behind the building to avoid any curious eyes inside the shoe store, and walked into the shop. The bell on the door tinkled and the kid and the woman looked up from the counter and smiled at him.

"Back so soon?" the woman asked.

"Yeah, I need to send some flowers to another

friend," Green said sheepishly as he stepped toward them, looking at the kid. "Were you able to make that delivery?"

The kid nodded. He had a big ugly-looking pimple on his neck. "Yeah, I just finished the run."

"That's great," Green said. "Were there any police officers there?"

The kid gave him a funny look. "Just the one that took the flowers. He wore a badge and a gun on his belt."

"But it was the father, right?" Green said, describing Kerney to the kid.

"Yeah, it was him," the kid said, "as far as I could tell."

"Super," Green replied, as he pulled the pistol from the waistband at the small of his back. He shot the woman first and then the kid, the silencer flattening the sounds into dull splats.

He stepped around the counter. Both were dead, the kid with a stunned look on his face, and the woman still wearing her frozen, customer-friendly smile. He took the truck keys out of the kid's pants pocket and concealed the bodies behind the counter.

Moving quickly, he put on a pair of latex gloves, found more keys in the woman's purse under a small desk, locked the deadbolt to the back door, and turned on the telephone answering machine. He got a wad of paper towels in the small restroom, wiped off the counter to destroy any fingerprints, and put the pen he'd used to write the note in his shirt pocket.

He pulled a piece of plain paper from the tray of the fax machine, and wrote out a message in block letters with a felt-tipped marker. Then he grabbed a fancy floral display from the refrigerated case and taped the message to the inside of the shop's door.

Green glanced around before locking up. No one was in sight. He wiped his prints from the handle of the door, put the flowers in the delivery van, and drove away unable to resist the laugh that bubbled out of him as he thought about the sign he'd put up. It read:

CLOSED DUE TO A DEATH IN THE FAMILY

That sure as hell was true, and would soon apply to Kerney and his family, too, if all went well.

Green eased into the passing lane, making sure to use the turn signal even though no cops were in sight. Within the hour he'd be done with it, back in his car, and heading for the open road.

Over a second cup of coffee, Kerney explained why he believed the killer was the bald-headed man and not Olsen.

Clayton, who agreed with Kerney's analysis, nodded. "So we're back to having an unknown suspect."

"Unless we can make an ID, this could drag on for some time," Kerney said glumly. "But if we stay smart and ask the right questions, we'll find him."

"Well, until then we'll just have to keep our guard up," Clayton said as he got up and put his coffee mug in the sink.

"I'm sorry all this crap fell on you and your family."

"It's not your fault," Clayton said as he returned to his chair. He leaned forward and gave Kerney a studied look. "Tell me something. Did you go into the delivery room with Sara?"

Kerney nodded, grinned, and his eyes lit up. "You bet I did."

As Kerney described the experience with unabashed delight, Clayton felt the last of the pinprick anger he'd always felt about Kerney begin to wash away. The thought came to him that his boneheaded rejection of Kerney hadn't been fair to the man. That it had been ground into him by his mother for as long as he could remember never to question who his father was, no matter how much he longed to know.

For the first time Clayton wondered if he'd been angry with the wrong person. Maybe it was time to stop trying to be the perfect, politically correct Apache man his mother always expected him to be and instead concentrate on being Kerney's friend.

Clayton smiled as Kerney described his shaking hands and pounding heart when he'd looked at Patrick for the first time and cut the umbilical cord. "Isn't that a kick?" he said.

"You've done it?" Kerney asked.

"Twice."

The doorbell rang and Kerney got to his feet. "It's probably more flowers," he said.

He checked out the window to be sure and recognized the van, although the man waiting with flowers in hand wasn't the same kid who'd delivered earlier. He took a couple of bills from his wallet and swung open the door.

Green smiled as he brought the pistol from behind the vase and pointed it at Kerney's gut. "Hello, shithead," he said. "Try to act natural or I'll kill you where you stand."

"Don't do this," Kerney replied.

"Where's your bitch and her baby?" Green asked.

"In the bedroom sleeping," Kerney said, raising his voice slightly.

"Good. Keep your hands at your side, step back slowly, and let me in. Be cool."

"Whatever you want," Kerney replied as he backed up.

Green waved the pistol. "Keep moving."

Kerney stopped when his legs hit the edge of the coffee table.

Samuel Green closed the door with the heel of his shoe and put the flowers on the foyer table. "How do you want it?" he asked. "You first, or the bitch and the baby?"

"I thought you wanted me to watch them die," Kerney said, raising his voice another notch.

"I'm flexible," Green whispered. "Keep your voice down."

"But not very bright," Kerney said. "You didn't do your homework with Olsen."

"Fuck you," Green said, his voice rising a bit.

"Where is Olsen?" Kerney asked, trying to keep the conversation going. He hoped that sooner rather than later, Clayton would come looking for him.

Green smirked. "Talking won't keep you alive. But I'll answer your question. He's at the bottom of a very deep hole."

"How imaginative," Kerney said. "You made all these creative finesse moves, and where did it get you?"

"Don't try to rile me, Kerney. You still don't know who I am, do you?"

"I'm working on it."

Green heard a flush of water running through the pipes beneath the floor. "Sounds like momma is up," he said, waving the gun. "Take me to her."

"Kill me now," Kerney said.

"No way, cowboy."

Kerney led the way past the open kitchen door. Clayton was nowhere to be seen. He turned the corner of the hallway just as the door to the guest bathroom behind him began to open.

"Hit the deck," Kerney yelled as Green swung toward the sound and fired two quick rounds, chest high into the door. He reached for Green as the man pivoted back to face him. Two bullets shattered the bathroom door and hit Green in the back.

Kerney stepped away and let him fall. "Clear."

From the bathroom floor, Clayton reached up and opened the door. He saw Kerney frozen in the hallway, a body at his feet, Sara behind him holding a pistol, and heard the sound of a baby crying.

"Sorry about that," Clayton said, getting to his feet. "I had to use the bathroom."

Chapter 15

The gunshots brought the two surveillance officers to the house in short order. After they arrived, Kerney asked Sara to take Patrick and stay with Gloria Baca until things quieted down. Knowing the place would soon be filled with cops and techs, she willingly agreed.

While Kerney called Gloria and explained the situation, Sara thanked Clayton for saving their lives, hugged him, and got him to promise that he wouldn't leave town before speaking with her again.

From the portal, the two men watched Sara bundle Patrick into his car seat and drive off, followed by a detective who had orders to stay with them as a precautionary measure. When she was out of sight, Kerney looked at Clayton and shook his head, afraid if he opened his mouth he'd say something dumb or insipid.

Clayton read the unspoken gratitude on Kerney's face. "Don't say it."

"I don't know what to say," Kerney replied, "except I'm glad you were here."

"So am I," Clayton said. "Do you think it's over?"

"God, I hope so."

"Who was that guy?"

"I'm not sure," Kerney answered. "Let's take a closer look."

In the hallway, Kerney bent over the body, removed the cap, wig, and mustache, and studied the man's face. There was something vaguely familiar to it, but nothing registered clearly.

"Nope," Kerney said, and without thinking he rose up and kicked the nameless, dead son of a bitch in the side as hard as he could.

It took most of the day to sort things out. Richard Finney, AKA Samuel Green, had been a fourteen-year-old runaway who'd robbed and brutally murdered an elderly Laundromat owner. He was one of the two potential suspects on Kerney's list Molina and his team had been unable to locate.

With a number of other officers Kerney had been sweeping the neighborhood near the crime scene on the night of the murder when Finney came at him from behind a vacant house, screaming obscenities and swinging a hammer. He shot Finney in the groin from a distance of four feet. At the time, he had no idea how young Finney was, but would have shot him anyway to stop the attack.

Kerney sat in Andy's unit while his friend read Finney's old juvie case file. Still rattled by the events of the day, a few moments of silence were a welcome relief.

"I guess losing your balls is enough to make anyone hold a grudge," Andy said, closing the case file and handing it back to Kerney. "But why didn't he just come after you? Sure, Potter handled the case in juvie court

321

and Manning did the psych evaluation. But Finney made a straight-up confession, and Manning thought he could be rehabilitated."

Kerney shrugged.

"And why did he wait so long to do it?"

Kerney shook his head.

"Why the Olsen disguise?" Andy asked. "Was it some sort of 'look how smart I am' kind of thing?"

"Who knows," Kerney said. He leaned back against the headrest of Andy's unit and thought about the two dead people at the flower shop, and the skeleton of a woman that had been found buried in the yard of the burned-out house where Finney had once lived.

He watched the crime scene techs loading up their gear. The DA had come and gone, as had the ME. Finney's body was en route to the autopsy table, and Clayton was inside the house going through a mandatory police-shooting interrogation with Sal Molina.

Mentally, Kerney did a body count. Aside from Potter, Manning, and Drake, there was Kurt Larsen, Mary Beth Patterson, the two flower shop victims, and the unknown woman buried in the yard. That made eight. If he'd aimed a little higher, Finney would be dead and those innocent people would still be alive. He wondered if there were more bodies Finney had left behind that no one knew about.

"At least something good came out of it," Andy said. "After all, Finney did ice Olsen before he could murder again."

"Yeah, there's that," Kerney said.

Andy's call sign came over the police radio. He keyed the microphone and answered. The water pump in Clayton's unit had been replaced and the vehicle was operational.

"He'll want to go home," Kerney said.

"What are you going to do?" Andy asked, eyeing his friend, who looked drained of all emotion. And why shouldn't he? For almost a week, everything Kerney cared about had been on the line. Just hours ago, a murderer intent on killing his wife and newborn child had been stopped only a few steps short of his goal.

Kerney looked out the window wishing Andy would quit talking and let him clear his head.

"Got any plans?" Andy asked to goad a response.

Kerney smiled weakly. "I'm going to get to know my son, spend time with Sara, celebrate with the in-laws once they arrive, push the house project along, go down to Mescalero to visit with Clayton and his family before Sara has to report back on duty, and be grateful for all that I have."

"Sounds like a full agenda," Andy said.

"Yeah." Kerney saw Clayton step onto the portal of the house and opened the car door. "That's one hell of a good man."

"Tell him that," Andy said.

"I plan to," Kerney replied as he pulled himself out of the vehicle.

Over the next several weeks, life slowly returned to normal, helped along by the visit of Sara's family, frequent phone calls back and forth with Clayton and Grace, and the calming effect of Patrick Brannon, who seemed, in ways Kerney couldn't quite put into words, self-assured and contented, which of course made him all the more amazing.

After the family celebration ended and the relatives departed, Kerney and Sara filled their days with frequent picnics at the ranch to watch the new house go up, shopping for the items on Sara's wish list, and staying close to home, due to Patrick's insistence that he be fed every two hours and be allowed to sleep whenever he wanted. They coped with it by taking lots of catnaps and alternating feeding and diaper-changing shifts.

Determined to spend as much time as he could with Sara and Patrick, Kerney went on unpaid leave when his vacation time ran out, occasionally dropping by the office to deal with a few important matters, not the least of which was Sal Molina's retirement party.

Arrangements had been made to visit Clayton and Grace on an upcoming weekend, so Kerney booked a suite at a resort lodge in Ruidoso and made reservations to take everyone out to dinner while they were there.

The night before they left, Sara snuggled up to him on the couch.

"You haven't said a word about the fact that I have to report back for duty in two weeks," she said.

"And I'm not going to," Kerney said. "It's not an issue anymore."

"Why is that?"

"Because," Kerney said, taking her hand in his, "I know without a doubt that nothing can break this family apart."

Ten minutes after Santa Fe police chief Kevin Kerney
picked up his rental car at the Bakersfield airport, he was
stuck in heavy stop-and-go traffic, questioning his decision
to take the less traveled back roads on his trip to the central California coast.

Congestion didn't ease until he was well outside the city
limits on a westbound state highway that cut through
desert flatlands. Ahead, a dust devil jumped across a
straight, uninviting stretch of pavement and churned
slowly through an irrigated alfalfa field, creating a green
wave rolling over the forage.

Kerney glanced at his watch. Had he made a mistake in
trying to map out a scenic route to take to the coast? By
now, he'd expected to be approaching a mountain range,
but there was nothing on the hazy horizon to suggest it.

It really didn't matter if he'd misjudged his driving time.
He had all day to get to the Double J horse ranch outside
of Paso Robles, where he would spend the weekend looking over some quarter horses that were up for sale. He hit
the cruise control and let his mind wander.

Kerney had partnered up with his neighbor, Jack Burke,
to breed, raise, and train competition cutting horses. Kerney would buy some stock to get the enterprise started,

Jack would contribute broodmares, pastureland, and stables to the partnership, and Jack's youngest son, Riley Burke, would do the training.

The sky cleared enough to show the outline of mountains topped by a few bleached, mare's tail clouds. Soon, Kerney was driving through a pass on a twisting road flanked by forked and tilted gray-needle pine trees and into a huge grassland plain that swept up against a higher, more heavily timbered mountain range to the west.

Finally, his road trip had turned interesting. He stopped to stretch his legs, and a convertible sports car with the top down zipped by, the woman driver tooting her horn and waving gaily as she sped away.

Kerney waved back, thinking it would have been nice to have his family with him. He'd arranged the trip with the expectation that he'd enjoy his time by himself and away from the job. But in truth, he was alone far more than he liked. Sara, his career Army officer wife, had a demanding Pentagon duty assignment that limited her free time, and Patrick, their toddler son who lived with her, was far too young to travel alone.

Kerney had hoped that the new house they'd built on two sections of ranchland outside of Santa Fe would change Sara's mind about staying in the Army, but it hadn't. Although she loved the ranch and looked forward to living in Santa Fe full-time, she wasn't about take early retirement. That meant six more years of a part-time, long-distance marriage, held together by frequent cross-country trips back and forth as time allowed, and one family vacation together each year. For Kerney, it wasn't a happy prospect.

He looked over the plains. The green landscape was pleasing to the eye, deeper in color than the bunch grasses of New Mexico, but under a less vivid sky. He could see a small herd of grazing livestock moving toward a windmill, the outline of a remote ranch house beyond, and the thin line of the state road that plowed straight across the plains and curved sharply up the distant mountains.

He settled behind the wheel and gave the car some juice, thinking it would be a hell of a lot more fun to drive on to

Paso Robles in a little two-seater with the top down and the wind in his face.

Kerney arrived in Paso Robles and promptly got lost trying to find the ranch. A convenience store clerk pointed him in the right direction, and a few minutes later he was traveling a narrow paved road through rolling hills of vineyards, cattle ranches, and horse farms sheltered by stands of large oak trees amid lush carpets of green grass. He drove with the window down, finding the moist sea air that rolled over the coastal mountains a welcome change from the dry deserts of New Mexico.

He'd been offered free lodging at the ranch along with a tour when he arrived, and he was eager to see how the outfit operated. The condition of the horses would tell him most of what he needed to know before deciding whether or not to buy. But the people who cared for the animals and their surroundings would also indicate whether his money would be well spent.

Kerney turned a corner onto a wide open vista, eased the car off the pavement, and got out to take in the scenery. On a hilltop behind and above him stood a large mission-style villa with a portal consisting of a series of arches supported by Georgian columns and topped off with a red tile roof and overhanging eaves. Paired bell towers with identical arches towered above either end of the second story. Two vineyards cascaded down the gentle slope on both sides of the villa. Taken as a whole, the place reeked of wealth.

To the west, densely treed coastal mountains rose up from a green, rolling valley that wandered down to a creek bed. A sign fronting the ranch road into the valley announced the Double J Ranch. In a series of fenced and gated pastures, broodmares and their foals gathered under shady oak trees.

The ranch headquarters bordered the creek bed and consisted of four white houses around a semicircular driveway within a few steps of a birthing barn and a long row of covered, open air stalls adjacent to small paddocks. Beyond the stalls was a barn that Kerney guessed was used to house the stud horses.

Sara had asked for pictures, so Kerney got the camera from his travel bag and took some shots, doing a rough mental count of the mares and foals in plain view. There were more than a hundred, signifying a very large breeding operation.

He drove to the ranch buildings and parked near the birthing barn, which had a small adjacent office building off to one side. A man in his early forties stepped onto the porch as Kerney approached.

"Mr. Hilt?" Kerney asked, as he approached.

The man nodded. "The name's Devin," he said with a welcoming smile, extending his hand. "You must be Kevin Kerney."

Kerney smiled back and shook Devin's hand. "Thanks for putting me up."

"I'm afraid you'll have to share the guesthouse with another party," Hilt said. "The boss has a buyer coming up from Santa Barbara sometime later today."

"That's not a problem," Kerney said, as he took a look around. "This is quite a place."

Hilt laughed. He stood six feet tall in his cowboy boots and had a sturdy frame topped off with curly brown hair cut short. "This isn't the half of it. Around the bend a mile away we've got a training track, stables, and pastures for colts and two-year-olds. That's where the boss, his wife, his mother, and the ranch manager have their houses. This area is just for my family, the trainers, and guests."

"It's pretty posh," Kerney said. "I can't remember ever seeing a more beautiful ranch."

Hilt laughed again. "It does make working for a living a bit more pleasant." He pointed down the driveway at a pitched roof, single-story clapboard house surrounded by a picket fence. "That's the guest cottage. Want to settle in first or take that tour I promised you?"

"Let's do the tour," Kerney said.

"Perfect," Hilt replied, as he moved to a pickup truck.

Hilt drove Kerney around the spread, passing on bits of information along the way. It was a quarter horse ranch with about four hundred head and a breeding program that foaled more than a hundred newborns yearly. Four stallions at stud were syndicated at over a million each. Most of the horses were owned by the ranch.

The owner, Jeffery Jardin, lived most of the time in southern California, where he owned a high-tech manufacturing business with major defense and military contracts. But his passion was racehorses, and the ranch showed that he pursued it seriously. Kerney guessed the size of the spread at about five hundred acres. He wondered what the value of the land was in the pricy California market.

Hilt told Kerney that in the morning he'd meet Ken Wheeler, a former jockey who oversaw the operation and culled the horses that weren't suitable for racing. Kerney hoped he'd find what he was looking for: two riding horses for personal use, one stud to service Jack Burke's mares, and some two- or three-year-old geldings Riley Burke could train as cutting horses.

Tucked into a separate part of the valley away from the road stood the training track and another set of fenced pastures that held good-looking colts and two-year-olds. Open-air covered stalls and a barn stood adjacent to the track. At one end of the stalls a circular pen contained a hot walker. Driven by an electrical motor, the device had four arms that looked like oversized propeller blades mounted on a triangular-shaped base. After training runs, the horses were hitched to the arms and mechanically walked to cool them down.

On a hill overlooking the track were three houses, one a two-story Victorian with a low-pitched hipped roof and spindlework porch railings. It was flanked by two more modest single-story houses built with brick and wood cladding. All were nicely landscaped and sheltered by oak trees.

As Hilt pulled to a stop in front of the barn, he pointed at a smaller Victorian house on the far side of the track. "That's where Ken lives," he said. "He'll meet you at the office tomorrow at seven. Want to look at some pretty horses?"

"You bet," Kerney said, as he climbed out of the truck.

Hilt spent the better part of an hour walking Kerney through the barn and stalls and into several nearby pastures. The horses were slick and well cared for, and the grounds, barns, and stalls were clean and tidy. Kerney learned the ranch employed a full-time veterinarian, two tech assistants, two trainers, and a variety of stable hands, groomers, exercise riders, and laborers, many of them Mexican. Low-cost housing was provided for a dozen key employees.

The two men entered a pasture, and several colts came trotting over to greet them. Hilt recited their bloodlines while Kerney gave them the once-over. He found himself enjoying Hilt's company and the talk of horses. He stroked a chestnut colt's neck and ran a hand over its withers, thinking it was decidedly refreshing to get away by himself and forget about being a cop.

Back at the guest cottage, Kerney found an overnight bag and briefcase on the floor of the largest bedroom, but no sign of the man who was sharing the accommodations with him. He dumped his stuff in another bedroom and looked around the cottage. Whoever decorated the place had a penchant for green and an obsession with frogs. The carpet, wallpaper, tile work, and even the kitchen ceiling were all various shades of green. Ceramic, glass, and pottery figurines of frogs sat on every table, dresser, and countertop, and framed prints of jumping frogs, singing frogs, and comical-looking standing frogs hung on the walls of each room. It seemed like a big silly joke that had gotten slightly out of hand. Still, it made him smile.

The kitchen was fully equipped and stocked. But Kerney decided to take himself out to dinner and do a little sightseeing before it got dark. Hilt had told him of a good restaurant in a nearby village, and given him directions.

He changed into a fresh shirt, fired up the rental car, and drove away, pleased with how the day had gone.

Always an early riser, Kerney was up at five. He showered, dressed, and sat on the porch of the guest cottage in the cool predawn air, drinking a glass of juice and enjoying the sounds of whinnying mares in a nearby pasture. Last night, after an early dinner, he'd driven to the ocean in time to watch a spectacular, romantic sunset, which only made him miss Sara's company.

When he'd returned to the ranch, an imported luxury sedan was parked in front of the cottage, and the door to his bunkmate's bedroom was closed. To avoid disturbing the man, Kerney had read quietly in his room for a few hours before turning in.

From the porch he could see a night watchman moving down a line of corrals where broodmares about to foal were kept under observation. Kerney strolled over to join him. In front of the office was a five-gallon bucket filled with horse biscuits. He stuffed some in his jacket pocket and caught up with the watchman. Even in the dim light, he could tell the mares were pampered ladies. He fed biscuits to those who came up to the corral fences to greet him.

He wandered up and down the stalls that held the mares with their newborn foals. Workers, including a veterinarian checking on the expectant mothers, soon began arriving. Barn boys started cleaning stalls and filling feed bins. One young man raked a herringbone pattern in fresh sawdust that he'd spread down the center aisle.

After watching for a while, Kerney went back to the cottage. There was no sound of movement behind the other guest's closed bedroom door. Hilt had told Kerney that the man had an early morning appointment with the owner, who personally handled the sale of all racing stock. Kerney knocked on the door to give the guy a wake-up call. He got no response, so he knocked again and called out. Still nothing.

He opened the door and turned on the light. Lying face up on the duvet covering the bed was a fully dressed man probably in his late sixties. One look told Kerney the man was dead.

He stepped to the body, checked for a pulse at the carotid artery to make sure, and backed out of the room, touching nothing else.

The last thing Kerney had expected to see was a dead body. He went to find Devin Hilt, knowing full well his morning would be shot as soon as the local cops showed up.

* * *

According to the California driver's license found on the body, the dead man was Clifford Spalding, age seventy-one, from Santa Barbara, a two-hour drive down the coast.

Sergeant Elena Lowrey of the San Luis Obispo Sheriff's Department thought it quite likely the deceased had died of natural causes. There were no visible wounds to the body; no defensive marks, no signs of a struggle. But until the coroner agreed with her observations and the autopsy findings confirmed it, she would handle the call as a death due to unknown causes. If everything looked copacetic, there might be no need to call out the detectives and the crime scene techs.

She stood at the foot of the bed for a minute and watched the coroner begin his examination before stripping off her gloves and exiting the cottage. Outside on the front lawn three men waited: Kevin Kerney, who'd discovered the body; Devin Hilt, who'd called 911; and Jeffery Jardin, the ranch owner.

Behind them, near the barn and stables, two employees, who looked to be Mexican nationals, worked at cleaning out a cool-down corral while keeping a wary eye on the proceedings.

Lowrey, who had an Anglo father and Mexican-American mother, bet that neither man held a green card. She had no desire to pursue it. Her grandfather, a migrant worker, had been deported years ago because of a disorderly conduct conviction stemming from a clash with police at a farm workers rally. He could never legally return to the States, although he did sneak in for occasional visits, especially when Ellie's kid sister, the baby-producing sibling of the family, added another grandchild to the clan.

She stepped off the porch and spoke to Jardin. "Can I use the ranch office to take statements?"

Jardin, a man in his sixties who sported a great tan, a full head of hair, and a worried expression, nodded.

"Thanks," Lowrey said, switching her attention to Kerney, whom she guessed to be around fifty and was good-looking for a man his age. He stood six-one, and had a nice build and deep set, pretty blue eyes.

"I'll start with you," Lowrey said to Kerney. "It shouldn't take too long."

Kerney nodded and followed the sergeant to the office, noting that even with the body armor she wore under her uniform shirt she cut a trim, well-shaped figure. A shade over five-five, she wore her thick dark hair rather short.

Kerney had come to the ranch as a potential buyer, not a police chief, so he doubted anyone knew he was a cop. Nonetheless, he'd told Hilt it would be best to keep everyone away from the cottage, a suggestion Devin readily accepted. Like most civilians, Hilt had no desire to stare in the face.

Kerney sat with Lowrey in the ranch office and answered her questions directly. He'd never met the man and didn't know him or his name. He only knew that he would be sharing the cottage with another visitor who was looking to buy horses. He'd returned from dinner last night to find a car outside and one of the bedroom doors closed. He'd simply assumed that Spalding was sleeping or desired some privacy. He'd read for a time before retiring and had heard no sounds from the man's room. Nothing out of the ordinary had occurred during the night to arouse any suspicions about Spalding's welfare. He'd discovered the body after attempting to wake Spalding with a knock on the bedroom door. He'd touched only the light switch in the bedroom and Spalding's carotid artery to confirm he was dead.

Lowrey asked for the name of the restaurant where he'd dined, which Kerney provided, and asked how long he'd be staying at the ranch.

"I leave tomorrow," Kerney said.

Lowrey nodded. "We might have to ask you to stay over, Mr. Kerney, until we clear things up."

"If it's possible, I'd rather not do that, Sergeant," Kerney said as he took his police commission card from his wallet and gave it to Lowrey.

The sergeant glanced at it and gave Kerney a reproachful look. "You could have told me who you were up front."

Kerney shrugged and took his ID back. "I knew we'd get around to it," he said. "Besides, until you say differently, I'm a person of interest to your investigation. But I would like you to extend the courtesy of allowing me to go home tomorrow."

He replaced the ID in his wallet and gave her a business card. "You can confirm who I am. Call the dispatch number and ask to speak to Deputy Chief Larry Otero. They'll patch you through to him."

Lowrey nodded. "I'll do that. Until we know more, this looks like an unattended natural death."

"So it seems," Kerney said, as he got to his feet. "But it's always best to do it by the book."

"Why didn't you just tell me you were a police chief?" Lowrey asked.

"Because I came here as a civilian," Kerney said, "which occasionally is a very nice thing to be."

Lowrey smiled, and a dimple showed on her right cheek. "Point well made, Chief. Will you ask Mr. Hilt to join me, and stand by in case I have any more questions for you?"

Kerney nodded and left the office.

If Clifford Spalding had expired in his own bed, the coroner, Deputy Sheriff William Price, would probably have done a quick death assessment and let it go at that, trusting the autopsy to pinpoint the cause. Instead, he decided to be a bit more thorough. First he checked the eyes for any signs of changes in the vitreous humor, which usually turns cloudy within eight to ten hours after death. The fluid was clear and there was no evidence of the minute blood clots caused by strangulation that show up as tiny red dots.

He inspected the mouth for any sign of blockage or corrosive burns, the neck for bruising or ligature marks, hands and arms for defensive wounds or needle marks, and fingernails for any traces of skin. He ran a gloved hand over the skull and found it to be intact with no telltale indication of blunt trauma. He stripped off a glove and felt the armpits with the back of his hand. They were cool to the touch.

There were early signs of rigor mortis, which usually occurs within two to four hours after death. That, along with the absence of any changes to the vitreous humor and the coolness of the armpits, indicated that the man had been dead for six to eight hours.

The body was clad in an undershirt, slacks, and socks. Using scissors, Price cut the undershirt and pants away, turned the body facedown on the double bed, and used a rectal thermometer to take the body's temperature. Then he checked the room temperature. The difference between the two readings brought his estimate of the time of death down to no more than six hours ago.

Blood pools and settles after death, appearing as a purple discoloration of the skin, and the lower back showed signs of it. Price pressed a finger against the spot and the color didn't blanch white, which was another good indicator that Spalding had been dead for about six hours, and, more important, hadn't been moved.

He looked over the body one more time. There were no surgical scars. The gluteus maximus and leg muscles were firm, indicating the man had been physically active.

Price guessed that either a heart attack or a stroke had killed the man. He took off his gloves and went to give Ellie Lowrey the news.

After admitting that he had almost no experience with cops or dead people, a nervous Devin Hilt confirmed what he could of Chief Kerney's story. Ellie Lowrey probed with a few more questions just to reassure herself that all seemed as it should before letting Hilt go and calling Kerney's deputy chief to verify his identity.

Bill Price came in just as she was about to begin her interview with Jeffery Jardin, the ranch owner.

"The body shows no signs of death by unnatural causes," he said.

"You couldn't seriously think that Clifton Spalding was murdered here," Jardin said in a bit of a huff.

Price smiled benignly. Civilians were always uneasy about the thought of homicide. He'd faced the same reaction from people time and again over the years. "We always try to rule that out first," he said.

He turned his attention to Lowrey. "I'd say he died in his sleep, either from a heart attack or a stroke, about six hours ago. The autopsy will tell us more."

Lowrey nodded. "Thanks. Ask the EMTs to keep everyone away from the cottage until I finish my interviews. I'd like to take another look around before we wrap it up."

"You got it," Price said, stepping out the door.

"Are you people always so suspicious?" Jardin asked.

"Careful would be a better way to put it," Lowrey replied. "How well did you know Mr. Spalding?"

"Well enough, on a business and social basis. Over the past ten years, he's bought about six horses from me, some that he ran in qualifying and small purse races. He didn't seem to care if they won or lost. It was a hobby for him, or rather for his wife, who I think basically liked the social scene at the track. He stabled his horses here and used my trainers. My ranch manager arranged for jockeys and the horses' transportation to and from the track. We basically did everything except race the horses under my colors. His wife keeps two of the horses he bought for pleasure riding, although they're good enough to race. I usually dealt with her."

"That's a pretty expensive hobby his wife has."

"Clifford could afford it. He owns, rather did own, a number of resort hotels up and down the coast."

"You said you knew him well," Lowrey remarked.

"For about the last ten years," Jardin replied, "after he married his second wife. I met them when they were first looking to buy racing stock. After that, I'd see them at the track, and we'd get together occasionally for dinner and drinks. Claudia, his wife, is a good twenty years younger. She divides her time between Santa Barbara and Santa Fe. Clifford built a house for her out there where she could keep some horses. I think she's in Santa Fe now."

"If you usually dealt with Spalding's wife, why did he come here this time?" Lowrey asked.

"Claudia had her eye on a horse she liked, and Clifford said he wanted to buy it for her as a surprise anniversary present."

"Do you have Mrs. Spalding's Santa Fe address?"

"My ranch manager should. He made the arrangements to have the horses she keeps in Santa Fe transported there."

Jardin glanced at his wristwatch, an expensive, wafer-thin gold timepiece that probably cost more than Lowrey's personal vehicle.

"Just a few more questions," she said, "and then we'll be done."

Kerney waited on the porch outside the office with the ranch manager, Ken Wheeler, and watched the coroner come and go. No longer a jockey, Wheeler had still managed to keep weight off his wiry frame. He sported a wide mouth that seemed ready-made to break into easy smiles, and had tiny ears that lay flat against his head. At six-one, Kerney towered over the man.

Wheeler told Kerney that he had two twelve-year-old halterbroke mares, four three-year-old geldings that didn't seem to have the heart to race, and a young stud named Comeuppance available for sale.

Wheeler thought the mares, once saddle broke, would serve well for pleasure riding, the geldings were surefooted and quick enough to be good cutting horses, and the stallion would do just fine at stud, if the new owner didn't expect fast runners from his lineage.

Kerney knew if he decided to buy it, the stud horse would be his most expensive purchase. "Is that his only flaw?" he asked.

"I believe so," Wheeler replied, his deep baritone voice quite a contrast to his diminutive size. "But you'll get to see for yourself. He's got good bloodlines, but none of his yearlings or two-year-olds look promising for the track. The boss says we sure aren't going to make any money keeping him, and I agree."

Before Kerney could reply, Sergeant Lowrey stepped onto the porch.

"Mr. Wheeler," she said, "could you get me Mrs. Spalding's Santa Fe address?"

"Sure thing," Wheeler said, as he slipped past Lowrey into the office.

Kerney raised an eyebrow. "Santa Fe, New Mexico?"

"She has a house there," Lowrey said, "and according to Mr. Jardin that's where she is. Do you know her?"

Kerney shook his head. "Do you want my department to make contact with her?"

"That would be helpful, Chief." Lowrey handed him a business card. "Ask your officer to call me first."

"Will do." Kerney reached for his cell phone. "What did the coroner have to say?"

"So far, Spalding's death appears to be from natural causes." Lowrey paused and gave him a once-over. "Quite a coincidence, isn't it, Spalding's wife having a place in Santa Fe?"

"In this particular instance, I would say that it is," Kerney replied.

"Are you sure you've never met her while you've been out riding the range?"

"That's very funny, Sergeant," Kerney said, slightly piqued at Lowrey's sarcasm. "Actually there are times when we still ride the range. But now that the streets of Santa Fe are paved, my officers mostly drive squad cars."

"Maybe you met her at a horse show or a rodeo," Lowrey countered.

"Not that I recall," Kerney said. He turned away from Lowrey and dialed Larry Otero's home number.

After talking to Larry, he waited for Lowrey to reappear. Instead, Wheeler came out of the office and told him Lowrey had a few more questions to ask and would be with him shortly. Kerney agreed to meet Wheeler at the track when he was finished, and cooled his heels waiting on the porch.

It didn't surprise him that Lowrey wanted another go-round. The "coincidence" that both Kerney and the dead man's wife lived in the same city would spark any competent officer's interest.

Finally, Lowrey called him back into the office. Kerney sat in a straight backed chair, while Lowrey perched against the office desk and studied the coral and turquoise wedding band on his left hand.

"You're married," she finally said.

"Yes," Kerney replied.

Lowrey's eyes searched his face. "And your wife didn't come here with you."

"She's a career military officer serving at the Pentagon. Her schedule didn't allow it."

"You must not be able to spend a great deal of time together," Lowrey said.

"We manage to see each other frequently," Kerney said, watching Lowrey, who was busy scanning him for any behavioral signals which might signal deception.

"Have you been married long?"

"A couple of years."

"Children?"

"One son, ten months old."

Lowrey smiled. "Your first?"

"Yes," Kerney said. "Now, why don't you get to the part where you stick your face in mine and ask me if I might be lying about not knowing Spalding's wife?"

Lowrey laughed. "As I understand it, Mrs. Spalding is about your age, and spends a great deal of time alone in Santa Fe, away from her husband. You seem to be in the same situation with your marriage."

"I am happily married, Sergeant. Don't turn a perfectly reasonable coincidence into a soap opera about two lonely, unhappy people."

"Obviously, you and Mrs. Spalding share an interest in horses."

"Along with about five million other horse lovers."

"Mr. Spalding was rich and considerably older than his wife."

"So I understand, from what you've said."

"And neither you nor Spalding have ever stayed here before," Lowrey noted.

"Apparently not," Kerney replied. "Do you find a chance occurrence tantalizing, Sergeant? That would be quite a stretch."

"Perhaps you're right. Do my questions upset you?"

"Not at all." His cell phone rang. Kerney flipped it open and answered.

"What kind of fix have you gotten yourself into out there?" Andy Baca, Kerney's old friend and chief of the New Mexico State Police, asked.

"What's up?" Kerney asked, raising a finger to signal Lowrey that he'd only be a minute.

"I just got a call from my district commander that some deputy sheriff, a Sergeant Lowrey out of San Luis Obispo County, wants an officer sent to inform a Mrs. Claudia Spalding of her husband's death and to determine your relationship to the woman, if any."

"Interesting," Kerney said.

"I've got two grandchildren in my lap, one on each knee," Andy said, "ready to head off to the Albuquerque zoo to see the polar bears. What's going on with you?"

"I'll call you when I know more."

"That's it?" Andy asked, sounding a bit exasperated.

Kerney laughed. "I'll talk to you later."

"I'll be home by dinnertime," Andy said. "Unless you get locked up, call me then."

"I'll do that. Have fun." Kerney disconnected and smiled at Lowrey. "Are we done here, Sergeant?"

Lowrey smiled back. "We'll talk again after I've heard back from your department."

"I'll be around," Kerney said, thinking Lowrey was doing her job and doing it well. Still, he didn't have to like it.

Ellie Lowrey made another visual sweep of the cottage before the EMTs took Spalding's body away. After they rolled him out, she gathered up the dead man's luggage, put it in the trunk of her cruiser, and drove a back road to the sheriff's substation in Templeton.

The station was housed in a fairly new single-story faux western frontier style office building with a false front and a slanted covered porch. It had been designed to fit in with the old buildings on the main street left over from the town's early days as a booming farming and ranching community. Now the charm of the village and its convenience to Highway 101, which ran the length of the West Coast, drew droves of newcomers looking to escape the sprawl of the central coast cities, creating of course more sprawl.

As second-in-command of the substation, Ellie Lowrey served under a lieutenant who was on vacation with his family in the Rocky Mountains. She parked in front of the closed office, carried Spalding's luggage inside, and placed it on her desk.

She'd secured the dead man's effects to ensure their safekeeping, which required her to do an inventory. She got out the forms she needed and glanced at the wall clock, wondering how long it would take to hear back from the New Mexico authorities.

Ellie had decided not to rely on Kerney's department for information until she knew for sure whether there was or wasn't a personal relationship between the chief and Mrs Spalding. Of course, if there was something going on between the two, both of them could lie about it. It was best to get corroborating information from an independent source such as the New Mexico State Police, in case they did have something to hide.

Spalding's overnight bag yielded nothing but toiletries and a change of clothes. The attaché case was a bit more interesting. A manila envelope contained a photograph of the horse Spalding was planning to buy, along with a record of its race results and bloodlines. The cover letter from Jardin listed the price at a few thousand dollars more than Ellie's gross annual salary.

Other paperwork in the case pertained to Spalding's hotel holdings. Lowrey recognized a few of them by name: very swanky places in upscale California resort communities. A sleeve held a small number of business cards. Lowrey thumbed through them. One was from a Santa Barbara police captain who headed up the Major Crimes Unit. What was that all about?

Lowrey wrote the information in her notebook. Tomorrow was Sunday. She doubted the autopsy would be done quickly given the likely absence of foul play. If the results came back as death due to natural causes, she'd drop the matter completely. Until then, she would keep the case open and call the Santa Barbara PD captain on Monday to satisfy her curiosity.

Ellie got up and poured a cup of coffee. She felt good about how the morning had gone. She'd spent five years as an investigator before earning her stripes and taking a patrol assignment. It was fun to work an investigation on her own again. In truth, she missed her old job, but accepting a promotion to the patrol division had been the only way to move up in the ranks.

She returned to her desk and started in on the paper-work, hoping it wouldn't take all day for the New Mexico cops to find Spalding's widow and report back.